## ADVANCE PRAISE FOR
# LOVEBOAT, TAIPEI

"Abigail Hing Wen's *Loveboat, Taipei* is a poignant
and honest examination of first love, family obligations, and that
strange place between high school and college, where we
don't quite know who we are, and as such, anything could happen.
A unique story from an exciting and authentic new voice."

—SABAA TAHIR, #1 *New York Times* bestselling
author of *An Ember in the Ashes*

"Equal parts surprising, original, and intelligent,
*Loveboat, Taipei* is an intense rush of rebellion, romance,
and complex family dynamics. If you've ever wanted to
feel as if you're breaking all the rules without actually breaking
any rules, then this is the book you need to read."

—STEPHANIE GARBER, #1 *New York Times* and international
bestselling author of the Caraval series

"*Loveboat* is *Crazy Rich Asians* meets a Jane Austen
comedy of manners—fresh, fun, heartfelt, and
totally addictive. It's a story about finding your place
and your people—where you least expected."

—KELLY LOY GILBERT, author of Morris Award finalist *Conviction*

"Not a ship, but a cultural phenomenon;
get ready to board the Loveboat, where millions of
Chinese Americans get their first taste of love and freedom.
Abigail Hing Wen's debut is as fresh as a first kiss."

—STACEY LEE, award-winning author of *Outrun the Moon*

# LOVEBOAT, TAIPEI

## ABIGAIL HING WEN

HARPER TEEN
An Imprint of HarperCollinsPublishers

HarperTeen is an imprint of HarperCollins Publishers.

Loveboat, Taipei
www.epicreads.com
ISBN 978-0-06-295727-6 — ISBN 978-0-06-299634-3 (int.) —
ISBN 978-0-06-300797-0 (special edition)
Typography by Corina Lupp
Interior art by Shutterstock/Orgus88
19 20 21 22 23   PC/LSCH   10 9 8 7 6 5 4 3 2 1
❖
First Edition

Dear Reader,

*Loveboat, Taipei* is inspired by actual summer programs attended by thousands of Asian American teens since the 1960s. My husband and I both attended the program in Taiwan in different summers and eventually met through mutual friends. South Korea hosts a similar program for young adults of Korean descent.

The program has evolved over the years. I loved chatting with alumni from across different summers. Loveboat alumni will no doubt recognize many of the landmarks and also note the creative liberties I've taken in service of storytelling. The story and all characters are fictional, and any resemblance to real persons is coincidental.

For an overview of the history of the program, see Valerie Soe's 2019 documentary *Love Boat: Taiwan* (loveboat-taiwan.com).

Thank you for reading!

Abigail Hing Wen
邢立美 (Xing Li Mei)

*For Andy*

*March 31*

BROWN UNIVERSITY   *Office of College Admissions*

*Dear Ever,*

*Thank you for your interest in our Program in Liberal Medical Education. This year's pool of applicants was exceptionally talented, and, with regret, our committee was unable to offer you a space in our incoming class . . .*

---

*March 31*

BOSTON UNIVERSITY   *College of Arts & Science*

*Dear Ever,*

*Each year, we are faced with the difficult decision of turning away highly qualified candidates . . .*

---

*March 31*

*WASHINGTON UNIVERSITY SCHOOL OF MEDICINE*

*University Scholars Program in Medicine*

*Dear Ms. Wong,*

*While your credentials are impressive, we unfortunately can only admit . . .*

---

*April 1*

*UNIVERSITY OF ROCHESTER MEDICAL CENTER*

*Dear Everett,*

*With only ten slots in our program, I am sorry . . .*

---

*April 1*

*RICE UNIVERSITY   Baylor College of Medicine*

*Dear Ever,*

*Thank you for your interest in the Rice/Baylor Medical Scholars Program. Unfortunately . . .*

---

*April 3*
CWRU SCHOOL OF MEDICINE

*Dear Ms. Wong,*

*With regret . . .*

---

*April 3*
NORTHWESTERN UNIVERSITY   *Feinberg School of Medicine*

*Dear Ever,*

*Congratulations. I am pleased to offer you a place in our Honors Program in Medical Education. Since 1961, we have offered a unique, seven-year educational experience for motivated students aspiring to medical careers . . .*

---

*April 4*
NEW YORK UNIVERSITY   *Tisch School of the Arts*

*Dear Ever,*

*Our Dance Department is unable to admit you at this time; however, we would like to offer you a place on our waiting list . . .*

*May 1*

*Dear Northwestern University/Feinberg School of Medicine,*

☑   *I ACCEPT the offer of admissions and have paid my deposit
     of $500.*
☐   *I DECLINE the offer of admissions.*

*Ever A. Wong*

CHAGRIN FALLS, OHIO — JUNE 5

The envelope drops through our mail slot like a love letter.

The familiar purple insignia—the four-petal flame spreading like a dancer's fan—sends me plunging down the faded carpet of our stairs. I text Megan:

running late b there in 5.

Then I snatch up the letter almost before it kisses the doormat.

My thumb traces the school's name in the upper corner. This can't be real. The last time an identical envelope arrived, crisp-cornered, smelling of new paper and ink and smudged with fingerprints, was two months ago. Like a full-colored dream breaking into a gray reality: of the lavender swish of tulle skirts, satin-rose ribbons unfurling, the weightlessness of leaps toward a sapphire sky.

NYU's Tisch School of the Arts.

Can it be—?

"Ever, there you are."

"Mom!" I spin around, scraping my arm against the rickety bookshelf Dad built. I fold the letter out of sight behind my back as Mom charges from the kitchen, waving a printout. Her jade-green blouse is buttoned to its modest neckline, as usual. A familiar panic digs into my gut. "Mom, I thought you were out."

"The church had extra volunteers today. I have good news." She waves the page, covered with Chinese characters. Another ancient herbal concoction to improve my circulation? I don't want to know, and anyways, she'll be making me drink it soon enough. "We applied for you and—are you wearing makeup?"

*Damn.* I seriously thought she was out. Normally, I'd have waited until I was down the block to pinkie on my microscopic touch of lip gloss.

"Just a little," I admit as she snatches a tissue off the side table. Behind my back, the envelope cuts into blisters on my palm.

"Mom, I'm late to meet Megan." I try to angle past her to the stairs, but the hallway, crammed from floor to ceiling with portraits of Pearl and me at every age, is as tight as the inside of a suitcase. "She's at the field already."

Mom sets my tank top more securely over my bra strap, lips pursing, as they do whenever I mention Megan. She'd rather I spend my hours getting ready for Northwestern because my brain and the Krebs cycle don't get along. I barely scraped a B in AP Bio—and that tumor on my report card might be malignant.

The tissue comes at me. It doesn't even occur to her she's invading my space. "Yes, but I need to tell you—"

A soft crash in the kitchen is followed by a wail from Pearl. "I'm sorry! My hand slipped!"

A moment later, my little sister's head pokes from the doorway behind Mom. I hide a smile as she bites into a spear of peeled grapefruit. Her eleven-year-old face is mine in miniature: same shoulder-length black hair and pixie face, but with doe-brown eyes like Dad's, reflecting her infinitely sweeter disposition—and a mischievous glint as she meets my gaze. "Mom, help! I spilled the brown sugar."

"You didn't hurt yourself?" Mom's already starting for Pearl.

"No, nothing broke."

Dad appears at the top of the stairs. "Everything okay?" The steps squeak as he descends, belly straining at his favorite Cleveland Indians sweatshirt. Under his elbow, he folds the *World Journal*, the Chinese-language newspaper of North America, that covers everything from global politics to the ten-year-old Chinese American global chess champ to the Yale-bound former child prodigy who is the bane of my existence.

"Grab the broom, will you?" Mom asks me.

"No, I've got it," Pearl says. "Look, the sugar's mostly on the napkin. Still clean."

Not a penny wasted. Five years of running interference for each other, and Pearl has it down to a science. I mouth *thank you* at her then squeeze past Dad, sliding my arm around to my stomach, keeping my letter out of sight.

"I'm sorry, I gotta run." My feet scarcely dent the carpet pile as I race upstairs. Near the top, my shoulder sets the family portrait swaying on its nail, and I grab hold to still it.

"Ever, I need to tell you something." Mom never lets go— Pearl and I know that better than anyone. "This summer—"

"Sorry, Mom, I'm *so* late!"

The slam of my door flutters the old test papers on my desk and sets my pink pointe shoes, hung by their ribbons, swaying on my bedpost. My room holds my twin bed, my dresser, and a few dozen pieces of dancing gear: jazz shoes on the floor by my closet, my dance squad flag in the corner, leotards and tights and skirts.

I lean my back against the door and clutch the letter to the pounding in my chest.

Can it be—?

I'd applied to Tisch on a whim, in secret. My parents tolerated all my dancing only because my guidance counselor reassured them I needed diverse interests for college applications. Buried under the mountains of medical program applications, Tisch was a shot in the dark. When the wait-list letter arrived, I

4

figured that was what they told all their applicants: *Thanks, but you go on without us.*

Downstairs, Mom's impatient voice mixes with Pearl's lighter tones. My stomach does a backflip—I have about a minute before Mom breaks down my door.

With a trembling finger, I rip open the envelope.

2

Ten minutes later, I jog onto the field behind the high school. Puffy storm clouds close over the sky, the remnants of a typhoon kicked up in Asia, according to the weatherman. The grass is moist underfoot. A guys' soccer match runs full tilt, a mad dash of Chagrin Falls orange jerseys versus blue from Solon, a rival high school. Normally, I'd stop and look, as in *look*, but today, all I want is to talk to Megan, my best friend since kindergarten, when we both joined Zeigler's Ballet Studio. We've danced together all the way through high school, along with our twelve-member flag corp and dance squad.

She's by her Camry, hauling our black-and-gold flags from her trunk, already dressed in our outfit: black leotard with sheer lace sleeves that catch the light, the matching skirt rippling over her long, lean legs. She has a dancer's body—like a living, breathing Degas sculpture. As I veer toward her, I feel a familiar twinge of envy. I'd rather take remedial biology all summer than have my thighs so exposed, but this is the price of dancing, and I'm willing to pay it.

"Megan!"

"Ever, you got out!" She waves, then grabs the periwinkle tote bag slipping from her narrow shoulder. Her reddish-brown hair tumbles over her fingers.

"Hey. Megan." I gasp.

"Hurry up and change." She shoves my tote bag at me, which I'd left in her car last practice for safekeeping from Mom. She glances worriedly over her shoulder. "Stikeman needs this field for some staff thing. We only have an hour."

"Megan." I clutch my bag like a life preserver. "I got into Tisch."

The poles clatter to the asphalt and Megan shrieks loud enough to be heard in Manhattan. I'm enveloped in a storm of curls and the scent of rosemary.

"How? *When?*"

"Just now." My body shakes as if I haven't eaten in days. I've tucked the letter under my pillow, but those black lines of type are seared into my mind: We are pleased to admit you to the Dance Department . . . "They emailed too, apparently, but I've been on hiatus since graduation. Now I have to answer by next Friday. I don't know what to do."

"You didn't tell your parents, did you?"

"I climbed down my pipe before they could talk to me."

"*Ever.*" Megan grips my arm and walks me toward the school. "You've got to stop doing that. If you break a leg, how will you dance? What if you hurt yourself permanently?"

"I'm not going to break a leg."

She frowns. "So Tisch. You want to go—of course you do, right?"

"Well, even considering it feels ridiculous, right? I've got almost a full ride to med school. You know how my mom feels about dancing—all body, no brain. Practically prostitution. Anyways, we can't afford Tisch. If they knew I'd applied, that I got *in*—I really think they'd consider disowning me"

"What about financial aid?"

"It's not enough. The letter mentioned a scholarship."

"From Tisch?"

"No, an arts association. I'd have to audition in Cleveland right after we dance in the parade next Saturday. At one thirty."

"Ballet? Jazz?" Megan's grip is starting to hurt.

"Open-ended."

"How about this routine? You made it up—that'll count for something, right? Okay to do a duo?"

"I don't have anything else!"

She frowns, thinking hard. "We'll have to Uber from Public Square. Shit." She shoves me toward the bathroom. "Now we *really* need to practice. Go change!"

Five minutes later, I am seated back-to-back with Megan on the grass. I lift the bottom of my fiberglass flagpole to form a roof peak with Megan's in the opening pose. A familiar warmth spreads like honey inside me: the anticipation of rhythm and beat.

Low notes. Wind instruments.

Like flowers uncurling, we unfold through our spines. Our legs unwind. Our black flags, cut through by a bolt of lightning, glide together in a sunrise. We line up and pan our flags in opposing—"Shit, wrong way," Megan apologizes—directions, salute to either side, reverse, one slow spin, a faster one, waking from a dream.

Then the music explodes—and so do we.

I spin a half turn. The wind of Megan's mirror movements ruffles my hair. Black-and-gold vinyl snaps at my ear as I hurl my flag skyward and swing into a double pirouette, feet shredding grass, black hair whipping across my face. The scent of grass fills the air and I'm so, *so* alive—never so alive as when I'm dancing.

Megan collides into me, our poles scraping.

"Sorry!" she yells. "What's next?"

Megan is always thinking ahead to the next step. I never have to. The patterns we make, how they change over what space and with what energy and tempo—that's what my body knows.

"Bigwheels," I gasp. My hand slides to my pole's end.

As the music races to close, we pirouette apart, hips swaying in a few parent-forbidden measures of sexy. Our flags sail high, revolving in tandem, once, twice, then we sweep out and back to center, where I land on my knees and throw up my arms.

"Sorry I screwed up the transition," Megan groans. She shuts off her camera, which we're using to record this dress rehearsal.

"S'okay. We'll run it again." Panting, I fall on my back. My blisters sting, the punishment of hours with the fiberglass pole, and we've more to go. But as blades of grass tickle my cheeks, my heart ricochets off my rib cage in a soul-surging rhythm.

Could this be my future? A lifetime of dancing, this limber-bodied afterglow—instead of walking antiseptic-smelling hallways?

"You are one mean choreographer, you know?" Megan grabs my water bottle and takes a swig before passing it to me. "Once we perfect this for Public Square, Broadway will bang down our door."

"Ha." I'm obsessed with musicals—dancing on Broadway would be a dream come true. Megan's just saying, of course, but it's dizzying to think about.

"Seriously. How do you come up with all that? We are so hot!"

"We could be green-haired hags and you'd say that. It just comes together. Your dad gets a medal for scoring us this slot in the parade."

"Well, his firm's been sponsoring it for ten years. It's about time he got something back."

Megan yanks the gold ribbon off a box of Malley's chocolates, our staple reward while we catch our breath. "Too bad you didn't get to dance the spring show with the squad. That number was *the* best. And you choreographed half of it." She pops a truffle between her lips. "I still can't believe your mom pulled you out of rehearsal like that."

"I can. It's the part where she did it in front of the entire squad that still kills me." I bite into a dark raspberry, shuddering with the memory. "Poor Ethan, she acted like he had leprosy. All because I was partner dancing with a boy."

"I honestly don't get her. I mean, you're eighteen."

"It's just that way." It's a mixed blessing to have Megan in the know, when her family's so laid-back she can't understand. "Chalk it up to her Chinese-Baptist roots. You know, she still hasn't given me the birds and bees talk? All I've picked up from her is—"

"'Sex is a by-product of marriage to be endured, preferably through a hole in the blanket.' So you've told me." Megan laughs and I almost smile, then she sobers. "Are you going to tell them about Tisch?"

"I don't know." Something tightens in my chest. "Med school's been the path set for me since before I could walk." The fulfillment of my parents' lifelong dream for stability. Respect. "The deposit's already paid. Dancing . . . they already hate how much time I spend on it. They've always expected I'd let it go after high school, when I join the real world." They know I'm in the parade, but I've downplayed it so they're not coming—I can't risk them cracking down on the time suck, not to mention my outfit.

My chest constricts further, and I rise up onto my elbows. "I can't think about it right now. I just need to nail this dance."

We run our routine and watch our videos a half dozen times, until Megan finally collapses, pries off her shoes, and massages her toes. "I need a break."

I flop onto my back beside her and dig my thumb into my palms. A few blisters are bleeding—*ugh*. I rub them on the grass, out of sight. Even a glimpse of my own blood makes me want to vomit—how will I handle a career of hemorrhages and puncture wounds?

Overhead, gray clouds close over the last patches of blue sky. A rumble of thunder vibrates the ground beneath me.

I'm tackling the small problems, but not the big one.

I can't help but think . . . if Dad gets that bonus Mom's hoping for. If I catch them in the right mood—

"Three o'clock," Megan whispers. "Don't look now, but there's a cute guy checking you out."

Unlike Mom, Megan knows when I'm not quite ready to talk. "Soccer boy?"

"Yep."

I pinwheel my flag over my face, helicopter-style. I can't deny it—maybe it's because I dance myself—I'm a sucker for athletes. Not because they're popular, but because of the discipline it takes to do what they do. Also the way they *move*—confident, purposeful—staking out their bit of space on this earth.

Sitting up, I cast a discreet glance toward the soccer net. The team from Solon in their blue jerseys has formed a circle and are kicking a Hacky Sack. An Asian kid makes eye contact, then we both look away. It's like an unspoken code between us. When you've grown up one of three Asian American kids in your school of less than five hundred kids, you don't do anything to draw attention to your Asianness—his or mine.

"Not interested."

"I'd go out with him."

"He's not noticing *me*, he's only noticing I'm Chinese." I grab my phone. "Which, to be fair, I noticed right back." Sure enough, the guy heads off with his soccer pals as I open the dance scholarship website to register. "See, he's gone."

Megan sighs. "Because you give every guy like him the when-they-ice-skate-in-hell vibe. Just because he's Asian American—"

"Based on sheer probability in the state of Ohio, I'm more likely to end up with a fifty-nine-year-old, two-time divorcé than another Asian American. *That* is my future." I say it like I'm joking, but the truth is, boys don't see me as dating material. Which is why I've only ever kissed one guy—and in the end, he didn't pick me.

"Okay, you're being ridiculous. What about the redhead? He's not fifty."

"Ha. Just give it up—" I break off as a blue convertible pulls up with a crunch of asphalt.

Right on cue.

"Dan!" Megan squeals, shooting to her feet.

The big hockey player steps from his car and swoops her into a hungry kiss. They've been apart for over six months, since his last visit from his freshman year at Rice. The kiss only lasts three seconds, but it feels like an eternity. I scuff the ground with my foot, familiar ribbons of envy tightening round my heart.

"Hey, Ever." Dan's strawberry-blond hair is longer than it was at his farewell party. But his chipped-tooth grin hasn't changed. My leotard feels transparent. And as his hazel eyes meet mine, crinkling with that smile, that afternoon behind the shed returns with a rush.

Those big hands on my hips. His tongue pressing my lips apart. He taught me everything I know about kissing that I didn't learn from practicing on oranges with Megan in middle school.

And then Mom and Dad ran him off.

"Dan wants to go for a ride." Megan wraps her arms around me; despite our grueling workout, her hair still smells like rosemary. I sense her guilt for happiness at my expense, her query, *you're okay, right?* Megan knows about that kiss, knows it's in the past. *We're still friends because you have the biggest heart this side of the Mississippi,* she's said. The truth is, most days, I try not to think about them. Together. She squeezes me tighter. "Let's pick up tomorrow? We're gonna land you that scholarship."

"Thanks." I squeeze her back, not wanting her to worry. Then, because she's standing there, I make myself dare to hug Dan, too. Like he's just another friend—

"Everett!"

I jump. My foot tangles in Dan's. My ear scrapes his bristled cheek as I leap back to face an audience I hadn't realized was watching.

14

Mom. She charges from our car, jade blouse snapping like a parachute. Behind her, Dad pulls his Cleveland Indians cap lower, like he's trying to shrink a few inches. He limps forward, that old injury from a fall mopping a spill at work.

I cross my arms over my leotard, a futile gesture. Dan shrinks back as Mom comes at me, a battering ram of fury. Fat droplets of rain pelt my head and shoulders as Mom grabs my lace neckline, jerking me off balance despite the fact that, at five feet one, she's two whole inches shorter than I am.

"You're wearing *this*? In public?"

I try to yank free. My leotard is *long sleeved*, for crying out loud. Megan tugs Dan out of firing range, but she needn't bother: his eyes are like a wild horse's, facing a blaze that's already scorched him once.

"Why are you here?" I choke out.

Mom shoves a page into my face. Creamy stationery creased into thirds. The precious purple flame insignia wrinkling under her fingers.

My Tisch School letter.

**3**

"What is this?" Mom demands. "What else have you been hiding?"

"Why didn't you tell us?" Dad's eyes widen behind his tortoiseshell glasses.

"Is this why you only got into one medical school?" Mom asks.

"No! Of course not!" God knows I'd thrown body and soul into my applications and interviews, knowing how important they were to my family. But even though Northwestern's program ranks higher than even Brown's, Mom and Dad blamed my Bs in bio when I didn't get into a bunch of places I applied. "How did you get this?"

"A woman called asking if you were accepting," Mom says through clenched teeth. I imagine the explosion on the phone, then the frantic search of my room. Mom shakes my letter as if it's crawling with red ants. "There's no future in dancing! You want to live like Agatha when you're old? You want *us* to live like that?"

Agatha. Mom's favorite object lesson from church, who comes in for free senior lunches with her lipstick as crooked as though a toddler crayoned it on, and warbles about her days with the Cleveland Ballet.

Dad's face is as stunned as if I'd taken out a gun and shot him in the chest. "Did you tell Northwestern?"

"Of course not," I say, and Dad's shoulders relax. "I haven't said anything to anyone!"

But I can read the thought bubble that hovers over Megan's head:

*Just tell them what you want. They can't keep treating you like an infant.*

"You think Dad wanted to push an orderly cart all these years?" Mom demands. "He did it to put food on our table." Because the state licensure board wouldn't honor his medical degree from China without him going through a residency he couldn't afford with a wife and baby on the way. Because this world crushes all our dreams. I know; God, I know. This time, she doesn't add what she often does: *But it's worth it. You got to grow up in America. You'll have opportunities we can't even dream of.*

17

And grown up I have, knowing that it falls to me, as the elder child, to earn back the cost of two lives.

*But why did you let me dance when I was little? I want to cry. Why give me honey when you knew my future was diabetic? Why let it in to fuse with my muscles and seep in under every square inch of skin?*

"You've worked so hard," Dad murmurs. He means for med school. But I can't help rubbing the swollen blisters on my palms.

Overhead, storm clouds have turned the sky to ashes.

"Tisch—" I can barely get my words out. "I applied on a whim. I didn't even get in at first. It wasn't serious—"

"Then you *don't*"—Mom crumples my letter into a ball—"need *this*."

She could have gone pro with that shot. My letter sails into the dumpster.

"That's mine!" I scream.

I fly forward and grab the rusty edge. Blisters burst as I heave upward—but my shoes slip, it's too high, too choked with moldering garbage to salvage my heart now pulsing on the other side of this metal wall—then Mom grabs the back of my leotard and pulls me off and clangs the lid shut with a whoosh of rotting air.

"What is *wrong* with you?" she cries.

My shoulders shake. I feel cold. So cold, despite the June humidity. Dan's backed up against his car. Megan clings to our flags. I wish they were anywhere but here. Megan's brown eyes plead: *tell them tell them tell them . . .*

I fight to steady my voice. "I just need to dance next weekend in the parade." No need to tell them about the scholarship audition, not until I win it. "I'll study bio between practices. I'll be ready for med school. I promise."

"Ever—" Megan protests, but I shake my head at her. We can't afford Tisch. That scholarship is my only chance and until I win it, there's no point telling Mom and Dad anything.

Mom and Dad exchange a look I don't like.

"Not just biology," Mom says stiffly. "Mandarin."

"Mandarin?" This must be what that Chinese printout was about, but seriously? Saturday morning Chinese school had been torture: a thirty-minute drive to affordable classes in Cleveland, copying characters by the hundreds into charts, reciting ancient poems without understanding a word. "I dropped out of Chinese school in second grade." After my teacher complained I had the fluency of a two-year-old, and the shame got too much for even my parents to bear. No way do I have time for Mandarin this summer.

But somewhere in the recesses of my mind, an alarm bell begins to clang.

"I was trying to tell you." Mom pulls another piece of paper, folded into quarters, from her pocket. Glances at my friends. Later, she'll regret her outburst in front of them, but it's too late now. "Your father and I feel it's time you learn your culture. We got you into a program. In Taiwan."

"Taiwan?"

My parents have always talked about taking us to visit Fujian, the province in southeast China where they were born, and met in college. They left after Dad finished med school. But we've never had the money to go. Family hasn't been a draw either. Mom's parents passed away before I was born, and Dad's four years after.

All I know about Taiwan is that it's an island off the coast of Fujian, and my uncle Johnny, married to Mom's sister in Vancouver, was born there. She might as well have announced we're blasting off to the moon. We can't afford a trip there, not with my tuition ahead, and Pearl's on the horizon.

"It's a good opportunity." Dad removes his cap, suddenly earnest. "You'll learn *fántǐ zì*—traditional characters."

I barely know what he means. "I can't take off for a week—"

"Eight weeks," Mom says. "It starts this weekend."

"This . . . *this weekend?*"

She nods. "Sunday."

"I'm not going!" I rage. "I got into Northwestern! I did everything you asked. I haven't done anything *wrong*!"

"Wrong? This isn't a punishment." To my surprise, Mom's near tears herself. "Aunty Lilian said the program's very good. Lots of young people enjoy it. And your ticket's so expensive. No refund!"

"Wait," I cry. "You *bought* a ticket already?"

"I sold my black pearl necklace!"

Her black pearl necklace.

The present from her father, who died when she was fifteen, younger than I am now. How many times have I seen her bring the string out on his death anniversary, polish the pearls with a scrap of red silk? She's told the story so often, how Gong-Gong brought it back for her from a failed business trip to Hong Kong.

And in Mom's necklace is the echo of their every other sacrifice—her slippers scuffing the hallway as she folds laundry, covering my chores while I studied into the night; the scar where she cut her finger chopping black chickens to nourish me during finals; Dad chauffeuring me to my clinic internship; all their worries over my med school applications.

Megan clutches Dan's hand.

*Tell them tell them tell them . . .*

A war rages in my heart. That guilt that comes with Mother's Day, when I can't feel as grateful as I should. Not even close.

It's one thing to dance around the little controls Mom exerts on my life. Quite another to shed a hard-fought-for future of financial security and respect for our family. My parents would slit their throats for my happiness, and in return, my future is their future.

I should have known better than to let myself get swept away.

My shoulders slump. I can't meet Megan's eyes.

"I'll need to find my passport," I say, then head for the car, leaving my heart in the dumpster, gasping like a dying fish.

4

Dad knocks as I sit hard on the lid of his plaid suitcase, trying to coax the stubborn, tasseled zipper around its last corner so I can make my flight this afternoon. I know it's him knocking, because he's the only one who does.

"Come in," I grunt.

He holds a soft black case. His graying hair is combed over his balding head. He's fifty-five, and his narrow face is tired and lined like a map of the Rocky Mountains, unlike Megan's lawyer dad who could pass for her older brother.

"Need a hand?"

"I got it."

He ducks coming in, as if my doorway isn't high enough. I take my room for granted most days, but now that I'm leaving, my Degas posters, lavender satchel, secret peanut butter cup stash—the space feels like my only sanctuary.

"This isn't for you to take to Taiwan. But I wanted you to have it."

The zipper's hopeless. I take the case from him and spill a stethoscope into my hand.

"My med school adviser gave it to me when I graduated. I've been saving it for you. Do you—do you like it?"

The chrome is still shiny. He's never used it: the soft Y-shaped neck, the round chest piece that can hold a heartbeat. I weigh it like a baby in my hands, this symbol of a respected profession my family has only watched from the outside.

It's more my size than his, as if it's been waiting for me.

The floorboards creak under Dad's weight.

A few years ago, Pearl and I watched *Mulan* on Netflix: the girl in ancient China who steals her father's armor to save him, returns home a hero, and tries to earn her father's forgiveness by thrusting her honors at him. Only to be told that the greatest gift was having her for a daughter.

Pearl and I bawled. And then we found out Dad had watched it on a flight from Singapore years ago.

"Did you cry, too?" Pearl had the guts to ask, while I hovered in the background, waiting for his answer.

Dad had scrunched up his face, goofy-like, as he did only for her. "I did."

"Really?" I blurted, startled into engaging. Did miracles still happen? Did he actually get it?

"Which part, Dad?" *Oh, Pearl, how do you dare?*

"When the Huns invaded China," came his honest reply.

Now we're standing in reverse. He wants me to love it, this gift, and I just . . .

He takes my arm, a rare contact. "Taiwan's not a punishment," he murmurs. "It was bad timing. I might be able to join you the last days if I can line up my business trip." To a hospital he consults for on the sly. It's a few extra dollars and they fly him out twice a year. Maybe that will be me one day: moonlighting. Sneaking out of the hospital in my white lab coat to dance on legs that have forgotten how to move.

Mom bursts in, pressing Dad aside. "Ever, I found you a neck pillow." She thrusts it at me, then unzips my suitcase lid. "Are you ready?" She inspects the contents, then yanks out my periwinkle dance bag and dumps my leotard and pointe shoes onto my bed.

"You won't be needing all that in Taiwan," she says, and bustles off.

Dad opens his mouth. "Ever—"

"I can't pack with all these interruptions."

I drop the pillow, set his stethoscope on my banned leotard, and fall back onto the evil zipper. I'm an automaton. Everything I'm doing is like their hands moving through mine.

I don't look up, even after my door closes behind him.

To: tisch.admissions@nyu.edu
From: ever.a.wong@chagrinfallshigh.edu

24

Dear Tisch Admissions,

With regret, I decline your offer of admissions.

Ever Wong

Twenty-one hours of connecting flights later, I sling my carry-on onto my shoulder and stumble bleary-eyed after my seatmate, down a metal ramp into Taipei's Taoyuan International Airport. My head still roars with the noise of the jets. My mouth tastes like talc and I regret the foil-wrapped teriyaki chicken that's threatening to make its way back up my system.

The airport glitters. Shiny white floor tiles shimmer with the reflection of a stampede of passengers. Perfume and body odor choke my lungs as I'm swept at dizzying speed past stores featuring Swatch watches and Dior shades, glass cases holding boxes of pineapple cakes, a fast-food counter serving black-lacquered bento boxes. *"Kuài diǎn, kuài diǎn!"* Someone pushes past me from behind.

I catch a glimpse of myself in a store mirror; dark-haired, small, and terrified-looking, surrounded by strangers. Trying not to panic, I yank my crumpled welcome packet from my backpack. My contact is a Chen Li-Han. My ride should be waiting outside baggage claim.

Now I just need to get to him in one piece.

Down an escalator, past larger-than-life billboards of Asian models I can't help gawking at, through a hallway . . . until at last, I spill into a rectangular room roped into lines that snake toward a row of immigration booths. Chinese characters mix with English everywhere and Mandarin announcements blare in my ears. At home, we only speak English, except when Mom and Dad use Mandarin to keep secrets. I've picked up a few basics at the Chinese Church, where service is translated line by line: "Let us pray" and "Please sit." And I know the dim sum cart (*har gow, shu mai, chang fen*)—and that, I thought, was all I'd need. I hope that's still true. I hope, I hope.

Back at the Cleveland airport, Dad had taken my arm and murmured, "Safe travels." It's a ritual, left over from family lore—the great-uncle who went to Germany and never returned, the niece lost at sea—like throwing a pinch of salt over your shoulder. If we neglect it, misfortune might ensue. It's always been us saying it to Dad as we dropped him off.

But I'd snatched back my arm. Marched through security, ignoring the paranoid twang that comes from that family immigrant history—*what if he dies before I come home?*

And what if I get lost and can't get back?

What if I get kidnapped?

What is everyone saying?

What have I done?

My breath comes fast and shallow.

Don't panic.

I just need to make it through this airport, then I can bury myself in character charts and try not to think of Pearl being

7,627 miles away or Megan dancing in Public Square with Cindy Sanders who's taking my place in the parade, or Dan—I can't think of him. With any luck, I'll hide under the radar of my Chinese school prison guard and won't have to speak to anyone for eight weeks.

At a booth, an officer behind glass blasts me in Mandarin.

"I'm sorry." I hand him my American passport. "I don't speak." Frowning, he takes a mug shot, scans my index fingers, hands back my passport, and waves me through.

Somehow, I make it to the luggage carousel, where Dad's whale-sized suitcase revolves in a loop. I squeeze between two travelers arguing in Mandarin and drag my suitcase free—it's heavier than I remember—then I'm jostling along with another herd of travelers into an arrival hall, flowing with a river of more Asian people than I've ever seen.

Panic!

A sea of faces rushes me, crowds waving cardboard signs printed with blocky characters and names in English. Someone cries a greeting and jostles me from behind, and then I'm falling, and then caught by a steel rail that divides me from the crowds: women in stylish blouses, men in beige slacks, though it's hot enough to melt crayons on the floor. And humid. My shirt and hair are plastered to my body already.

I make my way past the crowds and outside into a blast of sunlight. Horns honk. Oddly squarish cars rush by, their roar splitting my head into four.

"*Chien Tan?*" I ask a woman with another sign. "I'm looking for—"

A claw-like hand grips my shoulder, connected to a man with no hair and a face like a horse. The stench of cigarettes and cilantro breaks over me.

"Nǐ yào qù nǎlǐ?"

"Wh-what?"

"Nǐ yào qù nǎlǐ?"

His grip tightens. Panic overrides all remaining sense.

"No!" I rip free, whirl about-face, hell-bent on retracing my steps back onto my plane.

But two policemen in blue guard the exit.

And then my luggage, heavy with inertia, keeps twisting me round, tipping my world. My ankle gives way—then the pavement rushes to meet me, no railing this time to prevent me from making an undignified Ever-shaped splat on the ground.

A yell rips from my throat.

My suitcase yanks itself free.

Then a firm hand on my upper arm stops me inches from the ground. I eyeball a pair of blue jeans–clad legs. Black Nikes.

"Whoa, there," he says, and I gape up at an angle at the most handsome guy I've ever seen.

# 5

The guy hauls me to my feet as if I weigh no more than a monkey. I *feel* like a monkey—a clumsy one in desperate need of a shower, hair-combing, and breath mints.

"You all right?" he asks. "Jet lag's pretty bad off these flights. It's four in the morning for us."

He's making excuses for my emotional wreckedness; for looking like I just got spit out of a jet engine—and it's the kindness of this stranger that undoes me. As he releases my arm, I dash it over my damp eyes.

His jet-black hair is rumpled into careless spikes, like he doesn't need to bother with first impressions. He's paired an olive-green shirt with hip-hugging jeans that mean he either has very good taste, or knows someone who has. He's tall and leanly buff—I've never seen a real-life guy with so much prime real estate in arm muscles.

"Hi—hi!" I stammer wittily. "Um, hi!"

He tugs an earphone free. It sings with a homey Beatles song that reminds me of closing down the Patio Grill, where I worked last summer, only there has never been a guy like him there.

"Are you Ever Wong?" He rights my suitcase with a firm thud and scowls. "You're an hour late. We've been waiting for you."

Five minutes into the ride to Chien Tan, I realize there's something familiar about Rick Woo of the swoon-worthy arms. Is it his name? Face? Maybe I'm loopy from jet lag, but surely I'd have remembered an Asian guy of his sheer size and bulk. He takes up half our bench, which creaked and sagged toward him when he sat beside me. He moves with a sense of controlled—almost graceful—power, as if he's never taken a wrong step in his life. Meanwhile, my upper arm slowly purples with his handprint, a reminder that I nearly wiped out before him and every occupant of this fifteen-passenger van.

"Have we met before?" I venture.

"No." Rick falls into a silence that doesn't invite further conversation, his initial kindness evaporated like a splash of water left behind on the airport pavement. He fidgets with his cell phone, which isn't getting a signal. It drops and he swears and picks it up again, removing and reinserting his tiny SIM card. Oh, no. I forgot to buy one at the airport like Dad told me to. I've never been as addicted to my phone as my classmates, but now I can't even make a desperate lifeline call to Megan.

Upside: I don't have to take calls from Mom and Dad either.

Rick restarts his phone. His knee jiggles and he drapes his thick-wristed arm over it, running his thumb along the inside of his fingers in an odd, fidgety gesture. His wall of silence would have felt less awkward if the other kids weren't jabbering a mile a minute around us, as they have since I slipped into my seat.

Is he really that annoyed they had to wait so long for me?

Li-Han, our driver who is also, apparently, head counselor, meets my eyes in his rearview mirror. He's about ten years older than us, rail-thin under his fluorescent-yellow Chien Tan shirt, with a thick shock of black hair, black-rimmed glasses, and a bulldoggish jaw. He speaks in Mandarin, and with a jolt, I catch my Chinese name—*Ai-Mei*—which he'd used to check me off his list. *Ai*: love, and *Mei*: beauty, which has always felt less pretentious in Chinese. But no one but my grandpa, who named me, ever used it in real life, and he passed away when I was four.

On Rick's other side, by the door, a beautiful girl with pencil-straight black hair spilling over her creamy shoulders wraps up her flirting match with a hawk-nosed guy named Marc. Beside him is a prematurely graying guy named Spencer Hsu, who apparently is taking a gap year to work on a Senate campaign this fall. I haven't gotten the girl's name yet, and I feel a pang, wishing Megan were here—everyone seems to know each other already.

The van jolts over a pothole as the girl leans over Rick. Her heart-shaped face tapers to a cleft chin. Dark-brown eyes curl ever so slightly down either side of her nose. Her tangerine dress tightens against generous curves and could have come off a runway—by comparison, my lilac V-neck shirt over jean cutoffs feels grungy. Even if I'd changed before deplaning, I don't own anything half as nice.

"Hey, there. Li-Han wants us to do icebreakers. Whatever. I'm Sophie Ha—yes, like *haha*! It's Korean—my grandfather was Korean. I'm from Manhattan, but I live in New Jersey now. My parents split up and sent me here for the summer, but I'd have come anyways. Where are you from?"

"Um, Ohio." Aren't Asians supposed to be reserved? But she's so open. And she glitters. Sunlight glints off three earrings on her left earlobe, a contrast to my modest single studs. She somehow reminds me of a combination of Megan and Pearl.

"Cool." She props an elbow on Rick's shoulder like he's a big pillow. His wide, arched forehead and soft nose remind me of my cousin, though his irises are amber instead of brown, closer to the color of his skin. Why does he look familiar? Headphones, shaggy hair, athletic build . . . there's a resemblance between Sophie and Rick. The shape of their eyes, the full lips.

"Are you guys related?"

"Cousins," she confirms, and I can't help envying all the benefits that must come with a hot boy-cousin your age, like a built-in network of guy friends, a sounding board for your unrequited crushes. "We went to the same high school. I was a cheerleader. I'm headed to Dartmouth."

"Oh, cool—I dance. Um. Dance squad. Ballet."

"Cool. Rick's off to Yale"—she rolls her head charmingly—"to play *football*." She kneads his shoulder and pretends to cheer, "Rah rah sis boom bah!"

"Quit it, Sophie." He slumps against his seat, frown deepening, looking out the window. "We've hit rush hour."

"I give up." She sighs. "Even *I* can take only so much of your sulking."

Wait a minute . . .

Yale.

Football.

Woo.

"*You!*" I blurt.

Rick frowns. "What?"

When I was nine, Dad showed me a photo in the *World Journal*: the skinny Chinese boy with the birthday just five days after mine, with bear-like brows that have since spread proportionately over the forehead of the guy beside me. Woo Guang-Ming (Bright Light, family name first) of New Jersey had won the national spelling bee, when I didn't even know a round existed beyond my fourth-grade silver-medal victory. *Maybe you should put more effort into spelling,* Mom suggested.

When we turned twelve, Woo Guang-Ming had his piano debut in Lincoln Center. *You should practice more! Harder!*

At fourteen, he won the Google Science Fair for some machine learning algorithm. *How can you go to medical school with a B in biology?* We'd lived the same number of years on this earth, and he'd achieved four times as much.

I told myself he had no soul. He spewed algebraic formulas on command. His fingers were sausage-swollen from his mom's chopsticks coming down on them at the keyboard.

The only time I didn't want Boy Wonder struck down by lightning was when he quit piano to warm the football team's bench freshman year. The *World Journal* was worried, my parents devastated. *Who does he think he is, Tom Brady? Will he not go to college?*

I rejoiced. For once, Guang-Ming had done something off the beaten path (for an immigrant Asian American kid). And sitting on the bench—a waste of time by *World Journal* standards. It was the end of the Guang-Ming dynasty and I'd never have to run into a clip of his latest article placed on my pillow again.

But then Boy Wonder got recruited as a running back for Yale, not the best football team, but who in the readership of the *World Journal* cared? It was Yale. He skyrocketed again in my parents' esteem and plummeted in mine. The only other *World Journal* prodigy I remember half as well died by suicide. His grieving parents commemorated him with a full page spread of his résumé.

"What?" Boy Wonder repeats.

Here he is. The yardstick for my never-measuring-up life, in the flesh.

"Nothing," I say, and Boy Wonder's frown deepens.

"Never met an Ever before." Sophie smooths things over. "Is it a nickname?"

"For Everett." I *really* wish Boy Wonder wasn't between us joggling his arm and leg, putting me on edge.

Sophie's brow wrinkles. "Isn't Everett—"

"Did you want to trade seats?" Boy Wonder cuts her off, scooting from me. Sophie raises a brow. I flush. Do I smell?

"We'll be on campus in like, five minutes. Calm down. Poor Ever will think you're like this all the time." Boy Wonder shoves his phone into his pocket and makes a fist that pops his veins out on his tan arm. What the heck is his hurry anyways?

Sighing, Sophie turns back to me. "So Everett's—"

"A boy's name, yeah." My flush deepens, my usual embarrassment quadrupled. I don't want to keep talking over Boy Wonder and annoying him. "My parents didn't realize it was." To which most respond, "How could they not?"

Boy Wonder glances at me. "Guess Everett sounds like Bernadette or Juliette. Easy mistake."

I'm surprised. He understood. Sometimes things that should be straightforward—like what's a boy's versus girl's name, or why your entire self-worth isn't at stake when you let down your parents—just aren't. If you didn't grow up like I did.

"Yeah," I say.

Not that this makes up for him being the bane of my existence.

"What's it mean anyways?" he asks.

35

Why am I so weirdly fascinated by the stubble on his jaw?

"Brave as a boar. Remember, I didn't pick it."

"Ever the Brave Boar. I like it," he says.

I can't help a small snort. He can't mean it.

"No, really. Better than my name. Came from *The Sound of Music*. Friedrich. My little sister's Liesl."

I press my lips together, then admit, "That's hilarious."

He groans. "No, it's not. We had to watch the movie a hundred times and every time, my parents would say"—he waves a hand jazz-style—"'That's how we got your name!' My sister got so sick of it she changed her name to Shelly last year in fifth grade."

I can't help smiling. "She sounds a little like my sister." And a family that picks names out of an old but decent musical—not what I'd have expected for Boy Wonder.

He looks out the windshield, knee still jiggling, thumb running under his fingers, bored again with this mortal conversation.

*Okay, fine.* I face out my own window, my cheeks heated. The world feels jarringly off, as if I've dropped into a parallel universe, crowded with strange, squarish cars, oblong street signs, speed limits in kilometers, and Chinese characters. Then the elevated highway lifts us into tree-covered mountains. Mint-and-orange pagodas jut through the leaves: square, tiered roofs with corners flared like swallowtail wings, stacked in towers that shrink as they ascend. Like my favorite jewelry box Dad brought from a trip to Singapore, expanded to house-sized proportions.

*Toto, I'm not in Ohio anymore*—and I'm not sure how I feel about it. Disoriented, still mad, but also . . . intrigued.

"*Ai-Mei, nǐ xūyào tíng xiàlái zuò shénme ma?*" Li-Han says.

"I, uh, sorry, I don't understand—"

"He's asking if you need to stop at a store for anything," Boy Wonder says.

I flush. I don't need his help. "Oh, uh, no. No, I don't. And it's Ever. No one calls me Ai-Mei."

Boy Wonder responds in fluent Mandarin, conveying my answer, and then some. He even pulls off the elder-speak demeanor shift—his tone more deferential and respectful.

Of course he does.

Maybe it's the universe's idea of a cruel joke that on this trip, which my parents have forced on me, I've bumped right up against their measuring stick.

"If you speak Mandarin already"—I can't keep the acid from my voice—"why'd your parents make you come?"

"Oh, they didn't." His amber eyes flicker to me. "I came on my own. Sophie and I have family here, so we visit every summer."

Boy Wonder *chose* to attend Chinese summer school. Enough said.

"It's different when you're at Chien Tan, of course," Sophie says. "What about you? Why'd you decide to come?"

"*I* didn't." My voice pitches slightly. "My parents made me."

Sophie laughs. "Well, no one's *making* you do anything here."

"What do you mean?"

37

"Our cousins have done this program," Sophie whispers. "Best kept secret. *Zero supervision.*"

*Oh, really?* "So what does—"

Boy Wonder flicks a warning finger toward Li-Han, who probably understands a lot more English than he lets on.

"Tell you later," Sophie whispers.

I want to ask more, but our van pulls into a driveway, past a concrete slab bearing two Chinese characters. To our left, a red pagoda building—the largest I've ever seen—rises from the mountains. To the right, a guard salutes from his booth and a wooden bar lifts to let us through.

"Chien Tan," Li-Han announces.

I peer anxiously out the window as Li-Han narrates in Mandarin. A pond laced with giant lily pads gurgles with fountains. Our van winds toward a small campus of redbrick buildings with rows of two-paneled windows. More Asian American kids my age bump a volleyball in a grassy courtyard surrounded by lush shrubbery, and beside a rock carved with the Chien Tan characters, a bride in a red qipao and her tuxedoed groom kiss while their photographer snaps away.

"Is this a tourist attraction?" I ask. There must be fancier places in Taipei to take wedding photos.

The van stops. Boy Wonder steps out after Sophie and extends his hand to me. "Li-Han says they met here four years ago."

Some traitorous part of me wants to take his hand, to see if it feels hot or cold, but the rest of me is irritated, with him and myself—it's not like I can't handle getting out of a van. I hop down on my own, ignoring it.

"Cool. What are the chances?"

"What are the chances?" Sophie flicks her black hair over her shoulder, laughing. "It's Loveboat!"

"Sorry? I don't remember reading about a boat."

"It's not a *boat*." Sophie shoots Boy Wonder a meaningful glance, but he's already leading us to the van's back. "That's the nickname. Like the old TV show. Add it to the tell-you-later list. Rick, let's hit the markets first."

"You go ahead," he says. "I need to find a pay phone. I promised Jenna I'd call as soon as I landed and I'm way late now."

"*Jenna.*" Sophie huffs. "You should date Ever," she adds, to my utter horror. "Look, she's perfect for you—you play football, she dances."

Boy Wonder rolls his eyes. "Jenna's my girlfriend," he tells me.

Oh.

So he has a girlfriend.

I guess in my imagination, Boy Wonder always went it alone. Like me.

The other kids have gathered around the van's back door. As Li-Han inserts his key into the lock, Boy Wonder fishes his phone from his pocket and thrusts it under my nose.

"Jenna Chu," he says.

His girlfriend smiles from his screen: a professional photo I couldn't have afforded if I worked a year at the Patio Grill. She's even more beautiful than he is—her heavy black hair frames a slender face, delicate nose, and rosy lips. At her throat, dangling from a fine gold chain, is a class ring set with a sapphire. People sometimes called me a porcelain doll growing up, which I half liked, half hated. But Jenna actually fits the description, down to the French manicure on her folded hands. I'm surprised Boy Wonder hasn't broken her by accident.

His arm brushes mine. He's standing too close—I step back and catch an odd expression on his face. Surprise. I tug on my ponytail, realizing too late that it's lopsided.

"She's really pretty," I say.

"She's much more than pretty. She's super smart, too." Boy Wonder's voice sharpens, and my face heats with embarrassment. I hadn't meant to imply she wasn't. Now he probably thinks I'm shallow. "She's going to Williams next year." Is it me, or is he sharing an unusual lot about her?

"Boring, you mean?" Sophie yawns. "'*Ricky*, what am I going to *do* with myself all summer while you're gone?'" she says in an obvious imitation. Li-Han swings open the van's rear doors.

"Shut up, Soph. She's got plenty to do." With impatient jerks, Boy Wonder hauls our bags onto the sidewalk until he snatches up a black suitcase and lopes up the stairs.

"Rick, you forgot your backpack," Sophie calls.

"Damn." He swings back for it, then catches my eye. "Watch your step, okay?" He grimaces. "I might not be around to catch you next time."

What the heck?

40

With that condescending remark, he loops his bag onto his shoulder and dashes back up the stairs as if his entire GPA depends on him calling Jenna before he takes another breath. At the sliding doors, he nearly mows over a petite counselor.

"Rick, *watch out*," Sophie chides, but he's gone.

And good riddance. Muscles can't fix whatever his problem is.

"*Zhè shì Pan Mei-Hwa*," Li-Han introduces the girl counselor as she joins us, straightening her yellow Chien Tan shirt over a red skirt striped with yellow, green, and black.

"*Huānyíng lái dào Chien Tan!*" Mei-Hwa Pan waves both hands in greeting. She speaks Mandarin like a native speaker, though her rounded features aren't quite Chinese. Her long black hair is bound in a heavy braid, tied with a green ribbon. Her face is open and friendly, and when she smiles at me, I almost ask her to please tell me what I've gotten myself into.

Then a girl from the back of our van shoves her bag into Mci-Hwa's arms. Mei-Hwa blinks, but follows on her heels up the stairs in the same direction Boy Wonder took.

I grab my own rolling bag. A long-necked black bird alights on the bushes lining the concrete steps. Ivy-shrouded walls close us off from the rest of Taipei, but not the sun beating mercilessly down on my head.

I have no idea how a Loveboat fits into all this.

But if I'm going to be stuck inside these walls with Boy Wonder all summer, might as well shoot me now.

6

There's no chance to ask Sophie about the "Loveboat" in private.

Potted plants divide the spacious, sunlit lobby into lounge areas furnished with chairs sculpted from twists of cherry-brown tree roots. Sophie and I join the back of a line to a registration desk. On the wall, six clocks made of polished cuts of drift-wood display times in San Francisco, New York, Taipei, Beijing, London, and Tokyo.

All around us, more kids drop suitcases, saying to one another, "Don't I know you from RSI?" A guy in a Berkeley T-shirt fist-bumps another guy half a head shorter: "Yo, saw you at Cal-Michigan! Sorry, man, next time." Three girls in near-identical pastel dresses fall into each other's arms, squealing, "How've you *beeeeeeen*? Did you see Spencer's here, too?"

Even Sophie reunites briefly with girls from something called a Center for Talented Youth summer camp.

"How do so many people here know each other?" I ask Sophie.

"It's that six degrees of separation thing. Only for us, it's like, two degrees, know what I mean?"

I don't. I don't know a soul here, but in this moment, the loneliness I feel is overridden by the larger strangeness of blending in. In the mall back home, heads sometimes turned when I walked by with my family, but now, my Asian Americanness is invisible, erased like a shaken Etch A Sketch. It's an unexpected relief.

As we inch forward, Li-Han walks toward us from the opposite direction, balancing a tray of plastic cups. Sophie grabs two, along with fat straws. "Classic," she says. "I hate all the syrups people put in nowadays." Dark brown marbles revolve lazily in the bottom third of a coffee-and-cream liquid. A plastic film seals its top.

"What is this?" I ask, mystified.

"Bubble tea!" Sophie jabs her straw through the film and sucks up the marbles. "You seriously never had it? Milk tea with tapioca pearls."

"I've heard of it." I'm wary—I've never drunk anything swirling with solids. But I imitate her, puncturing my top more forcibly than I intend, making Sophie laugh. I suck in a mouthful of cold, sweet tea, punctuated by the chewy spheres. "Oh. It's good."

Sophie laughs again. "Ever. You're a *Twinkie.*"

I frown. Like the Hostess dessert—white inside, yellow outside? Grace Chin from my youth group would come out swinging if anyone used that term on her, but I'm not mad. Just defeated . . . again. Even among a horde of Chinese Americans, I'm not Chinese American enough. A sudden burst of missing Pearl weakens my knees.

Then a shuffle of guys descend on us: tall, short, lean, heavy, hairy—even a mustache and scary goatee. They ask our names and I find they all share two things in common: they're top college–bound (UCLA, Penn, Stanford, MIT) and they're sweating as much as I am. The humid air practically licks me. The male attention, the eager-eye smiles and handshakes—it's all a little overwhelming.

Two girls stop to introduce themselves. "Hi, I'm Debra Lee." A girl with blue, pixie-cut hair carried up in combs offers a firm handshake.

"I'm Laura Chen," says her friend in a Yankees cap.

"We're Presidential Scholars," says Debra. "We met in Washington."

"We met the President of the United States."

"That's how we got invited on this trip."

"Oh, Deb, we better run." Laura checks her watch and flashes an apologetic smile. "We're meeting the commissioner with the other Scholars—see ya."

They speed off before either Sophie or I can get a word in.

"Oh, *pardon me*. A VIP awaits." Sophie rolls her eyes. "*Wow,* that was annoying."

"No kidding." I toss my half-finished bubble tea in the trash, all my appetite gone. It's obvious now. My parents have sent me here to be sanctified. As iron sharpens iron, so one well-honed nerd sharpens another—except these aren't ordinary nerds like me, they're prodigies on the order of Boy Wonder.

"Wong Ai-Mei." A woman in her forties, heavy-set in a green qipao, greets me from behind the registration desk. Her salt-and-pepper perm curls down like a helmet on her head.

"It's Ever."

"*Ai-Mei,*" she thunders at me with general-like authority. Clearly, it's not up to me what I'll be called this summer. "*Huānyíng. Wǒ shì Gāo Lǎoshī.*" Welcome. I'm Teacher Gao. Gao—"tall." It suits her. The rest of what she says is lost on me.

As she digs into a box behind her, Sophie murmurs, "Everyone calls her the Dragon. Sucks we're stuck with her as program head this summer." The name fits her haughty jawline and nose.

We are roomed by arrivals. The Dragon hands Sophie and me keys to room 39, along with a tote bag stitched with a red, white, and blue flag of Taiwan, a white sun instead of stars on its blue square. It contains a yearbook and folded map of Taipei.

The Dragon switches to English in my parents' Hokkien dialect accent to set forth the program's expectations: Mandarin, Chinese culture, study hard.

"What electives would you like?" she asks. "Each runs for two weeks, then we have field trips."

"I'm doing a double cooking class," Sophie says. "I already sent mine."

"Elective?" I say. "I haven't picked any." Sophie gets a binder of recipes while I flip through the materials: paper cutting, zither, Chinese yo-yo, kite making, mah-jong, Chinese chess, fan dancing, ribbon dancing, sword fighting, lion dancing, dragon drums, dragon boat racing, stick-fighting, Mulan-style, *wow*—

"Oh! Ai-Mei, your parents already sent in your electives."

My head snaps up. "They did?"

The Dragon hands me a sheet bearing my Chinese name at the top:

*Mandarin: Level I*
*Elective 1: Introduction to Chinese Medicine*
*Elective 2: Calligraphy*

"Hey, we're in Mandarin together," Sophie says, but I barely hear her.

They picked my electives.

Just like they picked them through high school: French instead of Latin, *a dead language*, Advanced Topics in Biology instead of Dance.

"Can I switch one to ribbon dancing?"

"Ah, I am sorry. Class is full."

"What about fan dancing?"

46

"Full as well."

"Stick fighting?"

The Dragon shakes her head. "Your parents asked for these. You can call them."

I imagine the dead-end conversation with Mom: *Chinese Medicine is for med school. Calligraphy is practical. Good for writing prescriptions the rest of your life.* Seven thousand miles away, their invisible hands are still tight around my life.

I answer through gritted teeth. "Fine."

"Please reserve an hour for homework each night, always travel with a buddy, bed check at nine thirty p.m. No boys and girls in a room with the door closed."

"Of *course not.*" If Sophie held her hand up, Scouts honor, she couldn't appear more sincere. "We wouldn't think of it."

I can't help but smile. Until the Dragon introduces the demerits system.

The wall to her right contains a grid of the Chinese names of all Chien Tan students, more than I can count. We get demerits for coming late to class, failing to turn in assignments, using cell phones during school hours, failing to be in by bed check, getting caught up after lights out. Too many demerits means a call home. Twenty strikes and we lose the two-week Tour Down South—a chartered bus tour of the island at program's end.

"*What?*" Sophie protests. Apparently, that trip's worth something.

I frown. Nerd camp with Wong-family level regulations. Everything about the Dragon—including her Hokkien accent and short, permed hair—reminds me of Mom. *Studies come first. Why do you need to go out with Megan when you see her every day?* My summer's shaping up even worse than expected.

As the Dragon turns away to file our papers, I lean in to Sophie. "You said no supervision."

"There are rules. You just have to not get caught. They've sent one or two people home in their whole history."

"One more thing." The Dragon's back. "Every year, the kids put on a talent show on the last night."

Of course they do.

"Maybe you'd like to participate?"

Right . . . how about a solo flag corp dance? I shake my head.

"Oh, I have no talents." Sophie cheerfully pushes back the sign-up sheet. I can't help laughing. Sophie is a bit overwhelming, but also seems pretty down to earth, and funny . . . not her fault she's related to Boy Wonder. With her around, maybe this summer will be more bearable.

We gather our bags and head for the elevators. Sophie waves to a few guys we'd met earlier. "Benji Chiu is a *doll*, isn't he?" she whispers. "And David's *Haa-vard*-bound—*so cute*, don't you think?"

"Mm-hm." I'm noncommittal. Benji brought his stuffed bear, Dim Sum—a little too cute for me. David—I'm definitely not a goatee girl.

"Ooh, check this out." Sophie rips a purple flyer off a bulletin board pegged with glossy pages offering massages, tutoring, summer concerts. She plunges into the empty elevator. "We

48

need a plan!" Sophie bats my arm with the flier. "The clubs! I've got a list of the best restaurants. Oh, and our glamour shots!"

"Glamour shots?" My stomach dips as the elevator rises. "Like what movie stars get?" For the girl stapling *Summer Reading List* posters to the guidance office bulletin board just last week? "I can't afford—"

"They're *crazy* affordable—trust me. I'll book our appointment. Also, Rick and I are visiting our aunt at the end of the month—you're invited, of course."

"Oh, um. Wow." How generous—she seems to have taken a liking to me and I find myself not wanting to let her down. "Are you sure?"

"Roommates are family. Especially ones who aren't speeding off to meet *the commissioner.*"

We laugh. "I'd love to come. But aren't we in classes all day? One hour of homework a night? Where are we finding time to do anything else?"

The elevator halts on the third floor, and I drag my luggage into a lounge of blue-silk couches arranged around a black-lacquered table. Sophie's eyes glint with mischief. "Two hours a morning, plus two hours of culture class in the afternoon. Who cares about homework and the rest of the time is ours." She lowers her voice. "What'll they do if we skip? Send us home? *No way*. They want us to have a good impression of Taiwan."

"But demerits—"

The elevator chimes behind us. To my surprise, the Dragon steps out, a crowbar in hand, face as grim as if she's breathing

49

fire. She's followed by Mei-Hwa Pan, the petite counselor Boy Wonder mowed over earlier.

"*Uh-oh*," Sophie breathes. "Something's up."

The two march past us to the third white door on the left, which the Dragon pries open with her crowbar. Her sonorous voice berates and scorches. We pass the doorway as a half-naked girl bursts out, giggling, clutching her pink dress to her bra. Behind her, a guy in a black shirt scrambles off the rumpled bed. Lights glint off his wavy, crow-black hair, tousled and falling in his face. He grabs his shorts—but not before I catch a glimpse of his . . . equipment.

Oh my God oh my God oh my God.

Back home, I'm not even allowed to watch kissing scenes—whenever one comes on during family movie nights, Dad always flips the channel. Now I'm too stunned to close my eyes. Seconds later, the guy's in his shorts, shuffling past the Dragon into the hallway. His arm brushes mine. Insolent eyes—dark, liquid, opaque—slide to make contact. His lips curve in a wolf-ish smile and I read a spark of interest, an invitation. A dare.

The girl giggles again. She's pulled on her baby-doll dress. "Let's go, Xavier!"

A hot name to match the rest of him. I feel a small shock as our connection breaks. The Dragon chases them down the hallway and Sophie clutches my arm in a Megan-like way. Her body shakes with silent laughter as we weave toward our room.

If Dad were here, he'd have swatted Xavier down the hallway

with his rolled-up *World Journal* and placed me under house arrest for my own protection.

Maybe nerd camp isn't so nerdy after all.

"So *that*—" I finally say.

Sophie's cheeks are red from holding back her laughter. "That's *Loveboat*."

I'm starting to get the picture.

Our door is stuck, swollen into its frame with humidity. I turn the key and shove, then Sophie turns the key and shoves; then she says, "Here, you keep the key turned and we'll shove together." With our collective weights, the door flies open with a whoosh of air.

"We make a good team." She laughs and swoons onto her pinstripe mattress. "Oh my God, Ever! That Xavier was the hottest guy I've ever seen."

"He's taken already," I point out. Not that the pink girl had stopped him issuing that once-over.

"*Taken?*" Sophie snorts and sits up, flipping her sleek hair behind her shoulder. "One out of four relationships break up because of Loveboat."

"Wow, really?"

"Yeah, my cousin was dating someone then she met a guy at registration and they've been together since . . ."

Sophie prattles on as I set my purse on my dresser and

cross toward our double-paned window to check out the view. Our room is clean but simple: two beds, two desks, two dressers, a hot water thermos. Three stories below, the lush green lawn separates us from a row of brick buildings. A concrete wall, twisted over with green foliage, encircles the compound. Beyond it, to the left, the blue-green Keelung River divides us from the far bank—a sprawl of rectangular high-rises of Taipei, and beyond those, a gray-blue mountain dominates the horizon.

The view could have been really nice—except for the baby-blue pipe that stretches across the entire river, supported by two concrete columns. A red maintenance catwalk tops it. For sewage? What an eyesore.

"What music do you listen to?" Sophie winds her earphones around a slim iPod shuffle.

"Oh, um—I love musicals," I admit, a little embarrassed. Most of my classmates were into rock, hip-hop, metal/goth stuff.

"What's your favorite?"

"Oh, lots. Anything Disney. *Les Misérables, Phantom of the Opera.* My best friend and I've watched *The Greatest Showman* about a half dozen times."

"I *adore Greatest Showman.* When Phillip ran into the burning building after Anne, I about *died.*" She lays a hand on her heart, so dramatic I have to smile.

"I loved her trapeze dance. When she's telling him they're impossible."

"The same songwriters did *La La Land,*" Sophie says.

"Really?" Cool that she knew that—she knows so many things I don't.

Sophie plugs mini-speakers into her phone. The opening beats vibrate her desk and I resist an urge to stomp in time to them, like I would in my room back home. She unfurls her sheet over her mattress, rattling off the names of musicals she's seen live on Broadway. I've only seen *The Lion King*, on a class field trip to Manhattan. She's great, but our lives back home must be so different.

"So, do you have a serious boyfriend?" Sophie asks.

*No, but my best friend does.* God, I miss her. "My parents said no dating until after med school. I need to establish my career first."

"Of course they did." Sophie smirks. "No dating, then all in a day you're expected to land the heir to the throne and produce grandchildren. I've had four boyfriends—not that my parents had a clue." She rolls her eyes. "Anyways, what are you looking for?"

"Looking for?" I'm still stuck on the *heir* and *grandchildren* parts.

Sophie hugs her naked pillow. "I have criteria—I call them the Seven Cs: Cute, Cool, Cash, Clever, Creative. Charisma and *Charm.*"

"Oh, wow." It's a power list, not qualities I'd even presume to want for myself.

"Every girl has lists."

I nod. "My best friend had a long one—blue eyes, six-foot-plus, good muscles, nice butt. She got all of them, too."

Sophie laughs. "Lucky her. What about yours?"

I push my pillow into my pillowcase. A girl the grade below me, Grace Chin, had a short list: Christian and Chinese. Mine was even shorter—*not Stanley Yee*—the only Chinese American boy in my grade, whom people have been trying to get me to date since kindergarten.

"Someone I can dance with. Completely unrealistic." But my heart finishes the thought. Someone to lift me high and weightless into the sky like in the musicals—if partner dancing didn't violate my parents' no-inappropriate-physical-contact rule.

I'm back by the dumpster again. My stomach knots.

"I bet you'll find him here." Sophie smooths her blanket.

"In eight weeks?" I laugh at her, but she just twitches her brows back.

"It's *Loveboat*. Lots of parents send their kids here hoping they'll find someone."

"Parents *do* that? On purpose?" And I thought *my* parents were interfering.

"Rick's and my parents are old-fashioned like that." Sophie shrugs. "But like I said, I'd have come anyways."

I should probably feel horrified, but instead, I feel a strange thrill. If Megan were here, she'd have shoved me out the door already with a, "Go for it, Ever!" Not to *find him*, but to do something besides hanging back, wishing things were different with Dan—and boys in general.

I unzip my own suitcase. To my surprise, my dance bag sits in the center, a periwinkle egg in a nest of my clothes.

A lump forms in my throat, and I try to swallow it down. Is this Mom's way of apologizing, even if it's too little, too late?

I lift it out but it's all wrong. Rectangular, heavy, folded in half, instead of soft with a leotard and tights—this is why my suitcase weighed so much. With growing foreboding, I flip the bag upside down, and dump out a blue-and-red . . . textbook.

*Principles of Molecular Biology.*

I once read about a burglar's lantern, made for sneaking around in the dark. A metal box built so not a single ray of light can escape without the owner opening one of its narrow shutters. I'm that flame. Every want I have meets with its metal walls, like a supernova locked in a titanium prison.

"What's wrong?"

I whirl on Sophie. "You know what my life is?" I tear out a page, crumpling it in my hand. "Get straight As. No more dancing. Insane curfew, dress like a *nun*—"

"No sex until you die?"

"The most sacred rule of all!" I fling the book down.

"Well, no more following rules this summer." Sophie shoves her purple flyer at me. "This Thursday, we're sneaking out."

I drop my eyes to the flyer:

### CLUB KISS

#### *NO COVER FOR UNDER 21S! FIRST DRINK FREE!*

A guy in black leather, chains, and tattoos jams on his guitar. His blond hair flies like fishnet. He's with a band called Three

Screams, from Manhattan, and he looks like the kind of guy my parents don't even know exists, and if they did, they'd never approve of me going to listen to him.

"Clubbing all night," Sophie says. "Drink what you want, dance, dress to impress, and your parents can go eat dirt."

How many invitations from Megan and the girls for dinner and a movie in Cleveland have I turned down because they'd keep me out past curfew, or because *boys* were going?

"There's a guard downstairs," I point out.

She pulls a wry face. "Yeah, they've beefed up security. But Rick says we can climb the wall." With her bare foot, she shoves her emptied suitcase under her bed. "This is Loveboat. One big party. All summer. And no one's going to ruin it." Sophie fans her yearbook pages at me. "Ever, you are *never* going to meet this many eligible guys in one place. Admissions is super selective. I've been waiting for this trip for, like, *forever*. I'm so *done* with all those rock band–poser boys I grew up with. I'm finding my man here." She points to me like she's passing a parliamentary baton. "And your game plan, madam?"

With a sweep of my hand, my two-hundred-dollar textbook clunks to the floor, and I back-kick it deep under my bed. I pick up her Club KISS flyer and jot my list on its back.

*WONG FAMILY RULES*
*Straight As*
*Dress Like a Nun*
*Curfew of Ten*

*No Drinking*
*No Wasting Money*
*No Dancing with a Boy*
*No Kissing Boys*
*No Boyfriend*

I write the last one with a thrill, like I'm signing up to skydive off a cliff—it's not going to happen, but oh, what if it did? I dangle the list before Sophie: all the reasons I'm a baby compared to the rest of the world, because I'm med school–bound, because I'm my parents' daughter, because I'm Ever Wong.

"This summer, I'm breaking all the Wong Rules."

"Well then you left out the most important one." She grabs my pen and adds to the bottom:

*No Sex*

"Not *that*." I snatch my pen back, hating myself for blushing. Even if it's the most sacred of the Wong Rules. Maybe I've read too many Victorian novels, but I'm saving that for love.

"Fine." Sophie laughs and stabs at *Curfew*. "That one's first. We just need a way out."

I peer out the window to study the concrete wall that rings the campus. "We *could* climb the wall. If we stacked chairs. But it's a long drop on the other side." The wall's a good fifteen feet high. I scan the courtyard until my gaze lands again on the eyesore pipe crossing the green river. It disappears beneath a highway overpass. On our side, it starts from a concrete pillar beside the buildings across the lawn. A red utility ladder leads up to it and presumably down the other end. It must be a hundred feet long, all exposed to the eyes of Chien Tan by day.

But not by night.

"*That's* our route," I say, and I realize my decision is made. Megan would kill me if she knew.

Sophie presses in beside me and peers out. "You're not serious. If we fell—"

"There's a catwalk." I give my partner in crime a tight smile, ignoring the stab of fear in my gut, the image of tumbling dozens of feet down into dark waters. "Thursday night. We're on."

7

Our first task, Sophie declares, is to find clubbing outfits.

But downstairs in the humid lobby, Mei-Hwa and other counselors are herding kids into a dimly lit auditorium for the opening ceremony. I peer inside. The room appears to have been built with a smaller crowd in mind because every seat before the red-curtained stage is taken, with more students jammed in along the back wall and overflowing down the aisles.

"Come on," Sophie whispers, and we duck around a group of guys, steering clear of Mei-Hwa.

"How many kids are here anyways?"

"Five hundred." Sophie pauses at a table, where dozens of eggs bob in a bronze vat of tea-speckled soy sauce.

"*Five hundred?*" With a ladle, Sophie scoops a marbled tea

egg out, drops it into a paper cup and presses it into my hand. "That's bigger than my entire high school."

Drumrolls echo from the auditorium, seductively deep and rhythmic. I crane my neck to see the stage, where two guys in sleeveless white shirts and black pants are raining whole-arm beats down on barrel drums. A Chinese lion, shaking its over-sized gold-trimmed head, leaps out from between them.

Sophie grabs my arm. "Come on. Let's get out of here."

I almost suggest we stay—I've never seen a lion dance on this level of incredible. From the doorway, a counselor in a fluorescent-yellow hat beckons to us, calling, "*Lai, lai.*"

But Sophie yanks me around the corner, scraping my arm on brick, and then we're pushing out double doors into blinding sunlight. A pair of gardeners kneels in the dirt, planting flowers.

"Go!" Sophie urges, and I sprint with her up the driveway and around the lily pad pond, past the guard booth to the street.

"Won't they come after us—yipes!" I leap out of the path of a cavalcade of fume-spewing mopeds. Their rush of wind tears at my hair and skirt with a sputtering of motors.

"No one knows who we are yet." Sophie's laugh bubbles as she tugs me firmly onto the sidewalk, then sets off at a brisk clip. "Don't get yourself run over, okay? Traffic here is a human rights violation."

The sun beats down on my head as I shell my egg and try to keep up with Sophie. I haven't eaten a tea egg in years, not after

I opened my lunch box to shrieks of horrified, "What are *those?*" and I begged Mom not to pack me any more weird Chinese food. Sophie devours her own egg, making moaning noises straight out of a scene I wouldn't be allowed to watch on TV. I bite into warm flavors of star anise, cinnamon.

"Oh, yum," I say.

Chien Tan's driveway opens into a major street, facing a tree-covered mountain topped with that enormous pagoda building. Directly across from us, a brick mural of Chinese farmers is built into the hillside. Up the street, we pass a small, red temple with the fanciest tiers of rooftops—like a paperback book opened and laid facedown, sides gently sloping, corners upturned like the prow of a ship. It's painted in a riot of colors— red flowers, intricate designs, Chinese scholars in blue robes. A long, green dragon, its back flaming with yellow spikes, undulates over the top.

"Wild," I say. "I kind of like it."

"There's stuff like that all over Taiwan." Sophie drops her empty cup into a trash can. "You'll see."

We veer off through a tree-lined park, then through narrow streets lined with three-story buildings, fronted by garage-sized stores. We pass hairstyling shops, a tea room, a whiskey store, all labeled with Chinese characters.

At last, we step into an outdoor market crammed with vendor carts, small shops, and tiny restaurants with only a few benches for customers. A man mists a mountain of Chinese cabbages. A stout woman, hair bound in a purple scarf, yanks dough into foot-long sticks and drops them into her copper vat of oil; another shakes out a bolt of red silk. Jewelry shimmers like colored fireflies.

On Sophie's heels, I wander deeper through tarp-lined stalls. Vendors call, "*Xiaojie, lai lai!*" and motion to their fruit stands or dress racks. Their energy draws me in. I'm stepping into a tradition that must date back hundreds, even thousands of years. Sophie pulls out her wallet at every other stall—she buys a Hello Kitty shirt, a cloth pencil case printed with tiny cartoon bears, bottled water for us.

"Don't you want anything?" she asks.

My stomach knots a bit. My family counts every penny, and I've never felt free to just buy whatever strikes my fancy, unlike Sophie, clearly. Our goal is outfits, and I need to save all my firepower for that.

"Um, yea, sure," I answer. "Still looking."

Sophie flips through a stack of DKNY jeans, tries on a yellow North Face jacket, hefts Coach purses in her hands. "Everyone knows these are knockoffs, but they're such a *steal*," she gloats. She dangles a striped Elle-labeled dress before my body. "What about this one? Cut's *perfect* for your body type. You're slim, but sturdy."

"Thanks, but not this one." I push it aside. "I want an outfit my mom would kill me in."

She laughs. "I like how you think."

"Hey, Sophie." To my dismay, Boy Wonder is coming toward

us, head cocked to make room for the hundred-pound burlap sack balanced like a baby whale on his shoulder. So he's skipped the opening ceremony, too. The 100 percent humidity clings to my skin, but somehow, Boy Wonder with his forest-green shirt stretched across his broad shoulders looks as cool as the shady underside of an oak tree. I grimace.

"Rice?" Sophie beats a fist on his sack, scandalized. "Are you transferring into my cooking elective?"

"I tried to sign up, but it was full." Boy Wonder hefts his sack higher. "This is for weights. Turns out real weights cost fifty bucks a kilo here, so I bought this instead. Ten cents a kilo." He grins, obviously pleased with himself.

My brow rises. Creative. And surprisingly unpretentious.

But Sophie sighs. "We've been here less than three hours and you're already working out."

"I sat on the plane for fifteen hours with my knees to my ears. Enough downtime to last me the rest of summer."

I agree—instead of jet-lagged, I feel charged enough to dance a loop around the entire city. Boy Wonder levers the sack to his other shoulder. His T-shirt rucks up, offering a glimpse of tanned, flat muscles, from which I swiftly remove my eyes—but not before he catches me. Damn bad timing.

"At least you're in a better mood," Sophie says. "Good call?"

"Yeah, I got my SIM card working. I have a landline in my room, too."

"No fair, really? We don't."

"My roommate's some VIP kid. Xavier. Haven't met him yet."

"Of course they'd give the VIP kid to you." Sophie catches my eye and quirks her brow. *Xavier.*

"Whatever. Jenna says hi. I found her this." He touches the head of a carved bird tied with a red ribbon, jutting from his pocket—so Boy Wonder's the Wonder Boyfriend, too. Of course. I still can't believe Sophie suggested he date *me*—no way would I bring down a house of parental blessings on myself like that. Why can't Mr. Perfect SATs at least have the modesty to *look* the part: scrawny with thick glasses and acne, for starters. And Sophie's right—his mood's done a complete 180.

"We're hitting Club KISS Thursday," Sophie says. "Ever's idea."

His thick brow rises. "Not wasting time, are we?"

"Carpe diem." I shrug, keeping it cool. Latin, not Chinese, on the streets of Taipei. So there.

"Carpe noctem," he answers. Seize the night.

*Deodamnatus!* Boy Wonder's trumped me again—how many languages does he know anyways? I indulge a fantasy of me using that big, hard body as a punching bag.

"Meet outside our room at eleven," Sophie presses on. "And *please* don't wear yellow. It makes you—"

"Look jaundiced, so you've said." Boy Wonder rolls his eyes at me. To my dismay, my heart skips a beat. "Aunty Claire will be thrilled to hear you begged me to chaperone. Even bribed me with such excellent fashion advice. I'll be there. Don't want any broken hearts."

"It's the real Rick Woo again. Welcome back. Tell me this isn't a result of you and Jenna having phone sex."

"Mind out of the gutter *please*."

"Well, no worries about us." Sophie links arms with me while I try to block out unwanted images. "No guy's breaking our hearts."

"Oh, it's not you girls I'm worried about." With a smirk, Boy Wonder heads off, sack still balanced on his shoulder.

"We don't need a chaperone!" I call, but he's gone.

An hour later, I gaze uncertainly into the full-length mirror of a curtained dressing room. My black chiffon skirt skims a whole two inches above my knees. I twist to examine the corset-like back of the black halter top: satin lacing, wide eyelets that show off diamonds of skin. It calls for a dance—leg lifts, pirouettes, strong hands encircling my waist. I don't care that corsets are old-fashioned, I love it.

But between the waistband of my skirt and my top, a wide, pale ribbon of skin gleams.

So shameful! Mom's voice rings. *You want boys to think you're a bad girl?*

My reflection winces. The *Dress Like a Nun* rule is going down this summer, but maybe not with this outfit. *Besides, what will Rick-the-Chaperone think*, I wonder, before I remember I don't care.

Reluctantly, I peel off the skirt and top and return it to the protesting vendor. It's really more than I can afford anyways. But it gives me an idea. Maybe I can find a dance studio to join in Taipei. The thought gives me fresh hope.

I navigate out the shop's racks of dresses and cross the alley to another shop, where Sophie is modeling before a mirror. She tugs down the hem of a gold lamé dress laced with delicate flowers. The silk clings to her full body and she lifts a bundle of gold chains over her head. They pour down the plunging V-neck into her cleavage. She's the definition of sexy—and not afraid to flaunt it.

"*Duōshǎo qián?*" Sophie asks the vendor. *How much is it?* "What?" she explodes, when he quotes her the price. "*Tài guì!*" *Too expensive!*

I watch, open-mouthed, as Sophie puts on a performance worthy of an Academy Award: she haggles, gesticulates, verges on changing her tearful mind, until she gets her dress to a third of the ask and the merchant smacks his hands with satisfaction.

"Wow," I whisper as he wraps the dress in newspaper.

Sophie shushes me. "He got a great deal," she whispers, then sprints off to a shop hung with Burberry coats.

I pull a black cocktail dress from its rack and lift it to my body. My reflection frowns. I look like a girl headed to a funeral. Even from 7,000 miles away, Mom's turned me back into a little girl, while Sophie will look exactly like an eighteen-year-old breaking out for a night of dancing.

A horn honks from the street intersecting our alley. I step

out of the shop to see a silver BMW with tinted windows, forcing its way through pedestrians to pull up beside the sidewalk. To my surprise, a familiar-looking guy in a black shirt swings a leg out the back door. Wavy black hair tumbles into his face. An opal earring glitters on his earlobe.

The boy making out with the pink girl—Xavier. Rick's VIP roommate.

I duck out of sight and move to a gap between two vinyl flaps, through which I watch Xavier jerk to a stop halfway out of the car. Inside, a man with a face like Xavier's grips his arm. Xavier's dad? Does he live here?

They exchange an impressive torrent of Mandarin in loud, angry voices that cause a few tourists to scurry by. I recognize one word from his dad, only because my cousins used it on each other when we were little: *báichī*. *Idiot*. Xavier flashes his middle finger, hops out, and slams the door. The silver car squeals away.

I draw farther back, shaken by the force of their anger. Xavier's body is all hard, furious lines as he stares after the car, arms at his sides, fists clenched. A reddish blotch shines on his cheek—a bruise? Did his dad *hit* him? Whatever his dad wants—better grades, not a toe out of line, prostrated nose-to-the-pavement filial piety—Xavier's not just *taking* it like an Ever Wong.

He's fighting back. Can it work? Is it even possible?

Dan floats to the center of my memory. My first real crush, who sat behind me in eleventh-grade chemistry. He was the only senior, and Will Matthews called him an idiot, too. He lent me a pencil, then I lent him one, and we started partnering in labs, helping each other decipher the teacher's chicken-scratch on the blackboard. Dan was struggling with solubility calculations and asked for help.

"Sure." I'd danced with excitement into the eye-wash station. "Want to come over?"

I'd been an innocent then.

When Dad opened the door to Dan—freckled, blue-eyed, towering half-a-head over him and asking for me—Dad's jaw dropped. As we worked on the coffee table, he hovered waspishly close, flipping his newspaper, blowing his nose trumpet-loud.

Dan came two more Tuesdays. He wasn't an idiot; he was acing world history. His brain just wasn't wired for calculations. And maybe I'd smiled too much while he was over. Laughed too hard when he used my pen to play connect-the-dots with the freckles on his arm. Because when we slipped outside behind the backyard shed and he took hold of my waist, we were together for only five minutes before Mom was raging over us like a stung bull, swatting at us both. *Have you no shame?* Her cries, long after Dan had sprinted down our driveway, still echo in my ears.

I ran to find Dan in class the next day, desperate to explain. But when I arrived, he was emptying out his desk behind me. "Sorry, Ever," he'd murmured. "I just can't get in the middle of that." Before I could speak, he slipped away to a seat at the back. Then bolted after class before I could catch him. As the days turned into weeks, I lost the courage to speak. He lent me a pencil when I asked, but never borrowed mine again, and if he hadn't started dating Megan, I wouldn't have known him well enough to congratulate him when he graduated.

I snap back to the present. On the roadside, Xavier's shoulders have slumped. There's something vulnerable, almost little-boy lonely about him, left in the dust of his dad's fancy car. He jams his hands into his pockets and heads into the crowd, dodging a family sucking from fresh coconuts through straws. The crowd closes over him like stage curtains.

Before I can lose my courage, I return to the shop across the street and tap the vendor on the shoulder.

"I'll take that skirt and corset after all," I say.

**8**

"Thursday, after lights out."

"Thursday. Thursday night."

In the morning, the whispers buzz through the humid hallways, stilling whenever a counselor walks by. Everyone's invited. I get my phone partially working at the lobby store, but maybe I'm on the cheap plan, because my internet won't load, and I can't get calls or texts. The cheerful woman behind the counter shows me how to download WeChat, the Chinese messaging app. It means I can reach Pearl and Megan secretly, and Mom and Dad can't reach me—I'll take silver linings where I can.

I send Pearl an invite to sign up for We Chat. Miss you, I text her. How's it going? It's okay here. My roommate seems cool, but she spends money without even blinking. A bunch of us are sneaking out clubbing Thursday.

Hey, I text Megan, along with her invite. How's Dan's visit going? Things are okay so far, although lots of kids here seem to know each other already. Cousins and camp friends. Classes are whatever, but I'm looking for a dance studio. Sneaking out clubbing Thursday too—hope we don't get caught.

I'm staring at the screen, hoping for an answer. But they're asleep on the other side of the world.

I arrive in classroom 103, an airy white cube cut into five rows of white desks and orange, curved-back chairs. To my dismay, the Dragon, draped in a green jumpsuit, stands at the whiteboard, taking charge of the remedial language learners herself, apparently. She's printing symbols: the Chinese alphabet, which I only vaguely recall from Chinese school. Getting a failing grade won't be hard—at least one Wong Rule is guaranteed to bite the dust.

One body then another bang into me from behind, nearly knocking me off my feet. Blue-haired Debra and Laura in her Yankees cap rush by for the front row.

"Sorry, Ever!" they chorus.

Goatee-Harvard David, another Presidential Scholar, races in on their heels. The scent of his cologne oversaturates the air and stings my nostrils.

"Think they'll let us accelerate into Level Two if we test again

71

end of the week?" he asks. "Rick Woo's in Level *Ten*, the bastard."
He sounds admiring.

Honestly, do they really care what Level they are? I'm rarely
into climbing mountains, and definitely not one that doesn't
count for anything. I make a beeline in the opposite direction to
the back, out of teacher-calling range. I'm just happy to hear I'm
not stuck in class with Boy Wonder.

As I take my seat, Xavier steps through the door, wavy hair
tumbling into his face, his posture slouchy under his finely cut
blue shirt. His dark eyes alight on me, cool and sardonic. Crap.
I pretend to flip through my workbook, hoping he's walked into
the wrong classroom. Two rows ahead, a trio of girls coo over
albums of themselves in sexy outfits—the glamour shots, which
are, apparently, a quintessential Loveboat experience. All the
girls are booking appointments.

The seat beside me slides back.

"I'm Xavier." His voice is smooth and low, dark chocolate
with hints of cherry. If he remembers Sophie and me staring at
him (all of him) when the Dragon barged in, he doesn't give any
indication.

"Um, I'm Ever."

"Where you from?" The vulnerable Xavier has vanished,
too, replaced by this artsy-hot guy with a mocking smile. Even
the blotch on his cheek is gone.

"Ohio."

"There are Asian people in Ohio?"

His perspective on my home state is off, but not by much. I can't help a small laugh.

"Where you from?" I ask.

"Manhattan." A big-city boy, no surprise.

"You're Rick's roommate, right?"

"Yeah, I'm stuck with Whole Foods all summer. We won't be seeing him here—he doesn't slum it."

"So I hear." I don't even have to ask what he means by Whole Foods—Rick could be the poster boy for clean living. "Boy Wonder strikes again." I scowl. The corner of Xavier's lip turns up and I return his smile—we understand each other just fine.

"Hey, guys, how's it going?" Matteo Deng, a Euro-preppy rugby player, takes a seat in front of us. His family in Italy are wealthy clothing boutique owners and his accent's Italian. He's brushed his permed black hair into a thick plateau on his head.

Before I can answer, a hand closes on my bicep. A pale blue scarf tickles my cheek.

"Ever, I need to ask you something," Sophie whispers in my ear. "Xavier, Matteo, excuse us a minute?"

I follow her out the door. Her blue dress swishes and her scarf flutters like a kite tail down her back.

"Something wrong?"

The hallway is deserted, but she lowers her voice anyways. "Matteo bought me bubble tea this morning, and Xavier was flirting with me at breakfast. Now they're both in our Mandarin class! Should I encourage them? Invite them clubbing?"

This is the emergency? Really? "You're seriously boy-crazy." I laugh and she gives a charming shrug.

"It's—"

"Loveboat. I know. Well, do you like them?"

"Matteo's *adorable*. Have you heard him talk? Although I heard he yelled at Mei-Hwa when she dropped his laptop bag, but he was probably jet-lagged. He apologized. As for *Xavier*." She clutches her stomach dramatically. "Oh my God, Ever. He makes me *so* nervous."

"Um, hello. Pink girl?"

"Oh, Mindy." She swats at a gnat. "They met at the airport a week ago and she apparently threw herself at him. She was at breakfast. They didn't even sit together."

Less than twenty-four hours into the program, and Sophie knows everyone and everything already.

"Fine, invite them both," I say.

"Okay. I'll do it after class." She draws a quivery breath. "Help me if I chicken out?"

I hide a smile, tuck a lock of hair behind her ear. Back home, I'm on friendly terms with the girls on the dance squad, but really just have Megan. With Sophie, our friendship feels strangely effortless.

"Definitely," I say.

She beams and we slip back inside.

"*Ai-Mei. Bao-Feng, nín wǎnle,*" says the Dragon. "*Duǎnchu.*"

"Shit, seriously?" Sophie mutters. She grabs my elbow and steers me faster toward the back.

"What?" I whisper, alarmed. Not understanding a word is going to get old very quickly.

"We got a demerit each. For being late."

"*What? We were here—*"

"*Zhūyīnfú hào. Gēn wǒ chàng.*" The Dragon taps the alphabet on the board. In a deep voice, she sings to the tune of "Twinkle, Twinkle, Little Star": "*Bo po mo fo de te ne, le . . .*"

As we reach the back, Matteo throws Sophie a wolfish grin and she giggles nervously. Behind Matteo, Xavier still slouches in his chair, bare legs crossed at the ankles.

Sophie pulls out my seat beside Xavier and drops into it. I'm a little surprised—my purse is still hanging off its back. Maybe she didn't notice? I pull its strap off and slide into the seat beside her as Xavier gives me another of his dark glances. *He* noticed. I turn my gaze to the Dragon and pretend to sing along.

Whatever, right? It's Xavier. I might feel bad about what happened with his dad, but that doesn't mean he's not a Player. Someone to be handled with care.

We sing the alphabet twice more. "*Bo po mo fo de te ne, le . . .*" It's more torturous than Chinese school, because back then, I was six. Fortunately, or not, the gunners up front sing loud enough to cover for the rest of us.

Over the next hour, we learn the four main tones and the neutral one. Our voices slide up and down like a song. We combine two letters with a tone to sound out full-blown characters. Then the Dragon shoves aside one board to reveal another bearing five sentences written with the Chinese alphabet and Romanized letters, English translations mercifully printed beneath.

Matteo swivels in his seat with a squeak of chair legs. "Be my partner," he purrs at Sophie in his alluring Italian accent. No wonder she's swooning over him.

She glances sideways at Xavier, then smiles at Matteo. "I thought you'd never ask." Slipping from her chair, she moves into the empty seat beside him.

"Guess you're stuck with me, Wong." Xavier shifts into Sophie's empty chair. "You go first."

"What are we doing? I can't understand anything," I complain.

"Taking turns reading and answering the questions."

"Then you go first. You actually understood the assignment."

"No, you." He folds his arms over his chest.

"Fine. *Nǐ hǎo. Wǒ de míngzì shì Ai-Mei. Nǐ ne?*" I read the phonetics in an American accent that makes me cringe. *Hello, I am Ai-Mei. And you?* You'd think growing up hearing Mom speaking to her sister on the phone would help. Apparently not.

"Xiang-Ping," he answers.

I read the rest, finishing with: *What is your favorite movie?*

"*Fong Sai-Yuk.*"

"What's that in English?"

"*Fong Sai-Yuk.* Only the greatest kung fu flick in history."

"Kung fu flicks?" I make a face. "Ha."

"What's so funny?"

"My *dad* watches those."

76

His brow rises. "Well, maybe you should, too. You won't see fight scenes like that anywhere else. The choreography's amazing."

"Choreography?" I've never thought of kung fu as choreographed, but he's speaking my language—who am I to judge his taste?

"Maybe I *should* watch," I say. "So prejudiced, sorry."

"You should be."

I smile. He's very cool and guarded, but also kind of funny in a dark, wry way that makes me feel less on guard myself. Maybe I've been too quick to write him off.

Sophie drops a pencil and reaches back to retrieve it, flashing us a well-timed dimple. "*No English*," she chides in a scarily accurate imitation of the Dragon, before returning to Matteo.

Xavier turns the tables and asks me the first question in fluid Mandarin. He barely glances at the board. With all the proper tones, his low voice takes on a song-like quality; he's even better than Boy Wonder.

"Did you grow up here?" I ask.

"Was born here before moving to Manhattan." He shrugs.

"*You* should be in a higher level."

"I only speak. Haven't learned to read and write."

"Got it. Most of the kids in Chinese school were like that. Which was why I couldn't keep up."

Sophie tips back her black mane of hair so she's looking at Xavier upside down. "Ever mention we're going clubbing?"

The reminder twists my stomach. Less than a day in and I

already have a demerit. Am I really going through with this? With so many people in the know, how can the Dragon *not* find out our plan?

Xavier's dark eyes glitter at me. "Not yet."

"Matteo's in. You should come," Sophie urges. Then the Dragon makes us sing "*Liǎng Zhī Lǎo Hǔ*," a rhyme about two little tigers that Mom taught Pearl and me years ago. To the tune of "Brother John," we sing it once, twice, three times, in a round, then again, again, again. She writes a big red A in the upper corner of the board.

"*Hěn hǎo*. Very good," she praises us. "*Hěn cōngmíng, xiǎo péngyǒu*. So smart, my little friends."

"Kill me now," Sophie mutters.

"Seriously." I grimace, stabbing my workbook with my pencil. I may not be a Presidential Scholar or Level 10-er, but as hard as I might try not to, I'm going to ace this class.

9

After lunch, I stop by the computer terminal in the lobby. I look up dance studios in Taipei and run across studios focused on ballet, jazz, modern, Chinese dancing. If my parents had to choose one, they'd pick ballet for the discipline and focus. Twelve years of training at the barre gave me my foundation and got me into Tisch, but over the past few years, I've branched out—flag corps, jazz with the dance squad. I'm not a purist, I love all styles, love picking up new moves—I'd join all these studios if I could.

But ten minutes later, still no luck. Every studio is out of my price range and I can't ask my parents to pay—they'd tell me to focus on Chien Tan. But this is my last hurrah, my farewell to dancing. I need to find a smaller studio, like Zeigler's, maybe farther out from the city. Maybe something so small they don't even have a website—

"You done yet?" Mindy pokes my shoulder. Her pink tank top shows off her plump arms and her eyes are bright with blue eye shadow—but her expression is stormy. "Electives are starting. I need to get online."

"Sure, sorry." Relinquishing my seat, I head out the front doors into a blast of humidity. Introduction to Chinese Medicine is next. I hope it's not a hands-on acupuncture class. I say a prayer as I take the steps down: *please no needles*.

On the lawn, kids are gathering into three groups. Chinese Medicine is housed in the big white tent directly opposite. By the pond, a group of kids rain mallets down on barrel-sized drums. Beyond the volleyball net, a line of girls are receiving blue silk fans from a rattan basket held by Chen Laoshi—Teacher Chen. I join the line behind Debra and stretch my calves and laugh as Laura pretends to modestly cover her face behind the gold-etched silk, knocking into her Yankees cap. A dance unfolds in my head.

When I reach Chen Laoshi, she hands me a fan. I flip it open with a snap, tip my wrist, and flutter it out of line like a bluebird in flight.

"Cool move," Debra says.

The fan is snatched from my hand.

Chen Laoshi frowns. *"Zhèxiē jǐn shìyòng yú shànzi wǔ xuǎnxiū kè."*

"Sorry?"

"Only for the fan dancing elective."

"Oh," I stammer. "I didn't realize." The next girl in line taps her foot, waiting for Chen Laoshi, but my feet are glued to the grass.

"Can I switch electives?" I blurt. "I dance. Back home." I've never gone this long without. "Please"—my voice cracks—"I really want to join a dance elective."

She gives my shoulder a soft squeeze. "*Yòng guóyǔ*," she chides. *Use Chinese*. "*Bàoqiàn, zhè mén kè yǐjīng mǎn le*." She motions me off gently, her kindness worse than if she'd planted her sandal in my face. The universe has conspired to tear dancing from me before I even set foot on Northwestern's campus. If only Tisch—

But I can't think about Tisch.

I'll just have to find that studio.

I cast a longing gaze at the drum elective. The deep-barreled beats tug at my soul as my feet carry me farther away from both electives, toward Introduction to Chinese Medicine. Under the white tent, the humid air is as thick as a blanket. Xavier and some guys I met on the airport shuttle and at dinner last night are passing a steel bottle around. Xavier hands it to Marc Bell-Leong, who flicks his milk-chocolate bangs out of his eyes and takes a pull.

"Is that—?" I ask.

"Drinking age is eighteen in Taiwan." Xavier slouches with his hands in his pocket.

"Really?"

"Yep." He tugs out the chair beside him. "Pull up a seat."

I drop down, less nervous around him after Mandarin. The bottle moves from Marc to politician-Spencer, then Harvard-David, making its way around the table. Looks like my chance to break a rule in broad daylight. But I've never even *tried* alcohol—at Amy Cook's wedding last month, Mom, who grew up Baptist, whisked both our champagne glasses from under the waiter's bottle. I hadn't even questioned her.

"It's the strong jawline." Marc runs a thumb and forefinger down his own slender jaw. He's in conversation with the guys.

"The arm muscles?" David takes a swig and groans, "Ugh, that's strong." Scratching at his goatee, he passes the bottle to Sam Brown, a thick-fingered pianist from Detroit whose mom was born in Taipei. David drops onto his fists on the grass and pumps a series of push-ups, grunting each time he rises. Sam passes the bottle back to Marc and drops down beside him and they rise and fall together, acting all macho. I guess it's working because a few fan dancers stop to watch.

"Show off." Marc rolls his eyes.

David grunts. "You can't keep up."

"Can." Marc drops down beside them and they hold a contest, three bodies rising and falling like keys on a piano, until Sam collapses with his face in the grass and Marc and David keep pushing. Something about their energy appeals to me, but the one-upping is annoying.

Xavier's shoulder brushes mine. He leans in. He's not doing the macho thing, which surprises me, but I like that about him.

"There's a closet where they keep the extra stuff," he nods toward Chen Laoshi. "I'll nab you a fan later, if you want."

"Oh, um." So he'd noticed. "I don't want you getting in trouble."

"Would be my pleasure." His grin holds a grim edge.

The steel bottle is now with a guy named Peter. Getting closer. A familiar voice reaches my ears and I glance up. Boy Wonder, his NY Giants cap pulled low over his face, is speaking to Chen Laoshi while the fan dancers flick their blue silk fans open and shut like a field of blooming flowers. Chen Laoshi laughs, hugging the basket of fans.

Boy Wonder's not even *in* the elective.

What. A. Brown-Noser.

I scooch my chair around to turn my back.

"He's tall," Spencer says. "Also the hair on his chest. He's a rug."

"Still think it comes back to the strong jawline," Marc says.

Sophie walks up, tossing her floral blue scarf over her shoulder. "What hottie are you talking about? I want in." She swings an empty chair over, and settles beside Xavier with a half-wink that only she could pull off.

"Sorry, Sophie," Marc says. "It's your cousin so that would just be gross. We're debating what makes Rick the most masculine Chinese American guy we've ever met. Objectively."

"What a waste of oxygen," I say, and Xavier snorts.

Sophie laughs. "Hate to break it to you all, but he's straight. And taken."

"We're not after him. Just assessing."

"Also, he's *Taiwanese* American," Spencer says. "Like me and Xavier."

"Which is covered by *Chinese* American," Marc says.

"I disagree."

"I'm *Asian* American," Sophie says. "I'm part Korean. Ever?"

"I don't know," I admit. "I haven't really thought about it." I'm American. I'd never wanted much to do with my Asianness . . . but that was before.

"So if Rick's masculine, what are the rest of us?" David growls. "Effeminate Asian guys who can't get girlfriends? I *hate* that stereotype."

Marc looks David up and down. "You weigh less than Ever."

David scowls. I cut him a break and slap the side of my thigh.

"It's my legs, from ballet. I have more muscle here than all of you put together."

Sophie bubbles more laughter. David grunts. Marc makes a show of inspecting under the table. "Never want to be on the receiving end of a ballerina's leg."

I grin, surprised by my own boldness. I don't have close guy friends back home. How weird that just a day into Chien Tan, I feel as though I've known these guys all my life. Because it's camp? Because I was shyer back home, and now feel empowered among people who don't know the awkward history of my adolescence?

Is one of these the guy to kiss?

The steel bottle goes from Xavier to Sophie—and I realize that despite the camaraderie, no one's even tried to pass it to me.

"You're all coming Thursday, right?" Sophie says.

"Getting busted in a foreign country is not a headline I need for my future political career," Spencer says.

"Live a little." Marc squints at Sophie. "You sure there's a way out once we're over the pipe?"

"Ever and I will scope it out." Sophie passes the bottle over the table to him.

"Hey, Marc." I reach for the bottle, as Sophie says, "Eleven, meet—oh, ah, hm."

Li-Han, our instructor, drops a stack of thin-sheeted booklets onto our table's center. The bottle vanishes into Marc's shorts. David snatches up a booklet and flips through as Li-Han pushes his black-rimmed glasses closer to his face and moves to the other tables.

I take a booklet, then wish I hadn't. A human porcupine lies prone on the cover: a naked man with every inch of his backside, from neck to heel, stuck with needles. My stomach heaves and I flip it upside down.

Over by the fan dancers, Chen Laoshi is handing Boy Wonder a blue fan from her basket, smiling flirtatiously. Why shouldn't she? She's not that much older, and Boy Wonder probably dropped *Yale* and *football* a half dozen times. In flawless Mandarin.

As Chen Laoshi gathers her fan dancers around her, Boy Wonder heads toward us, the folded fan tiny in his hand.

"Speak of the man," Marc says as Boy Wonder nears.

"Rather not," I mutter.

"What about me?" Boy Wonder's brow rises, clueless, and everyone bursts out laughing. "Glad I amuse you," he drawls.

"You in medicine with us?" Marc asks.

"I'm in drums." He jerks his head over his shoulder. Then his eyes seek out mine. "Here." He lobs the fan at me and I, too startled not to, catch it.

"Oh, um—" Before I can stammer a thanks, his phone chimes with a Taylor Swift song, and he snatches it to his ear, knocks off his cap, and catches it with his free hand.

"Jenna! There you are."

"Can't she wait? No calls allowed now," Sophie chides, but with his T-shirt flapping in the wind of his own speed, Rick races off toward the dragon drums.

I open the fan. The scent of rosewood wafts on a soft breeze. The gold threads gleam against the blue silk. I could dance a forest sprite's caper or the role of a lady in a castle's courtyard with this.

Li-Han upends a paper bag over our table. A pile of gnarled roots drops out and its bitter dust sets me coughing.

"Cool, what is this?" David snatches one up. He's serious.

Li-Han answers in Mandarin I can't understand, nor do I care. Any elective would be better than Intro to Chinese Medicine. Over by the dragon drummers, Boy Wonder paces with his phone to his ear, smiling, his stupid, strong jaw backlit by the sun. A line of kids balancing oars on shoulders march by—the dragon boat racing elective—concealing him from view. When they pass, Benji and another guy are trying to lift the oversized Chinese lion head, its large eyes batting coyly, onto Boy Wonder's head while he ducks out of range at superhuman speed, and spins a full circle for good measure.

"Jeez, you're fast!" The guys are awed. Rick is laughing, phone glued to his ear. One day into Chien Tan and he's not only dodging demerits for illegal phone use, he's got a fan club.

But that club doesn't include me.

I toss the fan to Sophie, who's stood to head to her cooking elective.

"You take it," I say. "It matches your scarf."

# 10

I can't wear this.

Thursday night, I gaze at my reflection in the mirror Sophie bought for a dollar and taped to our door. Sophie, generous to a fault, gave me a makeover fit for a queen. My smoky eyelids and pouty lips, by my prudish Ohio standards, could get me arrested.

But it's my outfit that scares me most. The ribbon of pale skin gleams between my skirt's waistband and the skimpy black corset top that exposes those diamonds of skin on my back. I'd fallen in love at the market, and was all set to break the dress-modestly rule, but I can't go out in something so . . . *revealing*—

"We better head down. It's almost eleven." Sophie puckers her lips at her reflection and applies a second coat of lipstick. Her gold lamé dress glitters. "Xavier and Matteo are meeting us by the kitchen." There's been a quadrangle of flirting in Mandarin all week, from Xavier to me and Sophie to him to Matteo—par for course all over Loveboat. The gossip chain is buzzing loops about who's after whom, and tonight, I can't help feeling, will set more in motion.

"Give me a minute." From my drawer, I pull my soft black shirt with its quarter-length sleeves. I pull it on, covering my bare shoulders, midriff, corset seam. My phone on my dresser chimes.

> Pearl: Mom and Dad driving me nuts summer reading schools 2 months away wish you were here did you find a dance studio

The missing punctuation marks tells me she's dictating her text and having her laptop read to her, which she does to help with her dyslexia.

> Me: Hang in there. If you read them now, they can't be on your case anymore. I found a studio but too expensive, still looking
> Pearl: theyll find something else
> Me: Ugh, I know. Hang in there. Love u!

"Ready?" Sophie grabs the doorknob, then frowns at me. "We're going *clubbing*. You're going to be too hot in that."

I set my phone down beside two notes from Mei-Hwa to call my parents, which I've ignored. My legs flash in the mirror under my black chiffon skirt, an unseemly amount of skin. I tug my skirt down farther.

"I don't get hot," I lie.

"Are you sure—"

A knock sounds. Sophie tugs on the stubborn door. "Oh for heaven's sake," she fumes, then yanks with both hands and the door flies open. Boy Wonder, hair rumpled carelessly, steps through in a fitted canary-yellow polo over black pants.

Sophie throws up her hands. "Yellow. Rick, *I give up.*"

He grins, a sallow picture of innocence. She was right—yellow is *so* not Boy Wonder's color. If the game tonight is dress to impress, he's not playing.

Which, if he were any other guy, would be sort of impressive.

"I'm just here to chaperone, remember. Besides, you look nice enough for the both of us." He catches my eye.

"Ever." His eyes widen. I'm suddenly conscious of my magnified eyes and lips, the way my black shirt hugs my long torso and the skirt shows off my legs. His bear brows knit over his forehead in a scowl. "Your ribbon's undone."

"Oh." I reach behind for the knot Sophie tied earlier.

"Here." Boy Wonder comes around to my back, his voice impatient. My corset jerks tight around my rib cage as he knots my ribbons below the hem of my overshirt, once, twice, extra-secure. Like I'm twelve and he's my *dad*. Utter humiliation.

And he doesn't even notice. Next thing I know, he's peering out the doorway.

"Coast is clear. Come on."

A sliver of moon hangs in the sky as we emerge from the dormitory into the narrow lot behind the kitchen. The ivy-covered wall rises before us and the sour stink of trash wrinkles my nose. I keep moving past a twig broom, stacks of plastic crates, and a truck-sized dumpster, putting as much distance as I can between me and Boy Wonder.

But the others are close behind. As I reach the building's edge, Xavier glides into the moonlight beside me. His hand is in his pocket, wrinkling his designer black shirt that glints with silver threads. His dark eyes cut to me and a smile curves the corner of his lip.

"I like the skirt, Ever."

Unlike Boy Wonder, he's dressed for clubbing. His opal stud gleams on his ear—my parents would *so* disapprove of me standing anywhere in his vicinity. My hand strays self-consciously to the back of my corset, though he can't see the diamonds of skin there. I force myself to return his gaze evenly.

"I like the attitude."

"Mr. Yeh." Sophie tucks her arm through his. "Good of you to join us."

His corner-smile deepens, as if he can't be bothered with the effort of a full one. His arm brushes mine as he moves ahead.

I inhale the musky scent of cologne and my stomach dips—everything about tonight feels new and dangerous.

"Sauvage by Dior," Sophie whispers. "Isn't he *yummy?*"

"Ever, do something for me, okay?" Boy Wonder's voice, close enough to tickle the back of my earlobe, makes me jump.

"What?" My voice comes out uneven. He smells like the outdoors. Like grass and freedom.

"Keep your distance from Xavier."

"What?" I turn to him but our noses bump and I spring back with a small yelp.

Before he can answer, a crowd of kids comes between us—ten, then fifteen, then two or three dozen—sexy in sequins, bangles, lots of pale, moonlit skin. Way more than I was expecting. Someone giggles, then is shushed by a dozen voices. Just ahead, Xavier's leaning against the ivy-covered wall, thumb hooked in his belt loop, talking with Laura sans Yankees cap, and Debra, both cute in little black dresses.

Everyone's ready to break loose, except Rick-the-Chaperone.

The more I think about it, the more his warning annoys me—once again, it's *exactly* something my parents would say. Yes, Xavier might be a Player, but that also might make him the perfect guy to break a few rules with tonight.

"Where next?" Debra shakes back her blue hair.

I banish Boy Wonder-the-Chaperone from my mind. "The catwalk. There's a ladder. Sophie and I checked it out. Once we cross the river, look for cabs."

"And keep *quiet*," Sophie adds.

We slip along the wall toward the concrete pillar with its ladder leading into the night sky. There's one flaw to our escape plan. The moon shines like a spotlight on the blue pipe. Which means that for the entire two minutes it should take to cross the catwalk, we'll be exposed to every river-facing window of Chien Tan.

"Good thing there are so many of us," I whisper as Sophie begins to climb, the heels of her stilettos hanging off each rung. "They can't send us *all* home." But a knot cinches in my middle.

The ladder runs up into a metal tunnel formed of curved rails. It smells of rust. As I climb, a breeze whips my chiffon skirt against the backs of my thighs. I clutch it tight, silently hurrying Sophie, hyperaware of Boy Wonder's weight on the rungs below. Why didn't I let him go first?

But at last, I scramble over the pillar's top, three stories high, where the winds whip hair into my eyes. "Hang on," I call. The wind steals the words from my mouth, and sweeps the earthy, slightly fishy scent of the river at me. I grab hold of the painted rail and peer into the dark waters below. Then wish I hadn't. At the twist of vertigo, I yank my eyes back toward the sea of lights beckoning from Taipei ahead. The promised land. A line of silhouettes are already filing across the catwalk.

"Hurry," Sophie murmurs. I clutch the rail and focus on taking one step after another on the metal grid. My back prickles with the imaginary eyes of Chien Tan windows.

"They've reached the other side." Boy Wonder's ticklishly close voice makes me jump again. I need to stop overreacting to every little thing he does. Seriously.

"Cool," I say coolly.

I take another cautious step after Sophie. Another. Another. Another.

Then a rattling shakes the catwalk beneath my heels. The force sends me crashing into Sophie's sweat-soaked back. She emits a yelp as I fight for balance. My foot slips off an edge. My ribs hit steel and my shoe flies off, arcing toward the black waters. Scrambling for a hold, I catch a handful of air, then Boy Wonder's arm encircles my waist, halting my trajectory like a seat belt.

Down below, the darkness swallows my shoe like a silent river god.

"You okay?" His mouth against my ear shoots a shiver into my tailbone as he rights me. "Your shoe. Maybe we should go back."

"*No. Way.*" I yank free and tug off my other shoe. My heart pounds. He's blocking my way now.

He frowns. "You'll cut your feet—"

"Oh my God, I don't need a chaperone—"

A beam of light flits over the catwalk ahead.

Sophie swears. "Someone's awake."

I look back over my shoulder—and the beam catches me full in the face.

"Go," I yell. "Go go go!"

Spots swim in my vision and I drop my other shoe. I shove past Boy Wonder, grab Sophie's shoulders and stumble us across the last yards, cringing with every clank. The catwalk rattles and shakes with the rush of students behind us.

We drop into an empty parking lot surrounded by a concrete wall, lit by a row of five street lamps. A tabby cat shoots off with an ear-piercing yowl. It escapes out a gate flanked by two stone pillars, which open onto a street.

I should feel panicked, but instead, a laugh tickles my throat. "We're crazy!" Beside me, Sophie gasps for breath. "Come on." I grab her hand and pull her along. The gravel is hard and cold beneath my feet.

"I'll find a cab." Boy Wonder brushes against me as he lopes past. "Watch the glass."

Just in time, I dart around the broken bottle.

Ten feet beyond the gate, yellow cabs have lined up at a curb. Headlights gleam off chrome bumpers and engines purr in the humidity.

Stunned, I jerk to a stop. "No freaking way."

Sophie whoops. "Taipei knows us better than we know ourselves!"

"*Xiǎo péngyǒu, tíng, tíng. Huí lái!*" Distant voices from the left cut through the night. The glow of a flashlight spins closer as two guards in black and Li-Han emerge from the shadows a quarter mile down the street.

"*Shit.*" Sophie tugs me toward one of the middle cabs. "Don't let 'em recognize you!"

Then a flood of students boils out from the gate behind us like a well-dressed herd of buffalo.

"Let's go." Boy Wonder yanks open the front door and gestures at me. "Go—come on!"

"Don't be all chivalrous. You go!" I shove him in by his shoulder, waving Laura and Xavier into the back. "Go, go, hurry!" Kids soar in after Xavier. A girl crams into Boy Wonder's lap in front. Cabs screech away until only Sophie and I are left on the curb, Li-Han and the guards fast approaching. I can see the blue stripes of Li-Han's pajamas as I push Sophie into the back of the last cab.

"*Wong Ai-Mei, lái la!*" thunders a voice.

My Chinese name freezes me to the pavement.

From across the street, the Dragon herself is running at us. On the curb behind her, a light glows inside a black sedan. Her lime-green nightgown billows like scaly wings around her body.

"*Ai-Mei, nǐ yào qù nǎli?*"

"Ever, get *in!*" Sophie kicks her door wide open.

I spring forward but the Dragon's hand clamps onto my bicep. Her grip is like steel, pinching my flesh.

From the shadows of the cab's back seat, Sophie's eyes meet mine, uncertainty bubbling. No sense in all of us getting caught.

"Just go!" I shout, but the cab doesn't budge.

The Dragon's grip tightens. "Ai-Mei—"

Suddenly, an explosion like fireworks goes off by her car, shooting white sparks in every direction.

I take the moment of distraction to tear free and dive after Sophie, scrambling over skirts and pants as I pull myself through. Cologne fills my nostrils and the door slams against my foot and someone yelps.

"*Go!*" I shout.

"*Kuài diǎn!*" Sophie shouts. *Hurry!*

Our cab lurches forward and I slam sideways into a wall of chests. I struggle upright, my knees tangling in a boy's pants. I brush hair from my sight as Xavier seizes my waist, steadying me on his lap.

"What happened?" I gasp, pretending not to notice the heat of his hands.

Sophie's laughing. "*Rick* happened."

Up front, Boy Wonder holds up a small disk between thumb and forefinger. "Fire snaps."

A startlingly Pearl-like move. "Did you destroy her car?"

"Her car's fine. Can't say the same for *you*."

I wipe a trail of sweat from my forehead. "I'm so busted," I moan. I brace for a patronizing *I told you so*.

Boy Wonder's teeth flash with a grin, and instead, he says, "Then we better make tonight worth it."

**11**

Club KISS is as terrible as its name. Smoke fills the lounge of middle-aged men who line the walls, eyeing girls on the dance floor. Overhead, a strobe globe shoots rays of light in every direction, while a spotlight illuminates a makeshift stage of black boxes dripping with microphone and amp wires. Girls in skimpy tops crowd it, screaming, waving at a third-rate band who turned out to be from *Minnesota*, not Manhattan. A base vibrates my entire skeleton.

"They're awful!" I yell. But I'm not a music snob. If it has a pulse, I'll dance to it, and Sophie and I head-bang on with Laura, Debra, and some girls who live down the hallway from us. My socks—donated by small-footed Spencer—slide along the floor.

Something happens when I dance. If someone met me on the streets of Chagrin Falls, they'd assume I was on the quiet side, studious, hardworking. The side I let most people see.

But when I dance, I become music in motion. A goddess. Myself.

Sophie kicks off her own shoes. She grabs my hand, spins me under her arm while I sashay my hips and whoop. I imagine Mom's jaw dropping, Dad removing his spectacles, if they knew all the *culture* I'm picking up already. I've slayed my first Wong Rule—curfew—and wearing lip gloss, too.

I tug at my shirt, pulling it tight against the corset back it's hiding. The AC is cranked high, but will I dare take it off as the night rolls on? Because sometime tonight, another Wong Rule is going down. In style.

Debra holds out her phone for a selfie. As Laura crowds in, I sashay out of the way—no social media for Mom and Dad to stumble across. Opposite me, Sophie dances a sultry circle, scanning, scanning, scanning the crowds. The strobe globe throws stars across her pouting lip and enormous faux-lashes that only she could pull off.

"Who're you looking for?" I shout.

"Just looking!"

Then Boy Wonder pushes through the dancers and grabs Sophie's shoulder. The upper half of his canary-yellow shirt is dotted with sweat. His damp hair gleams like onyx. "They've brought in a guy from Snake Alley. You've got to try this—it's the best in Taipei."

Sophie pulls free, tossing her hair in a silky parachute. "Snake Alley—no way!"

"What's Snake Alley?" I ask.

"A disgusting tourist trap," Sophie says. "It's in one of the night markets, farther down south."

I follow Boy Wonder's gaze to a table at back, where a man in a leather apron pulls a dragon-green snake from a wooden cage.

A literal, slithering snake.

Well, well. Boy Wonder has some exotic interests.

"What's that for?" I ask as a wave of dancers jostles us sideways.

Boy Wonder smirks. "See for yourself." Grabbing my hand, he tugs me into the crowd of dancing bodies.

His hand over mine is rough, calloused. Big. A boy's hand. But it means nothing; if he weren't hanging on, the crowds would tear us apart. Sure enough, when we reach a thick chopping block on a table, he releases me.

Then I wish he hadn't.

Inches away, three snakes writhe in a mass of scaly coils: red-and-black, yellow diamond-patterned, the mottled, dragon-green. Dark red blood stains the block, overlaid by new, damp blooms. Just behind them, the thin-faced snake-minder wipes stubby-nailed hands on his apron.

"As your unofficial chaperone, I have to advise against this." Boy Wonder gives me an infuriatingly superior grin.

"Ha. Whatever." But my stomach clenches. So we're going to eat snake. I've eaten barbecued eel, but never stared my food in the eye. Never seen it slither through the sludge of its comrades' blood. The metallic scent makes me light-headed, as always—I almost fainted when I shadowed at the Cleveland Clinic, when I had to observe a doctor stitch up a gashed knee.

"Let me guess. We're grilling our own snake-kebabs."

"If only." Boy Wonder cocks a finger-gun at the snake minder.

"What do you mean?" I ask, but he's already maneuvering toward the bar and bartender.

"I'll get tickets."

"I can cover myself—" I protest, but he's out of earshot.

Fine.

Whatever challenge Boy Wonder's got planned, I can handle it.

A brown snake rears, hissing onto its coils. I force myself to face it, trying to brave my coming fate without throwing up. Or passing out.

"Want to hold one?"

I jump as Xavier slides up beside me. I haven't seen him since the cab ride, when I leaped off his lap and out the door. The silver threads gleam in his shirt. As he extends his bare forearm toward the snakes, his scent breaks over me—that musky scent, plus something I can't identify. He moves like a cat, cornering me, but not entirely in a bad way.

Then the dragon snake coils like a rope onto his arm.

My heart stops.

The corner of Xavier's lip rises in a teasing half smile. He rotates his arm, letting the snake's skin refract the light like jewels. Its forked tongue flickers over the pale inside of his forearm.

As the snake slides up his arm and nestles inside his collar, Xavier takes my hand. His is warm, like a mug of tea. A thrill of fear digs at my gut as the snake spirals down to his wrist. The heavy ridges of its underbelly glide over our joined hands and my skin crawls as I imagine the prick of its tiny fangs.

"He *definitely* likes you." Xavier shifts his grip to my fingers, folding them over his index finger.

I laugh shakily. "How can you tell?"

"How?" His smile deepens. Before I can react, he lifts my hand in a gesture I recognize from my Victorian novels.

And presses his lips to my knuckles.

My breath hitches.

Then Sophie's voice rings out behind me. "I'm *not* tasting *anything* that comes from those!"

I jerk free. Boy Wonder and Sophie are navigating the crowd toward us, Marc and Spencer in tow. A length of blue carnival tickets dangles from Boy Wonder's hand.

"Oh, Ever, did he bite you?" Sophie rushes forward.

"N-no, of course not!" I stammer, then realize Sophie means the snake, not Xavier.

Boy Wonder's eyes drop to my hand, as if a lip-shaped glow is still burning there.

Then Xavier turns back to the block, allowing the snake to slither off, as though nothing of importance has been interrupted. Sophie sets her chin on his shoulder, and Xavier idly squeezes her waist—gah, he really *is* a Player.

"You ready?" Boy Wonder hands the tickets to the snake-minder.

"Whatever you're getting all dramatic about can't be that bad." I toss my head, Sophie-style. "Snake tastes like chicken, doesn't it?"

Boy Wonder grins as the snake man drops a hatchet onto the bloodstained butcher's block with an ominous thud.

"Wait," I say. "He's not—right here—?"

With practiced fingers, the man arranges six glass vials on a tray. From an unlabeled bottle, he spills a clear shot of liquor into each one. Here's my chance to break Wong Rule #4, but, um, why is he grabbing the brown snake?

He grips it a few inches below its triangular head, then plants his snake-filled fist on the block.

His hatchet bangs down.

The snake's fanged head flies at Spencer, who yells and slams it with a kung fu chop. Too stunned to scream, I sway on my feet as Sophie shrieks, "GROSS!"

"That's an ulcer waiting to happen." Spencer wipes blood from his arm. "Sorry, Rick. I'm not drinking that!"

"Drinking?" Alarmed, I eye the limp snake. Its severed end spurts dark red blood. I'd assumed the snake was headed to a kitchen. A frying pan. "Wait. Isn't he *cooking*—?"

Into one vial after another, the man squeezes the snake's cut end. Dark red blood pulses out, pinking the liquor.

Boy Wonder grins crookedly. "Snake-blood sake."

"Wait." The table edge bites my palms. Mr. Perfect, it seems, has a dark sense of adventure, perhaps as hell-bent on breaking loose as I am. But I'm back in the Cleveland Clinic, the gashed knee blooming like a crimson flower. "Wait . . ." I croak.

The rusty scent of blood reaches the cavities behind my eyes. The crimson flow slows and the man shakes the snake over the sixth vial, catching the last red droplets. Then he shoves the limp snake into his apron pocket and plunks the tray before us.

Boy Wonder, Marc, and Xavier each take one. Spencer refuses.

Three are left.

"Sophie? Ever?" Boy Wonder's glance is challenging.

Snake.

Blood.

Sake.

"No way." Sophie's ordered a glass of wine. She waves it. "Girls don't drink snake blood."

"Anyone want a second?" Boy Wonder offers.

"One's plenty." Marc rotates his bloody glass in his fingers, staring into it. "Jesus. It's *warm*." Under his milk-chocolate bangs, parted down the center, his face pales. Beads of sweat form on his upper lip.

Only Xavier's face remains unimpressed.

A scenario crashes into my mind: me passed out on the floor, blood spilling from a cup that hasn't even touched my lips. There must be less exotic ways to break the *No Drinking* rule, like a nice mango cocktail.

I reach uncertainly for a glass. It *is* warm. Warmed by the heating lamp that beat down on the poor snake while it was writhing alive.

My hand shakes as I peer into the cloudy pink liquid.

Boy Wonder's brows rise.

All three guys, holding their tiny glasses, are watching.

Fighting nausea, I lift mine. "I'm in."

"To the freaking best summer of our lives!" Sophie clinks her wine glass all around. "*Gānbēi!*" *Bottoms up!*

I throw back my head. The warm, salty blood and sake set my throat on fire. It tastes bitter. Like metal. Medicine. Heat sears my chest, opening up a pipe there I've never felt before. I squeeze my eyes shut and fight it down.

Don't throw up. Don't throw up. Don't throw up.

My head feels stuffed with rice, then it explodes in a million directions. Kaleidoscopic tingles dance through my body—and it's not just the sake. I've faced down my fear of blood. I'm still standing. I've broken another Wong Rule—at this rate, I'll be done with them before the sun sets in Ohio.

Sophie cradles her glass and shakes her head, scandalized but smiling. Marc vomits into a spittoon. Xavier closes his eyes.

But Boy Wonder's watching me, emptied glass in hand. As our gazes lock, he cocks his ear toward his arm. My own hand is there, gripping him like a lifeline.

"Oh, sorry!" I've left four nail marks in his tanned flesh.

But there's a new glow of respect in his eyes that warms me as much as the sake.

"You've outmanned Marc."

Marc scowls. His hawk-nose wrinkles and he wipes his mouth with the back of his hand.

"Like it?" Boy Wonder asks.

"It was *terrible*." I smile. The heat of the sake pulses through me like a river, warming my fingers and toes.

So, I've impressed Boy Wonder.

With a new surge of confidence, I grab his free hand, then Xavier's, and drag them both into the strobe-lit fog. "Come on. Let's dance!"

Hours later, I'm still dancing.

I'm rocking it up with Debra and Laura, who dance like fiends. I grab Debra's arm and lean into her. "How do you do it?" I yell over the music. "You meet presidents. You dance!"

Debra gives me a wry smile. "What?" she yells back.

"You two *rock*." In my hand, I hold my third—fourth?—mango cocktail. I can't understand the shortsighted, small-mindedness of banning such deliciousness. I can't even taste the alcohol. Bless the bartender, who's taken a liking to Sophie and me and serves us drinks on the house all night.

Speaking of whom, where has that girl gone?

"Have you seen Sophie?" I yell. Debra shakes her blue head of hair, smiling as if I've spoken pig Latin. I repeat myself a few times, dancers jostling me against her. My socks want to stick to the floor.

From out of nowhere, Xavier seizes my elbow. His wavy black hair is damp with sweat and slicked back. I haven't seen him since Sophie dragged him off to the bar hours ago.

"Dance with me." His hold shifts to my rib cage. The strobe lights illuminate his sharp cheekbones. His eyes glitter as they hold mine, daring me to decline.

I dance with him. A cocktail sloshes onto my arm and his, but I don't care. He draws me close, and the rhythm of his movements find mine. I'm glowing, grinning—at him, the dancers behind him, the bartenders everywhere.

I'm dancing with a boy. Another Wong Rule bites the dust.

His warm fingers glide under my shirt and along my bare waist, settling against the small of my back. For the space of a heartbeat, a part of me freezes, like I've been misted with liquid nitrogen.

But all around us, couples have melded together, bodies grinding to the beat.

I'm not running and hiding just because a boy's invited me to do more than flirt.

So as the tempo of the music ratchets up, I throw myself into its beat. I pump my hips, nod low over my shoulder, crook one hand behind my head, the other still holding my glass. His eyes sweep my body. His neck gleams with sweat. My hair's damp. I writhe with him, matching thrust for thrust. His hip wedges against mine as he pulls me deeper, deeper—

And then I feel him.

Oh my God. Oh my God. Is that what I think it is?

Then Sophie's towering over me in her golden dress, necklace refracting the strobe lights. She drapes her arm around my shoulders, drawing me from Xavier.

"Maybe you should cool it with the drinks, baby girl!" she shouts over the music.

"There you are!" My laughter rings out. Everything's hilarious. "It's past one! Can you believe we're still out?"

She takes my glass and sets it on a speaker. Smiles at Xavier. "I'll be back," she says. "Just need to help Ever out."

"I don't need help," I protest, but Sophie's arm tightens around me. Her own back is damp with sweat.

Dancers slam against us as we weave toward the sidelines and I grin and knock back. It's like running through a maze of those big hanging bumpers at the kids' play space in Cleveland. One thump sets my head spinning.

"Rick, help." Sophie's talking to him. He's pocketing his cell phone, his thumb digging at the inside of his fingers in that odd, fidgety gesture of his. His jet-black hair is spiked as if he'd been clinging to it earlier. Beams of light cut across his unsmiling eyes, clenched jaw.

"Who'd you call from *here*?" I ask. At least, I think I do. It's hard to hear myself.

And why the thunder brows, when he was laughing over the snake beheading a while back?

Boy Wonder's arm wraps low around my waist. His body dwarfs mine as he walks me to the door. Wind gusts in the cloying scents of cigarettes and sweet incense. My stomach undulates like I've descended a roller coaster.

Then I break from Boy Wonder to hurl its contents onto the asphalt.

12

My head jostles against a muscled chest.

I open my eyes into darkness. I'm walking down a hallway, passing doors and brass doorknobs. No, not walking. My legs dangle. I'm cradled in someone's arms. Someone who smells yummy: like grass, sweat, freshly chopped wood.

Someone with a firm-footed gait.

"Where's Sophie?" I stir, panicked. I have a vague memory of pulsing lights, writhing with Xavier . . .

"Hey. It's me. Take it easy."

Rick.

I groan. My head pounds like dragon drums. I become aware of the regular pulse of his heart against my cheek.

"I can walk myself." I struggle, push against his hairy chest.

But when my feet touch ground, the world spins. Rick's arm goes under my knees again and he lifts me as if I weigh no more than a feather pillow. The warmth of his bare skin heats my cheek. Where's his shirt?

He chuckles, his voice soft and furry in the darkness. "If you're going to drink, you need to set limits. Didn't anyone ever tell you?"

"Nobody's told me anything about anything," I say, belligerent, then another wave of shadows crashes down.

I wake in my bed. Moonlight slants through my double-paneled window.

Rick's face appears beside me, leaning in from a chair. I hadn't noticed before how full his lips are.

"I found your key in your pocket."

A sudden suspicion dawns and I glance down. I'm wearing his canary-yellow polo shirt over my black chiffon skirt. The coarse fabric slides over my stomach as Rick pulls my blanket to my chin.

"Don't worry. Sophie took care of you at the club."

I blush, mortified he read me so easily. A paper cup of water presses into my hand. "Here, drink this."

"Did you carry me home?" No way could he have carried me over the catwalk. He must have come in the front gate.

"It was either that or drive around in the cab until you woke up."

Like a drunk date, when I wasn't even his date. I moan.

He grips my shoulder. "Are you hurt?"

"I've sprained my dignity."

His grip loosens. Then he laughs, so long I grow suspicious he's more drunk than I am. He's so weird, yo-yoing mood and all. Is something wrong?

Finally, he says, "Where the hell did you learn to dance like that?"

"Like what?"

"Like you belong on a stage."

"So you were watching my moves?" I imagine Rick's eyes following my body through the pulsing lights. It gives me a curl of pleasure.

"And here I thought you were just a big brain," he teases.

"Who's the brainiac?" I mumble. My big brain's floating in fog. My scalp hurts.

He takes my cup back. "Your hair's twisted under you."

His fingers brush my cheek. They slide into my hair, pulling a lock free, relieving some of the tension. I should pull away, but I can't remember why, and so I let myself enjoy this unfamiliar intimacy of his fingers in my hair, tugging a second bundle free.

"Doesn't it get tiring, being so perfect?"

He laughs, but this time, there's no smile in his voice. "I'm far from perfect." Oh, yeah? Did he once earn an A-minus? Or—gasp—a B?

"Tell that to my parents," I mutter, low so he can't hear me.

"*World Journal?*" He heard me.

"I wrote you a letter when I was eleven. My parents made me do it. To get homework advice."

"Did I reply?"

"Nope. Bastard."

"Is that why you hate my guts? Well, let me guess. You figured out your homework problem on your own."

"They wanted me to get *general* advice. Start a correspondence."

"I *am* sort of every immigrant Chinese parent's dream guy."

"I burned your photo in effigy after." My eyelids are mudslides; I can't keep them open.

"Good thing I already have a girlfriend."

"Yes, the *poor girl*. You're probably the tree that sucks up all the nutrients from the soil. Nothing else can grow around you." A yawn nearly swallows the last of my words.

But through the growing darkness, I feel him shrink away. I've struck a chord.

*Sorry, didn't mean it,* I want to say. But the effort feels titanic.

And then the darkness claims me.

"Wake up, Ever! Wake up! We overslept!"

Curtains screech on their rails. Sophie's voice along with blinding rays of sunshine pierce my fragmented dreams. I'm lying on my stomach on my bed, sheets tangled in my legs, arm numb from dangling over the edge. My head throbs as if all my arteries have migrated into my skull.

"How'd I get here?" I mumble.

"Rick took you home." Sophie flies about the room in various states of undress. "Good thing, too! Grace Pu was rolling around like a drunken walrus in the parking lot. Her so-called friends considered leaving her there! Oh my God, Ever, I have *so much* to tell you but we're *late!*"

I sit up, rubbing sleep from my eyes. Sunlight gleams off Sophie's bare stomach as she snaps on her black lace bra. My black shirt and corset top that never even saw the club lights hang from the back of my chair, ribbons dangling, wrinkled from a wash and squeeze.

A vague horror closes off my throat as my night rushes back. Rick witnessing messes that should never be witnessed by any living breathing creature, let alone him. His shirt I will launder—twice—before returning it, if he even wants it back. And . . . right here, had I said things I shouldn't have? *So you were watching my moves . . . You're probably the tree . . .* I need to find him and explain. Apologize. Except that I can never face him again.

"Did Rick say—"

"Move it!" Sophie flings my green dress onto my stomach and shrugs into a striped tank top. "The Dragon's making rounds. If she finds us here, we're stuck, and Yannie's booked solid the rest of the summer. We won't get another chance with her."

"Yannie? Who's Yannie?"

Once again, Sophie's urgency's contagious. I shrug out of Rick's shirt.

"Our photographer! For our glamour shots! Didn't I tell you

last night? Yannie's the best. All the slots were taken but I got us in on a cancellation—we'll just have to skip Mandarin."

"If you told me, I can't remember," I groan. My head is splitting into four pieces—the morning of my first hangover is *not* the day I'd have picked for glamour shots. How is Sophie flitting around like a moth on crack?

"Well, it's your lucky day! Once the boys start leafing through your album, *no guy* here will be able to resist you!"

I start to laugh, but it hurts my head. "No one's looking at my photos, least of all *guys-who-von't-be-able-to-ree-zeest-me*." Though posing for sexy glamour shots might be the perfect way to quit dressing like a nun, since that's all I seem capable of. I yank off my crumpled chiffon skirt. As if in protest, a napkin flutters to the floor, flashing like the cream-and-blue wings of a butterfly.

There's a drawing on one side.

"What's this?" Mystified, I lean over to retrieve it.

A pastel sketch.

Of me. Dancing.

A side shot, my head thrown back, inky hair streaming, nose tipped toward the ceiling. One arm is raised. I remember that song, that move—in a few strokes, the mysterious artist has captured the tension and energy in the lines of my body. And tucked it into my pocket.

"What's that?" Sophie draws her brush through her damp strands of hair and comes over, then gasps. "It's amazing!"

"I have no idea who drew it."

"You have a secret admirer!"

"Maybe." I blush. That would be a first. Is Boy Wonder also a Michelangelo? The thought surprises me—just because he took me home doesn't make him an admirer. Quite the opposite.

"*More* than an admirer." Sophie points to the lips, *my* lips, delicate and sensual. The artist has even captured the precise contours of my chest and shadowed the spaces around my legs, the trapezoid in between, in satin red. "This guy *wants* you, Ever."

*Who?* I can't deny how naked the drawing makes me feel.

A rap in the hallway, a fist on wood, makes me jump. Sophie presses her ear to our door, while I hide the sketch in my purse.

"The Dragon," she hisses. "She's next door. Quick. Let's get out of here."

The moment the Dragon steps into our neighbor's room, Sophie and I yank open our door together, shoot down the hallway, and take the stairs two at a time. We sweep past a blue flyer advertising the talent show, then under the demerits board, with its new smattering of check marks. Three red marks follow my name. My stomach tightens.

I tiptoe on Sophie's heels past the narrow door windows revealing classrooms already full of students—clubbers now ready to study, avoiding demerits. "If the Dragon's on the fence about calling my parents, skipping class might seal my fate," I whisper.

"If we don't do the glamour shots now, we'll never get to do them."

I heave a breath. I'm in this far already. "Fine." But I peek through the classroom 103 window. Anyone else sleeping in, braving the Dragon's wrath?

Only one seat besides ours is empty—Xavier Yeh.

My face burns and I hurry down the hallway after Sophie. Last night, dancing with Xavier had seemed like a brilliant idea, but now I want to crawl back under my covers and hide. I'll have to see him in class every single day, knowing I gave him a boner, and him knowing I know.

Sophie swears under her breath. We've reached the lobby. At a table with Li-Han and two other counselors, Mei-Hwa slams down three ivory tiles. "Pong!" They're playing mah-jong. Their Hokkien accents remind me again of my parents. Except my parents don't play games, they go to work, come home exhausted, bad-tempered. Mei-Hwa flexes tiny muscle-man arms and does a sassy dance in her chair. Li-Han drinks from a can of Mr. Brown coffee, and says something that makes Mei-Hwa punch his shoulder. She's Taiwanese Aborigine, it turns out; her parents from the Plains and Puyama tribes, part of the indigenous peoples who've lived on this island forever. Strange how she isn't much older than us, but she's our counselor.

"We'll have to go around them," Sophie says.

Then Mindy steps out of a phone booth, still clad in rumpled pink pajamas. Since catching her with Xavier the first day and her booting me off the computer terminal the next,

I haven't seen much of her. She knots her greasy hair into a ponytail and rubs eyes red-rimmed from crying. Her splotchy face looks scrubbed raw.

Her gaze falls on us and tears spring from her eyes. "Bitch!" she cries, and pelts up the stairs and out of sight.

Flooded with guilt, I stand rooted to the floor. I've always been on the other side of pining after a guy, never in this position.

But I'm not after Xavier. I was just—dancing.

The counselors are glancing up from their game. Sophie hustles me out a side door into the courtyard, still damp from a morning storm.

"Sophie, maybe I should talk to her—"

"It's not you, it's me," she whispers. "You're just guilty by association. Come on. Hurry." Not until we've jogged past the lily pond, does Sophie lean into me and whisper, "Xavier and I hooked up. Last night."

I stop dead in my tracks. "Hooked up? As in—?"

"We did it."

"Last night?"

"And this morning!"

She links arms with me, prattling on with far more detail than I need or want: how they'd made out the whole cab ride home, fumbled down the darkened hallway, tumbled into a spare bedroom on the first floor.

"And *oh my God*, Ever! Now I *know* why all those girls were after him."

I hadn't noticed before, but Sophie's lips are puffier, a darker shade, even without lipstick. A pink, quarter-sized hickey graces her neck. I can't imagine sleeping with a guy after knowing him only a week. Mom's judgments, of girls who spread their legs for boys, echo in my head. But none of her words apply to Sophie, who glows as though she's swallowed the sun.

"You're not mad, too?" Sophie asks. "I mean, I know you were dancing with him . . ."

"No. Of course not." Even if a rebellious part of me wishes I'd gotten grazed, I've dodged a bullet. Dancing with Xavier was one thing—hooking up something else.

"You barely know him!" I say.

"Are you kidding? Every day here's like a week." Sophie waves. "It's Loveboat, and Xavier's a keeper—in my book, at least," she amends, as though half the Chien Tan girls aren't drooling enough to drown him. "You wouldn't *believe* the stories my aunt's told me about his family. The Yehs practically own half the island, they've built an electronics empire—they own Longzhou!"

"Longzhou? Wow." We'd dropped by the twelve-floor department store on our hunt for clothes, but it was light-years beyond my budget—crystal chandeliers, endless escalators, Hermès, Chanel. Look-but-don't-touch.

So Xavier is an heir to an empire.

And Sophie knew that before coming into the program. But she'd kept the information to herself, after sharing a classified report's worth of intel all week: *Marc's dad owns a laundromat in Los Angeles and he wants to be a starving journalist—too bad because he's adorable. Chris Chen's headed to Berkeley and comes from decent money.*

I'm most surprised by the competitive streak she's revealed. Xavier means more to her than she's let on.

"But what about Mindy? Doesn't it bother you—?"

Sophie rolls her head along with her eyes. "Look, all guys play the field—at least the non-nerds. She's the girl who slept with him once. I'm the girl he found afterward. And all those codes about dating—honestly, the only one that makes sense is 'All's fair in love and war.' Even if they were betrothed from the cradle, it's not over until they tie the knot."

I frown. I don't know about codes, but I've always assumed a guy with a girlfriend is off limits. Like Dan and Megan. Rick and Jenna.

"Do you trust him?"

"Why do I have to?" Sophie smiles. "'Go in with your eyes wide open,' that's what Aunty Claire told me. Besides, I know his type. He needs a girl strong enough to meet him head-on. Look." She pulls back her hair to reveal Xavier's opal stud, gleaming on her earlobe—a slap on my mommy-like wrist. Who am I to judge when I've the experience of a junior nun?

"Just—be careful, okay?" I say, then start forward again, with no idea where I'm headed next.

13

We ride the Taipei Metro red line south to a stop whose name I can't read, then rise on a very long escalator into a street filled with a funny mix of shiny high-rises, three-story rows of buildings, and those colorful Taiwanese rooftops—jumbled together like three different sets of children's blocks. The photographer's studio is on the second floor of a narrow building beside a Daoist temple, where smoke from incense sticks rises from a brass burner.

I'm thankful to arrive, if only for the break from Sophie's incessant chatter about Xavier. A brass bell chimes overhead as I follow her into a perfumed room of polished wooden floors accented by red silk rugs and velvet ottomans. Citrus-scented candles flicker on a mantel.

A middle-aged woman in a plaid beret turns from a tripod facing a white backdrop curtain that unfurls in a room-sized square. *"Ah, xiǎo mèimei dàole!"* Her royal-blue button-down flutters in the AC as she lifts her camera to her face.

Poof! Poof! Poof!

White lights swim in my vision. I blink against them. I'd expected a simple mall portrait studio like Mom brings us to every year. Not this fancy boudoir. Life-sized portraits paper the walls: a girl fingering a wide-brimmed hat, a guy slinging a ruby jacket over his shoulder, couples pressed cheek to cheek.

"Will she really make me look—like those?"

"Even better." Sophie helps herself to a piece of candy from a crystal bowl, as at ease as if we were in her own home.

I'm afraid to even sit down. If I were home, I'd be eating potato chips at the public pool with Megan, hiding my one-piece under my striped terry towel. I don't belong in an extravagant studio like this, lining up to get air-brushed like a movie star. My head throbs from my hangover. I feel like a total imposter.

Sophie chats with Yannie, who speaks Mandarin and Taiwanese, but not English. They are moving to a cash register on a glass counter and I kneel by a coffee table littered with traditional vinyl photo albums and an iPad displaying digital ones. I flip through the iPad: girls in backless dresses lying on lacy bedspreads with their heels kicked up, or golden beaches at sunrise—the colors sharp and bold. I trace the sweeping train of a lemon chiffon gown and try to imagine myself in it.

Then I sort through the albums. I come across one devoted

to an acrobatic troop from Shanghai, dressed in fun costumes like green-and-pink flowers, glowing stars, scaly sea creatures, posing on trapezes and as awe-inspiring human jungle gyms.

An idea strikes, and I set the album down. "Sophie, does Yannie shoot for other theater or dance companies?"

Sophie interrupts herself to translate for Yannie. "Yes, she has some in the albums over there." She points to a shelf in the corner.

I pull out several leather-bound albums—a kung fu master class, a dragon drum troupe, a dance last spring by an expensive studio in Taipei I'd found online. But I'm looking for one I haven't run across yet.

At last, I come across a modest album labeled, "Szeto Ballet Studio." I bend over the costumed casts: *Cinderella, The Nutcracker, Sleeping Beauty. Coppélia* last August—I've danced in all of them at Zeigler's. The same girls pose season after season, a year older each time. It's as small a dance studio as they come. With a jolt of excitement, I run my fingertips over the address embossed on the back. I can drop by when we finish, but will they have space?

*"Āiyā! Wǒ fēicháng xǐ huān tā, dàn wǒ fù bù qǐ."* Sophie lifts her hands to her temples and shakes her head. *I love it so much but I can't afford that!*

I'm not alarmed, not after witnessing Sophie's killer negotiation skills in the market. Sophie will slowly give in until she gets the deal she wants, and miraculously, the photographer will feel equally pleased we value her work so highly.

At last, Sophie turns to me. "She'll give us two for one, since we're doing it together. Three outfits each, and she'll cut us a deeper deal if we pay American dollars."

"How much?"

When she tells me, I swallow hard. It's less than what it would cost in the States but wipes out a third of the savings I brought as spending money.

In my purse, my phone chimes with a text. My fingers brush my mysterious sketch as I dig my phone out.

Pearl: Mom wants to check how Mandarins going better call back soon

My stomach clenches. Mom's grasping fingers are after me. How much longer can I dodge them? I text back:

Thanks for the warning

I drop my phone back into my purse, then join Sophie at the counter. I run my hand over the gold embossing that frames a gorgeous girl in the album open before her.

Glamour shots. I can't imagine a more wasteful use of money.

Another Wong Rule downed.

I flip the album closed. "Let's do it."

Through her entire first shoot, Sophie yammers on about Xavier as she poses in a yellow batik wraparound, standing in three-inch

heels on the white backdrop before Yannie's camera. "We really connected, Ever," and "We never even got his shirt off!"

In the corner, surrounded by dresses on racks, I hold a pomegranate-red gown to my body and examine my reflection. Nothing's right—I've lost count of how many I've tried. I hang it back on its rack with a discouraged thump and dig into an accessories trunk of silk scarves, ropes of pearls, and elbow-length gloves.

But at last, when Sophie's session ends, I wobble in knee-high boots to take her place, tripping over the wire to the inverted umbrella that reflects light onto the backdrop. I've finally decided on an indigo mesh dress cross-tied with black satin sashes over the shoulders, bodice, and waist. Yannie's hairdresser braided a matching indigo sash into my black hair in a reversal of the dress. The white leather boots are a perfect contrast and I love the overall effect.

But as I face Yannie's silvery equipment, I feel like an imposter, as if I've shown up to a Cleveland Ballet rehearsal to the confusion of the entire corps.

An alarming burst of instructions flies from Yannie. I throw a pleading glance at Sophie, who breaks off agonizing whether Xavier liked her in gold to translate: "Lift your chin. Look straight into the camera. Bend your knees more and keep your chest pushed out. *More*—good!"

I force my fingers to unclutch my skirt. At Yannie's instructions, I stretch out on a white chaise that smells of perfume. Cock a leg. The velvet glides against my skin as Yannie repositions me, shooting my front, back, profile. She plays with the lights. Throws stars onto the backdrop. My body sinks into the cushions as I finally begin to relax.

"Beautiful!" Yannie removes her beret and scratches short, blond-dyed hair.

By the end of my first session, I'm flushed with the attention. Any compliments I've received over the years—my dramatic eyes, my silky black hair, my porcelain-doll features—usually made me cringe with the focus on my Asianness.

But now, an ember inside me flares brighter.

I change into a white jumpsuit as Sophie poses in her second outfit: a black dress covered by a blue trench coat that she slips suggestively down her bare shoulders with each shot. "This is the photo I'll slip under Xavier's pillow," she jokes. Then her smile fades. "Ever, I need your advice. So many girls are after him."

Honestly, how can such a smart, resourceful girl be so single-mindedly boy crazy? She told Rick no one would break her heart and told me she's going in eyes wide open. But she's so earnest, desperate in a way that seems out of character with her confidence.

Still, years of being Megan's wing woman means I play a darn good moral supporter. I think about options as I side-knot a long, wine-colored sash around my waist and let the ends dangle. I smile at my reflection: elegant, with a hint of martial artist—I like it.

"What about inviting him to your aunt's house at the end of the month?" I suggest. "You'll get him off campus that way."

"Oh, great idea! I'll call her and ask—I'm sure she'll say okay. She's the one who told me about his family." She starts for the dressing room, then turns back. "Oh, and Ever? *Please* don't take this the wrong way. But we only get three outfits so maybe go more . . . *sexy*? Not like that little-girl dress last night—and *definitely* not that preschooler jumpsuit. I mean—have *fun*, okay?"

She blows me a kiss that's 100 percent sincere. This is how Sophie Ha loves on her friends, like her no-yellow-clothes advice to Rick. Which means I'm in her club, and which also means that despite my trying very hard to break the Wong Rules, my pawn hasn't advanced at all.

I stammer something like *sure, okay.*

But it's all I can do not to stomp my way back to the costume racks.

I trade up my jumpsuit for a pink-and-black lace leotard that reveals skin in suggestive patches. Way more risqué. Yannie's hairstylist sweeps my hair into an updo that bares my neck. As Yannie snaps away, I strike a few dance poses, showing off my flexibility by grabbing my leg from behind. I grin, baring my teeth in a monster face for the mirror.

"That's more like it," Sophie says.

"My parents would kill me if they knew I was doing this. I've *definitely* violated the *Dress Like a Nun* rule."

Sophie, long-limbed in a white Italian bikini, walks to the

back of the studio, dialing her aunt. She makes a skeptical noise. "Wait until my next shots—*then* you'll see a real rebel, baby girl."

I lower my leg, fighting annoyance. I *am* rebellious.

Sophie chatters with her aunt through the rest of my second shoot. When she hangs up, she's beaming ear to ear. "We're on! She'll send a car to pick us up that Friday." She hugs me and squeals, knocking over my wide-brimmed hat. "Ever, that was the *best* idea! My aunt lives in this amazing mansion—even Rick says so. Xavier's going to be so impressed—and you'll love it, too."

"Rick . . ." Damn, of course he'd be there. I retrieve my hat.

So you were watching my moves—

Why, Ever? Why?

Another text chimes on my phone. Then another. And another. Another. Another. Pearl—is something wrong? I dive for my purse, nearly knocking over Sophie in her bikini as she steps onto the backdrop.

I hunch over my phone, my back to Sophie.


Call us.
Are you eating well? Studying hard?
Did you find the biology book? We heard you have spare time to study.
Hope you are taking full advantage of learning Mandarin!
It is hot there but dress modestly!


"Something wrong?" Sophie asks.

I clench my fist, unable to answer at first. I power off my

phone and jam it deep into my purse, under my sketch. "Nothing." Except that my parents have struck again. Violated Pearl's privacy and invaded my life. My stomach pulls taut and I pivot toward Sophie. "I just—oh my God!"

My roommate stands barefoot on the backdrop, her back to Yannie's camera. Her bikini lies in a silky, white heap on the floor. She's naked.

Not practically. *Actually*. Yannie's lights shine off her golden skin, illuminating paler bikini patches. They bring out her rosy undertones. I gape at her, awed by her daring. She places her hands on her hips.

"Ever, you're such a *prude*! This is art, not *porn*."

But a triumphant smirk hovers on her lips. She's sexy incarnate. A surge of jealousy thumps through my heart as she strikes pose after pose, as Yannie snaps away at the unbroken line of her backside.

I remember an afternoon in the park when I was six. I was eating a green apple, sitting on the grass in a skirt, when Mom pounced in a scolding panic, scaring me, reducing me to tears. Apparently, I'd spread my legs too wide. Exposed myself to all the people in the park who might or might not have been looking.

The grip of that shame has only tightened as my body developed more parts to feel ashamed of flaunting.

And I don't want her shame to control me anymore.

I change my outfit for yet a third time. Sophie wraps herself in a bathrobe, digs into a bowl of hard candy, and drops onto a couch to watch my last session.

With a nervous gulp, I step barefoot onto the backdrop, sliding a rebellious lock of hair behind my ear. I've decided on as provocative an outfit as I can stomach. The diaphanous skirt slits to mid-thigh. The sleeveless top, open at the front, flows like angel wings to either side. A single golden safety pin holds the fabric together over my chest, so flower-petal delicate that I can't wear anything beneath.

No bra.

No panties.

*Truly* risqué, Sophie-style.

I take a deep breath.

At Yannie's instructions, I raise my arms in a freeing Y. I arch my back. My neck. The pin stretches over the barely-there fabric. The slit inches seductively up my leg.

Sophie kicks her heels over the couch arm, translating. "Tuck your chin in—perfect! Now toss your hair—makes you freer. Yes—gorgeous! Not bad for my baby roommate!"

I grit my teeth—Sophie can be so patronizing. But the shyness of my first shoot is gone. I've never felt so naked. Or so sensual.

A few dozen poses later, Yannie flashes me the okay with her thumb and forefinger.

"One more pose," I say.

If Sophie can do a naked back shot, so can I.

Turning my back to Yannie's camera, I shrug and let the entire outfit slip to my ankles. Fully nude, I step out of its soft ring and nudge it with my toe off the backdrop. My heart pounds and though only Sophie has a view of my front, I cup one arm over my breasts and fan my other over my crotch.

For the first time, Sophie falls silent.

Stiff with terror, I hold the pose as Yannie's flashes radiate off the backdrop. I open my arms to present in second position. I throw back my head, letting my hair cascade to the small of my back. I curve sideways like the marble statue of a water nymph—*Dress like a Nun*—that rule has most definitely gone down.

At last, the rapid-fire clicking stops. Yannie speaks in Mandarin.

Sophie's no longer smiling. "We're done."

"Already?"

"I told you. She's got another customer in a few minutes."

I don't budge.

This is art, not porn. And as girly as it is, I want to see my body as I've never seen it before. As beautiful and free and daring as my roommate—no, even *more* daring than Sophie, who, after calling me a little girl all morning isn't saying a word now.

"Just one more pose," I say. "For my eyes only."

"And mine." Sophie rolls her own eyes. "I'm picking them up with you, aren't I?" But she translates for Yannie, who raises her camera.

I wrap my arms around myself and tense, like that moment right before the stunning opener to a new dance routine.

131

Outside, I imagine the footfalls of Yannie's next customer. My time's up. It's *now*.

My hands fall to my sides, wrists gently flexed, and I twist to face Yannie, baring myself to the storm of a thousand flashes of light.

**14**

"I shouldn't have done it." Regret haunts me as I walk the moped-lined sidewalks with Sophie toward the Metro, to Chien Tan for her, the Szeto Ballet Studio for me. "That last pose—"

My cheeks burn with the memory. When I close my eyes, I can still see Yannie's flashing lights, still feel them on my naked skin. The worst is that, left to my own devices, I'd have worn the white-and-wine jumpsuit and returned to the States happy as cream cheese. Why? Why did everything my mom say make me want to do crazy things?

"Calm down." Sophie twists her hair into a knot and secures it with a clip. She frowns, impatient. "Not like anyone's going to see your photos. Unless you were planning to hand them out."

"If my parents find out, they'll disown me."

"Well, they won't find out. You're so paranoid about them. Honestly, Ever. All this insecurity is getting annoying."

She's trying to stop me from worrying, but I can only imagine Megan's wide-eyed horror. Pearl's, too.

*This isn't like you, Ever!* they'd say.

And would they be right?

The fact that I'm not sure scares me.

Sophie and I separate at the Metro, and I walk another few blocks to the blue line, still trying to shake my worries.

*It's done. No one has to know.*

Szeto Ballet Studio is forty-five minutes from campus, on the outskirts of Taipei. I cross a few quiet streets to a modest, two-story building, swing open a glass door—

And step into heaven.

Faded pink walls enclose a reception room of dated but well-loved Chinese wooden furniture. The air smells of lilacs. Past a desk, I come upon a mirror-lined studio and a dozen girls my age, black ponytails whipping as they bend and stretch along a polished double bar. Tchaikovsky's "Waltz of the Flowers" plays. A red-haired woman calls in time, an unbelievable mix of Mandarin and French, "*Sì ge rond de jambe, shuāng rond de jambe, arabesque—fēicháng hǎo, Lu-Ping! Hěn hǎo, Fan-Li.*"

My own heart lifts with the familiar liturgy. Then an elegant Chinese woman, black hair pulled into a tidy French braid, glides toward me. She's in her forties. Her graceful carriage tells me she was once a dancer herself.

"May I help you?" American-accented English—I guess she can tell from my clothes. She seems surprised.

"Um, I'm here with Chien Tan and saw your *Coppélia* album at a photography studio. I'm, um, a dancer"—I stumble over the word—"and wondered if you have space in your classes or summer ballet."

"Chien Tan, of course! I'm Madame Szeto. You're welcome to join us." She walks me back to the reception desk and hands me an amateur playbill. "We're performing excerpts from *Swan Lake* in August. At the community theater."

"Oh, *Swan Lake*! One of my favorites!" The Princess Odette cursed into a swan, her dress of white feathers, her evil double, the love story that makes me cry. "How—how much are lessons?"

My hunch was right—she must not have raised prices in ten years.

The cost for the summer, week by week, will still wipe out the rest of my savings.

But it's a chance to dance.

"Are there auditions?"

"No need. Only the solos require auditions." She opens her ledger.

"Which solos?" I blurt.

Her brow rises. "All but the Prince. Odette—"

"Odette!"

"—Odile, Von Rothbart . . . to be honest, the roles will likely go to the girls who dance with us year-round. You may try out, but would need to prepare a two-minute piece—"

"Sure." I knock a pointe shoe off the counter and hastily replace it. "I can do that."

"Well, most of the girls have been preparing for weeks—I don't want you to be disappointed." She opens a notebook. "I could squeeze you in Sunday after next—eight a.m.? I realize it's early."

Not for the chance to dance a role whose choreography I've studied obsessively! I might even improvise a bit to show off what I can do. I'll take the Metro from Sophie's aunt's house. I read the brochure. The performance is the second weekend of August—when Chien Tan is on the Tour Down South, the highlight of the summer. But so is dancing, for me. And this will be my last dance. My farewell. I'll find a way out of the tour.

"I'll take the slot," I say. "Thank you," I stammer as she inks *Wong Ai-Mei* onto her ledger. She hands me a card for a dance shop for clothes and shoes and I clutch it like a lifeline.

Back outside under the hot sun, even though I don't approve of showy cartwheels, I put my hand on the sidewalk and turn one anyways.

The Dragon's lecture at dinner leaves our ears stinging. She stands on a stage under red paper lanterns, facing our dozens of round tables, but there's nothing festive in her expression.

"You are intelligent young people with bright futures. Why do foolish things that could harm yourselves? Anyone else leaving campus past curfew will be severely punished and may be sent home."

Yesterday, I'd have welcomed the chance, if I were brave enough to stomach my parents' anger and disappointment. Now, I don't want to go home. I'm free to dance. Spend money the way I want. Kiss a boy if I find one. I was drowning back home, and Chien Tan is a lifeboat.

"Looks like we're off the hook for strike one." Sophie pushes her empty dinner plate toward the lazy Susan, then opens a box of gourmet cakes she got Xavier to buy her. Four square cakes, burnt-butter tops stamped with intricate designs, nestle on a red silk bed. She hands me one. "Sesame seed balls or lotus cakes for afternoon tea?"

I bite into sweet lotus paste. "Um, *yum*. Both?"

"What about dessert? Shaved ice or make-your-own mochi? Too much sugar?"

Seems it will be full speed ahead planning the visit to Aunty Claire's for the next two weeks. But I don't mind. I'm looking forward to meeting Sophie's family—not to mention she's filled my head with stories of rooms and meals straight out of *Beauty and the Beast*.

"How about one per day?" I suggest.

"Did you buy those cakes yourself? Or did you get your rich boyfriend to do it?"

At Mindy's voice, Sophie pauses mid-bite. She chews and finishes swallowing before twisting around to face Mindy in a baby-blue dress.

"Nothing wrong with knowing what you want," Sophie says coolly.

"So, you admit it." Mindy folds her arms across her chest. "You're after him because he's from the richest family in Taiwan."

Sophie gives her a level stare. "I like nice things. So what?"

Mindy's arms unfold and her hands ball into fists, then she storms away.

Sophie lets out a breath. "She's jealous. It's understandable."

My cheeks feel singed. How much does Xavier suspect his family's money is a draw for the girls who are after him? I've never given much thought to a guy's money; I always assumed I'd be the one supporting my family. But maybe a guy like him has to think about it.

"You didn't mean all that, did you?" I ask.

Sophie pops her last bite of mooncake into her mouth. "When I was seven, our landlord used to pound on the door of our crap apartment every few months. I still remember hiding under the covers. And after he left, I'd ask, 'Will we have to move?'" and my mom would cry, 'You promised you'd take care of us,' making my dad feel like the little shit that he is."

"Gosh, Sophie." She has such good taste and incredible clothing—I'd assumed she came from money herself. Nothing like this. "I'm sorry."

"My mom's life is exactly what I'm *not* going to have. So yeah, Xavier coming from the richest family in Taiwan—I'd be lying if I said I didn't care. But that doesn't mean I don't like him."

I frown. His money *shouldn't* matter, but she's right, too—it's not something you can ignore about him either.

138

Sophie hunches toward me. "Maybe your artist is Benji. He's going to RISD to study art."

I automatically glance around for his stuffed bear, Dim Sum.

"God, I hope not." I shudder, then realize how cleverly she changed the subject.

With Sophie sitting squarely between Xavier and me in Mandarin, I have a front-row view into their growing relationship, and also the space I need from Xavier. The few times he catches my eye, I find an excuse to turn to Spencer Hsu on my other side.

Matteo, as far as Sophie is concerned, has fallen off the planet.

Over the next week, we practice bartering in the marketplace and talk about our families (*jiātíng*), boyfriends (*nán péngyǒu*), and girlfriends (*nǚ péngyǒu*). Xavier makes Sophie go first with the partner readings every time, like he did with me. She forges right ahead—it seems characteristic of their relationship.

As for me, I ace every quiz. What little pride I have won't let me write down the wrong answer. Even if it would help me break a Wong Rule.

I wash Rick's shirt in the basement laundromat, but I can't muster up the courage to return it to him. It's dryer-warm in my arms as I climb the stairs, debating whether to run it again with my next load. And when I see him in the lobby, dropping off a postcard for Jenna, I spin on my heel and dash off in the other direction.

In Chinese Medicine, Marc, David, and Sam dub themselves the Angry Asian Men. Between sets of push-ups and swigs from their steel bottle—I finally get a detergent-flavored sip—they compile a list of Asian-guy stereotypes:

"Kung fu master," Marc says.

"Nerd engineer," Sam says. "Followers, not leaders."

"*Effeminate*," David growls from mid-push-up.

"Own it, bro." Marc shoves David's head down. "That goatee isn't fooling anyone."

"Shut it!"

"This is war." Sam cracks his knuckles. "We need to take back these stereotypes."

"Yeah, how?" David asks, and they huddle around their bottle, plotting.

I turn to Xavier. "Why aren't *you* angry?"

He shrugs. "I grew up in Asia." And he doesn't come close to any of the stereotypes. But he doesn't contradict the guys either. He acts like he doesn't care, but I think he sort of does. I get the feeling there's a lot he doesn't let show, like his relationship with his dad. I wonder what else he's hiding under all that tousled hair, but it's not something I feel safe asking about.

A week and a half into Loveboat, the romances ratchet up. Someone leaves an anonymous flower on Lena-from-South Carolina's pillow (everyone knows it's Spencer). Debra and Laura steal Rick's football to lure him to their room, Jenna be damned.

Sophie works through a dozen different menus, down to which wineglass name tags to ask her aunt to bring out.

As for me, I move my feet to the beat of music from Sophie's speakers and study my mysterious sketch. I sneak by Benji's open door, looking for artwork, but only spot Dim Sum sitting glassy-eyed on his pillow. Once I discover my artist, I have a fantasy of flinging my arms around his neck and breaking the *No Kissing Boys* rule. *Maybe* I'd kiss baby-faced Benji. But would I be brave enough to kiss Sam? Or David, despite the goatee?

Messages to call home pile up on my desk, but now that Pearl's WeChat account has been commandeered, I only email her—she's lonely, her friends are away for the summer, she's trying to make progress on her Mozart Sonata in C, forcing herself to read all those notes through her dyslexia. Mom and Dad want me to call. Megan's well, but hard to reach—she's on a cruise with Dan and her parents, and although I initially try to keep her posted, too much is happening. *Fill you in when I'm back,* I email her.

Evenings after dinner, I toss dance bag and pointe shoes over my shoulder and race out to Szeto Ballet Studio.

"*Kànzhe wǒ, xuéshēngmen.* Eyes on me, girls." Madame demonstrates each combination in her muted flow across the floor: "pas de bourrée, pir-ou-*ette.*" I greedily emulate the glide of her legs, the flawless sweep of her arms. She speaks Mandarin, then English for my sake, and I start to pick up all sorts of dance words. "Turn the foot out more, but lovely arms, Li-Li. Bend your elbow like so. Very graceful, Pei." She's a stickler for technique but finds something encouraging to say to every girl. In my second class, she grips my biceps in firm fingers: "*Engage* your arms more. Pull them apart to here and feel how that locks in your balance. *Feel* the lines of energy, side to side and pulling from your head to your toe." She lifts my chin higher. "When you love the dance, it shows, my new bird. Let it show."

She *sees* me. Her praise is a dip in a warm bath of honey. I barely get out a "*xièxiè*" in thanks. I haven't loved ballet as much as modern and jazz, but under her, that's changing. If I get a solo, *Odette*, I'll get to work one-on-one with her. And so I double down—tighten my turns, push my leaps higher—then waltz on a bed of clouds back to Chien Tan.

I've never slept well, and almost two weeks into Loveboat, I still haven't adjusted to the jet lag. Plus tonight, the song in my head demands satisfaction. My feet itch to dance, my body to follow its lead.

I slip from my bed and change into tank top and shorts. On the opposite bed, Sophie's arm is flung in a pale hook over her head. Her inky hair spills over her pillow. In the moonlight, her face is softer, like a little girl's. She murmurs and rolls over to hug her other pillow and I tug her sheet over her bare shoulder.

Our stubborn door almost does me in, but I finally yank it open with a wrench that echoes down the hallway. I hold my breath as it fades, count to twenty, but nothing stirs in the darkness.

Slants of moonlight stripe the hallway tiles, which are cool under my bare feet. I make a game of leaping over each stripe, landing without sound, sashaying around the next. I waltz into the lounge, where empty bottles litter the table and the scents of beer, rice cakes, and red bean soup from an illegal Crock-Pot still linger. I've had so much fun hanging out each night, but now, I'm enjoying this loneliness, with just the music in my body.

The double doors to the balcony stand slightly ajar. I step out into the light of an enormous crescent moon in a milky halo. It dims the stars around it. The humid night air envelops me like a blanket as I raise arm and knee and turn a pirouette that lands me before the stone railing.

"Hey."

I spin around. To my left, the hulk of Rick's shadow shifts. Moonlight gleams off his rumpled hair, painting silver highlights into the black. He's sitting on a bench in a sleeveless jersey, muscled arms locked around his knees. Just behind him, a clay drainpipe glints against the brick wall.

"Rick! I was—"

I break off. Dancing, obviously. Tiny moons flicker in his amber eyes, which are as hard to read as always. I can't tell who's more annoyed by the interruption, him or me.

"I'm washing your shirt," I blurt. "I mean, I've already washed it. Twice. I want to run it one more time. It's clean, I promise. I mean, I'm not letting it sit around molding." Good grief. I clamp my mouth shut.

"I trust you."

"I'm so sorry you had to see me like that."

"You don't strike me as the girl who usually needs taking home."

"Oh, I'm *not.*"

He shifts to one side of the wooden bench. "Want a seat? It's a good moon."

Sitting under this gorgeous moon with him is a waste. I should be here with Marc or Sam. Anyone but Boy Wonder.

But I find myself taking a seat. "I don't think I've seen one quite that big." A darker band of sky encircles it, populated by stars, then light pollution from Taipei drowns out the rest of the stars down to the horizon.

"I like looking at the stars," he says. "It puts things in perspective, seeing how small we are compared to the universe."

Surprising humbleness. But I get it.

"They're so permanent," I say. "So old compared to our short lives."

"Did you know there's a black hole that emits the note B-flat fifty-seven octaves below middle C?"

"That is the weirdest random fact I've ever heard."

"But cool, right?" His teeth flash with a smile.

"Yeah, it is," I admit. "Are you into astronomy?"

"I read all the Usborne books on stars and planets when I was little."

"Oh, me, too." I shouldn't be surprised, but I never imagined that kid in New Jersey reading books that I loved. "Why are you up so late?"

"Couldn't sleep." A pause. "Thinking about Jenna."

So, he misses her. Hence the romantic moon. Sophie mentions he calls her and sends her a postcard every single day. He's a good guy, to have taken home a drunk girl he barely knew. Maybe I haven't given him as much credit as he deserves.

"Are you up late most nights?" he asks. "You've been missing a killer breakfast."

And he noticed? "Um, yeah. I've been sleeping in."

"Why are you up now?"

"It will sound weird."

He shrugs. "I'm weird."

"Seriously." I smile. "Sometimes I get these songs in my head. I see the dance playing out in my head. Then I need to dance it. Hence the pirouette." I nod toward the railing.

"That *is* weird."

"Thanks."

"Weird but cool. How long have you been dancing?"

"All my life. I was four when my parents put me in ballet."

"No wonder. So, you're a ballerina?"

"No. I grew up on ballet. I loved it—still do. But I love the dance squad just as much. And other dancing—jazz, modern, combining them. I know it's not serious, but I—I just love it."

"I get that. I can pick up almost any sport and be pretty competitive, but football's my favorite. All the strategizing. The team. What do you like about dancing?"

Funny how conversation with Rick is easier in the semidarkness when I don't have to look at his perfect face.

"It's the energy of the group. Everyone moving independently, but still coordinated."

"Like football."

"Is it?"

"Every play's incredibly strategic. The whole team needs to be coordinated."

"Have you played long?"

"Since high school. It's one of those sports you can pick up later and still be competitive. Enough for Yale at least. I'm not in Marc's category. He could go pro in track if he wasn't so committed to journalism."

"He's hilarious," I say. "All his Angry Asian Men talk. Taking back stereotypes."

Rick's silent a moment. "Marc's a hoot. We're running buddies now."

Yes, I've seen them jogging along the river together. I pull in a breath, then take a chance. "I found a sketch in my pocket after Club KISS. Of me. It was amazing."

"Oh?" His amber eyes are unreadable. "Who did it?"

"I don't know. I'm trying to find out," I confess.

"Show me the sketch tomorrow and I'll poke around, if you'd like."

"Thanks. Maybe Benji?" God, how presumptuous. "Sophie says he's going to RISD—please don't say anything to him."

"I'll be discreet," Rick says.

A hinge creaks down the hallway. The soft clip of footsteps draws near, and I bolt to my feet. "Shit, someone's coming." I can't even guess at the punishment if we're caught, a guy and a girl in a skimpy tank top together hours past curfew.

I bolt toward the clay pipe, tripping over Rick's outstretched legs. It's a water pipe that runs from the roof two stories above, all the way to the ground. I reach over the railing and grab hold: solid, clay-rough, hand-sized, much sturdier than the thin metal one outside my bedroom back home. The courtyard, the concrete steps leading to the main entrance is a three-story drop, but half-way down the wall, a narrow ledge intersects with the pipe.

"You're not going down that?" Rick whispers, disbelieving, but I've already climbed onto the railing and grabbed the pipe, fireman-style. Using the brick wall for toeholds, I ease down the pipe until my feet reach the ledge. Inches from my nose, a splash of bird poop stains the bricks.

I step sideways onto the narrow ledge, balancing on my toes, as Rick lands beside me. His bulk sets me off-balance, but he grabs my shoulders and hugs me to his side, hanging on to the pipe for the both of us. He's warm and smells like grass, tooth-paste. My heart pounds so loudly it's going to give us away.

Rick's arm tightens warningly. Above us, Li-Han appears in paisley pajamas, standing at the balcony railing. He looks up at the moon, which refracts off his glasses and illuminates the long cut of his cheeks. A short, green can of Pringles gleams in his hand. We're completely exposed—if he glances down, he'll see us.

I shrink deeper into Rick and hold my breath. We're both sweating into his jersey. His hand squeaks on the pipe and we tense.

But Li-Han merely crunches on a chip. Then another. Another. My back grows damper with perspiration and my foot begins to tingle like mad. I shift closer to Rick and rotate my ankle, trying to wake it. A pebble pings three flights down, clanks down the steps. Rick's fingertips dig into my shoulder, and we each hold our breath

Li-Han crunches another chip.

When Li-Han leaves at last, I expel a long breath. His footsteps slowly fade then Rick looks at me, a question in his eyes. I nod, then he climbs hand over hand back up the pole, and I follow until I throw a hand over the rail. Rick grabs my wrist and tugs me onto the balcony.

"We're crazy." I give a soft laugh of relief. "I can't believe we—"

"You could have gotten us in trouble." Rick releases me so abruptly, I stumble back, catching myself on the stone railing. "They'd have called our parents. Kicked us out."

Not a laughing matter to him, clearly.

I rise to my full height, brushing dust from my hands. "I'm the one who made sure we *weren't* caught."

"If you weren't here in the first place, we wouldn't have had to go down that pipe."

*What the heck?* "I have as much right to be on this balcony as you do!"

The bear brows scowl. He folds his arms, so certain he's in the right, because that's Boy Wonder.

Fine.

"Well *excuse me* for almost tainting your good name. That's all you care about, isn't it? If Mommy and Daddy call, you can blame it on me."

I don't slam the balcony door on him, but only because that will bring Li-Han running.

# 15

After the Dragon's threats, we laid low. But on Friday night, hours after I ace our first Mandarin exam, Sophie and I and a half dozen girls from our floor decide to chance it again. We tiptoe into the humid midnight and down three flights of stairs.

The Dragon has posted a guard at the back, and although a part of me doesn't believe we can pull off another break-out, we've planned tonight with care: splitting up into smaller groups, leaving past midnight, after the guard in his booth at the top of the driveway has gone home and even the Dragon should be deep in REM—plus disguises: I tuck my scarf more securely around my face.

In the lobby, we move stealthily past the potted plants, the cherry-root chairs. Outside, the waxing moon illuminates the lawn. We hurry around the lily pond, the splash of the fountains drowning our steps. A laugh escapes my lips and Sophie pinches my arm.

"Shh," she breathes.

We near the guard's booth, the street coming into view. A cab passes and we quicken our pace.

Then a muted voice behind us calls, "*Xiǎo péngyǒu, tíng-tíng.*"

Li-Han in his paisley pajamas is jogging after us, shoving his glasses toward his face. On his heels, Mei-Hwa gasps for breath, the colors of her Aboriginal skirt muted by moonlight.

"Run!" Sophie cries. I yank my scarf tighter. We're hailing a cab on the street by the time Li-Han emerges around the bend behind us, then our doors double-slam. We're laughing so hard Sophie can barely give the driver directions to Club Babe.

"They're not really trying to stop us," I gasp as we pull from the curb. I can't help feeling guilty. "Mei-Hwa looks like she'd rather come out with us than chase us."

"She's not the enforcer type." Sophie finger-combs her hair into order. "Anyways, it's a game."

"How so?"

"They need to make a show of trying, but they don't *really* want to catch us. If they did, then what? Drag us back by our hair?" She shakes her head. "The program wants us to have a blast, so kids'll keep coming to Loveboat."

"The Dragon seemed serious," Laura says.

"We got a *lecture*." Sophie scoffs.

"Maybe it's that Asian nonconfrontational thing." Debra

adjusts the rings on her fingers. "When have your parents ever stood up to anyone?"

"My parents never rock the boat," Sophie says.

I adjust my tank top straps. "*My* parents would stop me."

"Maybe they're more Americanized."

"No, my dad's put up with crap from his boss for years. They're only confrontational when it comes to *me*."

Sophie laughs. "Too bad for them they're not here," she says.

I smile. "Too bad." Turning back, I see Mei-Hwa watching us from behind Li-Han, who is scowling, texting on his phone.

Out of his line of sight, Mei-Hwa gives the cab a small wave before we round the corner.

A contingency of other Chien Tan kids are already rocking it up at Club Babe.

Sophie makes a beeline for Xavier at the bar. Boy Wonder's here, too, and as it turns out, he's a terrible dancer—big motions, no variety, just rocking to the baseline, nodding to the beat. Hallelujah, *finally*, an imperfection! But he doesn't dance much anyways. He sticks to the bar with the guys like abalone shells on rocks, and in my book, the farther he is from my space on the dance floor, the better.

But during a lull in the music, I find myself ahead of him in line for a glass of water. He's wearing forest green, a much better color for him. I keep my eyes on the pitcher of ice water ahead, pretending I don't see him.

Then he taps me on the shoulder.

"Hey," he says.

"Hey," I say, and face forward again.

"I'm sorry I was rude the other night. I was—I mean, I don't really care if we get in trouble. It wasn't your fault. I probably come across like Jekyll and Hyde. I just . . . I have a lot on my mind this summer."

Why did he have to go and apologize? I'd already put him back on the proper shelf in my own mind. Now he's a guy who not only recognized his own behavior but is big enough to say sorry. I want to ask what's bothering him, but we're not there yet.

"I've definitely noticed that about you," I say finally, turning to face him.

His eyes flicker. "Really?"

"Yeah. But thanks for saying something."

His shoulders settle. I hadn't realized how tense he was. "You're not afraid of anything, are you?" he says. "I mean, we were three stories high."

"I'm afraid of lots of things." I pour us each a glass of water. "Just not heights. I used to sneak out of my room at home like that."

"I'm still poking around about your artist. You're right. Benji's a really good one. So are a few other guys."

"Oh, um. Thanks. I didn't realize you were checking."

153

His smile is almost shy. "I said I'd help. Might help if I take a look at the evidence."

Maybe he's just being kind. Still, I fish the delicate sketch from my purse.

He whistles, and I can't help a flush of pleasure. "You look—so real." If Rick's the artist, he's a good actor. But, of course, he's not—he's the most devoted long-distance boyfriend on the planet.

"It *could* be Benji." He tilts my sketch so my dancing figure catches the strobe lights, making me move on the page. "I've gotten to know him. I'll get him to show me some of his other work. I'll be discreet, I promise."

He's surprisingly committed. "Cool. Thanks, Rick."

He sets my sketch on the bar and pulls a lamp closer to illuminate it. Traces his thumb down the curve of my hair, like he's trying to unlock the secrets of the sketch. I watch him, resisting the urge to snatch it back from under his fingers.

We "sneak out" every night for the next week.

The game repeats—cat and mouse between us and our chaperones, whose attempts to catch us grow more half-hearted with each jail break. Mei-Hwa even starts looking the other way as we pad down the hall in our dresses and heels. I'd say she's seriously neglecting her job, but this works out better for all. She can stay in her pajamas, and we don't get sweaty sprinting for the gate.

Free drinks drive our agenda—we stop at Club Kinki for its complimentary booze hour, then grab a cab to Club GiGi, then on to the next. We stay out until four and wake before dinner, and no one bangs down our door; instead, everyone fails a pop quiz—another Wong Rule downed.

It's a first for me, but I brush aside the pinch of guilt. Besides, with enough demerits, the conflict between the Tour Down South and *Swan Lake* goes away. When the Dragon marches toward me in the hallway, I spin on my heel and duck outside.

Three weeks in, the intensity of living together, eating together, studying, and breaking out together has bonded us tighter than I've gotten with most of my high school. Secrets, crushes, hurts, humiliations—every topic is fair game around the table of truth in the late-night lounge. Two more sketches appear: one under my door, the other tucked into my purse—me sorting I Ching sticks with a fortune-teller; me in a black dress, emerging from a cab, eyes lit with anticipation.

"Who could it be?" Sophie marvels as we slip down the hallway for a night at Club Omni.

"I don't know." All three sketches are set in public places with dozens of Chien Tan kids. "He's doing a good job hiding." There's a thrill in my heart. A secret admirer. When except for that brief flame that was Dan, no guy has ever been interested in me.

At the club, I dance with Debra and Laura under pulsing green lights to one awesome song after another until I collapse beside Rick at the bar and drain his water in three gulps.

Somehow, I always wind up next to Boy Wonder.

"Hey," I gasp.

"Hey." A brief smile flashes then fades. His mood's swung tense again: his elbow on the bar, his right thumb running over the inside of his fingers in that fidgety gesture. Now that he's warned me about his moods, I don't mind as much. I hope whatever's bothering him ends soon. The strobe lights illuminate four pale scars across the inside middle of each finger.

"You must have needed stitches." Only a few days ago, I wouldn't have asked. "What happened?"

He closes his fist and drops it. "Just a little accident last year."

"Did you try to scale a wire fence?"

"Something like that." Turning to the sharp-boned bartender, he orders two guava cocktails, my new favorite, in Mandarin. I've added more key food words to my vocabulary.

"I've got mine." I dig into my pocket, but he's already paid.

"My treat."

"Um, thanks. I've got the next round."

Rick clinks his glass against mine. "It's not Benji. He draws comics. Not the same style at all. A few guys are after you, but I have more artistic ability in my pinkie toe than they have in their entire bodies."

"A *few* guys?" I splash more water from a pitcher into my glass. "Who?"

"Not your type." Rick waves them away, chaff on the wind.

"Well, whoever it is, he struck again." I pull the new sketches from my purse. "Maybe I haven't met him yet."

156

Rick holds the pictures to the light. Studying them. "Oh, you've met him."

"What? How do you know? Wait, do you know who?"

"No, but he's talked to you. See, look." Rick points to my sketch's mouth. "Your lip quirks like that when you're excited. Wouldn't be able to see that if he *wasn't* talking to you."

I laugh, self-conscious. I feel my mouth quirking like the sketch. "Um. No one's ever pointed that out before."

Rick's still studying my sketches and I pull them from his fingers and tuck them away. He glances up at me, surprised.

"Well, what about you?" he asks. "You have any leads?"

I've met dozens of guys on Loveboat, from all over the United States and Canada. I've definitely felt some sparks here and there, another thing that's new for me.

"Well, Sam and I had a good talk about me growing up the only Asian girl in my class and him growing up half-black, half-Chinese in Detroit."

"Sam's cool. I'll check out his drawings. What about David? You've become his premed adviser, from what I hear."

"And guys say that girls gossip." I face the dance floor, hiding a flush of pleasure. "I'm *so* not helpful. These BS/MD programs follow a different process. I won't have to take the MCATs."

"I'm sure you were helpful." He sets his elbow on the bar, brushing my arm. "You told him interviews were key."

"He told you that? That's from my guidance counselor. They find out what kind of human being you are then." I frown.

"What's wrong?"

"Just remembering."

"Your sketches?"

"Applications. Killing myself over the Krebs cycle, all those hours writing essays. Interviews, waiting, agonizing. I never want to go through that again—but it's only the beginning."

"Yeah. Senior year was hell. That's why I'm here—I needed a break. Simplify life for one summer before the shit hits the fan again, you know?"

"I'm happy to be here," I admit. "I didn't think I would be."

The band switches to a popular slow song and a collective sigh floats from the dance floor. As arms snake up around necks, my smile freezes. He's not going to ask me to dance, but why must my mind even go there? My eyes fall on Sophie, her fiery-orange dress pressed like flower petals to Xavier's all-black, her white arms around his back, cheek on his chest, swaying with her eyes closed. She really does seem to like him, although I wish she wouldn't constantly urge him to buy her things—pineapple cakes, a stone pendant. They feel like her way of keeping score.

Beside them, a couple locks lips on the dance floor. Another couple grinds slowly to the music, oblivious to the world. The air ripens with hormones. I avert my eyes, only to meet Rick's.

My blush deepens. I set my glass between us. "So tell me why Boy Wonder quit piano to warm the football bench?"

The corner of his lip turns up, and I get the feeling he knows exactly what I'm doing. "You want the sanitized version? Or the truth?"

"Nothing's straightforward with you, is it? Both."

A dimple I haven't noticed before flashes low in his cheek. "Seventh grade, the guy who played piano after me at Lincoln Center had music seeping from his pores. I wasn't that guy. I could play, but I couldn't feel it—not like he did. I realized it wasn't piano, it was mastery I wanted. So, I figured out what I would be willing to put that kind of time in for."

"Football."

"Curse you, Woo." Marc reaches past Rick and grabs his cocktail, his bangs swinging into his eyes. "That's how you took my slot at Yale." With a wink at me, he finishes off Rick's drink. I grin.

"You're running track for UCLA," Rick retorts. "You're one of the smartest guys I know. If it makes you feel better, Benji took my spot at Princeton, though he turned them down."

"You can't know that," I object. "You can't say you didn't get in because he did."

"Think about it." Marc waves at the Chien Tan crowd. "Everyone here applied to the same schools. All of us Asian Americans are in the same bucket. One Asian American boy with perfect SAT scores gets in, another doesn't. Quotas."

"You and your Asian American soap box," Rick says. "They say they don't have quotas."

Marc scoffs. "*They say.* Like they'd ever admit it."

Rick's thumb digs at his scars, his voice edged. "The world has way more space than the Ivy Leagues. If you're good, you're good."

159

"So, the real reason you dropped piano?" I prod.

"I was the smallest guy through middle school. Half the girls got picked before me in gym. The team captains who got stuck with me would roll their eyes. Pure torture. End of eighth grade, the high school football coach came to recruit and promised undying glory and respect. I went home and begged my mom on my knees to let me quit."

"And she agreed? Just like that?"

"She's never been on my case about school or activities—not that she doesn't have her own issues with my life." A shadow flickers over his face. "Also, she has rheumatoid arthritis, so she's not the toughest cookie in the jar. And my parents were going through a divorce. Guess that gave me leverage."

"Oh, I'm sorry." I chew on my lower lip. Jenny Lee's mom has RA too, and she's in a wheelchair. I was so wrong about him being some parent-driven drone.

"Bell-Leong, you in?" yells a guy from the game tables.

"Thanks for the drink, Woo." With a playful salute, Marc slips off. Rick tucks a big green bill under Marc's glass, then pushes a plate of sticky rice cakes toward me.

"So, what would it take for you to be a pro dancer?"

"Pro dancer?" I choke on a bite of cake. "You got that from seeing me clubbing?"

"Yep." Unfazed.

"I'd have to audition for the New York Ballet. Or a Broadway show." I make it sound as impossible as it is.

"Well, why not try?"

"Because *no one's* a dancer."

"No one's a football player either, not that anyone goes pro out of Yale."

"I applied to Tisch," I admit. I haven't spoken about it since Megan. "I got off the waiting list."

"NYU, right?" Rick whistles. "That's a serious program."

Still feels presumptuous to say it. That someone who'd gotten an acceptance letter withdrew, then Tisch admissions pulled out their bucket of waitlist hopefuls and, somehow, picked . . . me.

"I turned them down. We could never have afforded it." Even with that tiny scholarship I'd clutched at like a drowning person for a single afternoon. Quickly, I add, "But I'm auditioning Sunday for *Swan Lake*. Should be fun."

"Cool. Where at?"

"Just a small ballet studio. I'm taking the Metro from your aunt's."

"Can I watch?"

"Seriously? You want to?"

"Professional curiosity. I've been to a dozen football tryouts but never a dance audition. Do they weigh you? Examine your muscles?"

I laugh. "You're in for a disappointment. I do a short piece—"

A thump against my backside knocks me into Rick, splashing water from his glass onto us. "Oh, sorry—" Turning, I look up at a big, sandy-haired guy covered in tattoos of Chinese characters, ordering a mai tai from the bartender.

"Heeey, cupcake." He grins down. "Wanna dance?"

*Cupcake?* Gah. "No, thanks. Taking a break."

"How about taking a break with me? You're the sweetest little Asian girl I've seen here." Two hundred pounds of meaty guy crushes me against the bar. He reeks of alcohol and sweat. I shove back, but it's like trying to move a brick wall.

"I'm"—*shove*—"good"—*shove*—

"Sorry, man." Rick smoothly hauls him off. "She's with me."

Coolness. I'd like to kick the guy where it counts. Instead, I tuck my arm through Rick's and flash the guy a sheepish smile.

"Hey, man, didn't see you there. So sorry." He practically falls on his face apologizing to Rick—and has Rick grown a few inches?

"Sorry," Rick says to me, after he's gone. "Didn't mean to rescue you, but you weren't into that guy, were you?"

"No, you read me right. Thanks." I force my fingers to unpeel from his arm. "How annoying he apologized to *you*. Like I'm your property."

Rick grimaces. "I know his type."

Guys with Asian fetishes. "Maybe he's not," I say. But it's one of those things I bet most Asian American girls have dealt with. I explained it to Megan last year over one of our long coffees, why it's not flattering, why it's based in stereotypes that have nothing to do with who you are, how it reminds me that I look Asian on the outside, no matter how I feel inside. I make a face. "I guess you know they're out there, but it's still jarring when you run into them."

I reach for my glass, but Rick catches my hand. "Hey, do something for me?"

His palm is calloused. This close, I catch that grassy, out-doorsy scent of his, as though his days on the field have permanently infused his skin.

Suddenly, I can't quite meet his eyes.

"What?"

"If you want to check someone out before you go for him, you can always ask me. I'll let you know if he's okay."

My voice comes out high. "Why the interest in my dating life anyways?"

I'm still not quite meeting his eyes. But before he can answer, raised voices from the dance floor draw our attention, and he drops my hand. A pair of dancers yell as they're shoved aside, then Xavier storms around them. He slams into me, his sweat-dampened shirt smearing my arm. Fury bubbles in his eyes as they meet mine.

"Watch where you're going, man." Rick's tone is sharp as he grips my elbow and steadies me. Then Sophie leaps onto Xavier's back, piggy-back-style, her orange dress streaming behind her like the tail of a comet.

"I didn't mean it!" She clings to him while he tries to shake her off. Heads are turning all over the club. "Xavier, I'm sorry. I know it's none of my business."

"Sophie." I seize her arm. What the heck is going on? I've never seen either of them like this before. "Sophie, please calm down."

Xavier finally succeeds in peeling her off. As she grabs for him again, Rick catches her by the waist and tugs her back. Xavier vanishes into a mosh pit of grinding bodies.

"Soph, I told you, he's not worth it."

"Oh, like you of all people are the expert on *that*?" She shoves him off, sending his cell phone skidding over the floor. Then she flies after Xavier.

I'm sober as I retrieve Rick's phone and hand it back. I didn't miss the dig at Jenna, but I don't have the courage to ask. As for Aunty Claire's—will Xavier want to come now? Are Sophie's plans over before they get off the ground?

Rick runs a hand down his face. "I hate it when she gets like this."

"Like what?"

"About guys. She has the worst judgment. Four boyfriends and none of them deserved her."

He's so protective—she's lucky to have him for a cousin. But he also seems to have a blind spot when it comes to his room-mate.

"She usually seems happy with Xavier."

"No one deserves that guy." Rick frowns at his phone. The screen's cracked and dark.

"You warned *me* off him—didn't you say something to her?"

Rick's eyes shift. He won't tell me. Not the whole truth. He pockets his phone. "I didn't see them coming. Then it was too late. She wouldn't listen."

"But why me then?"

He shakes his head. "Just watch out for her, okay? I'm glad you're her roommate." He drains his glass, chews on ice. "My prior offer still stands. You want to date someone on Loveboat, I'll check him out for you." I open my mouth to accuse him of changing the subject, but he continues, "Sophie wouldn't listen to me, but I'd do the same for my little sister."

Little sister.

I've leaned into him, my shoulder pressing into his upper arm. *Little sister.* A step above friends, but a metaphorical finger to my shoulder, pushing me back an inch. I open a gap between us. He and Sophie are the same: generously embracing me, her roommate, as family.

I hold out my hand. "I promise to check with you, *Gēgē.*" *Big brother.*

"For family," he drawls, "no charge."

We shake on it, sealing our new relationship.

**16**

A typhoon rages to the north of Taipei, sending showers down around the city. Thursday evening, on my way back to the dorms, a gust of rain-spattered wind blows me through the lobby doors of Chien Tan. It tugs at the bag of paper lanterns I picked up for Sophie's weekend, which starts tomorrow afternoon. She's been oddly close-lipped about her status with Xavier, but plans are still full speed ahead.

The lobby is full of kids playing Go and mah-jong. Mei-Hwa's face glows as she plays a toe-tapping Taiwanese Aboriginal pop song on David's laptop, swaying in her seat, on a mission to converting as many students as possible to her collection.

"*Ālǐ Shān De Gū Niáng.*" She chatters in Mandarin, slim hands gesturing.

"It's not bad." David says. "Not bad."

As I shake water from my hair, a wisp of a courier in an orange reflective vest wheels his bicycle in beside me, hitching a brown-paper package higher under his arm.

"*Xiǎojiě, wǒ zhǎo Woo Kwāng Míng.*"

"I'll take it to him." I accept the box, which is heavier than it looks. Cute bunny stickers hop along the top and bottom, and in between, Rick's name and address are scripted in copperplate English and Chinese, along with its sender's.

Jenna Chu.

The box slips. I catch it by its strings before it hits the floor and explodes. Wrapping it in my arms, I hurry toward the dining hall.

He'll be thrilled. Of course he will be. How nice to hear from his girlfriend, even at a summer program across the ocean.

At a table by the windows, Rick, along with Marc, Spencer, and Sophie—no Xavier—are digging into the daily feast. Steam rises from a tower of round bamboo baskets full of *xiǎolóng bāo*, a universal favorite. If Sophie is upset, she doesn't show it: she has everyone snorting into their teacups with an elaborate story of revenge she took on a guy unlucky enough to have jilted her. I discreetly tuck the bag of paper lanterns under her seat.

"Rick, this came for you." I drop the box into his lap like a five-hundred–pound weight, then take the seat two down, by Spencer, and pour myself a cup of red oolong tea.

Rick's eyes flicker from the package to me. "Oh—cool." He

seems pleased, though not as pleased as I expected—and I *really* need to stop overanalyzing him.

I spoon steamed bass onto my plate, keeping my nosy eyes to myself as he tears the brown paper. Maybe I'm just always obsessed with the guy who isn't available, so I don't ever put myself on the line. Maybe that's all that's happening with Rick, and why I keep revisiting that moment I took his arm at the bar.

"Sweet," Spencer says, and I glance up.

Rick unties lavender ribbons from a white box to reveal trays of chocolates shaped like squirrels, birds, acorns—homemade, by the looks of them. Silver confetti spill onto his lap as he lifts them out of the loveliest care package I've ever seen. I envision Jenna with her soft, black hair in a twist, pouring melted chocolate into molds, sprinkling confetti. She's even included dry ice to keep it from melting—no wonder the express delivery.

"Wow, wish someone would send me one of those," Spencer says.

"She must have spent *hours* on these," Sophie says.

"Not *hours*," Rick says. "She's really efficient. She likes making things like this." He's so protective. He offers the chocolates around. I take an acorn, which turns out to have a perfect raspberry dot in its center.

"It's yum." I stab my chopsticks into my pork chop, trying to tear off a piece. I'm happy for Rick that he's so well loved. I glare at my chop—why is it so tough tonight?

Sophie decapitates a bird with her teeth. "How much food can she send you before she has to pay export tax?" So this isn't the first care package.

"*Shut. Up. Soph.*" Rick scowls. "She misses me. That's all."

He tucks a thick letter into his backpack, passes the last tray of chocolates to a table of grateful counselors, then reaches for the steamed fish.

The sun is high in the sky the next day when the wrench of our stubborn door opening wakes me. Sophie enters, draped in Xavier's black shirt. I sit up in bed. Last night, she'd left Club Elektro arm in arm with him. Her hair is tousled, lips swollen. Kneeling between our beds, she unfurls a red silk rug. A web of intricate vines and white flowers unfold across the plush silk.

"Wow, he got you that?" I rub my eyes, as stunned by her state as the extravagant present.

"He left it outside the door for me." She removes a gold safety pin that I imagine held a steamy love note.

"It's *gorgeous*. He has such good taste." Is it his way of making up for their fight? It's a really nice gift, the nicest one yet, even more so because she didn't ask him to buy it.

"It must've cost a fortune." She brushes the pile so it lies even. "I mean, he could buy the entire market, but still."

"So you guys patched things up? How?"

"My feminine charms." She wiggles her arms and hips in a

little dance, smiling mysteriously, then flops back on her bed. "*Oh my God*, Ever—I seriously would bear him a dozen babies." Sitting up, she waves the menu for tonight's dinner. "And everything's going to the next level tonight. Silver or gold settings?"

"Silver." I reach for one of the silk goody bags we're stuffing, and pour a handful of hard candies inside. My job is to play supportive friend as she impresses Xavier with her family, then occupy them to give her space to slip him away for a seductive Saturday night on her aunt's private rooftop garden. I'm determined to help make her weekend perfect.

"Fish or steak? Or both?"

"Both? Surf and turf?" I tie a satin bow, add the goody bag to the growing mountain on Sophie's desk, and reach for another bag. She really is a combination of Pearl-like cute and Megan-manic energy, although there's no one like Sophie Ha. "Don't think it'll matter."

"Ever, what would I do without you?" She hands me a stack of cute stationary. "I found these yesterday. Take some," she urges, more of her daily generosity. "You know, if Xavier was coming by himself, it would be too much pressure. You know how Asian families get about meeting the significant other. Especially my uncle. He really admires the Yeh family."

"My parents would *definitely* freak out if I brought a guy to meet the family."

"So that's why this is just friends from the program coming over. I mean, of course they know he's my boyfriend. But with you and Rick there, it's balanced. Perfectly."

I flip through the stack as Sophie moves to her mirror, a cyclone of nervous energy. She's barely eaten in days. And the silver, the elaborate menus, the goody bags—does she really know what she wants out of this weekend?

"Hey, what's this?" Sophie swoops down at the door, then waves a square of origami paper at me. "Ever! Secret admirer strikes again."

"What? No way." I slide off my bed. A new sketch. Blotches of color—blues, rust, and greens—that, when held at arm's length, form . . . me. Balancing on the brick ledge in the courtyard yesterday, my arms out, one leg tipped out, my turquoise dress swaying to one side with a breeze. "It's *brilliant*." And by whom? Rick, Marc, and a bunch of guys had been playing a scrimmage game of football with an audience—anyone could have sketched this.

"Wish someone would draw me like that! Fourth one, isn't it?"

"Yeah." I turn it over, looking for some clue, some hint to the artist. "I should feel creeped out, shouldn't I?"

"This guy isn't a creeper. He's romantic. Maybe it's Marc—he totally likes you."

"Marc's not into me that way." And *he* feels like a brother, way more than Rick. "Besides, I think he likes boys. It might be someone I haven't met yet."

Or Rick . . . what if he's pretending to help me find the guy, but it *is* him. My parents—I can imagine how happy that would make them—a fresh surge of anger floods through me. No way would I ever give them that satisfaction.

"Well, whoever he is"—Sophie yanks on our door, which has swollen even more with recent storms—"he can't"—yank—"keep this talent under wraps forever!"

Grabbing my towel and toothbrush, I follow Sophie toward the bathroom, past Grace Pu and Matteo Deng passed out like a pair of cats on the lounge couch. Matteo, as it turns out, does have a temper, holding red-faced screaming matches with Grace up and down the hallway that usually ended with something broken—a bulletin board, a lamp, his toe—but they've made up again, clearly.

Inside the bathroom, Laura glances up from the sink, where she's hunched over in her floral nightgown. Her bedsheets are bunched in her arms as she scrubs at a period stain. As we enter, her face flushes beet red.

"Those suck," I say. At the same time, Sophie says, "David should wash those."

Laura's face deepens to an alarming eggplant purple. Her eyes slide from mine to Sophie's. "Oh, *no,* I wouldn't make him do this."

Oh.

*Not* period stains.

My own face flushes as Sophie's eyes meet mine in the mirror. I really am a baby.

"Just be careful." Sophie runs her toothbrush under the faucet. "A girl went home pregnant a few years ago—"

"*Ai-Mei? Nǐ zài nǎlǐ ma?*" Someone knocks on the door, calling my name.

"Shit, it's Mei-Hwa." Laura snatches her dripping sheets to

her chest and backs into a stall, trailing water everywhere. No one since Xavier and Mindy has been busted for violating the no-boys-and-girls-in-the-same-room rule, but no one wants to become the next object lesson either.

"Um, just a minute!" I grab a paper towel and dry the floor, then step in front of Laura's stall as Sophie opens the door. Mei-Hwa pokes her head in, running a nervous hand down her waist-long braid. She bites her lip, looking as though she wished she were anywhere but here, and peers at me.

"*Nǐ shēngbìngle ma?* Are you sick?"

"No, I'm good." I shut off the third faucet, then curse myself for drawing attention to it.

"You missed classes all week." She's using English—I'm in trouble. "We switched electives Monday and you haven't been to a single Calligraphy class." Mei-Hwa fidgets with the green ribbon on her braid. My heart sinks. Sophie's missed classes, too. Not as many as me, but still, no one's tracked *her* down. "Gao Laoshi is getting ready to call your parents."

"Oh!" The Dragon strikes again. "No need." I push past her into the hallway, leading her away from Laura. "I was just heading to Calligraphy."

I grab a sesame bun from the dining hall, then head outside into the back courtyard, where a stone carp the size of a baby beluga spouts water into a basin. The afternoon sun beats down on my hair, but the air is muggy with the promise of rain. As I round a corner toward the gym, the swing of a long stick nearly takes off my head. I duck as the wind of it tugs at my hair, stumbling back against the wall.

"What the—!"

"Oh, sorry, Ever." Rick hauls me by my arm to my feet, flashing a lopsided grin. A tiger-striped bo staff is in his hand. He yells and ducks himself as another staff comes swinging. He swings back at a guy I don't recognize, shoulders surging under his blue shirt. Dropping into a fighter's crouch, he charges his partner. All through the side yard, the cracks of rattan bo staffs punctuate the air as pairs of fighters battle it out while Li-Han calls instructions.

I've walked into the stick-fighting elective. I watch, envious, mesmerized by the action.

Spin, turn, jab.

Attack, counterattack.

Rick blocks another blow.

"You're up early," he says. Asshole—it's just past one.

"Too early." I give him the finger, low, earning a startled exclamation from his partner. Then I duck around them and head into the gym, Rick's chuckle ghosting behind.

Calligraphy occupies four tables across the gym, by the bleachers. On my way there, I pass the ribbon-dancing elective: Debra and other girls undulate silk ribbons attached to sticks, drawing

174

yellow, red, and orange spirals and curlicues in the air. Their graceful instructor demonstrates a basic dance and I find myself improving on it: If they moved in two counter revolutions. If they widened the arcs of the ribbons . . .

Some of the girls have great form and rhythm. I should be dancing with them, but Madame Szeto, *Swan Lake*—I'm finding my own way.

The calligraphy tables are divided into individual stations: stacks of large sheets of rice paper, black inkstones, bamboo jars of long-handled brushes. I take a seat. A few easels by the bleachers display samples of calligraphy. To my surprise, they're nothing like the soul-sucking character charts of Chinese school. They're works of art.

"Ever Wong." The familiar low voice draws my name into a song. Xavier pulls out the chair beside me. With a jerk of his head, he flicks his wavy black hair from his eyes. His arm brushes mine and my face heats. He's sitting too close.

"Your dad must have picked your electives, too." I scooch a few inches away. I need to be friendly, but distant. We haven't been together without Sophie since they got together.

"Something like that." His dark eyes sweep mine with a challenge, looking at me like he did that first day. Mayday. Mayday. I glance around for support, but I don't know the kids in this class well.

"So," he says. "We're headed to Rick and Sophie's aunt's this afternoon."

"Yeah," I say, "should be nice." Then I turn my back and flip through my book of fancy characters.

There's a knack to holding a *máo bǐ*—a calligraphy brush with a soft head of rabbit, goat, or wolf hair. Lefties are encouraged to switch to right or the stroke ends don't come out right, but our teacher is a lefty herself, and lets me slide. We practice slow versus fast strokes. I get a mini-lesson on grinding ink, which I do to the rhythm of the ribbon-dancing songs. I wish my Chinese school teacher back home had let us use brushes and inkstones instead of copying characters by the hundreds. Maybe I would have lasted longer.

In the courtyard, the stick-fighting elective is going strong— the thwacks of bo staffs audible through the glass doors. My fingers itch to spin a staff—but I'm stuck with paintbrushes. Still, lulled by the ribbon-dancing music, I find myself sinking into the character work, focused on getting the strokes right.

"Xiang-Ping, this is very nice, but the assignment is to *copy the poem*." The teacher's voice is strained. They've had this conversation before.

Xavier's page holds just a single character: a square with a dash in the middle. The character for *sun*. He's mocked it, too: childish rays blast from it.

He shrugs, making no move to pick up his brush. His demerit list is easily the longest, thanks to his refusal to turn in a single assignment, in Mandarin or Chinese Medicine.

"Aren't we all bored to death being treated like babies?" Sophie defended him, when the subject came up one night.

Now, our Calligraphy teacher laughs helplessly, and turns to another student.

Before I can look away, Xavier gives me a lazy smile that reminds me of his kiss on my knuckles.

Then he dips his *máo bǐ* into his inkwell and begins to paint on a fresh sheet of rice paper. By the roundness of his strokes, I can tell he's not drawing characters.

"You'll get in trouble again," I whisper. Not that he cares.

Sure enough, he shrugs. I find myself inching closer, but he hides it with his arm.

"What are you painting?" I finally ask.

His teasing grin crinkles his eyes. "Show you in a minute."

He makes me wait another five. But at last, he hands the paper to me.

I feel a lightning bolt of shock. Familiar blocks of color form this gymnasium setting. The *máo bǐ* hang like a row of cattails on their drying racks. Ribbon dancers swirl in the margins.

And in the center of it all is painted, in a style I'd recognize anywhere . . . a girl.

Me.

**17**

"*You're* the artist."

Prickles run down my back. Xavier was drawing me before he and Sophie even got together. I wouldn't be human if I denied that a part of me is incredibly flattered. One of the most sought-after guys on Loveboat has rendered my portrait five times.

This guy wants you, Sophie had said.

He smiles. "Did you think it was Whole Foods?"

"Of *course* not," I say. Too quickly. His eyes flicker. I *knew* it couldn't be. But why this rush of disappointment? I *don't* want the Boy Wonder my parents would swoon over. And if Rick *had* been the artist, dating Jenna, sending me this unspeakable message while pretending to help me figure it out, my respect for him would have diminished.

"Why?" I ask Xavier.

"Why what?"

"Why are you drawing me?"

"Am I any good?"

Just like that, he's forced me to study it: My miniature hand hovers a *máo bǐ* over my rice paper. The first stroke of a character waits for a companion. Inky hair waterfalls along my face and my profile is turned—not toward the paper, but the bo fighters outside the glass doors.

Watching Rick.

I blush. Caught doing something I hadn't even realized I was doing.

"It's incredible." He sees the world in bursts of color and shapes, rather than coloring-book outlines.

Xavier exhales. He was waiting for my verdict—and it mattered to him. But why would he care? Right now, all I see is the guy trying to seduce me with his sketches—and almost succeeding.

Almost.

I push the picture back at him. "You can't draw me."

His lashes flicker. "Why not?"

My voice sharpens. "You're with Sophie. You should draw *Sophie*." It would be her dream come true—just as she's three times more excited to get her glamour shot proofs than me.

"Maybe I don't want to draw Sophie. Maybe I'm not with her either."

"*Maybe?*" I shove my chair back, scraping the floor. "I shouldn't even be having this conversation!" The teacher glances our way and I lower my voice. "Maybe sleeping with a girl means nothing to you, but it does to most girls, okay?"

His upper lip curls. "Sometimes things aren't always the way they seem."

We're talking in circles. This is dangerous. We're headed into a weekend that Sophie's spent every waking minute planning, endured a full-body waxing for—all for Xavier.

Megan will never know half of the bone-crushing agony I felt when she told me she was dating Dan, and there's no way I'd do that to Sophie.

Xavier leans into me. I catch the spicy scent of his cologne and snatch my arm away, hating myself for the part of me that's enjoying his blatant interest. Hating myself for the curl of curiosity of what it would feel like to have those soft lips on the places of me he's drawn.

I tear Xavier's painting in half, then fourths, then eighths. It's like stomping on a butterfly to spite the bully who hatched it from its cocoon, but I don't let on.

Xavier's gaze follows my movements, but he makes no move to stop me. His expression doesn't change. Class is ending. Students are clipping damp calligraphy pages to a clothesline to dry.

I drop the pieces onto his notebook, brace my paint-smudged hands on the table, and rise over him.

"Don't you dare say a word about this to Sophie," I say fiercely. "You're *her* boyfriend. You bought her that *rug*."

His mouth sets in a line. He's used to being accused, as well he should be.

"Just for the record," he says. "I've never slept with Sophie."

What?

Uncertainty flutters like a trapped moth inside me. The pieces of painting swirl over his hand.

But I've heard every detail from her lips myself—all the girls have. I have no idea why, but he must be lying. Thank God Rick never *did* find out Xavier was my artist—he'd have told Sophie and then what?

"You know what? It doesn't matter." With a jerk, I grab my calligraphy book. "And for the record, you're an asshole. Stop drawing me."

I storm to the clothesline, clip my page to it, then escape out the door.

But I can't escape the fear that our weekend has just grown exponentially more complicated.

# 18

"Where's Rick?" Sophie tugs impatiently at the skirt of her orange-striped dress, which shows off cleavage to the point that it's distracting even me. We are standing on the lowest step outside Chien Tan, as the driver loads her suitcase into the back of Aunty Claire's Mercedes van. She wrinkles her skirt in a nervous gesture. This weekend means so much to her—and as for me, the Wong Rules are taking a back seat to supporting her. Anyways, I've only got *No Boys/No Kissing Boys* left, and at this rate, that one's going nowhere.

"Aunty Claire's waiting." She climbs into the van as Xavier climbs in from the other side, setting an orange Osprey backpack on the floor. I avoid looking at him. "Rick better hurry."

"I'll go find him," I offer.

She grabs my hand and tugs me close to whisper in my ear. "*Please*. Rick needs to come. Uncle Ted will give Xavier the third degree if he's not there to run interference."

"I'll drag him by his hair if I have to." I set my dance bag at her feet, but when Xavier reaches for it, probably to add it to the luggage pile, I snatch it back as though he were trying to steal it. Sophie is too busy dialing her aunt to notice.

"Ever," Xavier begins, but I head off, glad to put distance between us while I can.

It's funny to be going into a weekend *not* devoted to sneaking out clubbing. Almost a relief, if I'm honest. The lobby swarms with kids and backpacks headed to visit families, with as many gathered to stay, gearing up for the talent show at the program's end. Two guys toss Chinese yo-yos. Another pair performs magic tricks with a man-sized rubber balloon.

"Have you seen Rick?" I ask Debra and Laura as they strum on guitar and zither.

Debra's fingers dance on her strings. "Sorry, no."

"Maybe upstairs?" Laura sweeps her bangs from her eyes.

Five minutes later, I knock on Rick's door. It opens with a soft click. Rick's desk comes into view: hosting a blue retainer case, a half-used tube of acne medicine, and a bar of soap, separated from a mountain of Chinese and American snacks he's stockpiled—bags of dried fruits, nuts, suncakes, a can of Pringles, six-packs of iced tea. Xavier's half of the room is more spare: a hamper of laundry, blanket barely dented, as if Xavier's trying to pretend he's not here.

"Please calm down," Rick says. "I told you. My phone's still broken. The time zone threw me off."

Rick stands at his window over the burlap sack of rice he bought for weights. His black hair, damp from a shower, darkens the collar of his forest-green shirt. He presses his landline phone to his ear. His thumb rolls along the scar inside his fingers in that gesture of tension I've come to recognize.

Even from here, I can hear the girl on the other end:

"I'm *sick* of your stupid excuses! You and your whole *family's*—"

"Jenna, I said I'm sorry. If you could fly out here—"

"If you want to *fuck* with me, Rick Woo, then you never should have gone to Taiwan. You could have done that right here in my own bedroom."

I cringe. Try not to let her words paint images in my head that I don't want there. I half expect him to explode at Jenna—but I'm dreading it, too.

"Jenna, I know it's hard to be apart. I need you to be patient. Please. Jenna? *Jenna*—wait!"

Rick swears and drops the phone, his easygoing stance replaced by a body webbed with stress lines. I want to go to him and siphon it off.

Then he slams his fist through the center of his rice sack. Rice grains rattle as they pour from the split fabric onto the floor.

He catches sight of me, and jumps a foot into the air, knocking over his lamp with a crash. The door slams behind me, gusting a breeze that ruffles the workbook on his desk.

"Sorry," we chorus. I'm not sure who's more mortified—him or me. He rights his lamp, then kneels and begins to sweep the rice into a pile.

"I'm sorry you heard that."

"What's wrong?" I grab his trash can and scoop double handfuls of rice into it.

"I don't even know. She wasn't happy I came on this trip. We've never been apart longer than a few days."

"Really?" Even I've been away from home for a week, for school field trips. Is that the problem then? She must really depend on Rick. I feel a curl of sympathy. I know a few girls like that on my dance squad: smart, fun, pretty girls who for some reason can't set foot out their houses without the boyfriend they always seem to need around.

"Didn't she think about coming on this trip, too?"

"Couldn't. She's volunteering at a horse camp for disabled kids. I'm trying to get her to fly out for a week, but she's terrified of flying."

"The ticket's *really* expensive."

"Not for her. Her dad's an executive in the Bank of China Hong Kong."

"Oh." I flush. All my sympathy evaporates—buying an international plane ticket at a hat's drop, no pearl necklace sold off. I can't even imagine it. I roll to my feet, brushing rice from my palms. "Sophie and Xavier are waiting downstairs."

"Crap." He dumps the last handful of rice into the trash. "I completely lost track of time."

I shake the sack's remaining grains back down, then fold it in half and lay it on his desk by a stack of postcards. The top one is inked with Jenna's name and several lines in bold, blocky handwriting. Her four-page letter, filled with copperplate cursive, rests beside it. I can't resist a peek. The top page is the last, which reads at bottom:

*Shells and I went to Sweet Connections today. Wish you were home already. Still trying to understand why you had to go. I found you a cool song—will save it for when you're back and we can listen together.*
*Love you forever.*
*Jenna*

A Polaroid photo shows Jenna with her arm around a girl in pigtails, Pearl's age, with Rick's amber-flecked eyes. They're grinning like a pair of thieves over ice-cream cones. Shelly. Rick's sister. This girl is totally in love with Rick. Her sweetness feels at odds with the girl on the phone, and yet this letter-writing pal of Rick's little sister must be the girl he loves—and I'm standing here reading his private mail.

Rick's staring at his phone, as if he can bring her here by telepathy.

"Rick?" I clear my throat. "Are you still coming?"

Rick starts. "Oh, God." Seizing his Chien Tan bag, he opens his drawer and crams socks and boxers into it. Then he slaps his bag down on his dresser and shoves the drawer shut. "I can't take my family right now."

I frown. "What do you mean?"

"Last Christmas, my sister and I visited with my mom. Every day, I got an earful from five aunts and uncles: 'Rick, you need to drop that girl like an anvil and find the right one.'"

"They've met her?"

"Yeah. The summer before, in the States. My mom *fasted* for three days trying to get me to break it off."

"Fasted?" Guilt-wise, Rick's mom puts Mom and her black pearl necklace to shame. My gut clenches as I remember Dan sprinting down our driveway. How dare they try to dictate who we love? "That's *bullshit*, Rick. My parents never let me date either."

"Oh, they *want* me to date." He laughs, a brittle unlike-Rick laugh. "My family's more traditional than the Qing dynasty. I have twenty-two first cousins, and I'm the only boy with the Woo last name. They're all depending on me to pass the family name along." He drags a hand over his face, defeated again. "Just not with her."

"Why don't they like her?"

"Stupid reasons."

I grit my teeth. "I'm sure they are."

"This year's going to be 'What about Loveboat? Two hundred fifty nice Chinese American girls—HOW CAN YOU WASTE THIS OPPORTUNITY?!?'"

I seriously want to kill me some Woo family members.

"Can I do anything?"

"It's hopeless." His thumb worries his scars. "The only thing that will get them off Jenna's back is if I bring home a girl who *isn't* Jenna."

He crashes backward onto his bed, two hundred–plus pounds in no hurry to go anywhere. Sophie is waiting downstairs. Do I go let her know Rick's not coming and ruin her perfectly balanced weekend? Even without his fasting mom, this family visit sounds like torture. But better than moping alone after that call. And I *want* to help him—he took me home passed out drunk and never said a word, got me the fan, even if I gave it to Sophie, tried to help me track down my artist, even pretended to be my boyfriend to rescue me from the cupcake guy—

Cupcake guy.

"So, what if you *did* bring a Loveboat girlfriend home?" I blurt. "Pretend I'm her—like you did for me at the club. That'll get them off your case, wouldn't it?"

As soon as the offer leaves my mouth, I know it's a mistake.

But Rick lifts his head off his pillow. He gives me a speculative look. "You mean, introduce you as my girlfriend to my aunt and uncle?"

I back away, toward the door. "It's a terrible idea. Forget I said anything."

"No! No, it's perfect, actually." Rick sits up. Grabs his football

188

and spins it on his knee. His eyes narrow. "Really perfect. My family will *love* you."

"They will?" Is that a compliment or insult?

"Totally." He gets up, drops his football. "They can't say I didn't try. And when you break up with me a month later, that's the perfect excuse for why I'm back with Jenna. This could be a way to get them off our case permanently." His eyes widen, earnest, oddly desperate. "Ever, you really won't mind?"

Curse me and my stupid ideas. His family must be a murder of trolls to inspire such insanity on his part. And I'm just as insane.

"We're not going to *act* like boyfriend and girlfriend, right?" I cringe at the high pitch to my laugh. But I can't. I can't hold hands with Boy Wonder.

"Course not. This is Loveboat. Especially with Sophie bringing Xavier, if we tell them we're together, they'll believe it. Ever, I owe you one. You're brilliant."

*No, I'm a fool.* But his gratitude is like a bar of dark chocolate. I can't resist.

"I'll have to leave early Sunday for my audition."

"No problem. I'm coming, right?"

"Right."

"So, no problem."

"What if Jenna finds out?" *Or my parents?* After all the rule breaking, *pretending* to break one—the *No Boyfriend* rule—feels the most risky, with the most to lose.

He grabs his laptop and opens his email. "The only person who'd tell is Shelly. I'll tell her not to repeat anything she hears."

Fighting panic, I grab his Chien Tan bag off his dresser and start for the door.

"Hey, I've got that." He grabs for it, but I yank back, snapping a strap.

Bad sign, but I'm already rushing out the door. "What are little sisters for?"

19

A pair of guards in crisp blue swing open wrought-iron gates onto a wide driveway. Our driver pulls through, touching his fingertips to his brow in salute.

Sophie was not exaggerating. The Zhang residence sits in the heart of Tianmu, one of the most expensive neighborhoods in Taipei. Along the stone walls, baby-pink rosebushes—"imported from England," Sophie says—rustle in a breeze. Blue-gray flag-stones and English grass carpet the grounds all the way to a two-story mansion of white stucco and green-shuttered windows.

"Hey, Sophie, I need to tell you something." For the fourth time, I try to catch her attention. Rick and I have been trying to update her and Xavier on the change in our dating status since we hit the road, but between giving Xavier the scoop on her family and now, the mansion, she hasn't paused for breath.

Our van stops at the foot of a stone stairwell the width of an estuary. A white-gloved porter opens Sophie's door and she flies out like a sunbeam, squealing, "Aunty Claire! We're here!"

The update will have to wait. Two barking Shiba Inus, along with two black-haired kids around five and six, hurl themselves at Rick. The boy yells football stats in clipped British English. The girl, despite her picture-perfect rose-print dress cries and babbles—apparently her mother just informed her she's too young to marry Rick.

"Hey, Felix! You've been doing research?" Rick swings the boy onto his shoulder and spins, making him yell. He tugs on the girl's pigtails. "Fannie, you don't want to marry an ugly old troll like me."

"Yes, I do!" Fannie lisps; she's lost two lower teeth. I laugh. Rick will be a great dad—*um, wrong road!*—it's not as though I really *am* his girlfriend, assessing his potential life-mate qualities. *Arg!*

Eager to put space between us, I follow Sophie up the steps into a high-ceilinged foyer of white marble tiles and pillars, man-sized vases, a large bonsai tree, a curved staircase—all sparkling with light from a chandelier the size of a grand piano. A Japanese-style pond, built with flat stones into the floor, swims with orange carp.

"Aunty Claire!" Sophie swoops down on a petite, pregnant

woman and plants a kiss on each cheek. Then she threads her arm through Xavier's. "This is *Xavier Yeh.*"

"Welcome!" Aunty Claire, swelling belly and all, is stunning in her tailored sea-green qipao and string of emeralds. She bestows the same queenly greeting on Xavier, then on Rick, still bent double with Fannie and Felix clinging like monkeys to his back and neck. Rick detaches himself from his cousins, grabs my hand, and tugs me forward.

"And this is Ever Wong." Rick's tone is even, but he somehow sounds . . . proud. As if he's created me himself. "My girlfriend."

A stunned silence follows. I can't look at Sophie or Xavier.

Then Fannie screams and runs upstairs, wailing. Aunty Claire's eyes grow wide. I'm terrified she's about to scold Rick. *How dare you bring such a mouse home when your cousin brings the Heir to the Yeh Empire?!*

Then her arms go around me. Jasmine perfume fills my nostrils.

"*Goà-khò!*" she cries in Hokkien. My goodness! "Sophie, you should have *warned* me!" She holds me at arms' length and drinks me down with gorgeous eyes. "Rick, *you* should have warned me! Ever, sweetie, my home is yours. Do you have any favorite dishes? I'll send my maid to the market."

"No, no." I find my voice. "No. Anything is great." And where will all her enthusiasm go when I dump her darling nephew? Sophie frowns and I feel another stab of guilt.

Then Rick's arm encircles my waist, warm and possessive. "I knew you'd like her."

"I'm giving you the Eleanor suite," Aunty Claire says to me. She starts up the stairs, then turns back. "Rick!" she cries, exasperated. "Carry her bag!"

As Aunty Claire heads deeper into her mansion, I snatch my body as well as bag back from Rick. My heart pounds in my throat. His hand and arm have branded themselves through the fabric of my clothes into my skin.

"We're just *pretending*, remember?" I whale him in the stomach with my bag, earning an *oaf*. The guard chokes with a laugh.

"Sorry," Rick whispers, sheepishly. "Wanted to look convincing—everything will hit the family emergency phone tree by tonight. Won't happen again."

"Better not," I snap, then march after Aunty Claire to the largest suite in her museum-mansion.

Besides a porcelain Jacuzzi, my room is dominated by a gold-trimmed mahogany box: a bed fit for an empress, heaped with a striped duvet, walled in on three sides by wooden rails carved with vines, dragons, lotus flowers, and topped by a lattice canopy. Amethyst brocade drapes flank tall windows that overlook a sparkling pool. By the door, I run my hand along a shuttered slot designed for room service.

Sophie darts in and shuts the door behind her. As her eyes

take in the royal bed, I bite my lip. Was this room supposed to go to Xavier on her behalf? Now the benefit is wasted on me—and Rick and I have upstaged her weekend plans.

"What's going on?" she hisses.

"Rick wouldn't come at first." I try to explain how we came to be fake-dating, but Sophie shakes her head.

"How does he expect this not to get back to Jenna?"

I frown. "He said no one would tell her."

"This family gossips like there's no tomorrow."

My stomach dips. "He seemed sure." It's Rick's problem. But I'm so distracted that I have to knot and reknot the ribbons on my pointe shoes twice before I succeed in hanging them from the canopy to remind myself of Sunday's audition.

If his family doesn't like Jenna, there'd be no reason to talk to her about his new girlfriend, right? I just need to double down supporting Sophie's plans, which means laying low, not getting outed, and making her-and-Xavier look good.

"How are things with Xavier?" I ask carefully.

A tic pulses in her eye and she touches it with her fingertips, stilling it. Then she smiles.

"Great! They're totally *great*," she says.

Downstairs, the doorbell chimes the tune of "Auld Lang Syne."

The family and Xavier have gathered in a spacious living room with the most intricate ceiling: dark square latticework framing panels painted with Chinese mythology. Jade sculptures populate the room: Dragons and phoenixes. A five-mast ship that Dad would love, sailing through clouds. A jade-and-cypress screen, softened by strips of sunlight pushing through the kind of white wooden blinds Mom's always wanted.

Rick grasps my hand, whispering, "Aunty Claire put out a call to the entire clan. I'm so sorry about this."

"About what?" I try not to fixate on the grip of his hand as he tugs me toward a collection of velvet settees. Then the doorbell chimes again and our afternoon spins out of control.

Aunts and uncles pour in as Aunty Claire's maids bring out porcelain tea sets etched with ancient Chinese landscapes. She has a collection of over a hundred teas, but we don't get a choice: her maid pours a fragrant *Dà Hóng Páo*.

"It costs more per ounce than gold," Sophie whispers into my ear.

"Um, wow," I say as a gray-haired uncle, Oxford polo shirt so crisply ironed he could slice cheese with it, seizes Rick's hand. "Guang-Ming! And you must be Ever!" He pumps my hand. I should have changed into a nicer blouse. A skirt instead of shorts. "Have you visited the National Palace Museum? Do you believe those wonderful treasures belong to Beijing or Taiwan?"

"I, uh—"

"Don't embroil her in your politics, Jihya," Aunty Claire calls as she heads to answer another chime of the door.

"And Bao-Feng!" Jihya embraces Sophie. "On your way to Dartmouth for your MRS, I hear?"

Sophie laughs and kisses his cheek. "Exactly, Uncle. But let me introduce you to Xavier . . ."

Dozens more cousins, aunts, uncles, and great-aunts and great-uncles gather around us, each new arrival an interruption of introductions, handshakes, hair-tousling for Rick, who takes it all with good humor. Two elegant grandmothers chat in Japanese and everyone else speaks Mandarin and Hokkien at light speed. I catch a few words: *pretty, too skinny, sexy!* Rick grins at me—more amused than apologetic. No wonder he didn't want to deal with his family's Jenna bashing—every single uber-educated person has an opinion, down to little Fannie, playing with a frog: "*Too old,*" she declares flatly. In English, for my benefit.

"I can't speak Mandarin," I murmur to Rick. Can they tell I don't come from money? I feel strangely anxious, wanting their approval. "Will they hold that against me? *You?*"

"Don't worry." He squeezes my arm reassuringly, sending an unwanted pulse of pleasure through me. His affection feels out of character with the brooding, gruff Boy Wonder. I almost tug free, until I remember the entire family is watching. Like hawks. How did I get myself into this mess when, until a week ago, I would have happily shoved Rick off a cliff?

On the couch, Sophie snuggles against Xavier, who remains upright, so they look more like a cat leaned against a pillar than a couple. He slips his hand from hers to reach for his teacup—deliberately? She bites her lip, then turns to hug a cousin: Su, who's visiting from California with her fiancé, Kade, a tennis champ in a black leather jacket.

"We met on Loveboat, too!" Su pulls me into a hug that squeezes all air from my lungs. "We're getting married next year!"

"Sophie mentioned you," I gasp. "Congratulations!"

As I find my seat again, Xavier's eyes meet mine—cool and sardonic. "Looks like we're both in the hot seat," he murmurs.

"Seems so." I take my own cup of tea and blow on its surface. I want to ask why he came. He knows Taiwan better than I do— he must have suspected the family would react like this. I hope he believes Rick and I *are* together, even more reason for him to keep his painter-fingers off my likeness.

But somehow, I doubt it.

"And what are your plans for your future, young man?" Uncle Ted, a well-dressed man in his fifties, refills Xavier's teacup. He's Aunty Claire's husband, and though he didn't speak particularly loudly, all conversation suddenly ceases. Everyone leans in to listen.

Xavier sets his cup on the coffee table. "I don't know."

Uncle Ted frowns. He scratches at his trim, salt-and-pepper beard. *I don't know,* clearly, is not an answer on the approved list.

"Xavier can do anything," Sophie interjects. "He could be a banker. Or a lawyer. A doctor. It just depends on what he wants."

"I've met your father." Uncle Ted lifts his glass of wine. "Real estate. Electronics. Smart cars. The Yehs have their fingers in every key industry in Asia." He's not smiling. I can hear Sophie's lungs screaming for air, waiting for his judgment to fall. Then

Uncle Ted tips his glass at Xavier. "They're brilliant. I imagine you'll follow right in their footsteps."

Sophie smiles. The fabulous Yeh empire trumps all. Uncle Ted's insider knowledge makes Xavier's family sound even more glamorous than what Sophie told me.

But at the mention of his father, Xavier's head had snapped up. "Wouldn't count on it," he says. "Seeing how this Yeh isn't even going to college."

A ripple of surprise cascades through the uber-educated cousins. Sophie, too. I would have laughed, but truth is, for better or worse, Chien Tan is a selective program and every kid is college-bound—I'd assumed Xavier was, too. So why not? Is this related to his dad calling him an idiot, to the fight I happened to witness?

"Xavier follows his own path," Sophie puts in. "He has so many options, it's about picking the right one, not locking in too early."

Uncle Ted laughs. "Straight to work first? I approve—the boy inheriting the family business doesn't need to waste time with fancy degrees. At least not yet."

Xavier's eyes flicker to Sophie's. She's surprised him, in a good way. "Something like that." She's covering for him, so smoothly I doubt her family noticed. She'd seriously make an amazing ambassador.

"So, what about you, Ever? Have your parents lived in Taiwan long?" Aunty Claire turns to me. She's not more than ten years older than us. I can see why Sophie described her as the beautiful aunt she looks up to. And at her question, the entire clan grows toward me like flowers to the sun. Xavier smirks—it's my turn now.

"My family's not from Taiwan." My face warms under their scrutiny as I explain how my parents migrated from Fujian to Singapore, then to the States.

"We're all human beings" Aunty Claire waves all distinctions away. "But your parents must be so brave and smart, like Rick and Sophie's. Usually only the top students from here can go to the United States. It's why all you kids turned out so well. It's in your genes and upbringing."

"Benji tells everyone his dad drives a taxi, and he got into Princeton," Rick says, but Aunty Claire shushes him, waiting on me.

Do I downplay with Chinese modesty, or is that disrespectful to my parents, and a sign of bad upbringing? I split the baby with a *hm—cough*. Either way, she's moving too close to the sacrifice I've heard about my whole life. If my parents had stayed in Asia, they'd be surrounded by family like this, instead of us living as an isolated four in Ohio. Respected, blended in, no risk of the occasional *go back to China!* in the parking lot, like an arrow out of nowhere. If they'd stayed, Dad would still be a doctor. I know. God, I know—but being here makes it real.

To my relief, a housemaid interrupts with a platter of yellow mango halves, scored into cubes and inverted into easy-to-eat turtle shells. Jihya brings up a fistfight between rival legislators in Taiwan's parliament—apparently a regular thing—and the clan breaks into a finger-shaking debate in Mandarin, Hokkien, and English, verging on mango-throwing.

I laugh, but Rick grimaces. "Sorry they're so obnoxious," he whispers.

"They're not." I'm half in love with his family already—even Fannie—so energetic, physical, and rambunctious in a way my family isn't.

"Enough of this, we're boring Ever." Aunty Claire daintily crosses her legs under her qipao. "So tell us, Ever. I knew I'd marry Uncle Ted the moment I laid eyes on him, but you young people these days don't seem to be in a hurry. Out of all those eligible boys on Chien Tan, how did you decide on our *Guang-Ming*?"

Rick drops his mango half. "Oh, we just—"

"*Tiām-tiām, Guang-Ming.*" She puts a hand on his knee. "I want to hear from Ever."

"Well . . ." Sticking to as much truth as possible is probably the safest course. "Rick was the first guy I met."

"Oh?"

Her smile droops a bit, so I take another stab. "Well, honestly, I've known Rick my entire life. And I hated him at first."

"Really? How's that?"

"My dad reads the *World Journal* religiously. Every year or so, an article came out about this . . . *amazing* boy." Rick groans as Aunty Claire and the cousins murmur with approval. "I used to find articles about *Woo Guang-Ming* on my pillow. My parents had a fatter file on Rick than on me."

"No kidding?" Rick murmurs.

I meet his gaze and grin. "I called him Boy Wonder."

"I knew it." A cousin punches Rick in the arm. "We call him Football Man."

"Shut up," Rick says and everyone laughs. At the least, I can entertain his family about the legend of Woo Guang-Ming in the good old USA. "National spelling bee champ. Piano. *Yale*. Rick Woo was the yardstick no kid could measure up to—me included." Rick makes strangling noises. But he's benefiting the most from this charade, so let him squirm. "Of course, every Chinese parent in the States wants their daughter to marry Rick," I add for good measure. He told me so himself.

"You wouldn't *believe* the phone calls I get, asking me to set up this and that daughter with my nephew." Aunty Claire beams. *And he's chosen you.* The whole setup, the overwhelming family attention, is designed to woo me on Rick Woo's behalf. And it's working a little too much.

I hastily press on. "But when I got off the plane and *recognized* him, all that resentment fell away. Why beat him when you can join him?"

As Rick squirms, I smirk. Serves him right for taking me up on this ridiculous plan.

Then a wicked glint comes into his eyes. He takes my hand and folds his fingers through mine, sending a shiver through my body.

"I had no idea you felt that way," he murmurs huskily. I try to tug free, but his grip is iron. Warmth rushes to my face. I silently curse him. His mouth quirks with a smirk I've never seen on his face before. I send him death-threats with my eyes.

Aunty Claire sighs, toying with her wedding band. "Rick, I'm *so thrilled*."

"*Finally*," says a cousin.

Rick stiffens. His fingers loosen around mine, though he doesn't let go. Jenna's name hangs in the air. *And good riddance.* Aunty Claire and cousins have no choice but to love me because ANY GIRL IS BETTER THAN JENNA.

Why are they so allergic to her?

"And what are *your* plans for next year?" Aunty Claire intervenes.

I open my mouth to tell her about Northwestern.

But what comes out is, "I'm going to dance school."

Why not? None of this is real anyways.

I brace for disappointment. Instead, Aunty Claire clasps Uncle Ted's hand. "Oh, how lovely! Ted sits on the board of the National Theater here in Taipei."

"Really? Where *Romeo and Juliet* played?" I'd seen some flyers.

"Yes, and many others. The Mariinsky Ballet—it was the Imperial Russian Ballet in the eighteenth century. The Suzuki Company of Togo, Yang Li-hua Taiwanese Opera—you probably don't know these, oh, Yo-Yo Ma." She snaps her fingers. "The American cellist. We don't possess an ounce of talent, but we love to watch, right, Ted?"

Her husband kisses her mouth, a public display of affection

I've never seen between my parents at home, let alone before strangers. "We're at the theater every other weekend."

"You're patrons of the arts," Sophie declares.

Aunty Claire flutters a modest hand, but I shift to the edge of my seat. "Oh, *wow.*" I've never met a family like this. "That's amazing."

"How did you choose dance? What are your plans?" Under Aunty Claire's barrage of questions, I tell everyone about Tisch. The chance to learn from choreographers and teachers who've performed with dance companies around the world. I feel Rick's eyes on me, my gesturing hands. "I've been arranging routines for my school squad for years. One day, I hope I'll get to choreograph something amazing—like a musical on Broadway."

"Well, I hope we have a chance to see you dance."

"You could," I say, before I can censure myself. "I'm dancing in *Swan Lake* in August."

"We'll be there." Aunty Claire's eyes shine. "Your parents must be so proud."

I expel a breath when we finally break to view Aunty Claire's latest acquisition, a Matisse-inspired painting she bought at an auction in London. *Are* my parents proud of me? They wouldn't be if they knew how I've been spending my summer.

Trying to push them aside, I drift from the group to admire Aunty Claire's paintings of Bengali tigers, Spanish cathedrals,

Chinese horsemen, and French children—East and West mixed together. I like them juxtaposed. I bring my nose to the blushing blossom on a jade-and-carnelian tree. It smells like jasmine. A sixth sense makes me glance up. I meet Xavier's gaze across the room, where he's standing with Sophie and her cousins, a glass of wine in hand. I frown at him in warning—I'd better not find a sketch of me with my nose in these blossoms.

"You've picked my favorite, I see." Aunty Claire presses a tissue-wrapped package into my hand. "Just a small gift."

"Oh, no, I couldn't." I try to hand it back. It feels like a scarf or other soft cloth.

"Please. Rick is my *A-hia*'s son—my eldest brother. With their family in the States, I don't get to dote on Rick as much as I would like." She tucks my hand under her arm. "You know, dear, I meant what I said. I felt so lucky when Ted found me. Even in those early days when he was still a stranger, I knew everything was about to change. I'm so glad Rick met you."

An irrational part of me wants to wrap her enthusiasm around my shoulders like a cozy blanket. But the dominant, rational part still can't believe how ready they are to embrace me as the One for Rick. They really are as traditional as the Qing dynasty.

And here is where I subtly champion Rick's cause.

"I really can't believe it myself," I say. "I know Rick's last girlfriend was super smart. Comes from a terrific family. Pretty, too," I add, though now my mouth tastes like sand.

205

"I don't like to speak poorly of other girls. But you should know. Rick is like the giving tree in that American children's book. He gives and gives. He drove her everywhere. Talked to her until three in the morning about her worries, stayed up until morning to finish his homework afterward. Love should be between equals. Equal sharing, equal give-and-take.

"I don't know if Rick's told you, but he's trying to transfer to Williams. He says it's his idea, but Rick's parents are certain Jenna is insisting on it."

"He's withdrawing from Yale?" He's never even hinted at that. Or has he? I remember the edge to his voice when he told Marc what college you went to didn't matter. Come to think of it, he's never brought up Yale himself—Sophie did, and then everyone else.

Is *this* why his family hates Jenna? Ivy League snobbery? *A pox on their shallow houses!* He's willing to buck all family expectations, not to mention the far less important *World Journal* readership, for *love*.

"Are you monopolizing Ever?" Rick's hand ghosts against the small of my back, then it's gone, leaving behind a strange flutter of disappointment. But he's being respectful Rick, doing exactly what I asked him to do. Why would I feel disappointed?

"Girl talk." Aunty Claire lays a fond hand on my cheek.

"Well, if you don't mind, I'm hoping to give her a tour. I came here so often as a kid, it feels like my second home."

"This *is* your home, darling." Aunty Claire kisses his cheek. "Go right ahead."

"Sorry about that." Rick pulls me by the hand into the hallway.

"It's okay, I like her." I really don't think we need to hold hands *all* weekend, do we? I want to ask him about Yale and Williams, but now doesn't feel like the time. "She's so *gracious*. So positive." The intimacy of her taking my arm, touching my cheek, talking about the give-and-take in relationships—such a contrast to arms-length Mom. "I love your whole family."

"Do you? Jenna says they're loud and obnoxious." He flushes. "Sorry. I—shouldn't have said that."

Because he's comparing us?

"They are, I guess," he adds. Protecting Jenna again.

"What are you playing at, Rick?" Sophie snaps. She's coming from the living room, Xavier in tow. Her mouth is pinched. I tug my hand from Rick, who blinks with surprise but thankfully doesn't press the charade.

"I couldn't take another Jenna-bashing weekend," Rick confesses. "Ever's helping me out." The gratitude in his glance makes me feel like he's taking my hand back. "I owe you."

"They *adore* you," I say. "Of course they'll come around. You didn't need me to do this."

Sophie pushes open the French doors, leading us to the sparkling blue pool surrounded by white lounge chairs. "They *worship* Rick. Hence the Jenna-bashing. You just saw the whole clan in universal agreement. Imagine the entire clan yelling obscenities and that gives you a picture of last summer. But *this*"—she pinches Aunty Claire's package under my arm—"she bought this for her own wedding."

"Oh, please take it—" I shove it into her hands, but Rick's already speaking.

"I didn't expect her to take it so seriously. Or invite the whole clan—"

"You're the only Woo boy! Of course she would!"

"—but when Ever dumps me for a better man, the family will back off Jenna. They can't say I didn't try on Loveboat." He grins at me, unfazed—everything's going according to plan.

Except that I can't imagine that better man.

"So Ever's doing the dirty work because Rick doesn't have the balls to stand up to his family." Xavier flips a quarter through his fingers. "Why am I not surprised?"

Rick's eyes flash. "No one asked you—"

"It was my idea," I interject. "I'm happy to help."

Xavier catches his quarter. I brace for a barb, but he just pockets his coin and turns to Sophie. "Kade wants to show me his motorcycle."

"Oh, not that stupid bike." She weaves her arm through his. "I still need to show you the roof terrace—"

"Xavier, you coming?" Kade pokes his head through a gate at the deck's other end.

Sophie bites her lip as Xavier peels free. He saunters over with his hand in his pocket, as if he's perfected a languid stroll out of defiance against those who've tried to hurry him along his whole life. I still don't understand why he's here.

Sophie gives a small shake of her head, then tosses Aunty

Claire's package at Rick. "You better hope Jenna doesn't hear about this. Not if you don't want another—"

"We're in *Taiwan*. No one will tell her." He presses the package back into my hands before I can protest further. "Aunty Claire wanted you to have it."

"I wouldn't put it past Jenna to hire a private investigator," Sophie says.

"*Don't even start*." The growl in his voice has leaped five points on the Richter scale.

"Start what? Talking about how whipped you are?"

"Just because I try not to jerk my girlfriend around."

"Her insisting on a postcard and phone call a day is the very *definition* of—"

"Shut up, Sophie! Just shut up and leave her alone for once! I'm *sick* of taking your crap."

Rick's hands are in fists. Opposing linemen would have cowered from that glare, but Sophie swings her hair to her back, defiant. "And *I'm* sick of you coddling her like she'll break if you sneeze!"

I cling to my package, desperately wishing I could follow Xavier. But I'm with Sophie—why is Rick, so confident and self-assured in every other area of his life, the opposite with Jenna?

Because he's in love with her.

Rick's eyes stray to mine. His lips purse. He'd forgotten I'm even here.

"You don't know anything, Sophie." He storms toward the mansion, nearly colliding with Aunty Claire, coming out with a tray of guava-mango shakes. He ducks around her and vanishes inside.

"You children all right?" Aunty Claire sets the tray on a stone bench.

Sophie swats at a mosquito on her arm. "You know us."

"Then you leave poor Ricky alone." Aunty Claire places a hand on her swollen belly, uncharacteristically stern. "You keep giving young men a hard time like you do—" She glances around and lowers her voice. "And no one good will want you, Sophiling."

*Ouch.* Even my parents wouldn't go that far. She's joking, of course.

But the transformation that befalls Sophie is shocking.

She lowers her eyes. Two red spots burn on her cheeks while the rest of her fire goes out, as if Aunty Claire had sprayed her with an extinguisher.

Aunty Claire's not joking.

Neither was the uncle about Sophie earning her MRS at Dartmouth.

My family is controlling, but never talking about boys meant they'd never asked me to *please* them either. Sophie's family is nontraditional in some ways, but uber-traditional in others, especially when it comes to marriage. No wonder Sophie's so obsessed with finding a guy—for the first time, I feel a stir of pity for my glamorous roommate.

"Why don't you girls come help me with dinner?" Aunty Claire squeezes my arm. "Would you like to call your family first, dear?"

"I called them this morning," I lie, taking one of her shakes. God, I miss Pearl. I owe her an email. "But thank you."

"Sweet girl." Aunty Claire strokes my hair with a fond hand as I fall into step behind Sophie, and it's all I can do not to duck guiltily.

# 20

An hour and a half later, after bathing sticky slices of *niángāo* in beaten raw egg and carving radish flowers with Aunty Claire and Sophie (who carved ten to my three—how does she work so fast?), I search the mansion for Rick, peeking between the reclining leather seats in the basement movie studio and moving steadily through silk rug–lined hallways and up curved stairways to the rooftop garden, blooming with sweet-scented gardenias and a guava tree. The warm breeze blows my hair over my face as I look out over the city skyline, the skyscraper Taipei 101 rising lonely above it all. My body aches to make something of this view—to dance—but I turn around and head back downstairs.

I knock on the oak panel of Rick's bedroom door a second time, but there's no answer. He must have gone outside. As I pass

Xavier's room, soft little moans and kissing sounds reach my ears through his door.

"I did it for you," Sophie murmurs.

I can't hear Xavier's reply, but Sophie's angry grunt follows, then the vehement scrape of a chair leg on wooden floor, as if they've pushed apart.

"What's *wrong* with you?" Her voice rises an octave. "You didn't hold back with Mindy from what I hear."

"I just don't think we should do this," Xavier answers.

More furniture scrapes the floor. A thud, like a book thrown down. Pages snapping. My feet have frozen to the silk runner.

Then the door flies open. Sophie rushes out. Stops as her eyes fall on me. She tugs the straps of her orange-striped dress back onto her shoulders as his door slams, blowing her skirt between her legs.

"You okay?" I ask, alarmed.

"He's a moron." She yanks his earring from her ear. "I was so stupid to get involved with him."

"You don't mean that," I protest.

"We're through." She hurls the earring at his door, which pings off and disappears under a grandfather clock. "I'm going to sit by the pool until dinner."

Kicking aside a pink bear, she pushes into her room and slams her own door—her carefully laid weekend plans chucked out the window. I raise my fist to her door as Xavier's flies open.

He's shrugging a black shirt over his head. Track lighting glints off his tan chest. Through his doorway, the bed sheets of his four-poster bed are rumpled, covers turned back, orange backpack on the floor.

As his eyes meet mine, he freezes. I wonder what picture of me he sees this time, standing frozen with embarrassment.

"Ever. This isn't what you think." The absence of a smirk or mocking in his voice makes my stomach dip. Xavier the Player is much easier to face than Serious Xavier. "Sophie and I—"

"It's none of my business." Skipping over the bear, I bolt for the stairs and down two at a time.

"Ever, wait," he calls, but then I'm out of earshot.

Fifteen minutes later, I find Rick running through a bamboo-lined path in Tianmu Park, a few blocks from Aunty Claire's. Dusk is falling, the sky violet streaked with pink clouds. The scent of camphor trees floats in the air and a gathering of men and women move beneath them in a tai chi dance, like monks in a Shaolin temple.

Rick's gray shirt, soaked in a vase-shaped bar down his front, clings to his chest. His body is locked as if he's bent his entire will on outrunning his demons, whatever they are. Sheer determination, that's how he became Boy Wonder.

He catches sight of me and slows.

"Hey."

"Hey."

Wiping his face on his sleeve, he jerks his head at the path.

"Want to walk a bit?"

A surge of nervousness. "Sure." I fall into step beside him and we move down a stone path, shifting aside for a rickshaw to pass with a squeak of wheels.

"Xavier was right." Rick shoves his hands into his pockets. "It wasn't fair to make you do this for me. I'm being a coward."

"I'm the one who offered."

"I just—need to get them to stop hating on her." He slouches, fists plowing deeper. "Maybe I shouldn't have come this summer."

"Why did you?"

"I told you before. Rite of passage. I needed a break."

"From Jenna, too?"

"No, of course not." His eyes open wide. He shakes his head. "Yes. Yes, maybe."

"How'd you get together in the first place?"

"She moved in next door in sixth grade. Her parents asked me to walk her to school and she started waiting for me after school, too. In high school, she'd drop by with snacks after football practices and I invited her to freshman homecoming. Been together since."

"Does she know how much your family dislikes her?"

"Yes. I've tried to keep it from her, but it leaks out in little ways." His thumb digs at the scars on his hand. "We've had some bad fights. Aunty Claire's family was over one time when we were arguing and it naturally made the gossip circuit." He frowns.

"Is that why Sophie doesn't like her?"

"Not exactly. Things weigh on Jenna. Friend stresses. Grades.

She's an only child and grew up pretty lonely. Her parents travel a lot for work and expect a ton from her, and every bit of stress is like a stone she sews into her clothes—she hangs on to it all. Junior year she lost fifteen pounds. She came over every night and fell asleep in my bed while I did homework.

"I was juggling school and football and Sophie didn't like how much of my time she took up. I tried to encourage Jenna to develop interests—she used to volunteer at a children's clinic but she dropped out. She only wanted to focus on her grades and me—I didn't want that either."

"Your aunt said you're transferring to Williams for her."

"I didn't realize she knew." His frown deepens. "Williams hasn't finalized my transfer, which is why I haven't said anything. Sophie doesn't even know." His gaze shifts to a bird in the grass, attacking the last of a pork bun. "I know my family's upset, but it's hard for Jenna to be on her own. She'll be premed—"

"Premed?" I cringe. "Her parents want her to be a doctor, too?"

"No, *she* does. She wants to be a pediatric oncologist, working with kids with cancer—she'd be great at it. But uncertainty is hard for her. Your BS/MD program—she'd kill for that kind of certainty. Last year was hell. She applied to a bunch of those programs, got wait-listed everywhere."

I pluck a peach off a tree and roll its fuzzy roundness between my palms. And so this is why the transfer—Jenna needs solid, dependable Rick at her side as she navigates the stresses of college premed, all those stones she'll be sewing into her clothes trying to get into med school. I don't want to buy into his family's Ivy League snobbery, but something feels wrong. Did he really need to give up Yale? I know nothing about surviving long distance, and maybe it's excruciating. But Megan and Dan have made it work across six states. Williams and Yale are only a few hours apart. And what about football? Is he that afraid of losing Jenna?

He's still trying to peel those scars off his fingers. I touch his hand. "Were you with her when you got those?"

His hand stills. "How could you tell?"

"You do that whenever you're thinking about her."

He balls his hand into a fist, as if trying to undo all those other times he's given himself away. "Yes. It was an accident."

His voice is like a brick wall, keeping me out. Whatever happened, the memory has turned out a light in him. I let it drop.

"Do her parents know?"

His voice sharpens. "Know what?"

"How depressed she is."

"No." He drops his fist. "No, she's not close to them. She made me promise not to tell. Her dad would blame her for being weak—they always told her not to cry growing up."

"They might not get it." Would *I* feel safe telling my parents? "But you can't carry her all by yourself." I glance up at him. "You really love her, don't you?"

He expels a breath. "Yeah. Yeah, of course I do."

The peach is sour in my mouth. I toss it into the trash as we reach the park's opposite gate, and turn to retrace our footsteps.

The tai chi club comes back into view, on break, drinking from metal thermoses. A white-haired man distributes bo staffs to the men and women, who spin them like a field of windmills. We sit on a bench to watch and I extend my leg to one side and grab my toes, trying, with the familiar stretch, to re-center myself.

"You told my family you're going to Tisch."

Rick's not letting me re-center myself. "Joking. Obviously."

"Were you? Because whenever you talk about med school, you look like you've permanently lost the Rose Bowl."

"Whoa, is that like the apocalypse?"

He smiles. "Worse." His grin fades. "It's a real question."

I release my toes. "When I was little, I fell off my bike and gashed open my knee. My dad stitched me up, and said, 'When *you* become a doctor, you'll take care of it yourself.'

"Every day, he'd come home from pushing his cart around the Cleveland Clinic, all deflated and smelling like antiseptic, and I'd run and hug him. He'd tell me about some surgery he'd glimpsed, or someone's life a doctor saved, and how proud he was I'd be a doctor someday. The doctor he didn't get to be. He didn't say that last part, but I always knew it. And I was going to make his pain worthwhile and he wouldn't be so defeated anymore."

"When did you turn down Tisch?"

"The day before I flew here."

"You could try calling them." He sits up. "Explain you felt you had to."

"It's too late."

"School doesn't start for a month. Tell them you had family issues. That you didn't think it was an option. You could take those dance and choreography classes. You'd live near Broadway—"

"*STOP.*" I clamp my hand over his mouth. He's ripping open scars I've worked hard to let heal. "What are the chances another girl with my profile will drop out before September?" Another Asian American girl, if Marc's right about quotas. "Less than zero. Besides, you're giving up football for someone you love. So who are you to talk?"

I release him and he bites his cheek. I still feel the bristle of his chin on my palm. His eyes are wide, as if I'd tased him. He's paled under his tan.

Then he looks away. "I don't know."

After a moment, I say, "Med school's everything I've worked toward. My parents, too." All the meals Mom cooked while I studied into the night, covering my chores during finals, acting as my maid, Dad my chauffeur to my internship, all their worries over my applications because my future is their future. Paying my deposit and first semester's tuition. They'd never ask me to pay a penny, not like Megan's parents. I'm a Wong before I'm Ever, as much as Rick's a Woo carrying his family's name.

A flock of birds sails overhead, the rush of wings stirring the hot air. We both need cheering up. As the tai chi group windmills their staffs in slow motion, I slide off the bench and approach the white-haired man.

"Can we try?" I ask in not-too-shabby Mandarin.

"Of course, little sister." He offers one of his rattan staffs; the rest of his Mandarin is lost on me. I heft it experimentally, a plain, functional staff—five feet long, and an inch and a half in diameter, the wood splintering a bit at its tip. The familiar weight, so similar to my flag staff, is comforting.

"You want to try tai chi?" Rick's smiling a bit.

"I've got a better idea."

I point the stick at his chest. A real smile breaks over my lips. All those hours with my flag team are about to pay off.

"I *challenge* you to a duel. If I win, you stop moping around this weekend. If you win, you wallow all you want."

He blinks. One bear brow climbs into his forehead. "You're not even in the elective."

"Humor me."

"I also happen to be the best stick fighter in the class. I'm a natural."

I sniff haughtily. "I'll be the judge of that, Football Man."

His brow rises farther, then the rest of him follows to six feet one, forcing me to raise my eyes.

"Happy to decimate you," he drawls. "But I'm twice your weight."

"Give yourself a handicap." I circle him, herding him toward the cart of staffs. "No using your weight advantage."

Then, just to show off, I pinwheel my stick in a perfect 360.

Rick gathers his jaw off the ground. "*Someone's* got moves."

The old man slyly thumps Rick on the back as Rick selects a

stout bamboo rod, worn in its center by many hands. He holds it low, looking extremely competent.

"I'm not going easy on you."

"I wouldn't expect you to."

"And if I win, you'll dance in the talent show."

"*What?*" I lower my staff a fraction. "Not fair. I'm not doing the talent show."

"Don't see why not. Five hundred students and twenty-five counselors is as big an audience as you'll get for *Swan Lake* in Taipei. Bigger. And it would be your own."

"Fine, but you won't win."

"Famous last words." He gives a mock bow.

I begin to pinwheel my staff. My troop often practiced without flags, so handling a staff is as familiar as crossing my legs. Rick's eyes never leave mine.

"You're trying to distract me."

My hands flicker in deft motions, keeping my stick whirling in a hypnotic blur.

"Ya!" I charge.

Rick blocks lazily, smirking. The crack of wood on wood punctuates the air, reverberating in my hands. I swing again. Again. Force him back until his foot hits brick wall.

I grin tauntingly.

And then *he's* shoving *me* back, stick flying, all his years of athletic training bearing down on my head.

In a few minutes, I'm panting.

"Do you yield?" Rick taunts.

"Famous last words." I swing a blow at his head. He ducks, but the wind of it parts his hair down the middle. "Ha!" I read the expression in his narrowed eyes: *Way too close*—no way is Rick letting little Ever Wong take him out in a bo fight.

He lunges, but I dance aside.

"Show off."

My grin widens. Every move he makes, I imitate and make my own. He's strong and fast, but I'm way more agile. We duck, swing, press one way on the grass, then the other, in a dance that satisfies a hunger in my body. The energy of our joined steps crackles between us.

Just off the path, I slap my bo against his and throw my weight behind it, trying to force him back.

"Tactical error," he gasps. A trickle of sweat rolls down his neck. "No man moves a mountain. Or woman." I ignore him, shove harder. Our faces inch closer over our crossed sticks. His amber eyes, flecked with sunlight and a hand's width away, hold mine.

The corner of his lip tightens in a smile.

We're close enough to kiss.

The realization strikes me in the nose like the butt of a staff.

Panicked, I step back, releasing him. His eyes widen as he stumbles forward. I instinctively whip my stick down—and slam his knuckles.

"Ow!" His staff clatters to the ground as he shakes out his hand. "I surrender!"

"I'm so sorry!" I seize his wrist, horrified. "I was going for your stick."

"I'd rather you hit my knuckles than my stick."

His tone is sly, un-Rick-like. I drop his wrist like a hot coal, blushing furiously. "Oh, you get lots more hits for that!"

I pretend to beat him about the head, and Rick swoops down on his staff, rolls to his feet, and blocks, dodges, chuckles. My body sings with our movement—every fiber of muscle alive, in sync.

Then he seizes my staff.

Suddenly, I'm pressed against him, staves crossed. Sweat glistens at his hairline and my own neck is damp. His warm, grassy scent fills my lungs and my heart kicks into a higher gear.

Rick's staff clatters to the ground.

Then my chin is in his strong fingers. The pad of his thumb traces my lips, shooting an achingly delicious shiver into me. Our bodies pull tight over my staff, still caught in his hand, and my fingers close on his arm for dear life as he tilts his head down, as our noses brush, as his soft inhalation takes air from my mouth—

And he pulls back.

The almost-kiss crackles between us.

Jenna.

A cold space opens between us, my staff gripped solo in my hands.

Rick wanted to kiss me.

And as for me—he must have read everything in my face, too. I've never felt so naked, not even when I took my glamour shots. He's *Rick Woo.* Boy Wonder of *World Journal* fame and every girl's dream guy.

"Ever—"

*"Xiǎo mèimei, Xiǎo dìdì, Chīfàn la."*

Rick jumps. A maid in her black-and-white uniform, a woven basket hung on her arm, is coming down the pathway, calling us to dinner. Her eyes flit between us, crinkling with amusement—she's thrilled for the young Master Woo and his new girlfriend.

Fat raindrops begin to fall as Rick stoops to retrieve his staff, hiding his face. My hand rises to my mouth, my lips he didn't kiss.

"Ever—"

"She's lucky to have you," I choke out. "I hope she understands that."

Tossing my bo to the white-haired man, I sprint past Rick and from the park as the clouds open. My feet pound an unsteady rhythm through the falling rain. Rick doesn't come after me, and I don't expect him to.

I shouldn't have come.

Not this weekend. Not to this park. I shouldn't have proposed and then stupidly agreed to carry out this charade.

Because before I left home, I knew what my life was: med school, my parents' never-measuring-up daughter, pining after

Dan from afar. Then today, for one perfect afternoon, I'd had something else—a future in dancing, a family that accepted me, a boyfriend I admired and respected—

And none of it was real.

**21**

The Taiwanese folk song that played tonight weaves like a ribbon through the folds of my brain. A dance unfurls to join it: a double ring of girls in colorful dresses, hands joined, swirling in opposite directions around a pair of lovers. My body wants to dance.

There's no hope of sleep when I'm like this.

I'm alone in my empress canopy, legs tangled in cotton sheets. Moonlight slants through the openwork carvings, illuminating horses, fierce warriors in battle, my striped duvet. The air is hot and still, and under my head, my down pillow is soaked with sweat.

It's my second night in Aunty Claire's mansion, after a weekend's precarious balancing act: Sophie ignoring Xavier to flirt with a distant cousin and me avoiding Rick while pretending to be his girlfriend—all while making dumplings in Aunty Claire's airy kitchen, playing Go with black and white stones, getting magical massages on a padded table, and sitting down to crystal-and-silver meals of chopped lobster, oyster pancakes, and the freshest abalone on the island.

Tonight, though, my head throbs from the rounds of shots I drank with Rick's cousins and aunts and uncles. The teasing about grandbabies, until Rick had to intervene, *all right, that's enough.*

I sit up and grab the tablet on the bedside table, a loaner from Aunty Claire. Its white glow stabs my eyes as I search the internet for variations on "dance scholarship," reading up on the USA Performing Arts Scholarship and Young Arts Foundation.

But as I told Rick, everything is long past due.

My movement sets my pointe shoes swaying from their ribbons on the post from which they hang, knocking softly against the wood. I tug them down and lie back on my pillow and tuck them to my chest, like Floppy, my old stuffed bunny. My audition tomorrow—that's what I need to focus on. The last dance of Ever Wong.

I squeeze my eyes shut and think piqué turns: toe to knee then down, turning, spotting, turning, spotting, single, single, single, single, double.

What would it take for you to be a dancer?

You could call them—

I drop my shoes, which make double thuds below.

I've let Rick in too far. Now his voice and hope have inter-twined themselves into the most intimate secrets of my heart, along with that almost-kiss that I can't stop coming back to—but I *need* to stop. To untangle this ribbon that has somehow tied me to him without my being aware.

The grandfather clock chimes a solo. One o'clock. Sleep really is hopeless. Sliding from my mattress, I grab my new silk night-robe—the present from Aunty Claire for the girlfriend who isn't even the girlfriend. Still, I slip it on and press open my oak-paneled door, then pad barefoot over the runners down the hallway.

Everything in the dark feels muted and lonely. The stone and glass, the Asian vases, all meticulously dusted and arranged. Giant seashells remind me of Pearl, who loves them. But the scents of teakwood and white flower oil reminds me of Mom—and something recoils inside me.

In the living room, an orange cinder sparks. A fire burns in the grate, though the air is hot and humid. A log snaps, sending up a cloud of embers. The scent of ashes reaches my nose.

Someone's awake.

A thread of light glimmers a few feet from the fire.

Xavier's back is toward me. His black shirt is rumpled, as if he'd slept in it. In his hand is an ivory-handled *tanto*—worn by an actual samurai of feudal Japan, according to a cousin, soldiers who didn't fall on their swords like the Romans did, but dis-emboweled themselves.

"Xavier, what are you doing?"

He spins. The short sword glitters in an arc and firelight illuminates his tanned face.

"Ever." He lowers the tanto to his side. "I—I couldn't sleep." His eyes rake over me and I send a silent thanks toward Aunty Claire for this robe that hides my thin nightgown. I want to turn and run in the opposite direction, but instead my feet carry me into the room.

"I couldn't sleep either." The thick tatami rush-grass mats, imported from Japan, tickle my feet. The sword gleams again, then firelight illuminates a dark line welling from Xavier's palm.

"You're bleeding." A wave of queasiness washes over me. I should have fled while I had the chance. The sword is ancient. Not the thing anyone should be using to become blood brothers. "That blade could give you gangrene."

Xavier lifts his hand, as if surprised.

"Were you trying to take your hand off?" Fighting nausea, I grab his fingers, examining the fast-flowing cut. Years of helping Dad treat cuts and scrapes at church picnics means I at least know what to do in principle.

I cast about the room, but unlike my home, which is littered with boxes of Kleenex for Dad's hay fever, not a single box is in sight. I unknot the sash of my robe and yank it free, hoping Aunty Claire won't find out I destroyed her present—and then wonder why her good opinion matters so much to me.

Xavier's stillness as I wrap his hand with my sash makes me more nervous than his sketches—even in the darkness, I feel the weight of his eyes.

"I saw a first aid kit by the pool," I say. "Wait a sec?"

When I return, plastic box in hand, he's stretched up on his toes, returning the sword to its hooks. His eyes meet mine. I blush and draw the open flaps of my robe together.

"I got it," I say unnecessarily. Taking a deep breath, I begin to unwrap his hand. Every layer of the silk sash is soaked through with a Saturn-shaped stain. Blood. Blood. Blood. A wave of vertigo crashes over me and I sway on my feet. Yes, I drank the snake-blood sake, but this blood is human.

Forcing myself steady, I swab his cut with antiseptic, then swiftly bind it with gauze and tape. Only when it's humanely bound do I breathe again.

"I can't stand blood," I confess.

His expression flickers. "I couldn't tell."

My knees wobble. I sway again and he takes the kit from me, and I drop onto the mat, put my head on my knees, and close my eyes.

"You okay?"

"Yeah, give me a moment."

He hands me a bottle of wine left over from tonight's festivities. A French wine with a white label. I fit its glass top to my lips and take a long pull. Dark cherry, rich and strong. I take a second pull, a third, letting its smoothness warm my body and drive those bloody Saturns from my mind.

I only look back up again when he says, low, "Thank you."

A familiar shame follows. And fear. Even if I manage to

cram all the book knowledge of medical school into my sieve-like memory, this is what I'll have to face, every day. Torture.

"Sorry," I croak.

He expels a breath. "I'm the stupid one who cut myself. You all right?"

His reaction surprises me, maybe because it's so—human. "Yeah, I'm fine." And I did it, didn't I? I bound his blood-oozing cut. With a bit more courage, I help him pack up the box. "You've had your tetanus shot, right?"

He nods. The firelight plays over his face, reflecting in his eyes. Under his gaze, I pull my robe closed again. I wonder if he's sketching me in his mind and the thought, instead of making me angry this time, stirs something hot inside me.

Maybe Xavier is exactly what I need to forget Rick.

He holds his hand out for the bottle. "What's the real deal with you and Boy Wonder?"

"We're together, didn't you hear?" I ask, bitter.

"And my mom's the Dragon. I'm his roommate, remember? I hear his phone calls. I see his postcards." He hands the bottle back. "So . . . what? He has you *and* her? The jocks of the world always get what they want, don't they?"

I shouldn't drink this much, not after what happened the first night of clubbing, but I take another long pull. I ignore the jab at Rick, who doesn't seem to me like he's getting what he wants at all. Ignoring the stab of pain in my chest as I imagine what daily phone calls and postcards Xavier's witnessed.

"I'm just helping him out."

"What's in it for you?"

"Nothing." But heartache. Why *doesn't* he have the balls to stand up to his family for Jenna? "What do you care?"

"Maybe I feel sorry when I see unrequited love."

"Ha. None here." But I flush. I don't like him peering into my soul like this. "What's up with you and Sophie?" He's still here, after all, though her behavior makes it clear she's done with him.

"My dad would like her."

"But you don't? I honestly don't understand." Sophie's gorgeous and fun. Super generous. "Any guy would be lucky to be with her."

Xavier's eyes are on mine. Watching me.

"I left that rug outside your dorm room," he says. "I pinned a sheet with an *E* on it. For you."

*What?* The scene when Sophie walked in with the rug under her arm rearranges itself in my mind.

I'd assumed. She'd let me.

"I didn't know," I stammer, but his eyes tell me he already knows. I set the bottle by my foot. The wine has made the warm, still air suffocating. "You weren't lying before."

He gives a short nod. He hasn't contradicted anything Sophie's said about him either—just let his reputation as a Player-capital-P keep building.

"Why did you even come this weekend?" I ask.

His eyes flicker to the fire. "You wouldn't understand."

"I'm pretending to be a guy's girlfriend so his family will accept his real one. Try me."

"Maybe being with a girl who's into you is better than being alone with your worthless self."

*Worthless?* Handsome, sought-after Xavier Yeh of Longzhou fame and fortune?

"Why would you say that?"

His eyes flicker away this time. His hand drifts to a work-book I hadn't noticed, then he catches my gaze and moves his hand away. Xavier Yeh, class rebel and collector of demerits—is studying his Chinese reader on a Saturday night.

And it's as if his reader is whispering with a secret.

"Can I see?"

He reaches for the bottle. As I hand it back, our fingers brush—his are hot. Feverish.

He trades me his notebook. "Read it and weep."

He finishes off our bottle, climbs to his feet, and rummages behind a liquor bar by the window.

Alone on the floor, I open his workbook, mystified.

The pages feel fragile, as if they might rip if I turn them too hastily. An unfamiliar handwriting crams the margins. Copying Chinese characters. Copying their English translations.

"Bibent" instead of "didn't"

"Pensel" instead of pencil"

"dall" instead of "ball"

A cork pops at the bar.

When he returns, new bottle in hand, I ask, "Is this your handwriting?"

He sits beside me again, closer this time. His leg, bristly with hair, brushes my bare calf. His feet are long and lean. The heat of his arm presses against mine, but my body is slow to react, and I don't move away, and then I don't want to. I put the new bottle to my lips and drink a richer, darker wine that rushes warmth into my fingers and toes.

"Words don't like me," he says. "They bounce around the page. I can run my eyes over them a hundred times and still not understand what I've looked at."

Like Pearl. I remember how Xavier refused to write in calligraphy, except for that single, symmetrical character. How he always made me, then Sophie, go first in partner exercises, so he could hear me read aloud, then repeat back what we'd read. He's hidden it so carefully, and now he's showing it to me, the girl who shredded his painting into snowfall.

"Are you dyslexic?"

"Something like that." His voice is rough. "Another word for stupid."

I'm stunned. I've read about kids feeling that way about dyslexia, but those stories always felt like time capsules— outdated ideas frozen in amber, like the secret shame of the woman who gave birth out of wedlock in *The Scarlet Letter* or the witch hunt in *The Crucible*.

"It's not stupid," I say. "My sister's dyslexic."

"Really?"

"My dad tutors her. She had a special ed teacher through elementary school. Gets accommodations and uses voice dictation software. She loves music but note reading is hard for her, so she uses her ear to help—I mean, it's not easy, but she's top in her class."

He gives a short barking laugh. "My dad says it's an excuse. Western obsession with psychology. Chinese kids don't get dyslexia."

I swear under my breath. "Didn't you ever get special instruction?"

He shakes his head. "I had a tutor here in Taiwan when I was younger. He was about a hundred years old. He told my dad I couldn't learn." He locks his elbows around his knees. "My dad used to say he should've beat me harder to beat it out of me. Then I'd have learned."

I close his notebook. "He *beat* you over *dyslexia*?"

Xavier drains half the bottle before passing it back to me.

"My mom used to try to stop him."

"Used to?"

He's silent. Then, "She died when I was twelve."

"Oh! I'm sorry."

Xavier shrugs. "It's just my life. My father set me up in an apartment in Manhattan while he stayed in Taipei. I had an educational consultant. My teachers figured I couldn't read because English was my second language. Eventually, I figured out how to cover up. Money can buy you anything in middle school and high school." Xavier reaches for the bottle again. "Last March, when my dad visited, he found out I hadn't even applied to college. I figured there was no point. He fired the consultant, and I didn't bother showing up for finals. I don't even have a diploma."

"Oh, Xavier."

He touches the small of his back. "My dad gave me a new set of trophies and told me I was a disgrace to nine generations." His lips twist sardonically, and he takes another pull from the bottle.

Trophies. He means bruises.

But the message has penetrated over the years—so deep that Xavier believes it, deep down.

A memory of my own resurfaces. Mom with the chopsticks, hitting the inside of my bare thigh, once, twice, three times. I must have been young; I remember wailing, scrubbing my eyes on the hem of my Hello Kitty nightgown. I don't even remember what I'd done, except that we were in the study. Maybe I'd botched my spelling drills. The chopsticks only came out occasionally, and left no scars, but the shame has lingered.

"Let them wallow in their disgrace," I whisper.

The firelight makes his cheekbones prominent, like blades. His jaw tightens. With a single finger, he traces a line down my nose. Then over each brow. Then, from corner to corner, my lips. Drawing me. Seeing me.

Then he leans in, and kisses me.

His mouth is soft, sweetened by wine. The gauze bandage brushes my cheek as he tucks his fingers into my hair and cradles the curve of my neck. Under his lips, my back arches slightly—

What am I doing?

I start to pull away. But he gathers me to his chest. His arm slides down my back, his lips devouring me. He breaks for breath.

We need to stop.

"Xavier—"

His mouth silences me, parting my lips, making me gasp with the unexpected pleasure of his tongue. He tastes like the wine, the fire in the grate, and I'm pressing back against him, wanting him to take this Wong Rule–breaking kiss deeper and deeper, to heal that hole in himself and to keep making me feel so wanted—

Then Sophie's scream rips open the night.

# 22

"Sophie," I choke as I pull free of Xavier.

"You're my *guest*." She runs at us. Her rose-print robe falls off one narrow shoulder and she hauls it back over herself. Xavier's opal glints on her lobe—she's returned it to her ear. "You're my *guest!*"

"Soph—"

"Shut up!" My cheek explodes under her palm. "Shut up, shut up, you slut!"

White blurs my vision. I press my hand to my burning cheek. I've never felt so small and low, all my guilt blazing on my swollen lips.

*But I thought you didn't want him anymore. I thought—I thought—*

Her arm whips back for a second blow.

Then Xavier seizes Sophie's wrist.

"It's my fault! *I* kissed her."

The part of me not overwhelmed by horror is stunned by how swiftly he's stepped to my defense. Sophie flinches as if he'd struck her and wrenches free. She clutches the front of her robe. Her dark brown eyes are a lost puppy's, so vulnerable and hurt that, even knowing she's played us both, my heart aches for her.

Then her lips twist. "Oh, so *now* you've got a spine?" she spits at Xavier. She whirls as if to go, but pauses as her gaze sweeps the floor. Swooping down, she snatches up a sheet of paper. Her mouth works like she's trying to speak but can't find the words.

"*You.*" Crumpling it, she flings it at Xavier. It bounces off his chest to the floor and unfurls, refusing to keep its secrets.

Another sketch: Aunty Claire's blue porcelain cup raised to my lips.

With a sob, she bolts toward the stairs, her robe rustling around her like crumpled butterfly wings. An eternity later, I hear the slam of her door.

Xavier's hand finds my waist. "You all right?"

I jerk away, as if he's burned me. I honestly believed Sophie was done with him, but I should have known better. I'm back in the moment when Megan told me about Dan, only what I've done is a hundred times worse. What kind of friend am I?

"Ever, please talk to me—"

With a small cry of my own, I pull free and flee down the hallway to the Eleanor suite.

I awake to the pair of amethyst brocade drapes fluttering over their windows. The sun is high—it's nearly mid-day. Groggy-eyed, I slip from my bed and pad into the bathroom, still trying to shake the weight of last night. Aunty Claire's beautiful mosaic tiles echo with my unsteady footsteps. In the shower, as the water blasts, a gray frog leaps from the corner and my short scream reverberates off the glass.

"Oh, *Fannie*," I sob. "Frog—*go away*." It ignores me, and I leave it ribbiting maniacally while I drown myself in the hot spray, letting its sharpness chip at the ache in my heart, until at last, cold water chases me back to my bedroom, toweling off my hair and face. I feel heavy, like I'm draped in one of those lead blankets under an X-ray machine. I'll have to face Sophie again back on campus. And Xavier. And Rick—

My foot lands on a soft, paper-wrapped bundle on the floor by the door. Orange tissue paper tied with a matching ribbon. *What's this?* I detach a note and unfold a thick sheet of paper filled with blocky handwriting.

*Dear Ever,*

*I didn't want you to go to sleep tonight without my apologies. You've done nothing but help me this weekend,*

*and yet I overstepped boundaries. I have no excuses. Only
that I never want to jeopardize our friendship, which has
been a surprise and gift to me this summer.*

*Your friend always,*
*R*
*P.S. I found this in the market tonight and couldn't resist.
Hope you'll get a kick out of them in the winter.*

He must have dropped this package through the room
service slot last night. My eyes sting as I unwrap a pair of cuddly
sky-blue socks, printed with male and female dancers, spinning,
whirling, pirouetting. I slide my hands into their woolly warmth.
After this lavish weekend, after Xavier, these *socks*. They're so
goofy, so dear.

But he showed me Jenna's photo the first hour I met him.
This note is a reminder we're just friends, and once Sophie gets
ahold of them, his family will beat down his door with an heir-
loom ring and beg him to put it on Jenna's finger already. I've
succeeded beyond his wildest imagination.

And what could I say? I'm sorry for not-cheating on you;
I'm sorry for cheating on your cousin but things aren't what they
seem; I know you told me to stay away from Xavier, but—

My toes connect with a satin box. My pink pointe shoe flies
right, ribbons splaying in careless loops over the rug.

My heart lurches into my throat and my eyes dart to my
alarm clock, which never rang.

"My audition."

I've missed it.

Two minutes later, letter, socks, and clothes crammed into my dance bag, I race down the hallway toward the stairs. My heart is too crowded to make sense of anything but the need to get to Szeto Ballet Studio.

As I near Rick's room, I hear him in English, Aunty Claire hysterical in Hokkien, each reverting to the language they're most comfortable in, like my relatives when excited or stressed. I don't hear Sophie's voice, but maybe she's in there, hands on her hips as Rick sits up in bed. Shame claws through my chest.

At least I've cleared his path for Jenna.

"We were just pretending," Rick says as I pass his door. "Please don't blame her. She was helping me—"

"Rick, no!" I whisper. *You've ruined everything.*

And then I'm leaping down the curved staircase two steps at a time.

**23**

The sun is directly overhead as I reach Szeto Ballet Studio, breath laboring in my lungs. An oppressive dread rides my shoulders as I barrel through the door. My sweat-drenched shirt clings to my rib cage.

But as the faded pink walls and air-conditioning envelope me, and the strains of *Swan Lake* reach my ears, a sense of refuge closes around me.

I run toward the music.

The familiar ballet posters—*Coppélia, Nutcracker*—feel cliché after Aunty Claire's art collection. But that disloyal whisper is swept away when my eyes fall on Madame Szeto in the studio, the scooped back of her maroon leotard reflected in the wall-length mirror. Before her, a handsome man with trim black hair executes a stunning barrel-turn, arms out, legs whirling, while a girl in a white leotard sashays around him. Prince Seigfried, auditioning more Odette hopefuls. I'll beg her to squeeze me in. Stay past closing if she needs me to.

Darting into the dressing room, I dump out my bag and have my tights in hand before the door swings shut.

But it never does.

Instead, it opens again to admit Madame Szeto, ebony hair swept back into its usual graceful chignon at the nape of her neck. Her leotard pulls taut over her straight shoulders and small breasts.

"Madame, I'm so sorry—"

"You're no longer welcomed here." Her mouth, usually soft with fondness, pinches like a shriveled apple.

"I'm *so* sorry I'm late." Apologies tumble from my lips. "I was hoping—"

She seizes my bag and shoves my things back inside. The papery tear of Rick's note reaches my ears.

"Please, Madame," I say, but she grabs my arm and half drags, half steers me through the reception room, while I babble explanations and try to right myself. The firm hand that showed me how to hold my midriff now pinches my flesh like a talon. Maybe she can't give Odette to the girl who shows up an hour late, but why is she kicking me out?

"Please, I don't under—"

"Our young ladies have reputations to uphold. We cannot allow anyone to tarnish that. Not even a girl from *America*." She drops me like a filthy rag at the door and hurls my bag into my stomach.

"Can't I just dance with the chorus?" I cry.

"Leave, Ms. Wong." She holds the door wide. "Don't require me to call security."

"Security?" I cling to my bag. The doorjamb hits my shoulder as I back into merciless sun. "There must be some mistake."

She throws a wallet-sized photo at me. I snatch at it but miss, and it flutters to the cement.

"I don't presume to know how dance studios run in America, Ms. Wong, but in Taipei, we don't operate this way. Please don't come back. Same to your friend."

Friend?

My hand shakes as I stoop to recover the photo. Of a girl.

She's back-dropped in white, the only object in her rectangular world. Her hands open like fans at her sides. She gazes out at me, chin raised boldly, dark-red lips parted with a seductive intake of breath, coils of black hair swept up to show off every curve of skin from the slope of her neck to her coyly cocked ankle—and everything in between.

All oxygen is sucked from the world.

My nude glamour shot.

While I was sleeping this morning, Sophie must have picked it up from Yannie's studio.

And delivered it here.

The door squeaks as Madame Szeto begins to swing it shut. I grab its edge with both hands.

"Wait! Please let me explain."

I'm forced to pull my fingers away as she shuts the door in my face.

I am out of cash, so I walk the two hours back to campus. I've lost a week's tuition at Szeto's but I can't ask for it back. My feet feel as heavy as the concrete blocks that rim the shoreline against typhoons. Mopeds race by, spewing clouds of grit over me. My pocket bulges from the crumpled photo that I can't bring myself to look at. My lips sting—I need to speak with Xavier after running from him, but I don't know where we go from here. As for Rick—

My fingers rise to my chin. I can still feel the imprint of his fingers there.

I need to understand why he gave me those socks.

Why he told his aunt we weren't really together.

I need to explain.

I drag myself up the brick steps to Chien Tan and enter the lobby through a side door. It's unusually deserted. Panicked voices are shouting in the salon next door, but I can't muster up an ounce of curiosity. The demerits board covers one wall: our Chinese names in a long row, raining down demerit check marks, with a long column under Xavier's name, and a matching column beneath mine. It's so juvenile.

"Stop it! Stop it right now!" a girl shouts next door.

"*Do* something!" yells another.

246

"Guys! Cool it!" Marc yells.

*What's going on?*

Hitching my bag higher on my shoulder, I round the corner and crash into a sweaty back.

A ring of kids has formed around two wrestlers: Xavier's arms are locked around Rick's neck, both bent double as they lurch into Marc, who grabs at them, earning himself a punch in the stomach.

"Quit already! Let go!"

"Break it up!"

Other hands yank at them, but they're inseparable, a force of muscled arms and legs and rage, knocking over everyone in their path.

Before I can cry out—dive forward—Rick jerks free. His shoulder surges, then his fist explodes in Xavier's face.

"Rick, stop!" I cry.

Both boys turn to face me, mirror expressions of rage. Blood streams from Xavier's nose. Rick meets my eyes and flinches. Then Xavier grabs the back of his shirt and they're at it again like a pair of wild beasts.

"You asshole!"

"Coward!"

I've never been the girl fought over by boys, but I don't need any kind of ego to understand this fight has to do with me . . . but why? Because of the kiss?

"*Xiang-Ping! Guang-Ming!*" The Dragon in her green dress jostles past me, Li-Han on her heels. I never thought I'd be happy to see her. She snaps her fingers, barks orders, and Li-Han, Marc, and two other boys pull Rick and Xavier apart. They glower at each other. Xavier scrubs at his nose, which drips red petals onto his cream shirt. His eyes flicker to me, dark and unreadable, but Rick doesn't meet my eyes.

I watch in numb silence as the Dragon dispatches Li-Han, Marc, and Rick to take Xavier to the infirmary and have a talk— that's the Dragon's way. Rick looks as furious as if she's ordered him to donate both kidneys to Xavier.

"*Ai-Mei!*" My name is like shrapnel on her lips. "*Nǐ zài zhèlǐ děng!*"

"*Shén me wèntí?*" I blurt. What's wrong?

She motions me toward her office. Only now do I see that in her hand, the Dragon holds another naked photo, of me.

Sophie struck again.

**24**

I know what my punishment is even before the Dragon shuts the door of her office, a chaotic workspace of four long tables and a steel desk flooded with papers. The air is sharp with Chinese ointment. Photo collages of students from prior Chien Tan years cover the walls, none of whom, I'm sure, have ever been escorted here for the reason I have.

"*Zuò*," she commands.

Tight with dread, I sink into a chair before her desk. She dials my parents. I picture them on the other end, bolting upright in their floral-sheeted bed, Mom on her bedside phone, Dad on the wireless, as the Dragon speaks rapid-fire Mandarin.

Then she hands me the phone.

My hand shakes as I raise it to my ear. "Hello?"

"How could you do something so foolish?" Dad cries.

"We raised you better than this!" Mom cries. "Now you've shamed us!"

"You know what those boys think of you now?" Dad demands, words that puncture a veil between us—he's yet to acknowledge my first bra, let alone that *boys* might think *anything* of me. The shame of that little girl who spread her legs too far crashes down all over again.

"What if Northwestern finds out?" Mom's voice rises a decibel and I have to hold the phone from my ear; the Dragon can hear every word. "They'll kick you out. You may have ruined your *life!*"

Fresh panic erupts like lava in my chest. I clutch the phone. Sophie wouldn't send my photos to them, would she?

"They *can't!*" I cry.

"We trusted you enough to send you by yourself!" Dad shouts.

"This isn't why I sold my black pearl necklace!" Mom cries.

Black pearl necklace again?

"I didn't *ask* you to sell it!" I roar. "I didn't *want* to come here! All I wanted to do this summer was *dance* and you *stole* that from me!"

Great gulping sobs tear from my throat. The Dragon hands me a tissue, but even with her in on our dirty laundry, it feels so *good* to hurl that truth into the open.

"How can you be so ungrateful?" Mom cries. "We've done

*everything* for you. Lord, why did you curse me with such a daughter?"

"How can you call me ungrateful? I gave up dancing! I'm going to medical school! You never ask me what *I* want!"

And there's no answer. Just the murmur of my parents conversing, then Mom again.

"We will find you a ticket to come home."

I grip the phone. "*No!*"

"Go pack your bags. Be ready to leave in the morning."

"You can't make me come home now! I'm not ready!" I'm shouting, making no sense to anyone. I've forgotten how swiftly my parents can cut me off from privileges, even from seven thousand miles away.

In a last attempt, I appeal to the cardinal Wong-family sin. "You flew me here already—why send me home now? It's wasting money!"

"*You* made this stupid decision!" Mom snaps. "So *you* suffer the consequences!"

The line goes dead.

I barely remember stumbling from the Dragon's office. My chest burns as if my parents have filled it with live coals then kicked it in. I had begun to understand where they were coming from. Even felt sympathetic for what they'd given up by emigrating—home, acceptance—and appreciated that they've never pushed me to find a husband or called me a disgrace to nine generations.

All that's gone. I don't care what baggage they dragged over the ocean. They have no right to make me carry it the rest of my life.

As I enter the lobby, catcalls and whistles shatter the air.

A hundred eyes leer from every corner: guys at the Chinese chess game, the pool table, the foosball box. The automatic doors glide apart to admit Sophie, prim in her tangerine dress and arm in arm between Chris Chen, a tall guy whose teeth have started to stain from chewing betel nuts, and another guy whose name escapes me.

Sophie halts in the doorway, takes in the scene, and smirks.

*This* is what I'll face the rest of my stay. The price of my last days of freedom.

But even as I whirl toward the stairs, as I grip the rail, intending to bolt for my room, a flood of anger surges through me.

These guys *know* me.

They've broken out with me over the catwalk. Danced at the clubs and even gotten advice on med school from me, for crying out loud.

How *dare* they treat me like a piece of meat now?

And how dare Sophie?

Releasing the rail, I march up to her, ignoring the boys.

"That was *my* property," I say. "You had no right."

Sophie makes lewd kissing noises. "*Please* don't play innocent little victim."

"I'm sorry." A flush rises in my cheeks. I'd underestimated her. In so many ways. "But that silk rug in our room is also mine. So don't *you* play victim either."

She stiffens.

I glare around the lobby, and suddenly no one will meet my eyes. "If you guys want a live viewing someday from a girl you actually care about, then maybe instead of doing a hundred push-ups a day and ogling a photo that doesn't belong to you, you should *man up* and be the guy who deserves one. So anyone with my photo, *hand it over now.*"

I hold out one hand, palm up. I *hate* that it trembles.

No one moves.

My heart sinks. Can they really be so piggish and low?

Then David crosses from the foosball table and places a photo in my palm.

"Sorry, Ever," he murmurs, and drifts away.

My entire body trembles but I keep my chin high as seven more photos grow in a stack on the first. There were only a dozen or so guys in the lobby after all.

"How many are there?" I hold up the stack.

Sophie's lips thin into a line. She won't say.

"Don't even *think* about sending these to Northwestern. Or Dartmouth will get a letter, too." Her eyes flicker—with fear? Anger? Still shaking, I shove the stack into my pocket. "Look around, Sophie." The lobby's emptied out. "No one's left on your side."

Then I walk away.

I drop by the infirmary, only to be informed by the nurse that due to her flooded store room, thanks to the latest typhoon, she had to send Rick and Xavier to the local clinic. My photo has grounded me for life. I can't even go after them.

The afternoon darkens to evening as I wait anxiously on a couch of silk pillows in the boys' lounge, three doors down from Rick and Xavier's room. I don't know who will return first, or if they'll return together, just that so many things have gone wrong since the bo fight and Rick's fingers on my chin: I've lost Odette and my parents are yanking me home. Then there's Xavier, and the fistfight, and whether Rick's angry with me for doing the one thing he asked me not to do, and why couldn't he freaking stand up to his family for Jenna in the first place, and why I took that God-awful photo, and how many are still out there and is one going to end up on social media or make its way to Northwestern, and did I subconsciously sabotage myself by losing Odette because it would only make the titanium prison of the burglar's lantern more unbearable, and can I ever, ever go back to being the daughter my parents want me to be?

An angry sob issues from my throat. Raindrops spatter the windows that look out on the night. I reach for my cup of bubble milk tea, which tips and spills across the black lacquer coffee table. It drowns the seashell figurines of Chinese fishermen, which match the living room table back home. I glare at it: another Wong invasion.

They never even gave me a chance to explain.

Ignoring the mess, I rise to stand by the windows. Down below, the blue pipe stretches tauntingly across the black waters of the Keelung River. A pair of dragon boats, glowing like magical slippers, glides under it. I never got to ride one, feel the spray of water on my face.

"Ever, you okay?" Spencer pauses by the elevators, a wooden mah-jong box under his arm.

Unlike Rick, Spencer really is like a brother to me. So is Marc. And Benji.

"Have you seen Rick?"

"He left Taipei."

"Left?"

"This afternoon."

"Where did he go?"

"Li-Han drove him to the airport. I heard from Marc. He's flying to Hong Kong for a few days."

"Hong Kong!"

He never mentioned a trip there—only that Jenna's dad works for a bank there. By the time he's back, I'll be gone.

I'm never going to see him again.

"You coming out tonight? We're hitting the beer garden in Gongguan. Rick said that one's the best; too bad he's not here to join."

"Um, I can't." My bones have turned to jelly. "But have a good time."

I sink back down on the couch as Spencer heads off. The pang of loss surprises me. How did that happen? A week ago, I would've been relieved to be shed of Boy Wonder, but now . . .

The floorboards squeak. "Hey. Ever."

Xavier. He's wearing his favorite black shirt, the silver threads catching the muted light. His nose is a purplish hue, which fits the mysterious, tough-guy persona he projects, though not the real person he's allowing me to glimpse. A long, rectangular box is tucked under his arm, one of those boxes made to hold scrolls, with two halves that come apart like a tube of lipstick.

The memory of last night's kiss, his soft, sweet mouth devouring me, springs back up between us.

I rise from the couch, braiding my fingers together until they hurt. "You're back."

"And grounded. Twenty demerits, baby." With that sardonic smile of his, he holds out his hand for a high five.

I step back. "I heard Rick went to Hong Kong," I blurt.

He lowers his hand. "To meet Jenna."

"Jenna!" So she's overcome her fear of flying? And why do I feel this stab of betrayal? Our charade had been for her benefit. He's never pretended otherwise but somehow, I feel . . . rejected.

Xavier's eyes are oddly soft. Sympathetic. I remember the picture of me watching Rick's bo fight. Xavier sees me so clearly, and last night—last night, he made me feel so wanted.

256

"What's in the box?" I ask.

Xavier puts a hand to its top. Then releases it. "Nothing."

Something about the way he says it makes me reckless. Or maybe it's the kiss that emboldens me. Or that it's my last night in Taipei, forever.

"Let me see."

It's his turn to back away. "No."

I snatch at its upper half and he grabs it back with a small cry of panic, and then the top rips free, followed by a flood of rolled pages. Xavier snatches at them, his face desperate, but there are too many: a half-dozen Ever sketches flutter to the floor. Not hasty sketches like the ones he's given me, but full-colored, detailed, shaded, woven through with shadow and light and time and dedication.

Me dancing at Club Love.

Me gazing out on the lily pond, my hair blowing in a breeze.

Me wrinkling my nose at a gnarly Chinese herb.

Me sitting by Aunty Claire's glowing fireplace, a bottle of wine at my feet.

My eyes filling an entire sheet.

My lips.

My body trembles as I kneel before these beautiful sketches, pieces of his heart in purple and red and green. Gently, I gather the paintings and roll them back into a soft tube and fit them into his box and rise and hand it back to him.

"I'm sorry," I whisper.

He laces his fingers through mine. "Ever."

There's a warmth in his low voice. A shy invitation. And it's my last night. Before I return to the straitjacket of my real existence.

Xavier's arm goes around me. He cradles my head against his chest, his sensitive fingers massaging the vertebrae in my neck. My back arches slightly with the pleasure of his touch, then I pull back to look into his eyes.

The desire there makes my knees tremble.

It's my last night.

But if I take this step, there's no telling where it will lead. No telling what it will mean to leave behind not just my parents and their rules—

But myself.

Then I put my hand on the back of Xavier's head and pull his face to mine.

25

The sun is peering through the two-paned window when I awaken. I lie on my side on a cloud of down feathers, nude between cotton sheets and a blue duvet and the weight of Xavier's arm over my waist. His naked body presses against my back from shoulder to thighs. His breath warms the nape of my neck.

Last night returns like a dream: Xavier's hand on my back, guiding me to this room as our mouths moved together, the click of the door sealing our privacy, then his mouth on my eyelids, my cheeks, the hollow of my neck, his hands exploring, the ripping of foil between us, my fingernails in his shoulders.

My body is sore in places I didn't know could feel sore.

What have I done?

I stir under Xavier's arm, which shifts to my hip. Heavy and intimate and possessive. The subtle scent of him, cologne, sweat, male, reaches my nose. His body is imprinted all over mine—and what does this mean? I'd never been the focus of such ravenous want. Never imagined how irresistible its pull. Sex *isn't* the barely tolerable duty of procreation, like Mom always insinuated. It's two human beings fitting seamlessly together. Maybe it was the dancer in me, but I'd known instinctively how to *move*—

I wanted to wait for love.

Opposite me is Rick's unmade bed. Nothing has changed since Friday, except his clothes from the weekend are dumped on his rumpled sheets. His stuff is still here—snacks, soap, care package. The folded bag of rice on his desk lies by the stack of postcards.

Xavier's arm tightens, drawing me closer. "You're so sweet, Ever," he murmurs, still half-asleep.

And how strange he'd said the one thing he could have to make me want to leave.

Slipping from his arms, I hunt for my bra, panties. I don't *want* to regret what we've done, but I'm not the kind of person who can shrug this off. My gaze drops to a red smear, like a smudge of calligraphy ink, on a drooping corner of his bedsheet.

Blood.

*My* blood.

Biting back a small cry, I slip out the door.

The silver lining of flying home today is that I won't ever have to face Xavier again.

I'm afraid to return to my room and Sophie, so I head downstairs. The hallway is empty, and though I've walked them dozens of times, I feel lost and aimless as I wander the corridors. Somehow, I find myself in the dining hall. The breakfast bar is weighed down by pork-stuffed buns, a porridge bar offering five different toppings, platters of scallion pancakes, heaps of fried eggs and Chinese sausages. Salted eggs, Dad's favorite that he makes himself by slipping raw eggs into an old pickle jar of warm, salted water.

Rick was right: I've been missing out on a killer breakfast. Now, it's my last supper. I should eat, but I can't muster up an appetite. I've put a single pork bun on my tray when the Dragon arrives, her green skirt swishing.

"Ai-Mei, my office please. Your parents are on my phone."

More English. It's official. I'm out.

In her office, Mei-Hwa is sorting papers, a song playing on her iPod. She shuts it off and meets my eyes timidly, and I flush. "My favorite," she apologizes, though I don't know why—she has great taste in music. The Dragon sends her to substitute teach our class, then pushes her speaker phone toward me. The scent of Chinese ointment makes my eyes water and the air conditioner blasts my head.

"Hello?"

I grip the edge of her desk, brace for the flight number, instructions for how to spend my time on the plane, pickup plan, along with those wounding shots that only Mom can deliver. My lips sting from Xavier's kisses and a part of me fears that the Dragon can see them there, or that Mom will hear it in my voice.

"Ever, we can't fly you home." Mom's voice is like chipped ice. "The change fee is too high."

"Wait, what?" My eyes meet the Dragon's impervious ones.

"You stay until we find a cheaper ticket. But no more going out by yourself. All special activities canceled. Gao Laoshi said you don't do your homework. You have more demerits than anyone else. You sneak out past midnight. You take naked pictures! Good Lord, what's next?"

My fingers clench together in my lap. Her worst nightmares about me have all come true. And why, I don't know—but I'd needed Xavier last night, and maybe I used him.

"Nine o'clock bedtime. Counselors will guard you at night."

"No boba factory tour for you." The Dragon weighs in. "No lantern launching, no dragon boat racing, no talent show—"

My head snaps up. "I'm not even *in* the talent show!"

"*Educational field trips* only," Mom concludes.

"You can't *control* me." My throat aches as if I've swallowed a razor blade. I hold my voice low to keep it from cracking. "I'm *eighteen*."

Once again, the line goes dead.

**26**

I try to call Megan from the lobby phones, but she doesn't pick up. She's probably out with Dan, or still traveling with her parents. I hide in the fifth-floor lounge the rest of the day, skipping classes and avoiding Xavier. But there are four weeks left in the program, two more weeks of class before the Tour Down South. I'll have to face him eventually.

Hunger finally drives me to dinner in the dining hall, where I seek out Debra and Laura at a table near the back and hide myself among them. Across from me, Mindy shoots to her feet, tossing her black hair contemptuously over her shoulder.

"*Slut.*" She storms to the next table, where she puts her head together with girls from the second floor. All of them shoot me scathing looks.

My eyes prickle with tears, but Laura squeezes my arm. "You were so *brave*. You told those guys."

"That was such a shitty thing Sophie did." Debra spoons mapo tofu onto my plate. She knows it's my favorite and I dig in hungrily, grateful to have someone looking out for me.

"We *hate you*, you know?" Laura laughs. "I mean—if I had your bod, I'd pass my photos out myself." She hands me a napkin-wrapped package. "We collected six. How many are left?"

They're standing by me. I choke down a mouthful of spicy tofu.

"I don't know," I whisper. "I need to find out. The photographer knows, but I'm not allowed off campus. I can't speak enough Mandarin to even call."

"We'll ask for you," Debra promises. "We'll find them."

"Thank you," I say. But short of fishing in every pocket, notebook, and drawer on campus, the only way I'll get all of them back is if someone hands them to me.

I head to my room after dinner, hoping to avoid Sophie by going to bed early. In the lounge, Mei-Hwa lies stretched out on a blue-silk couch, head propped on the red-, yellow-, and green-striped pillow stitched by her grandmother. Over the top of her novel, she meets my gaze and her face reddens, then she hides behind its pages.

So. My babysitter. Who, I'm sure, has never done something as stupid as . . . well, any of the things I've done these weeks.

I sweep by without a word.

*"Ai-Mei. Wǒ néng tígōng bāngzhù ma?"*

Her tone is timid, not judgmental. I pause, my back to her. "My name is Ever."

"Ever. My other name is Gulilai."

I look at her. She's sat up and set down her novel. She tugs an earphone from her ear and I hear a song. "Your tribal name?"

She nods. "I always forget you don't understand Mandarin."

"Which name do you prefer?"

"I like them both."

"Is that what you're supposed to say?" It comes out more belligerent than I mean.

"No, I do like them both. I'm an ethnically Plains and Puyama girl, but I'm also Taiwanese."

She's me in reverse. A minority in Taiwan, like I am in the States. Somehow, she's making all her identities work: she wears clothes that reflect her heritage, and brought her grandma's pillow, and tries to convert people to her favorite music, and yet she goes by a Chinese name and reads an English book.

I touch her iPod. "What song is this?" It feels strange to use English, in this longest conversation we've had yet.

"*Lán Huā Cǎo.*" She tugs her earphone free of the iPod, and a girl's voice sings out the song she was playing in the Dragon's office. Her favorite. "It's an old Chinese folk tune. 'Orchid Grass.'"

My toes twitch to the beat. "I like it."

"You do?" She seems surprised, like I feel when the twelve members of my dance squad love my routines. And has she grappled with the same insecurities, the same fears of being accepted as someone outside the main culture? Have I given off a snobby vibe of my own? I find myself wanting to reassure her.

"I really do like them. Your songs have a way of sticking in my head."

"My parents played this one when I was growing up."

"I can't imagine sharing music with my parents."

Her brow rises. "Why not?"

"We just like different things."

"I miss my parents so much." She says it truthfully and without embarrassment. I envy her.

"They don't live in Taipei?"

"We live on the eastern shore, in a small village. Several hours away."

"Why did you take this job? Not to spend your summer chasing delinquents."

She laughs, a soft, soothing sound. "I wanted to meet kids from other countries, and help them learn about mine." She smiles and touches her iPod. "Orchid Grass" has ended. "If I can make even *one* person love *one* song of mine, I will have succeeded. Also"—her voice grows wistful—"my family needs the money. I have two younger sisters. My mom just had a baby."

I imagine Pearl. Mei-Hwa is a big sister, like me. And wasn't I just like her at the start of summer? Steady and responsible? Barely able to even *imagine* trouble, let along get myself into it?

"Do you . . . want to talk?" she asks hesitantly.

I meet her gaze. She bites her lip, as uncomfortable as I am. I'm glad we talked. Got to know each other a little bit more.

But no matter how friendly or sensitive Mei-Hwa is, she's still the Dragon's eyes and ears.

"Thanks, but I'm good," I say. "Thanks for sharing your song."

And with that, I slip away.

In my room, the closet stands open and emptied of clothes and hangers. My dresses lie in crumpled heaps, as though Sophie had kicked them around. My black chiffon skirt has soaked up a can of stale beer. Her dirty laundry still remains in her hamper, but she seems to have moved out. It's a small reprieve.

I mop and sort into the night, trying to put some order back into my universe. I find my lilac V-neck and jean cutoffs that I wore on the flight here, scrunched under my bed. I've come so far from that girl who showed up on Loveboat. I pad to my dresser, where I dig out the list of Wong Rules. *Drinking, wasting money, boys, sex.* I've devoted all my energies to doing what my *parents* don't want, instead of what *I* want.

And I've been impulsive, stupid. And selfish.

"*Wǒ zhǐ xūyào gēn tā shuōhuà.*" It's Xavier, outside in the hallway.

Mei-Hwa answers in Mandarin. Her voice rises, then a knock sounds on my door.

"Ever, it's me," Xavier says.

I grip my shorts in my lap. My body still remembers. Everything. I can't face him. Not now. Maybe not ever.

"Please don't push me away."

*He's afraid.* His fear tugs a chord in my heart.

But he's the one who *isn't* supposed to get hurt. The Player who deserves anything. Why must he be so vulnerable?

Mei-Hwa is scolding him, back in full-fledged counselor mode. I picture her tiny, determined frame, yanking him down the hallway, proof that size has nothing to do with power, and I almost want to go out to spare her and him the awkwardness.

"I'm sorry, I just can't talk tonight," I say finally, but they're gone.

I email Pearl to check she hasn't been scorched by the conflagration back home, then pour my heart out to Megan in a three-page email.

Finally, I delete the entire note and replace it:

Miss you SO much. Hope you and Dan are having a blast.

In the morning, I wake from the fading dream of a white feather tutu. I cling to its threads as they slip from me: Rick's laugh, Xavier's paint-smeared fingers. Why was I dreaming of them both? The light through the window is gray. No one's awake yet, the silence unnatural.

I study my list of Wong Rules. A new list runs through my head—instead of Straight As: work on projects I love. Instead of curfews and no drinking and dress like a nun: everything in moderation.

But those rules are reactions. Which means that list still belongs to my parents.

Not to me.

I crumple the Wong Rules into a ball and toss it at the trash can. Score. Outside my window, down in the courtyard, Marc and his Angry Asian Men are wading calf-deep through flood waters. My eyes fall on Rick's blue socks, folded together, on the edge of my desk. I pull their wooly softness over my hands and clap softly, feeling an odd, hollow sense of loss. Like I've misplaced something.

Without Sophie's mini-speakers playing music, the room feels stiflingly still. I adjust my radio alarm clock until I find a Taiwanese pop song with a toe-twitching backbeat. It's followed by an American eighties song.

Almost against my will, the music takes hold of my shoulders, then my hips, then my feet. Slowly, my stocking arms draw curves through the air, picking up speed as the music deepens. My fingers pulse against the stretchy knit, wrists flex parallel movements to the rhythm. I begin to dance. One song. Another, another, my feet beating out the rhythm on the floor. I whirl into the space between the dressers, my long-armed shadow stag leaps over the walls, until, deep in my body, I understand what I will never have words for.

As the fifth song fades, I spin a slow circle. My blue hands sketch a cylinder around my body, slimming to the song's last note. There's a pulsing deep inside me as my blood storms the chambers of my heart. Maybe it took hitting bottom this weekend to give me the wake-up call I needed.

I open my notebook, and write a new list. Neither in obedience to my parents, nor against them:

*1. Sort things out with Xavier*
*2. Help him with reading*
*3. Learn some Mandarin (would be nice to understand what my parents say in code)*
*4. Choreograph an original dance for the talent show, even if I can't be in it*
*5. Dance my heart out until med school*

I stack Rick's socks neatly and set them on the desk. Smooth out the tiny dancing figurines.

After a moment, I put my pen to the page again:

*6. Wait for love next time*

I write a new title at the top:

*The Ever Wong Plan*

Opening my door takes four yanks that threaten to pop both arms from their sockets. *Oh for heaven's sake,* Sophie's voice echoes in my head, and I feel a pang.

I head down the stairs to the landing, where the blue flyer still hangs by a piece of tape.

*Do you sing? Play an instrument? Juggle?*
*Sign up for the Talent Show today!*

I tear it from the wall and find Debra and Laura in the second-floor lounge, sprawled on red yoga mats, working out to Taylor Swift. I roll the flyer into a tube, more nervous than if I were approaching a guy for a first date.

"Hey, Ever." Debra finishes a set of leg lifts, and unsticks her butterfly-printed shirt from her sternum.

"What's up?" Laura rolls her mat into a tube of her own.

I show the flyer to my fellow clubbers. "I was wondering if you girls might be up for working with me on a dance routine." The talent show needs to be Chien Tan–themed, but that's not a limitation so much as a chance to take some risks. "I've got a dance based on something I put together for a friend and me back home. I can incorporate ribbons and fans from your electives. Music-wise, I'm thinking of a mix of American and Taiwanese songs."

"Cool," Debra says.

"Not too weird?"

"No, I'm in," Laura says. "I bet Lena would join us. She's a pro."

"We can practice in the B Building," Debra says.

"I have a confession," I say. "I'm technically not allowed in the talent show."

"The photos?" Debra scowls.

"Yeah." A dig in my stomach. "We can't let the Dragon know I'm involved. I won't be in the show. I'll just teach you the dance. Besides, after my photos, it's for the best that I'm not onstage." With all those eyes on my body.

"Bull," Debra says, but I press on before I lose my nerve.

"We can start tomorrow after electives."

"Tomorrow's temple tour. Thursday's Sun Yat-Sen Memorial," Laura reminds me. "Friday's the National Palace Museum."

So many obstacles already, with our schedule filling up as the weeks roll on. Funny how when you let yourself want, the fear of *not* getting it ratchets up.

But inch by inch, I'm on my way with the Ever Wong Plan.

"Saturday then," I say.

I owe Xavier an explanation. An apology and a talk. But I'm relieved not to spot him in the dining hall; he's never been an early riser. I move through the buffet line and place a pork-stuffed *bāozi* onto my tray as Marc passes by the double doors. He's dressed for running in track shorts and a sleeveless jersey.

"Marc," I call. Setting down my tray, I dart toward the door, only to slam into the Dragon. Her stout arms are filled with a stack of readers. Her heavy perfume wafts over me.

"Ai-Mei." Her measuring eyes sweep the length of my skirt and her lips tighten.

But before she can pronounce some judgment, I dart past her. "Marc!"

Halfway down the hallway, he turns. His hair, parted down the middle, falls in its usual chocolate milk streaks to his cheeks. His eyes light up and he swings a long, brown-paper-wrapped package from under his arm.

"Hey, Ever. I was looking for you—"

"Did Rick go to Hong Kong to meet Jenna?"

Marc's eyes shift as I catch up to him. "It was an emergency."

"What happened?"

"It's—complicated."

"Is someone hurt? Jenna's dad?"

He thrusts the paper package into my hand. "He asked me to give you this."

"What is it?" I unwrap the paper to an elegant bo staff: lightweight rattan marked with tiger stripes, tapering at either end.

"We were in the market waiting for Li-Han to drive him to the airport, and he bought it."

"What for?"

"Stick fighting."

I flush. "Obviously." I run my hand down its polished surface. It's flawless—no splinters for me from this pole. I twirl it a full revolution. I would have admired its balance if I wasn't so off-balance myself. Is he saying he remembers the almost-kiss? I love it too much already, and I can't afford that.

"Tell him thanks," I say stiffly.

"He said to tell you sorry and that he'd talk to you when he gets back in a few days."

"Sorry for what?" For the kiss? The whole messed-up weekend? Maybe he's trying to make up for Aunty Claire hating me.

Marc shrugs. "I figured you'd know."

I don't. And I can't read into his kindness, when most likely, that's all this is.

"I hope no one's hurt," I say. Tucking the staff under my arm, I start to head back to breakfast, then turn back.

"Who started the fight?"

"Rick." Marc bites his lip. "But they've kind of been at it since the beginning."

"But . . . why? I haven't—"

"Sorry, Ever. Not sure how much he'd want me to say." Marc balls up the paper, his expression pained. "He'll be back soon. Talk to him then."

I avoid Xavier in Mandarin by switching seats to the front by Debra and Laura, dashing out as soon as we're dismissed. The next days pass in a blur: homework in an empty classroom under Mei-Hwa's supervision, who rewards my efforts by eliminating a demerit. I chat with her a bit more about music and her family, while all of Chien Tan launches sky lanterns from the balconies of the Grand Hotel. No sneaking out clubbing for me either—but I don't care. "Maybe I got the whole clubbing thing out of my system," I tell Megan, when I finally catch her from the pay phone downstairs. "Or maybe everything else that's happened has overshadowed it."

"Or maybe you're just finally doing more of what *you* want to do," she says wisely.

Now I tap a rhythm on my thigh under my desk, plotting out my new dance as the Dragon teaches us radicals, the components of characters: three tick marks for water, a five-pointed explosion for fire, a bleeding heart for heart. I recite lines of poetry and sing *"Liǎng Zhī Lǎo Hǔ,"* and listen to a talk by Mei-Hwa on the more than sixteen Aboriginal tribes who make up 2.3 percent—a bit over 500,000 people—of this island's population, all the while feeling Xavier's eyes on the back of my head.

Rick's been gone three days. I hate that I'm counting.

At night in my room, I twirl his bo staff. A flagless staff has so much potential and I experiment with sweeps, lunges, jabs at invisible enemies. The staff hisses through the air and I remember slamming Rick's knuckles. I hadn't expected his absence to dominate my thoughts and even my dancing. Back at home, he was the hated Boy Wonder. And here . . . ?

I don't know what this means. Or if it means anything at all.

Thursday, Laura and I climb the steps to the Sun Yat-Sen Memorial, a square building topped by a yellow, swallowtail roof.

275

Inside, a two-story statue of a man who looks like my uncle Johnny, sits on a carved stone chair. He's flanked by Taiwanese flags in red, white, and blue.

"He was a doctor before becoming a revolutionary," Laura says.

"Way to overachieve."

"Right? It reminds me of the Lincoln Memorial."

"Me, too. Or is it the other way around? Maybe tourists from Taiwan look at Lincoln and think, cool, just like Dr. Sun Yat-Sen's, too bad they don't have sentries standing by to show some respect."

Laura laughs.

Friday afternoon, we board luxury buses for the National Palace Museum. Warm rain sheets down as we arrive at a stunning gate of five white arches topped by sea-green roofs. Laura and I open our umbrellas and fight the rain as we walk up a broad avenue of flagstones flanked by thick-leaved trees. The museum itself, a sprawling, beige palace, is nestled at the base of an enormous leafy mountain. Five matching sea-green-and-orange pagodas rise at its center, and on either side.

Halfway there, we run into Sam and David getting down on hands and knees, black hair dripping with rain. Peter and Marc climb on top to form a human pyramid while a fifth guy snaps photos on his phone.

"What are you doing?" I ask. I decide to pretend I don't remember David had one of my nude pictures.

"We're taking back our stereotypes," Marc says.

I'm confused. "Is this for an elective?"

"No, it's our statement. To the world. The Gang of Four Manifesto."

I laugh. They're an odd bunch: heavy-set Sam, wiry David with his goatee, soft-skinned Peter, and lanky Marc. "So what stereotype is this?"

"Haven't you noticed? The Asian dad in the movies snapping a million photos?"

"I thought you were calling yourselves the Angry Asian Men?" Laura says.

"Gang of Four's better," says the aspiring journalist. "They were the badass officials who led the Cultural Revolution and were charged with treason by the new government. Not that I'm on their side, but they have a great name."

Laura hands me her phone. "Take my photo with them, will you?"

As I snap a shot, my purse is knocked from my shoulder. Sophie sweeps by in a flutter of red silk, arm in arm with Benji. Last I heard, she was dating Chris, full speed ahead to find her man. Benji throws a panicked, Bambi-eyed gaze over his shoulder.

"She's not just boy crazy," Laura says. "She's insane."

"It's her family." Why am I trying to explain? *She wants a husband, not a hookup.* Laura raises her brows like I'm speaking pig Latin. With many of the girls refusing to associate with Sophie, I've won the battle in a way. But instead of vindicated, I feel strangely responsible, as if her unhappiness now is my doing. What she did was wrong, but I've wronged her, too, and I can't see how either of us will ever recover.

Some guys are approaching from behind. "Taiwan wants *freedom*." Spencer's talking politics as usual. "The entire country has a history of oppression—first by the Japanese occupation, then the KMT. And is the US coming to their aid if Beijing comes after them?"

"If it works for them," Xavier answers.

"Hurry, Laura." Panicked, I dart ahead before they can catch up to us. "I'm soaked. Let's get inside."

A red-carpeted staircase leads to galleries of incredible things: carved ivory globes nested one inside another; nuts and olive stones carved into animals, boats, demon masks. A jade statue of a boy and bear embracing makes me think of Rick. Maybe Jenna got wind of our fake relationship and is breaking up with him? Maybe her dad's involved. Or maybe I *want* something to be wrong, when Rick's actually strolling hand in hand with Jenna through the night markets of Hong Kong, Ever Wong a distant memory.

I try to immerse myself in these treasures of China, liberated/stolen by the KMT, depending on which side of history you sit. I skirt Xavier's group by a Mongolian yurt and line up with Laura and a few girls to view a famous Chinese cabbage chiseled from a single cut of white-and-green jade. We get a lesson on how to distinguish jade from rocks by shining a light through it.

At lunch, I find the source of things I'd chalked up to quirks of my parents: freshly pulped watermelon juice, passion fruit halves served with tiny plastic spoons. I even run across Mom's favorite—a purple dragon fruit dripping with dark juices, instead of the white, desiccated ones imported by the Cleveland Chinese grocery. The heft of it in my hand makes me uneasy and I set it back on its tray and move on.

After lunch, I find myself wandering alone into a large salon where a crowd fights its way toward a glass case. Sweat-laced bodies pile up behind me, and I'm inched forward like tooth-paste in a tube, until I'm squeezed out against the case. Fighting for breath, I brace a hand on the glass and peer at a cinnamon-brown slice of pork belly on a gold platter. Light glistens off a layer of fat and striations of fleshy meat. It looks good enough to sink a pair of chopsticks into and devour—and wonders of wonders, it's made of jasper.

"That stone is the one thing you absolutely had to see in Taipei," a voice teases behind me. "And now you have."

My heart jolts as Xavier maneuvers in beside me. His gold chain glints beneath the collar of his tailored shirt. He takes my elbow, protecting me from the crowd as we make our way out. His nose is still bruised: a patch of dark yellow over its bridge.

His touch, his scent, stirs my body with the memory of his kisses, our bodies interlocked.

"Hi," I say dumbly.

"Did it mean anything to you?" His low voice runs under the crowd's rumblings.

"The stone meat?" I swallow hard. "Funny how much our ancestors worshiped food."

His smile doesn't reach his eyes. "They had a lot of appetites we don't give them credit for."

I blush, fixating on a five-colored vase ahead, decorated with immortals, a hundred deer, fruits, fauna, auspicious blue clouds.

"You're avoiding me," Xavier says.

"I didn't know what to say," I admit.

His posture is easygoing, but his hands tense on the rail separating us from the vase. "It wasn't a random hookup for me."

I moisten my dry lips. "I don't want to regret—"

"Then don't." His hand brushes the back of my hair. "You're holding out for someone who's made his choice."

A new stab of anxiousness. Xavier's seen all the phone calls. All the postcards. But the bo staff . . . I wish I could *call* Rick but I've never needed his phone number and don't have it.

"Why were you fighting with him?"

Xavier's eyes shift. "He was pissed about the kiss at his aunt's. It wasn't his business."

I hate Rick for knowing.

But he *made* it his business.

"Maybe he hasn't made his choice," I blurt.

Xavier turns toward me, spreading an exasperated hand. "Then why's he with Jenna in Hong Kong?"

"How did you even know that?"

"I overheard his call at the clinic, okay? She was moving

her flight from Taipei. He was arranging to pick her up at the airport."

"Taipei?" I stammer. "She was coming to Taipei? I didn't know." Why didn't he tell me? For all I know, Rick's finally manned up and planned to force his family to accept her.

I'm such a fool.

The years of unrequited pining crash down on me with aching loneliness. After Dan, I haven't learned anything. Obsessing over a guy in love with another girl. A guy who's made clear over and over that he thinks of me as his sister.

My chest constricts. I move into the next room, where the taps of a chisel on stone echo from a guest-artist carving chops at a corner table. A panorama on a silk scroll dominates the rest of the room, a range called Mount Lu, with craggy peaks and evergreens, with blues so deep and rich I can taste them.

As Xavier comes up beside me, I start to move away, but his hand covers mine on the railing.

"Is this . . . would I have a better chance with you if I could read?" he asks quietly.

My head snaps up. "That has nothing to do with anything! How could you even think that?"

He looks away. His wavy hair has grown longer since the first day, and he's tucked it behind his ears, making him look younger. I look back on my behavior—running off the morning after, avoiding him because I've been too mortified to own my choice—I haven't been kind . . . at all.

"Does your dad not want you to paint?" I ask.

He gives me a quick glance. A short laugh. "My dad will buy art if it's a good investment. But no stupid son of his is wasting time mucking around in it."

"Well, he's not here. So, go do it. Paint your heart out the rest of this trip."

He runs his hand along the railing, still not looking at me. Then he pulls his notebook from the back of his shorts and thrusts it into my hand. It's warm from his body. Unwillingly, I flip through. There's a tentativeness to these drawings I didn't see in mine, as if he sketched them with one eye peering over his shoulder, waiting for a lash to fall.

A temple's stone pillars, carved with scaly dragons and gold-embossed characters. An artist in a paint-flecked smock raises his brush to an easel. A marbled tea egg lies on its own shadow. No girls, when I'd half-expected them. Just more of me. Fishing the last thread of shark fin from my soup at Aunty Claire's. Me at the breakfast bar this morning, scooping a salted egg onto my plate. My profile at the front of the classroom, facing Debra for a paired exercise.

The back of my head on his pillow, the curve of my bare shoulder, folded sheets pulled to my elbow.

I nearly drop the notebook. His drawings have changed. They're deeper. Fervid. Feverish.

I press his notebook back into his hands with shaking hands of my own. I move to the chop-carving table, where the artist is etching the triple characters of Chinese names into soapstones the size of rectangular lipstick tubes. Seals. To imprint the red stamps on paintings in this museum and at Aunty Claire's.

I buy a pale green chop, swirling with darker green veins.

"*Nǐ jiào shénme míngzì?*" The stonecutter is asking for the name to carve into it, but I shake my head and hand the stone to Xavier.

"You should carve your own," I say. "Chen Laoshi says most artists do. Kind of like a ballerina sewing her own ribbons on her pointe shoes—sorry"—I pull a deep breath and exhale through my mouth—"but you can't draw me anymore."

"Why not?"

"You know why."

"No I don't." He flips the chop, rubs his thumb along its edge.

"Don't make this so hard."

"I'm not the one making it hard."

"*Stop.*" I turn to go, but his arm wraps around my waist, holding me in place.

His next words are half-buried in my hair. "Ever, all I want is a chance."

I took advantage of a crush and fanned it into a flame.

All the phone calls. All the postcards.

I find myself leaning into him. I rest my forehead on his shoulder as his arms go around me and I'm so afraid I'm going to hurt him.

But I no longer have the strength to push him away.

"Maybe we could read together some." My voice is muffled by his shirt. "I'll help you with English, you help me with Mandarin?"

His arms tighten. He rests his chin on my hair. "I'd like that."

27

"Laura, step forward so we can see you. Lena, that's perfect."

All day Saturday and Sunday, I throw myself into preparing for the talent show as if my sanity depends on it. Maybe it does. We work out-of-sight in the back courtyard by the carp fountain, and I've adjusted Megan's and my dance to incorporate fifteen girls—instead of a flag duet, I block them into three groups of five girls with fans, ribbons, and snappy jazz moves, then braid them together as the song builds.

"Keep your circles the same size for those three measures, then break into the interweaving lines."

Sliding into instructions comes so naturally to me—and the girls are *good*. With five hundred kids to recruit from, we've gathered an all-star squad. But by the end of the weekend, the dance hasn't gelled yet. Honestly, it's a random mix of ribbons and fans.

Still, as I work with them, I feel an internal calm, a sense of groundedness deep in my core. My parents sent me to discover my heritage, but in the process, I'm also finding parts of myself, even if that self isn't who they want me to be.

Between classes and dancing, I place a lifeline call to Pearl from the lobby phone, asking her for tips I can pass to Xavier.

"He needs to find a reading teacher for dyslexia when you guys come home," Pearl says. "But you can still read with him. Dad did that with me when I was little, remember? Hours a night. Also clay letters. That was fun."

When did my little sister grow up?

"I remember." Dad on the couch with Pearl in his lap, a book spread over her skinny legs. They used to read long past her bedtime, until Mom chased her angrily to bed and scolded Dad. Dad's an absentminded teddy bear when he gets into something. But I don't want to think of him that way. It makes it harder to hang on to my anger.

In the evening, as storms batter the windows, Xavier and I work in the fifth-floor lounge. I bring our readers. He brings a box of dragon's beard candy.

"*Chuang qian ming yue guang.*" I read the phonetic pinyin of the poem assigned for homework. "I have no idea what I just said. Something something bright moon something."

"*Chuáng qián míng yuè guāng.*" He corrects my tones. "I'm pretty sure you said, 'Bright moonlight before my bed.' Most Chinese kids learn that poem in grade school."

"Why doesn't the Dragon give us the translation?" I grumble. "At least you and I make a good team. I don't understand half of what I'm saying, but you—"

"—understand what you're saying but can't read half of it." He grins. His front tooth is slightly crooked; I hadn't noticed before. "This is kind of fun."

*He's* fun. Self-deprecating in that wry way. I hope this is helping him, showing him those things he's believed about himself are lies. I want to give him something good this summer, even if I don't know if I can give him what he wants.

He's not pressing me beyond the reading.

Maybe we're moving back toward a friendship. I hope so.

The following Monday afternoon, the fifth week of Chien Tan and a full week since Rick left, my eroding demerit list permits me to renew outings—as long as I clear it with the office. When I meet the girls in the courtyard, I say, "Want to hold practice outside the National Theater today? Could be inspiring."

They're game. Arm in arm, singing "Orchid Grass," we move in a herd past the pond and up the driveway. As we round the bend, I catch sight of Sophie coming toward us in a yellow sundress, dwarfed by Matteo's rugby frame.

"I do *not* talk too much." Matteo's moon-shaped face and Italian accent are both stiff with anger. With a meaty hand, he yanks savagely at the collar of his striped polo shirt. His other hand is clenched.

"I'm sorry, babe. You don't—I'm just in a bad mood, okay? I promise I'll make it up to you." Sophie tucks her hand under his elbow, but his knuckles remains white on his fist. They cuddle on the bus trips to Chiang Kai-shek's former residence and the zoo, and I heard they've secretly moved into the spare room. But Matteo's explosive temper ended with Grace Pu leaving the program—surely, Rick wouldn't approve. And he'd asked me to watch out for her.

Sophie catches sight of us. Her gaze flits from me to our group. Her flawless makeup—down to her green eyeliner—and her crisp sundress contrast starkly with my shorts, tank top, and bare face. Noticing no longer comes with its old twinge of insecurity, but I still brace myself as I say, "Mei-Hwa dropped off your dry cleaning. I put it in your closet."

"I'll pick it up." Something like regret in her eyes gives me my own pang. I've seen her leave boxes of pineapple cakes in the lounge for others to enjoy, then slink off without taking credit. Typical Sophie generosity, but now her shoulders droop, her eyes are shadowed. We hit it off from day one. She's helped me break free of my straitjacket. I wish I could talk to Rick about her.

She starts to pass, then turns back. "Ever?"

"Yeah?"

"There's construction at the Metro. You might want to cross the river and grab cabs instead."

It's a good tip. It saves us fifteen minutes of retracing our steps, and cabs split four ways are cheap.

"Thanks," I say.

Sophie nods, then tucks her hand under Matteo's arm and moves on.

In my head, I add a bullet to the Ever Wong Plan—

*Sort things out with Sophie. Somehow.*

Our cabs drop us off at Liberty Square, a vast public plaza fronted by another gate of five white arches accented by blue pagoda roofs. It leads onto a wide avenue flanked by sculpted trees that runs toward the white temple and blue pagoda roof of the Chiang Kai-shek Memorial.

On either side of the avenue, two traditional Chinese buildings face each other: the National Theater and National Concert Hall. They're works of art themselves: wide stone steps leading to a platform surrounding each building, and red columns holding up two-tiered, orange roofs with dragons, phoenixes, and other mythological Chinese creatures marching down each swallowtail corner.

A breeze gusts through the humid air. I guide the girls up steps to the deck of the National Theater. A wall of glass doors reflects us like the mirrors of a ballet studio. Posters advertise upcoming performances by a Beijing opera and Julliard string quartet.

"We couldn't have asked for a more perfect place to practice," I gloat. "This is like Carnegie Hall. Or the National Theatre in DC."

"I learned to ride my bike here." Lena fingers her cross pendant, her gaze following a little boy pedaling his own bike under his parents' watchful gaze.

"Really?" I'd learned to ride in the park near my home, Dad hanging on to the back trying to keep up. "Were you visiting?"

"I was born here." In her southern drawl, I now hear the lilt of a Taiwanese accent. "I moved with my family to the US when I was eleven."

"I can't imagine coming here like it's your own backyard." Did Mom learn to ride her bike in a plaza like this one? Was Dad one of those boys playing cards in the corner? Did they listen to pop music and flirt, or were they always serious and focused?

"Ever," Debra calls. "You ready?"

I'd been staring out over the plaza watching ghosts.

"Yes," I say. "Let's do this."

"*Lán Huā Căo*" begins to play from Debra's speakers. "Orchid Grass," the old song Mei-Hwa shared with me. I love the simplicity of its melody to open the dance. My girls spread out on the platform, their reflections dancing in the row of glass doors. As the music blends into the next song, I adjust the blocking to balance the long swirls of ribbon with the rosewood fans and propless jazz dancers. The music spills over to a yet-unchoreographed song, spontaneous free dancing breaks out, and we spend as much time laughing as practicing.

At last, soaked with sweat, we flop down on the steps and drink from our bottles.

"Lena, you dance like you're made of water," I say, and the girls chime agreement. She has a body like Megan's, supple and slender. I'd never seen her dance before our group came together; she's never come clubbing, and is really involved with the weekly Bible study she started on the fifth floor. I was surprised she agreed to join us. And grateful.

"My mom's a dancer." She smooths her black hair back with her stretchy red headband. "She gave up her career to raise me. I considered dancing professionally, too, but I talked about it with my mom and the ballet world is too cutthroat. Worse than pro sports, where at least you win or lose the game. Ballet—it's so subjective."

"So what are you doing instead?"

"I'm applying to physical therapy school. I want to work with dancers. That way I'll get to stay in the dancing world and choose the hours I work, so I'll still have time to dance."

"You're so lucky you can talk to your mom about this." Why can she, but not I? Is it because we grew up in different cultures? If Mom and Dad were raised in America, or I in Asia, like Lena . . .

All the important questions in life, I ask my best friend or the librarian. I never talk to my parents about the books I read or the music I love or the dances in my head. I can't trust them not to take what bit of soul I offer them and hurl it into a dumpster.

"My mother told me to try to find another way to come at the dance, something to make myself more than a pretty body. But I'm not like you." She lays a hand on her heart, dimpling with an impish smile. "I'm just a dancer. Not like you—a *choreographer*—that's not something everyone can do."

I'm too stunned to give my usual, knee-jerk denial. Megan often called me a choreographer. *Am* I one? If I am, what does that mean?

But the sun is beginning to set behind Taipei. We need to wrap up.

"Ready for our last runs?" I ask.

The girls groan, but climb good-naturedly to their feet and spread out.

Their movements are coming together, arms, legs, angles flowing closer to synchronization with each run-through. But something is still off—that randomness I can't nail down. As I observe the final go, I understand what's missing.

"It needs a tent pole to bring it together," I say as Debra and Laura collide. With Megan's and my interactive duet spread out among the girls, the dance is a canvas without shape, waving in the wind.

"It's awesome the way it is," Debra says. "We just need to learn it."

"Seriously, it's great, Ever," Laura says.

"It's great because you are." I smile, appreciating their support.

But the choreographer in me—I try on the identity, which squeaks—wants more.

# 28

Tuesday night, I spend a quarter hour at my desk on Skype with Mom, trying to help her navigate a medical bill our insurance is refusing to cover. We're both tense, frustrated by the necessity of this call neither of us want to endure. Dad hasn't spoken to me since the nude-photo call. That he's still angry hurts more than I care to admit, but I try not to dwell on it. At least Mom hasn't brought the photos up again.

As we wrap up, she says, "Ever? I found a ticket from Taipei that's almost the right price. I'm watching for it to come down."

"*Mom.*" Just like that, my blood pressure shoots through the ceiling. "I'm behaving. I'm getting all As. I'm even getting tutored. I don't need to come home early, and besides, there's less than three weeks left."

"Your father and I, we made a mistake, sending you away your last summer."

United they stand, as always.

As I sign off, I push to my feet and find my legs trembling. I text Pearl:

Are they really still trying to bring me home?
Pearl: Yes. They talk about your photo every night.

I groan and grab my bo staff, twirl it in a hypnotic whirl until it hums, then spin a full circle myself while keeping it revolving in place, a trick I do for my flag dances. I'd impressed Rick with part of this move. He's been gone over a week, missing the dragon boat race he'd organized himself, from which I was banned. I want to tell him about this dance I'm doing for the talent show. I want to beat him in another duel. I take out my calligraphy inkwell and my thinnest brush, and paint my Chinese name onto the staff's tip:

王爱美

I blow on the paint until it dries.

All Rick's stuff is still here. He has to come back.

He has to.

Xavier's already on the couch when I enter the fifth-floor lounge, the top three buttons undone on his black shirt, his pencil gliding over the sketchbook in his lap. He's drawing out in the open, new for him. A reader and box of dragon's beard candy are stacked at his side.

With a finger, he brushes his wavy hair from his eyes. "You all right?"

I slump down beside him and open the box. "My parents are trying to fly me home after forcing me to come here in the first place. When I've finally gotten a group of dancers together." When I finally feel at home.

"I don't want you leaving either." He massages the back of my neck with cool fingers and I battle a twinge of guilt.

I shift away. "Don't."

He puts his hand into his lap. After a moment, he says, "If it's ticket prices they're waiting on, I doubt they'll come down."

"Let's hope not." But I'm not just fighting the ticket. I'm fighting the anxiousness, the guilt that welled like blood from a bad cut when I saw her tonight. The wrinkles deepening around her eyes. Her cup of herbal medicine she takes for the ache that won't leave her back. Her bulldog fight to stretch every dollar.

"I brought some rice." I hold up a plastic-wrapped handful, wheedled from the kitchen staff. "We can make rice-clay letters." Pearl's tip. We knead the rice into gray clay and form letters on the table until the rice starts to harden.

"Cool." Then Xavier holds up an ancient-looking DVD. "I

brought something different for tonight. *Fong Sai-Yuk*. You said you'd try it."

The kung fu flick. "I said *maybe*." I smile. "The first day, when I didn't know any better." And he remembered. "I'm game."

Xavier pops the DVD into the player and dims the lights. It's an old film, the acting overdone, but as the story unfolds on the screen, I sink deeper into the couch. I read the subtitles: an ambitious Chinese martial artist competes to win the hand of the daughter of a powerful hooligan, then journeys to save his father.

"I can't believe I'm watching this. I mean, my *dad* watches these movies. Some of the girl stuff is way old-fashioned, but the story's pretty good."

"I tell you, kung fu flicks get a bad rap. They're not all beating up guys. They're about honor. Glory. *Sacrifice*." He thumps his chest, making me smile.

I applaud when the credits roll. "Oh, *wow*. When Jet Li straps his dead friend onto his back and makes their enemies kowtow, it was seriously—"

"The greatest scene in kung fu movie history."

"Totally got shivers. You're right about the choreography. Thanks. I'd never have watched that on my own."

He tucks a strand of hair behind my ear. His fingers linger on my neck and this time, I don't pull away. It's past my bedtime, but Mei-Hwa hasn't appeared yet.

"Why do you trust me?" I ask.

His fingers trail down the bump of my shoulder, the line of my arm to my elbow, sketching my outline.

"You never told anyone about my drawings."

"I did before I knew it was you."

"Exactly."

Even if everything Loveboat feels fair game for the gossip circuits, it had never occurred to me that I *could* share he was my artist.

"It wasn't my secret to tell."

His fingertips have reached the back of my hand. "That doesn't stop most people."

I pull free. "Can I see your new sketches?"

He holds my gaze a moment. Then puts his sketchbook in my lap and shows me the five-arched gateway to the National Palace Museum. The jasper meat, creamy layers of glistening fat, as delicious as the real deal. With each page turn, his sketches grow in confidence.

"You should have your own act at the talent show," I say.

"For paintings?" He scoffs.

"Sure, why not? You could make a mural and hang it up there."

"I'd rather just show my drawings to you." His gaze makes me blush. I drop mine to the rectangular tube as he tugs a short scroll from it.

He unrolls a sketch of three old men in black hats, sitting in a row with a pots-and-pans vendor of the night market behind them. Their beards are gray, threaded with black. Their cotton clothes patched, dusty in parts. An unusual choice for a rich boy.

"I saw them, and I thought, maybe when you get that old, that's when you find peace. Maybe the secret's just living a fucking long time with the right people."

"Oh." A soft chord twangs in my heart. "I love this." A cloud of peace does hang over them. Wistfulness. He's baring his soul.

"I painted it for you," he murmurs.

Without realizing it, I'd hunched closer, my knee brushing his. I smell hair gel and cologne. I close my eyes and try to steady my breathing. What if I did go down this path with him? Him drawing, me dancing, both of us pursuing our art and cheering each other onward? He's rendered my portrait a dozen times and seems so sure of me.

"Xavier, I don't know—"

His soft lips silence mine. He tastes of powdered sugar. I pull back, but before I can decide whether I enjoyed the kiss or am angered that he stole it, footsteps pound down the stairwell. The door bangs open, and Sophie rushes through, her favorite tangerine dress wrinkled as if she's slept in it. Her knuckles press to her cheekbone. She averts her eyes from us, but above her hand, one eye purples like a damp ink block.

"Sophie, what—" Xavier rises, but she brushes by, smelling of coconut oil.

I push to my feet. "Xavier, I've gotta go."

I hurry after Sophie to our bedroom. With her hand still pressed to her cheek, she fumbles with the hot water thermos on our dresser. Snatching my towel off the back of my chair, I move toward her.

"Sophie, are you okay?"

"I walked into a wall." Both hands go to unscrew the thermos. The white of her eye is solid red—I swallow hard as she spills hot water onto her towel.

"You need cold, not heat. I'll get ice. Wait a sec." I duck outside and jog to the ice machine by the emergency exit, taking the opportunity to wipe the shock from my face. This can't be happening. Is it? Did Matteo . . .

When I return, I press the cold bundle into her hand. "Heat's good later, but not for a few days," I babble. "I hit my eye with my flag staff once."

She frowns, not wanting my help. Then she flinches and presses my towel to her face.

"Are you sure you walked into a wall?"

Her good eye glares. "You of all people have no right to lecture me about my love life."

She's right. "I'm worried about you," I say painfully. "You need to tell the Dragon—"

"It's none of your business." Towel to her eye, she climbs into bed and pulls her sheets over her head, turning her back. She lies still.

After a moment, I shut off the lights and climb into my own bed. Her shuddered breath reaches my ears as she stifles her crying. My fist tightens helplessly on my pillowcase. Without Rick here, she's so alone.

I reach over the edge of my mattress for the rattan staff, which I pull into bed beside me, needing its solid comfort. I want to stretch it across to her, build a bridge between us, but I know she won't take it.

And if I can't get through to her, then I need to get to someone who can.

In the morning, Sophie's gone. Her bed is made. She's folded my damp towel into a square and left a note on it that she's gone out with Matteo and won't be back until late. She's never done that before.

I dress and run downstairs, but she's not in the dining room, lobby, or courtyard. Debra walks across the grass toward me, holding a paper bag of hot *bāozi* from the 7-Eleven.

"Have you seen Sophie?" I blurt.

"She went out."

"Who with?"

"Matteo, Benji, Grace, I think—they're headed to Yáng-míngshān for the day."

The mountains—a day trip from Taipei. At least Sophie's not alone with Matteo, but her note has firmed my resolve to get help.

I climb the steps to Rick's floor, in the off chance that he's finally back and I can ask him for help. There's a pain in the center of my chest I've never felt before. What I told Aunty Claire about him was true. Since I was a little girl, a part of me was drawn to that boy with immigrant Chinese parents like mine who had managed to conquer his world. The truth is, if I *did* have a boyfriend, if I could set aside the annoying fact that my parents worship the ground he walks on, I'd want him to be like Rick.

So I've admitted it.

And he's with Jenna.

There's no answer to my knock. Xavier's dad picked him up this morning for a day with family. I head back downstairs to the front desk.

"Is Rick Woo still in the program?" I ask the clerk, hoping I don't come across as stalker-ish. "Has he left for good?" How silly of me to think his stuff was anchor enough to make him come back. Li-Han could pack a box and ship it to the States.

How silly to hope that *I* might have been an anchor.

"I'm sorry, but I don't know," answers the clerk.

"Can I get his cell number?"

He frowns. "I'm not allowed to give out private information."

I never wanted to set foot in the Dragon's office again, but I try her next. Li-Han is there, whittling a whistle from a stalk of bamboo, which he shoves out of sight when I appear.

"I don't think he's left." He scratches at his thick shock of black hair. "But aren't you leaving? Your parents are changing your ticket, yes?"

"I'm not," I snap. "They'll have to kidnap me and air-drop me home."

Xavier's still out with his dad, so we don't meet tonight. I'm glad he's gone. I still haven't figured out how I feel about his kiss. Whether I'm ready to go down this path with him. In my room, I pull my bo staff from my sheets. There's a certain move I love, a series of barrel-turns across the stage, but it's a male dancer's move from Prince Seigfried of *Swan Lake*. My room's too narrow to execute it so I head outside to the back courtyard and practice it there under the darkening sky, pushing my leaps higher, sharpening my turns, reveling in the power and the bo staff. A routine begins to gel, and I laugh when I recognize a few kung fu moves from *Fong Sai-Yuk*. Thankfully, only the stone carp is watching me: Ever Wong the dancing dork.

After my shower, I pull on my nightgown and wrap my wet hair in a towel. On my way to my room, my feet dance the new combination: rapid footfalls, a lunge, a one-footed turn—

A scream behind me rips me from the dream.

Sophie races up the hallway toward me, thrusting her arms into her floral blouse. She's bare-legged in nothing but black panties and her matching lace bra. Her blue skirt flutters from her arm.

"You bitch!" Just behind her, Matteo lunges in a drunken stupor, hauling up his pants with one hand. He slips, catching himself on a hand and knee. "You *fucking bitch!*"

Sophie's voice wobbles. "Stay away from me!"

They're back.

I bolt for our door and grapple with the terrible knob, shoving, shoving—*why must you always jam?* Desperation gives me strength and I ram it open, ram her through, tumble after her. She smells of men's shampoo, sweat, and fear. I shove the door shut as Matteo lunges, his beefy face a mask of rage and bloodshot eyes, spewing curses. The door shakes under his weight. I jam the bolt in place, then hang on tight. Under me, the door convulses as he pounds and pounds.

"Bitch-cocktease!"

The door shudders under his blows. The lower hinge splinters and dust bunnies fly over my bare feet while I pray the wood holds fast.

"What the hell, Deng?" snarls a voice outside.

Xavier?

My eyes widen, and Sophie's hand flies to her mouth.

"Fuck off, rich boy. You don't own this hallway." But Matteo's pounding subsides.

Xavier's voice is smooth. Calm. "Why don't we go get a drink, you and me? You need to clean up. I'll meet you downstairs."

Matteo grumbles something I can't make out. Then his footsteps shuffle away. After a moment, Sophie sweeps her hair from her face with a trembling hand. My shoulder's bruised, but Sophie is frantic like a hummingbird's wings. Her eyes are wide with panic, the purple eye swelling shut.

A tap sounds on the door. Xavier. "You girls okay?"

Sophie's eyes flare. "Yes. Fine." She motions for me to keep the door shut. "Thanks, Xavier. I'm fine."

"We're fine, Xavier."

"He's already passed out in his room. I'll be in the lounge down the hallway. Don't worry."

Xavier's standing guard. I'm grateful. "Thank you," I whisper through the crack in the door. I was only lucky he turned out to be a much better guy than Matteo.

After his footsteps fade, too, I turn to Sophie.

"I thought he was going to kill you."

She slumps on her bed, tucking her bare legs up. Mascara runs down her cheeks and she smears it over her face in a grayish splotch.

Her lips narrow, set and furious. "I bit him."

I drop beside her and grab her hand. "It was self-defense. We need to tell the Dragon."

Sophie pulls away with a bitter laugh. "Oh, that'll go over well. The cocktease got a shiner. What'd she expect?"

"*Sophie.*" I clench my nightgown in both hands. She can be so strong for others . . . why not when it comes to herself? "No guy should treat you this way."

"Yes, mum."

I give her a measuring look. "I don't think you know that."

Her good eye spasms and she rubs it impatiently. Then she pulls her legs to her chest and buries her face in her knees. She chokes out a sob. "I can't respect him. Any of them. I can't keep my mouth shut—and they *hate* me for it. Even if all the probabilities were on my side on Loveboat, Aunty Claire's right. No good guy's ever going to want me."

*Oh, Aunty Claire.* "She has an amazing life, but I'd never wish it on you if I had all the wishes in the world." I tuck a length of my friend's hair behind her ears. "Does landing a guy really mean this much to you?"

"A *rich* guy." She pulls away. "Just let me be the horrible person I am, okay? You have no idea. Even Aunty Claire has no idea."

"Try me."

"After the divorce, my mom went to work in a hotel and then some asshole manager slapped her butt and she shoved him onto *his*, and now she's cleaning toilets. I had to give up my dinners to my brothers. Mom comes home with a new gray hair a day. She got ugly in a single year—no one good wants *her* now. I'm never going to be old and poor and thrown away like her."

"You're not your mother. *You* are freaking going to *Dartmouth!*" I give her shoulders a shake. "You negotiate like a *shark* and you're smarter than ninety-nine percent of the planet. Last I checked, that includes most guys in existence. So why don't you go make your *own* millions of dollars?"

Sophie blinks as if I've spoken pig Latin. But then her legs come down.

"My mom told me not to apply to Dartmouth. Your parents harp on your grades. My mom was the opposite. She said I wouldn't get in, and now that I have, she's worried I'm setting myself up for failure. Like her, I guess."

*How can her mom be so blind?* flares the thought. But another part of me is starting to understand. Like Dad, crushed under the weight of his own wasted education. But instead of pushing her daughter to new heights, Sophie's mom has tried to keep her from the same failures.

"Sophie, you'll run companies someday. You'll get yourself on those most-powerful-women lists." I believe it. "Trust me."

She winds her blanket around her fists. Her eyes are moist. "I have never"—she chokes—"done anything as horrible as what I did to you."

"Yes, it was horrible." But I learned something about myself. That after hitting bottom, I'm strong enough to get on my feet again.

"I knew you wouldn't tell—and you didn't. I wanted to carve your face up for what happened with Xavier. But the whole time I knew you were a better person than me. I knew that was why he liked you more."

"I'm not a better person. I was jealous." In all the ways I was jealous of Megan I was jealous of Sophie. Of Jenna. "I was insecure—and I ended up hurting everyone."

She balls her fists in her sheets. "I printed twenty of your photos. I tried to get the rest back, but I don't know who has them. Or if anyone does."

Twenty. I swallow hard. That leaves five left in the world, unless any one of them made it to the infinity of the internet.

I flip open her blue fan and pass it to her. "Do you think, maybe, you might like to join my dance team?"

Her eyes widen as she takes it. Turns it over in her hand. "What would I do?"

"Dance with us."

She almost smiles.

"I've seen you. You know how to move. I can put you in the center, or the back, anything you want. Just promise me we'll talk to Mei-Hwa about Matteo in the morning."

"Mei-Hwa?"

I nod. "She's not the Dragon. But she knows her. She'll help us figure out the best way to handle this."

Sophie folds down the fan and rubs her cheek uncertainly. "It's not nice when girls tell, right?"

"Or to ever rock the boat."

We fall silent. Then she nods.

"Done." I hug her.

I find Mei-Hwa at breakfast and the three of us retreat to an alcove off the lobby. Mei-Hwa's thin face grows grimmer as we give her the account. Then she springs into action. Fifteen minutes later, Mei-Hwa, Sophie, and I are in the office before the Dragon. Mei-Hwa does all the talking in speedy, flawless Mandarin, about what happened to Sophie, and the shame this could bring on the program.

A half hour later, Matteo is sent packing. He's gone before the kitchen staff clears the breakfast buffet.

Sophie almost cries as she hugs Mei-Hwa, and so do I.

In the afternoon, Sophie, uncharacteristically sober, bruised eye hidden by makeup and the shadow of a straw hat, joins my dance team in the rain-soaked back courtyard. Last night's storm stripped the cypress trees bare of their foliage and like the trees, none of my dancers look happy with her arrival.

"Are you kidding?" Debra scowls under her blue hair and puts her mouth to my ear. "We've worked too hard to let her in to stab us in the back. Especially after what she *did*. Ever, think about it."

I squeeze her hand, grateful for her concern, even if it's misplaced. "It'll be fine," I whisper, then raise my voice. "Everybody! Let's do a run-through."

My dancers are gorgeous in their spandex, T-shirts, shorts, and leggings, fifteen strong and totally different body types all moving to the rhythm. Sophie sits on a bench and watches critically. For what, I'm not sure. She doesn't seem inclined to dance with us. I don't know how to include her, though I want to find a way, and then I'm distracted by the dance itself. As it progresses, that gap—the thing I'm missing—becomes more apparent to me. Like a hole in a parachute keeping the performance from taking its proper shape.

"You're not smiling, Ever," Laura says when we finish. "What's wrong?"

"I'm sorry. That missing tent pole . . ."

"I see it, too." Lena adjusts her red headband. "Why don't *you* do a solo? Something that *moves*. Covers the stage. We'll form up around you."

"I'm not allowed—"

"The Dragon doesn't have to know," Debra says. "Not until you walk onstage and by then, it'll be too late. You're our best dancer. If we're going to nail this performance, you need to be in it. You know it, too."

The Dragon *did* send Matteo packing, but her help today doesn't make me immune to her fire. I imagine the Dragon rushing the stage, seizing me by my collar: *Stop the music!* I imagine the Dragon *not* rushing the stage, me dancing before those guys who've ogled my naked photo. My skin crawls backward.

But Debra's right.

"We can't let her find out," I say. The girls swear on it.

"We have to be extra careful about practice."

"We will."

I start by improvising around them, weaving in and out of the three groups. I tug on Debra's ribbons, cut through the spaces, try out some of my new kung fu–inspired steps. The pleasure of doing this thing I love, surrounded by their energy, finally eclipses my worries.

"It's an improvement," I concede, reaching for my water bottle. "It ties the parts together. But it's still missing something— energy, *gravitas.*"

"You need a drummer." Sophie speaks up for the first time. "I'll ask Spencer. He's in the dragon drums elective. Also, what are you doing for costumes?"

"I figured we'd find dresses in the night market."

"I'd recommend blue, green, and orange for the three groups

so the audience can follow along better. Red or white for Ever to stand out. My aunt has a great tailor in Taipei who's really reasonable—I'll take charge. And one more thing. Your talent's wasted just doing the Chien Tan show. Our auditorium's all folding chairs and old curtains. I'll talk to Uncle Ted. The National Theater sometimes needs opening numbers."

I choke on water. "The *National Theater*?"

"So we'd do *two* performances?" Some of Debra's animosity fades.

"One for Chien Tan. One for Taipei." Sophie smiles shyly—thrilled and awed, as if she's walked into a stadium and caught a flyball.

I return her smile. Then I back up to see the group better. "All right, let's do another run—"

I bump into a firm body behind me. A warm arm. All eyes shift over my shoulder and widen.

I know who he is before I turn around.

I'd forgotten how beautiful he is in the flesh, even with his travel-rumpled jet-black hair and wrinkled olive shirt. He's slung his backpack on his shoulder, holding it there with a muscled arm. His earbuds are twisted together and draped in a loop over his neck.

His amber eyes meet mine, a sadness in them mixed with a newer light.

"Rick," I croak. "You're back."

**29**

I have to hold back from flinging myself at him. "I wasn't sure you were coming back."

"I just got in." His eyes travel over my team. "What are you doing?"

My face aches from smiling. My heart thumps with a million questions. "A dance. For the talent show."

"Ever choreographed it," Laura says.

"No kidding?"

"It was your idea," I say.

"I'm going to drop off my stuff." He hitches his backpack higher. Runs a hand through his hair, uncharacteristically nervous. "Will you—come by when you're done?"

The girls exchange glances and I pick up a fan off the ground, wanting to hide my face before I give away how nervous he's made me.

I fight to keep my voice casual. "We're still rehearsing. I'll be by in fifteen minutes."

Seven minutes later, I knock on Rick's door. The door opens with a waft of steam. Rick in blue plaid boxers peers out, a white towel over his bare shoulder, hair damp and slick from his shower. My eyes slide down his tanned chest to his muscled midriff—*oh my*—and shoot back to his amber eyes.

"Sorry," I blurt, flustered. "I couldn't focus. Came earlier."

He's as embarrassed as I am. "No problem. Let me change."

I catch his freshly showered scent as his door closes behind me. I turn my back and face the wood of his door, braid my fingers together. He's back. Of course he's back. He said he'd be. He said he'd talk to me then.

"Why did you go to Hong Kong?" I blurt at his wall. "Why were you gone so long? Was something wrong?"

"Yes and no. All set." His striped T-shirt eases my ability to look at him.

"Was Jenna with you?"

He blinks, surprised. "You heard about that?"

"Xavier told me."

Rick frowns. "He must have heard me on the phone with her. Here." He slips a stack of photos into my hand, modestly facedown. "I cleared out the guys' lounge but then everything

313

happened and I didn't get a chance to get these to you. I'm sorry. I should have called to let you know."

"Oh—" My face flames. The edges cut into my palm as I thumb through them—four—then shove them out of sight into my pocket. I'm not sure which is worse—that he's seen all of me, shoulders to toes, or that he's seen all of me and is as indifferent as if I were the Statue of Liberty. My eyes fasten to his knees. "I never meant for them to get out."

"I figured. You okay? Marc told you, right?"

"Oh, *Marc*." A laugh bursts from my lips. "He told me just enough to make me paranoid." I clamp my mouth shut—I hadn't meant to admit that. I still can't look at him.

Until he puts his hand under my chin, and lifts my head. In his face, I don't see judgment. Just concern. And a question.

Then he releases me. He picks up his cap and puts it on his head. "Let's go somewhere we can talk. There's a favorite place of mine across the river."

My chin still burns from his touch. "I'm not allowed off campus."

Rick glances out his window into the courtyard below. "I'll get you out."

Fan-Fan, the guard in the booth at the top of the driveway, merely winks at Rick as we pass. How easy it must be to walk through life when you're Rick Woo. But I'm no longer irritated.

314

Reputation matters. It can make your life easier or harder. Rick's earned his the good old-fashioned way.

The sun burns overhead as we cross several streets rushing with honking cars and mopeds, and an overpass over the Keelung River. I fill Rick in on losing Odette, the new dance with my girls, my parents' threat to bring me home, and he goes from pissed at Sophie to sober when I tell him about Matteo.

"If he were still here, he'd have to answer to me." Rick yanks me out of the path of an oncoming scooter. "My family has the worst track record. Half my aunts and uncles have had their marriages blow up because someone cheated or beat on someone. Including my parents. Soph's, too. Sometimes I wonder if this is how Sophie and I ended up where we did."

"Where you did? What do you mean?"

He glances away. "I'll tell you when we get to where we're going." The traffic thins as he leads me down a sidewalk toward a walled complex, fronted by a Taiwanese-style gate of dark wood beams hung with red paper globes. The four corners of its roof flare upward in the traditional swallowtail style, muted and elegant in dark brown and cream. "Thanks for taking care of Sophie. I'm glad you"—he hesitates—"and Xavier . . . were there."

Xavier. My stomach cinches. Rick seems to be waiting for a response, but I move past him and step over the threshold into the complex.

Carved-wood doors slide open to sunlit grounds like none I've ever seen: a jagged rock labyrinth, arched bridges of redbrick layered on gray stones, a maze of curvy white walls, inset with glassless windows shaped like flowers, pomegranates, clouds, even butterflies. A long, low brick mansion lies across the courtyard, with several smaller buildings to the right. A few families stroll the grassy knoll.

"I didn't even know this place was here," I say, awed.

"It's Lin An Tai. It's the former residence of an old family named Lin, from the 1700s. I came here when I was a kid." Rick moves toward an asymmetric archway curved like the leg of a harpsichord. "It felt like falling into a Chinese Narnia."

"Oh, it totally is!" It's so beautiful, it makes me want to dance.

"I've been coming here to think. It's kind of my secret place."

I follow him over brick walkways and through circular archways, emerging onto a pond floating with white flowers and lily pads, orange carp swimming beneath. Two pavilions, crowned by rusty-brown pagoda roofs, sit on adjacent shorelines. We move into one and I brace against the wooden railing, my feet moving gently to the music of insects, the gurgle of a distant waterfall. Rick stands beside me. Our elbows connect and neither of us pulls away.

"Why were you fighting with Xavier?" I ask finally.

He drops a pebble into the pond, making ripples that run into the lily pads. A second pebble follows the first. Followed by a third. I wonder how many pebbles it would take to fill this pond, with the things he's deciding not to say.

"First day of Chien Tan, David was running his mouth about girls in the yearbook, and Xavier made it known he was targeting you. In a total asshole way." I feel a stab of anxiousness—I don't want to know what Xavier the Player said that made Rick warn me off him, even if that's no longer how I see Xavier.

"I'd told him to stay away from you. After Aunty Claire freaked out about you and him, I went looking for him, but he'd left already, and then I came back to campus and found your pictures everywhere, and when I ran into him—I—I assumed. Then I guess I lost it."

My feet have stilled, rooting themselves to the floorboards.

"But Xavier and I—talked. At the nurse's. I saw one of his drawings of you. By accident. And I realized he was your artist. Maybe he was just putting on a show for the guys before. And I guess you probably knew he honestly liked you and you could take care of yourself. And that—" He pauses. "Makes me think better of him."

I can't help cringing as I imagine the conversation: Rick holding an ice pack to Xavier's nose. Checking out Xavier for me, like the big brother he promised to be.

"You shouldn't have told Aunty Claire we were pretending," I blurt. "You ruined everything."

"I wasn't about to let the family think things about you that weren't true." He crosses his arms, his brows kneading into a stubborn line. "You were doing me a favor. I was the one too chicken to stand up to them in the first place."

There's truth in that. And I'm relieved Aunty Claire knows I wasn't cheating on Rick.

"But she must think I cheated on Sophie."

"Sophie ignored Xavier all weekend." He frowns. "Anyways, you won over Fannie. She was disappointed you didn't take her pet frog with you."

"Her *pet*?" The ribbiting terror in my shower was a *gift*.

"But you made it better, too," he continues. "It took standing up for you for me to realize what I wasn't doing for Jenna. What I wasn't *willing* to do for Jenna. How wrong that was." A fourth pebble follows the others to its watery grave.

"Rick, what happened in Hong Kong?"

His forehead creases into lines. Then he starts from the pavilion, floorboards creaking under his weight. A dragonfly shoots over the grass after him, quick darting movements from flower to flower. I follow him to the Qing-style mansion and through sliding paneled doors into an inner courtyard, where sunlight spills over scalloped eaves onto a square of dirt floor. More carved, paneled doors on three sides slide open to bedrooms displaying historical Chinese furniture. The scents of parched grass and oiled wood float on the wind, but despite the peaceful setting, my mind whirs like the leaves sweeping ahead of us.

Rick tugs me down onto a bench. "All these years, I've stomped all over Jenna. We've done everything I wanted, never anything she wanted."

Honestly, it's what I'd have expected from Boy Wonder, before I met him.

"Did you ask her what she wanted?"

"I tried. She never wanted anything. And me—I guess I want the world."

"And you go for it. And I—" I swallow my pride. "I admire that about you."

"I told you Jenna needs certainty. Stability. I was always off doing crazy things, in her eyes—traveling for games, competitions, championships. Coming here all summer. I made her so nervous and I felt so guilty. All the time."

I'd worried he'd break Jenna. Is he saying he did?

"A year ago, I tried to end things. I told her that in the long run, we'd be better, stronger people apart than together. We were in her kitchen. Cutting a loaf of bread we'd picked up. And she—" He rubs his thumb over those white scars inside his fingers. "She started crying and saying she couldn't anymore, couldn't take her parents, school, *life,* without me. She grabbed the knife and—"

Oh, no. *No.*

"I grabbed hold." He opens his palm to sunlight. Under its harsh yellow rays, the four inch-long scars line up in their row.

"Oh, Rick." I press my fingertips to them. Stiff, dense tissue. Cut to bone. I remember how easily he'd pulled the cupcake guy off me at the club. Now I imagine him, terrified, hanging on to the blade with all his strength.

"So you stayed with her."

"I couldn't take the chance she'd eventually go through with it."

"But what if she was just—"

"Manipulating me?"

I hate that word. "What if she was just saying it?"

"This probably sounds like I have Stockholm syndrome, but she's not a manipulative person. Not intentionally. She was horrified when I got these." He curls his fingers over the scars. "She's never forgiven herself—just sewed on another big stone to her suit of failures. Part of me thinks maybe she did it because I was there and she knew I'd stop her. Either way, I couldn't risk leaving her."

"And you didn't tell anyone? Not even her parents?"

He hangs his head. "She made me swear. I told everyone it was an accident. We were chopping vegetables. The knife fell and I stupidly grabbed it."

What they've gone through—I can't seem to grasp it. How did she feel in that moment that the line was crossed? How did Rick? Guilt swells in my throat. Rick's whole family—Sophie, even me—have been hating on Jenna, who needs help more than anything. I put a hand on his arm. "Were you angry?"

"More terrified. I stayed, and things got better and she even started volunteering at that horse camp. After a while, in my mind, we were a done deal. We grew up together. We'd been together forever and weirdly enough, the only thing we didn't do was sleep together. Maybe it's the one thing I did right. Even though I thought—I know this sounds insane—but I thought I was going to marry her."

I pull free. "Oh my God, what is with your family? Rick, you're *eighteen*."

"And I've been taking care of my mom and sister since I was fourteen. I opened a bank account before I could drive. I'm the eldest son of an eldest son of an eldest son. You know the last thing my dad said when he left us? He said, 'You'll have to be the man of the house now." I hated him for it. For abandoning my mom when her RA flared out of control and the going got tough. But I took what he said to heart.

"And I couldn't be like him. Not with Jenna—I couldn't do that to her."

I can't believe how trapped he's been—is—not only by Jenna, but by his own principles, his impossibly high standards for himself, and his integrity. That night on the balcony under the crescent moon—he'd been worried about her.

"This is why you're transferring to Williams."

Rick plucks a long blade of grass. Twists it around his finger. The greeny scent of the crushed stem wafts on an uptick of wind.

"Every time I've come here on this trip, I wanted to show this place to you. Because you reminded me of my little sister, I told myself. You getting into one crazy situation after another with me. And out again." His entire finger is a grass tube. He releases the blade, which springs free in a soft coil. "That night on the balcony, when we climbed down the pipe, I—I almost kissed you. I'm sorry I was so rude then—I was mad at myself. I told myself it was because you were so pretty, and I was just a typical asshole.

"But at my aunt's, I finally admitted there was more to it than that. I called Jenna and told her we needed to break up." His eyes go strangely blank, as if he's buried away all other feelings trying to bury this one. He pulls out his phone and shows me a black-and-white photo of a robin flat on the earth. "She texted me this overnight."

The photo is eerily beautiful: the bird on its side, as if asleep, its tiny beak outlined against the dirt, its feathered wing spread forward to modestly conceal its feet.

"Is it—?"

"Dead."

My mouth goes dry. "What does it mean?"

"When we were younger, she used to bury every bird we found drowned in the pond behind our houses. She'd mark their grave with a rock and cry over them. She took this photo because she said it looked so peaceful.

"I was terrified she'd do something . . . irreversible. And I realized it was stupid to have tried to take care of her on my own. I called her mom and told her everything. She had no idea.

"Then both her parents called me. Her dad was in Hong Kong, so I made arrangements to fly out to meet him in person. Jenna had booked a ticket to Taipei, and switched her plane ticket there. I agreed to wait for her, but she didn't end up coming. She tried three times over the week, and just couldn't step onto the plane."

I can't help feeling a swell of compassion for her. I don't know what it means to feel that helpless. That frail.

"I can't believe . . . all these weeks, these years." Not the Boy Wonder I'd imagined and hated, but a scared kid, trying to do right. "Did you come to Taiwan for space?"

His eyes widen. He looks sick. "Sort of horrible, isn't it? She's terrified of flying and so I went where she couldn't. She told me once that I had no soul. Maybe she was right."

I once thought the same thing, and it shames me now. "You stayed with her *because* you have a soul. More than most. But you never—" I break off. "Does she have a counselor?"

"She saw one a few times. Hated him."

To struggle with all this on her own—no wonder she'd clung to Rick. "It takes time to find the right counselor. My dad's a big fan of counseling, maybe because of Pearl's dyslexia."

"Her dad said he'd do everything he could to find the best one."

I stand and cross to the doorway, facing the courtyard. The wind sweeps the dry grasses all the way to the jagged rock labyrinth by the entrance. I don't ask why he didn't tell anyone else. I know the philosophy: you don't tell on your family to outsiders. Police and authorities aren't to be trusted—what if they took you away? But he's been so *trapped*. This is why he was as hell-bent on breaking out as I was.

Jenna wasn't the only one wearing a suit of stones.

I sense rather than hear him approach from behind.

Without turning, I ask, "So you don't think of me . . . like a little sister?"

His hand falls on my shoulder and I pivot slowly to face him.

I don't know who moves first. But then I'm in his arms. His fingers grip the back of my neck. His other hand fists in the silk at the small of my back and his morning shadow scrapes my chin as his mouth comes down on mine.

His kiss hits deep in my chest. The *rightness* of his lips, his warmth, his arms holding me tight. There's nothing gentle or

323

tender in this kiss—he's strong enough to snap me in half and my fingers slide into his coarse hair as I pull myself to him. He tastes clean, like spring water and mint, and his tongue sweeps my mouth and stirs something deep inside me that I've glimpsed only when I'm lost in a dance. It scares and thrills me.

But at last, we both come up for air. He rests his forehead on mine, holding my gaze. Panting gently, matching me breath for breath. His lips are pink, kiss-swollen. His hands slide to the insides of my elbows. His amber eyes have darkened with a desire, a hunger that buckles my knees.

"What are you thinking?" I whisper.

"The timing makes no sense." His voice is hoarse. "I shouldn't want to be with anybody—after everything—"

His mouth takes mine again. My blood pounds through my veins. I want to slam the doors shut and tackle him to the dirt and let him quench all his hunger on me.

Then I put my hand to his and gently pull free. I shiver in the vacuum left. But I need to say this.

"You just broke up," I say with difficulty. "From a really hard relationship."

His hands return to my arms. "I'm not on the rebound, Ever. If I'd never met you, I wouldn't have known, but now I do. I want to be with someone like you. I want to be with *you*."

I believe him. Boy Wonder always knows what he wants . . .

"I don't want to lock you into another relationship. You need time."

"It wouldn't be a lock." His grip tightens. "Ever, I've never felt as free as when I'm with you."

I draw on every ounce of self-control to keep from flinging myself at him. But I can't, I *won't*.

I pull free of his arms.

"Is it Xavier? He was your artist. He—"

I put my finger to Rick's lip, silencing him. "We can hang out, okay? The Tour Down South is in a few days."

Those bear brows contort with a frown. "So we'll be tour buddies?"

I grimace. "Tour Buddies might be worse than Little Sister. But better than Fake Girlfriend, which wins worst idea on the planet."

"It was yours." His half smile almost makes me reconsider. A trill in the rafters explodes as two birds swoop down in an effortless dance of flight.

Why am I resisting?

Then it hits me. "I have an idea. I just hope it's not the second worst idea on the planet."

He looks apprehensive, suddenly. "What?"

"How about we be Dance Partners? For my talent show performance."

He wrinkles his nose. "Let me guess. A hippo in a tutu? *Fantasia?* I'll do it, of course, but I don't want to spoil your show."

I laugh. "No." I let myself hug him, fast, then let go. "Will you do a bo fight with me?"

## 30

"Ever, I love you, but this is a terrible idea," Debra says flatly.

She crosses her arms and leans against the basin of the carp fountain, whose never-ending spout of water splashes merrily. It's nearly nine o'clock, after my dance team's first run-through with Rick. The other dancers have left, but four of us—Debra, Lena, Rick, and I—are still in the back courtyard. Overhead, stars speckle the night sky.

"I'm expanding the definition of dance." I spin my bo staff, then raise it fast to block a lazy swing from Rick. "Mulan does it." I'm giddy from our hour of nimble-footed experimenting. Another guy might have frozen up jumping in cold, but Rick's rolled with it and we'd lunged at one another like a pair of tigers, brandished our bos, circling, filling in the space between the dancers. And the flow, the current between us, the crackle of *energy*—

"Not the stick fight. It's awesome. But you two." Debra points between Rick and me. "Someone has to say it. This is *Loveboat*. If you break up—"

"We're not dating." I dodge a jab from Rick aimed at my midriff.

"And my blue hair isn't growing out. You guys have a falling out, that's the end of this show we've all worked our asses off for."

"Come on, Deb." Lena the peacemaker tosses an arm around my neck, the other around Debra's. "It's perfect now, you said so yourself."

"And we're *not* having a falling out." I spin my staff as fast as I can, making my hair fly with its wind.

Debra turns on Rick. "What are you going to say when the guys rag on you for dancing with a bunch of girls?"

"Marc already did." He spins his bo, drops it. "For six miles up and down the Keelung River."

"Really?" I lower my staff, dismayed.

"I told him to go find his own dance team if he was so jealous."

I laugh, but Debra slings her bag onto her shoulder, still frowning. "Bed check time, Ever."

As Debra and Lena head off, I look up at Rick, still laughing. "This was exactly what the dance needed. Like snapping the last gear into a clock."

Rick spins his bo staff again, and it slips again. "I'll get this," he vows.

I whirl mine in another 360. "You're *so* competitive."

We start toward the dorms and he tosses the staff and catches it. "I don't want to ruin your show."

"You won't."

His arm sweeps wide and he pulls me into the dampest hug in history.

"Ug, you're soaked!" I shove him off and he grabs my arm and shakes his sweaty hair at me while I shriek, "Rick! Stop!"

The lobby doors open with a soft squeak. Xavier steps out, moving from lamplight into the shadows of night. His eyes are downward focused, on the sketchpad in his hands. The wind ruffles the wavy black hair falling into his face, his black shirt.

Then his eyes rise to meet mine and I jerk free from Rick.

"Xavier—"

The sketchbook drops as he pivots on his heel.

"Xavier, wait!" I call, but he's gone.

"I'm sorry." Rick's staff has stilled. "That was my fault. I'll go get him for you."

My hands shake as I recover Xavier's sketchbook and try to uncrush its corner. "No, it's my fault. I should have talked to him sooner."

"I have good and bad news," Sophie says, as her hairdresser lathers a mountain of shampoo into her dry hair. "Which do you prefer first?"

My own scalp is getting massaged off my cranium, and it feels amazing. Shampoo parlors like this one are another Taiwanese specialty we're cramming in to celebrate the end of classes, and our last night before the Tour Down South.

As for good versus bad news, bad news makes me think of that last still-missing photo. Even with Rick and my girls helping me, no one knows who has it, or if anyone does.

"The good news," I say.

"Your dress is almost ready for your solo. The tailor agreed to take half the payment in ad space so it's completely affordable. It's red, like we talked about—you're going to be so *sex-ay*."

Maybe my photos are on my mind, but I don't want to be sexy onstage. Not with all those eyes on me. I wish I could monitor the costume-making myself, but between dance practice and wrapping up classes, all I've been able to do is send internet pictures I liked with Sophie.

"Is it low-cut? How short's the skirt?" I sound like Mom. But it's not her talking this time, it's me.

"I'll make sure it's not too much. Promise."

"What's the bad news?"

"The National Theater is booked solid. Uncle Ted's trying to get us added onto a matinee performance as the warm-up show, but it's not looking good."

I'm more disappointed than I expected. Three tiers of 1,498 velvet seats—the National Theater would have been the biggest thing I've ever done. The crowning moment for the last dance of Ever Wong.

"Anything we can do to convince them?"

She shakes her head. "I asked Uncle Ted if we could do a weekday. He said we *might* be able to get a Monday slot, but it will just be us. No audience, besides Uncle Ted and Aunty Claire."

I bite my lip. "Do they know I choreographed the dance?" Would they support us if they did?

"I didn't tell them," Sophie says, and we both fall silent.

Our hairdressers rinse our hair with warm water from a handheld showerhead, somehow managing to keep the rest of us dry. As they towel off our hair, I say, "If we did Monday, we could host the *whole* talent show there. The Dragon would jump at the chance."

"The whole show?" Sophie purses her lips. "No Chien Tan talent show has ever performed at the Theater."

"Well, maybe they should. Mike Park's doing a stand-up comedy routine that aired on his local channel. Debra met a guy that played piano at Carnegie Hall. There are five hundred kids here to mine for talent!" My smile feels tight. Xavier should showcase his work. I have his sketchbook, more masterpieces, but many more blank pages. I tried to catch him in Mandarin and Calligraphy, but now he's the one slipping out ahead of me. He won't speak to me, not even to let me know he passed his final exam yesterday, which I saw when the Dragon posted our grades. Twenty percent was based on a conversation in Mandarin, which he must have aced, and which I passed thanks to *his* tutoring.

We were building a friendship, now I've lost it.

"I'll talk to Li-Han. And the Theater." Sophie frowns. "We'll need the Dragon's okay. I mean, she *should* be okay with it, but coming from us . . ."

"She can't turn it down if it's good for all Chien Tan." But I'm worried, too. "Let's cross that bridge when we get there."

We break to thank and tip our hairdressers, then start back toward campus. "You know, you're good at this," I say. "This making-things-happen business."

"You think so?" Sophie tucks her clipboard into her bag.

"Must run in your family." Rick and his bazillion competitions, championships, even his trip to Hong Kong. "You're as happy doing this as trying on dresses. Or getting good deals."

I smile but she doesn't laugh. "My mom or Aunty Claire, they'd tell me—" Her mouth quirks. "Nice girls aren't bossy."

Will we ever be free? I hug her a fierce one. "Nice is *so* overrated."

The Tour Down South runs at breakneck speed.

Rick and I share a seat at the back of Bus A, one of eleven luxury buses porting all Chien Tan around the island. Our caravan navigates highways raised on long concrete stilts, putting us on eye level with the leafy canopies of treetops. A plume of smoke rises from skylines of neighboring cities, with modern buildings accented by those swallowtail roofs and Chinese architecture. The cityscape gives way to farmland, glass-roofed greenhouses. Concrete dikes dam silvery-blue waterways. The mountains are giant scoops of green leaves.

At the Taroko Gorge, our bus drops us off between the two sky-high cliffs, covered with emerald mosses and cut through by a river that swirls aquamarine, turquoise, sapphire. Rick and I race ahead at a mile-eating pace. I can hardly believe it—this otherworldly blue water, my feet dancing-leaping over the rocks and Rick loping beside me—is all real.

"Everything there is to Ever Wong, lightning round," Rick says. "Answers only. Game?"

A dam's opened for him. We're talking nonstop.

"You have to answer, too," I say.

"Sure. Favorite book?"

*"Harry Potter."*

*"American Born Chinese."*

"Oh, I love that one!"

"Favorite food?"

"Mangoes."

"Country fried steak. With gravy."

"Seriously? *So bad* for you."

"No commenting!"

"Right, sorry."

"Marshmallow test—did you make it?"

"What?"

"You know, that test when we were, like, five years old. You can eat one now, or wait and get two, which is better."

"Er, um, I ate the one. You?"

"My mom got called away for ten minutes. I waited the whole time."

"Show-off."

"Yep. Greatest fear?"

"Getting injured so I can't dance." I frown. "Let's not go there."

In the night markets, we sample street food, from griddled mochi cakes to shaved snow to pig ears on sticks. Rick makes me try deep-fried stinky tofu. I retaliate with duck tongue. We fold grasshoppers out of bamboo leaves. He buys a miniature grandfather clock for his mom, who collects dollhouses; I buy a stuffed platypus for Pearl—and at every turn, he finds excuses to touch me, pushing money into my hand, running his palm down my back, around the curve of my waist.

"Tour Buddies, remember?" I swat at him, pretending to scowl. "Just Tour Buddies!"

"Sorry, I forgot again." He hides his hands behind him and grins like Cookie Monster. He's wearing that canary-yellow shirt I wore home from Club KISS, and even though it still makes him look jaundiced, I can't help wanting to grab those hands back.

Our buses pass through the Tropic of Cancer on our way to the southernmost tip of Taiwan, which is shaped like a swallow's tail. Rick's fingers linger on my arm as we walk dirt paths between deep green fields of vegetation to peacock-colored waters, stand at the juncture of three seas, which looks simply like the sea, with no recognition of the human divisions assigned to its ebbs and flows. I taste salt on the wind and we laugh as the enlarged Gang of Four—now the Gang of Five—Sam, David, baby-faced Benji, Peter, and Marc—line up with their fingertips together, in prayer before a rock shaped like Nixon's head.

"What are you now?" I ask, as a friend snaps photos. "Which stereotype are we taking back this time?"

"Five Wise Asian Sages," Marc answers without opening his eyes.

"We Asians," Sam intones. "Are *so* wise."

I feel a warm surge of affection. I'm not the only one taking charge of my identity this summer.

I lift my phone camera. "Smile for the Take-Back-the-Trope photo collection!"

Five wise sages bow deeply to me. "Well spoken, our daughter."

Time for dance practice has grown tight. With tombs and caves and temples to explore, our buses arrive later at each new five-star hotel, then we search out a space to practice away from the Dragon's eyes.

In a basement ballroom of our Kenting National Park lodging, reflected in a wall-length mirror, Debra plugs speakers into her phone and the sixteen of us run the whole routine. Spencer and Benji, recruited by Sophie, cart in wooden drums as big as themselves.

"Wow, where'd you find those?" I dance my fingertips over the leather drumskin, making them sing.

Spencer grins. "The night market sells all."

My dancers form up again, and Spencer and Benji rain down whole arm beats that echo off the walls, punctuated by the crack of Rick's and my staves. Locked in battle, Rick and I swing, dodge, feint. He misses a step, then tosses down his bo with a groan and I throw a jump-kick at his stomach and he grabs my foot and makes me hop wildly, fighting for balance, and my dancers beat him with their ribbons, and then he's laughing, and I'm laughing, and we're all laughing.

When we finish the next run, applause rings out. The double doors are crowded with hotel staff in checkered shirts and a women's tour group from Holland—I hadn't realized we'd gathered an audience.

"Did you come up with that on your own?" asks a honey-blond woman in yoga pants.

Sophie points to me. "She did."

"It's fantastic." Lena's eyes shine. "This is what I mean, Ever. Not everyone can pull something like this together."

I blush. A shutter on the burglar's lantern has cracked. Rays of the supernova are escaping. "It's still hard to believe this is happening." Or that it's mine.

Sophie passes around a box of green-tea cookies, then I check the hallway for counselors, and the team leaves two by two.

"You ready, Rick?" Spencer slides his dolly under his drum.

"Yep." Rick draws me into a quick hug. When he pulls away, a letter is tucked into my hand, and Sophie is gazing at us over her clipboard, her face speculative.

As he and Spencer head out, I gather up a few stray cups from our snack break. Then I grab the last cookie and set out with Sophie.

We are passing a housekeeping cart of blankets and sheets when Mei-Hwa brushes by, her skirt swishing red, green, and yellow about her. She gives me a small smile.

"*Wǎn' ān.*" Good night. Then she glides ahead, graceful in her own right. For a moment, I want to call after her—tell her we're dancing to "Orchid Grass," her favorite song. The one she introduced me to the night I hit bottom. But Mei-Hwa has a job, and if she found out what we're up to, she would be obligated to tell the Dragon, just as she did about Matteo.

"Did she see you dancing with us?" Sophie whispers as we hurry up the stairs to the lobby. We're already a few minutes past my curfew.

"No, of course not," I say with more certainty than I feel.

At the elevators, Sophie presses the button. She touches Rick's letter in my hand. "What exactly happened with Jenna?"

I choke on a bite of cookie. "He didn't tell you? They broke up."

"And she accepted it? Just like that?"

I blink. "I assume so. I mean, what else—"

"I have a hard time believing she'd let him go just like that."

I frown. He'd tried before to break up with her. Sophie knows that. But she doesn't know what really happened then. "Why were you so hard on Rick and her?"

"Where even to start?" She purses her lips. "Jenna's a smart girl. She likes science. She headed up the chemistry club at school, and she's in the knitting club, too. Shelly *worships* her. You'd think with her looks and brains and money, she'd be more confident. But even with Rick telling her over and over that she was beautiful, she had surgery to make her eyes bigger. She dropped volunteering at the children's clinic because some guy cracked a joke about it."

"Really?" I understand how she feels. My own eyelids, like Sophie's, are single-lined instead of double with an upper crease. I used to avoid looking in the mirror with my Caucasian friends, because my eyes seemed small by comparison. If I'd had the money and the chance to stop Cindy Sanders from pulling the corners of her eyes at me through elementary school, would I have taken it? Maybe half a year ago. But now, here among beautiful eyes like Sophie's, I wouldn't trade mine for anything.

"I know, who am I to judge, right?" Sophie says. "But I was fed up with him carrying her around like an invalid. She clung to him like he was her life preserver."

That's because he was. "He worries about her—"

337

"She's eighteen. Grow up already." She jabs repeatedly at the button. "This is the slowest elevator on the island."

I open my mouth and shut it again. To Sophie, to Rick's whole family, Jenna was the over-possessive girlfriend. Not someone in trouble.

I want them to know the truth. But her secret isn't mine to tell.

"I never imagined Rick joining a *dance*," Sophie continues. "I haven't heard him laugh like this since we were eleven, when I almost set my aunt's closet on fire."

"What? How?"

"I was checking price tags. In the dark, with a candle. Rick's never let me live it down." I smile at the image of Rick and Sophie, like Felix and Fannie, making mischief. Then my smile fades. I clutch Rick's letter to my chest.

"What was Rick like with Jenna?"

"You mean did he buy her presents? Touch her every time he breathed? Walk around like he's been crowned king?"

My heart sinks. "Yeah."

"No. She was more like his little sister, you know?"

I choke on a laugh. "No, I don't know."

"She asked me once if he liked boys because he barely kissed her." Sophie's smile fades. "She was always so insecure about him. A month ago, I'd have told her not to worry. He'd never let down someone who depends on him."

I love that about Rick. But I feel a twinge of worry, too—is he letting her down now?

"Hey, where's your bo?" Sophie asks suddenly.

"Oh, no." I swivel toward the stairwell. A few guests are emerging, laughing and talking. My stomach clenches. "I left it in the ballroom."

"We should get it." Sophie wrings her hands, eying the clock. "Or the hotel staff will give it to the Dragon and it has your name on it. They'll tell her we were dancing. She'll put two and two together and we're through."

The elevator dings. On cue, the Dragon emerges, heels clicking a staccato warning. Her dark eyes swing to us.

"Ai-Mei, it's past curfew," she says in Mandarin. Sophie curses under her breath. We're too late.

"Ever, you forgot this." Mei-Hwa appears out of nowhere, skirt swishing. The Dragon frowns, maybe at my American name, but Mei-Hwa just presses a blanket-wrapped bundle into my arms. It's stiff and bulky, like an overflowing coat rack.

"Oh!" It's my bo staff, disguised.

"Off to bed. You're late." Mei-Hwa shoves me toward the open elevator before I can speak. Then she takes the Dragon's arm, asking about tomorrow's schedule. The Dragon's gaze strays to the bundle in my arms. Thanking Mei-Hwa with my eyes, I grab Sophie's hand and drag her into the elevator out of fire-breathing range.

Dear Ever,

I'm sorry it's taken me so long to reply to your question about homework. I must have missed your letter when it arrived seven years ago. If I hadn't, perhaps the course of my life would have changed much sooner.

I'm afraid I don't have a lot of wisdom to offer you about homework except that I work my ass off. And picked classes I wouldn't mind spending hours on. I guess I am a bit of a perfectionist, which my favorite physics teacher said is good for school, but sucks for me. I hope you find a more efficient way to get it done.

I am needing some advice as well. I'm hoping you can help. I'm not the best at expressing what I feel. Not in words. But there's this girl. When I first met her, I felt this weird shock, like recognition. Like I'd dreamed her face a hundred times before, but now was the first time I could see it clearly.

When I think back to all the qualities I've admired in people I've met, I find them all in her. She is fearless. Strong and kind. She loves her family so much she struggles with letting them down, even for her own happiness. When I had a problem, she jumped in headfirst to help me. She makes me question the truth of mathematics. 1 + 1 was always 2. With her, 1+1 is exponential.

And when I dance with her, I finally understand. Dancing has to be between two people in balance to work.

*I've teetered on edges my entire life. Now, I'm still walking those crazy pathways, but I'm no longer off-balance. For the first time, I can look up at the sky. And it's filled with stars.*

~

*Ever, when I started writing you this letter, I thought my question would be, how do I convince you of what you mean to me? But now, I realize that's the wrong question. I'm not going anywhere. I'll wait as long as you want me to.*

*Yours,*
*Rick*

I fold his letter down and do a Google search: *How do you know when you're falling in love?*

31

The typhoons grow in severity, sheeting rain against our bus windows and blurring my view of the passing countryside. Our bus quiets as we drive by an entire Puyuma village submerged: tin roof peaks poking up through muddy water like islands swept clean of life. Debris floats everywhere: the spinning wheel of an inverted rickshaw, dead fish flashing silvery underbellies, a muddy doll with her hair and red-, yellow-, and green-striped skirt fanned out around her.

"Was anyone hurt?" Debra asks up front. Our tour guide tells her no, and conversations pick up again.

On the last full day of tour, we arrive at the hot springs resort Sophie has raved about since summer began. A wooden gate leads into a lush grove of trees. *Lán Huā Cǎo* plays from hidden speakers, setting my feet dancing as Rick and I pick our way down a stone path ankle-deep in flood waters, under dripping palm fronds that hang like curved combs, and through a grove of bamboo to the flat-roofed resort beyond. I'm hand in hand with Rick as we've been since his letter, though we haven't kissed again, as though we know that once we do, there will be no holding back that flood.

"I'm a sucker for Jacuzzis," I tell him as we move through the hallways toward my room. After six days of walking the entire southern shore of Taiwan, Love River in Kaohsiung, not to mention dance practice, my sore body is eager to sink into the heated pools.

"Alas, hot springs are separated between men and women." At my door, he hands me my bag, which he insists on carrying.

"Seems kind of old-fashioned."

"Those darn rules." He gives me that sly grin of his that brings to mind naughty things in the dark. His hand grasps the small of my back and he pulls me close, rubs his nose against mine. I close my eyes, anticipating, wanting the touch of his lips on mine.

Then he pulls away. Flashes a teasing smile.

I frown. "You know something I don't and want to lord it over me?"

"Rules are rules." He heads down the hallway, refusing to say more.

"And I'm still breaking them," I call.

Sophie and I tie on pale green yukata robes and set out for the women's hot springs on the ground floor. In a small reception room, a chubby-faced attendant hands us fluffy towels, then gestures with both hands up and down his body. He's about our age, and reminds me of my cousin George. He speaks rapid Mandarin.

"Sorry?" I lean in, not wanting to miss important instructions.

"Naked!" He gestures with alarming enthusiasm.

"Japanese-style." Sophie laughs as we duck through a pair of linen curtains printed with blue cranes in flight. "These hot springs are used nude. He has the key word for tourists."

"Rick told me they're separated by gender. 'Alas.'" I laugh. That sly tone of his. "*Naked.* No wonder."

Debra and Laura are disrobing in the bathroom already. Wall-to-wall mirrors reflect rows of cabinets where we store our robes and slippers. A teapot of red oolong tea steeps among a garden of porcelain cups. Warm air wafts from beyond a curtained doorway, along with the seductive gurgle of water and scent of minerals.

"I'm in heaven," Sophie sighs.

"Me, too." I wrap my towel around myself as the Dragon enters, stout in her own yukata robe, salt-and-pepper hair hidden in a plastic shower cap. My locker key drops with a clatter as her eyes fall on me.

"Ai-Mei," she scolds. "Did Mei-Hwa forget to tell you? No hot springs for you."

My own worries about my last nude photo isn't punishment enough. My parents have struck again.

"Oh, please let her stay," Sophie begins. "It was my fault—"

"It's fine, Soph." I'm already pulling my robe from my locker. For all I know, the Dragon has spies watching our dance, and the last thing I want to hear is, "No talent show for you." I hope Mei-Hwa isn't in trouble now, too.

Debra and Laura shoot me sympathetic glances; Sophie a guilty one. But underlying my disappointment runs a deeper undercurrent of sadness. My parents are trying to rein me in the only ways they know how.

But they can't undo the ways this summer is changing me.

"See you later," I say.

"Ever."

Xavier's voice makes me jump and nearly knock over a vase on a stand holding a purple orchid. He steps from a guest room door and leans against its frame, a sardonic smile twisting his lips like it did in the early days of summer. His T-shirt is paint-smeared and his long box of paintings is under his arm.

"Xavier. Hey." I take hold of my sash, needing something to hold on to myself.

"I was right, wasn't I? The jocks of the world get what they want, don't they?"

I flush. But at least he's speaking to me. "That's not why I like him."

"Then what is it? Those broad shoulders? Yale? The ass-kissing fan club?"

"That's unfair and you of all people should know that. Rick's—" I try to boil it down, what it is, when there's so much, his generosity, his humility, his kindness, his devotion, all the while feeling I shouldn't have to justify myself. "Sometimes we don't have reasons. We just love who we love."

Xavier's eyes flicker. I brace for a laugh.

"I know."

"Know what?"

"We can't help who we love."

He crosses his arms over his box, dark eyes brooding. I wish we could recapture that friendly comfort, but it's gone, elusive as sunlight during this typhoon season.

I let go of my sash. "Thank you for helping with Matteo that other night." It's a long overdue thanks.

He grunts. "Any decent guy would have."

And that's exactly what he is. A decent guy.

"I owe you an apology," I say. "For what happened the night after Aunty Claire's."

"Don't apologize." His jaw works. "You said it yourself. We were both in on it." He pulls the box from under his arm and pulls out a rolled sketch. "You forgot to take this."

The three old men. I hold the stiff, curling paper, trace my fingers around its border, admiring the detail in their beards, the patches on an elbow, the wistfulness he's captured.

"I love it. But I can't accept this."

He unbends a bent corner. "Why not?"

346

"It's too valuable. You can do so much more with it than give it to me."

He gazes at it helplessly. "Like what?"

My throat tightens. "You'll just—know. When the time comes."

"You're so fatalistic." His voice is rough as he rolls the sketch back into a tube. "Well, maybe I am, too. If I'd met you first."

"Xavier . . ." My hand falls helplessly. Was there a reason Xavier and I came together this summer? Outwardly, we're on the same journey—fighting to do our art despite our parents' opposition. And he made me feel attractive when I didn't believe I was. We could have kept it there, but I let it go too far.

"We have to reset." Is that even possible? "I want us to be friends. I want us to *stay* friends."

He slouches against his doorpost. Then he says, "Wait a sec?"

He disappears into his room. When he reemerges, he takes my hand and presses a small photo into my palm. He closes my fingers over it.

"I'm sorry," he says. "It was wrong not to give it back."

My photo. My hand trembles. "*You* had the last one."

"I dated a girl last year who told me I'd pay some day for all the girls I ran over. I guess she was right."

"Xavier, please. Don't—"

"Reset. I'm trying, okay?" His eyes are on his toe, scuffing the carpet. "I'm working on a mural. Maybe I'll even take your advice and stick it to the talent show." With a smile that doesn't reach his eyes, he slips back inside his room and closes the door.

"You can't miss the hot springs. They're the best part of Taiwan." Rick's hand on my elbow guides me ahead of him into the buffet line of the resort restaurant. A row of silver chafing dishes, warmed by tiny blue flames, gives off a mouthwatering aroma.

"You said Snake Alley was the best of Taiwan," I mock-complain. "And the shaved ice. And beer gardens. *And* night markets." Back with Rick, I feel better already about the sting of the ban, about Xavier. I scoop eggplant onto my plate and pass on the black-bean clams, he loads a dozen onto his plate.

"They're all the best." His warmth nestles against my back, magnet to my iron, as we wait for the line to move. "Marc and I found a bathhouse out on our run today. I'll sneak you in after lights out."

"Naked?"

"Those are the rules."

I'd quipped back before I could censure myself, but I feel a thrill. Yes, breaking rules has consequences, and sometimes they're in place for a good reason. But sneaking out is no longer about rebelling. It's going after things I want.

And I want this night alone with him.

"Which way to the onsee?" An over-enunciated male voice, a British or maybe South African accent, breaks through the low rumble of conversation in the restaurant. A tourist and his

348

brunette wife walk through the double doors. Beside them, a balding hotel clerk spreads his hands helplessly, speaking Mandarin. The tourist fusses with his white hat, like he's headed into the Australian outback. His wife pulls a Chinese silk shawl tight around her shoulders.

"Which *way* to the *onsee*?" The man turns to Mei-Hwa as she sails in, bird-like in a red blouse. She tugs her earphones from her ear.

"Sorry?"

He repeats his question with exaggerated loudness.

Mei-Hwa's brow wrinkles with confusion and she flips her long braid over her shoulder. "Sorry, I don't understand."

His voice rises with impatience. "We're *looking* for the *outdoor* onsee."

"She doesn't understand either. Let's go." The wife tugs on her husband's arm.

"Can't speak English properly," he says, loud enough to be heard in Taipei. "No one here speaks a damn word of English."

The color leaves Mei-Hwa's cheeks. Silence falls like a heavy curtain as all conversation ceases in the room. A smear of red crosses my vision. Yes, most staff in this rural part speak almost no English, compared to Taipei. But most Western tourists I've encountered have been respectful, even more so than some Chien Tan students. This man's *tone*—I've heard it before: the woman at McDonald's yelling at Mom, the store clerk who called Dad a stupid chink.

My first instinct is to pretend it didn't happen, as I have all my life. To spare Mei-Hwa the embarrassment, because maybe if we don't acknowledge the disrespect, it won't exist.

But then I set my plate on the buffet and stride toward them.

"You owe her an apology." My hands ball into fists. "She's not your servant. No one here is."

The man turns chili red. At last, someone speaks perfect English.

"We weren't talking to you."

"You were talking to the entire dining hall. And news flash— not speaking your language—*in their own country*—doesn't make anyone less intelligent than you."

Rick's hand braces my back. His disapproval radiates at the man, who scowls up at two hundred pounds of running back.

After a moment, he spits, "Apologies," in Mei-Hwa's direction.

"No problem, sir." Mei-Hwa really is that kind. "I hope you find what you're looking for."

His wife glares at me as she hurries him away. Mei-Hwa puts her hands to her cheeks and gives me a tremulous smile. She bursts into Mandarin, then interrupts herself. "Ah, I always forget you don't understand—thank you."

"Sit with us?"

"My parents called. I need to call them back, but I'll join you afterward." She plants a floral-scented kiss on my cheek, then leaves.

Back at the buffet line, Rick hands my plate to me, then takes it back when I almost drop it. My hands tremble. The dining room chatter is subdued.

Maybe I shouldn't have made a fuss.

But by the time we reach our table, Spencer and Marc are behind us. Sophie is talking to Xavier at his table, then she carries her plate over to join us.

"A woman yelled at my dad to go back to China," Rick says. "We were just walking down the sidewalk. I was six."

"Happened to my mom, too," I admit.

"My dad didn't say a word back," Rick says. "I hated him for that then. But now, I think he was tired of having to fight it."

We're breaking another taboo, talking about racism, but I've just broken a bigger one confronting that guy before the entire restaurant, instead of sticking to that Asian nonconfrontational thing. But these are rules meant to be broken. Something happens to a kid when they see their parent treated like that. Something happens to the parent.

"It's a thousand little deaths," I say. How weird to have come all the way to Taiwan to understand this. Rick takes my hand and squeezes.

"My family always had trouble crossing the US-Canadian border," I say. "Once we got detained overnight, my mom, Pearl, and me, coming back from visiting my uncle." Brusque interrogations while I eyed the guns strapped to holsters, Mom so terrified she dropped and broke her glasses, a night in a grubby motel room we couldn't afford. "When I was old enough to drive, I took over for border crossings. They cut me more slack. You learn to put on a certain face and tone so they leave you alone, right?"

"Or play football so they'll respect you," Rick says quietly.

My fingers tighten in his. Dancing taught me how to charm, a defensive shield. Maybe it's another similarity that drew us together, for better or for worse.

"It's not so bad in LA," Marc says. "In some places, Asians are the majority, even half Asians like me. Worst I got was name calling on the basketball court, but all kids are mean."

"Some people have it even harder." Spencer shreds his sesame biscuit. "One of my friends wears suits when he goes through airport security. He says otherwise, as a black guy, he'll get frisked and it takes too long. First on my agenda when I get to Congress is to overhaul the Department of Homeland Security."

"I'd contribute to your campaign," Marc says. "But I'm going to be a starving journalist. How about I cover you? 'A vote for *Hsu* is a vote for YOU.'"

"Rick will fund your campaign," Sophie says.

"Sophie will *run* your campaign," I offer.

"I could." She tosses her hair. "And once you hit the Oval Office, Ever will be your surgeon general."

"My dad would bust an artery from sheer joy." As for me, I imagine advising the President of the United States as his chief medical officer. No blood involved, just dispensing pearls of wisdom. I would be lying to say the prospect isn't exciting on some level.

But for the first time, I realize it's exciting as someone else's story. Not mine.

"If she wants to do it, she could." Rick kisses my ear, surprising everyone else around the table. How is it that he doesn't know my favorite color yet but understands this part of me so well, better than even I do?

I smile at him. "My first order of business will be to add warning labels to snake-blood sake. It's definitely hazardous to your health!"

Everyone laughs. We're only dreaming, of course. All our parents' lives have been full of struggle.

And yet we want to believe.

A familiar crash of wind shakes the building, setting the white paper lamps swaying overhead. Raindrops accelerate their drumbeats against the windows. Then the lights flicker out, plunging the room into darkness.

A chorus of dismayed cries rises.

"Blackout," Sophie says.

A lighter flares in Rick's hand, illuminating his chin. Matching glows appear at other tables.

The hotel manager addresses us in Mandarin, and Rick translates for me. "There's another typhoon over Taitung, on the southeast coast. Six villages flooded."

"*Six* villages." I recall the doll floating in the muddy waters. "Where will the families go?"

"Who knows?" Spencer says. "Our tour guide said the

shoreline changes every season because of typhoons. They're constantly getting hit."

"How can they live like that?"

"We're so privileged," Rick says, and even on the heels of our talk of racism, he's right.

Our mood is somber as we leave the restaurant. The hallway is lit by pale yellow emergency lights. I bump into Mei-Hwa, pulling her rolling bag. Its cloth is so worn she's bound it with rope to hold it together, something Mom would have done to save money rather than replace it.

"You're not leaving?" I ask, dismayed.

She didn't bat an eye when the tourist yelled at her, but now her eyes fill. "My home in Taitung was hit by the typhoon. My whole village is destroyed. I'm going back to help my parents."

"Oh, no! Your sisters. Your parents—are they safe?"

"Yes, but we've lost everything—our clothes, photos, furniture. Everything's gone."

Like a stage emptied of its dancers, all her joy's been swept away. A ragged sob issues from her throat. I wrap my arms around her, inhaling her floral scent as she clings to me.

"I'm on a scholarship at my university," she says. "How can I afford to stay? How will they survive? What will they do?"

I imagine her parents, already eking out their survival day-by-day, minorities in their own country, sacrificing to give their daughter a leg up. Except for the accident of my birth in the United States, I could have been Mei-Hwa.

The wind blows open the door, gusts a blast of rain over us. I feel helpless as I release her.

"We're doing a dance to 'Orchid Grass,'" I say. "Thanks for sharing it with us."

A genuine smile flits over her face, before it disappears into shadows again.

"Thank you, Ever."

"Please let us know if there's anything we can do."

She nods and wipes tears from her face, then drags her suitcase out into the unrelenting rain.

32

Gurgling water echoes in the darkness. Rick lights a candle. It illuminates a flagstone floor enclosed by a solid fence of bamboo poles, a pagoda roof that partially shelters the square space of this bathhouse, nearly a quarter mile from the main resort.

Rick's already pledged a hundred dollars of his own savings to my collection for Mei-Hwa. It's a start. But she and her family, our talk over dinner all weigh on my mind as I grip the knotted sash of my yukata robe. I dip my toe into each of two pools built of flat stones. The smaller pool is warm, the larger hotter than any Jacuzzi. They smell of minerals. A spring pours from their corners, continuously refreshing them.

Rick slides the Japanese doors closed. "You first. Promise I won't look."

I hear his smile through the candlelit darkness. Some of my worries give way to the thrill of being here with him. Maybe part of fighting the unhappiness in this world is to seize happiness when we can.

He turns his back to study a line of three showerheads facing as many stone stools while I disrobe and slip into sinfully silky waters. They scald with a delicious heat. My bare feet slip over smooth stones as I sink to my shoulders and find an underwater ledge to sit on. The bamboo walls and the closed doors shut out the world.

"Mmm," I groan. "Let's stay here forever."

Rick slips in beside me. His arm glides against mine. I try not to think of that bare chest, the hard muscles of his abdomen. Our hidden nakedness, with nothing but water between us.

"This is the first time we've been alone since you came back from Hong Kong."

"When we were in my room for three minutes? We should have stayed there. Why did I have to show you the Lin mansion?"

"Because it was the best in Taipei," I mock him.

"True." Rick sinks deeper, to his chin. His voice takes on a sly tone. "You know, some *onsen* label themselves nonsexual. Just to be clear. Although the gender separation's been a thing since the Meiji Restoration opened Japan to the West."

"How do you know so much, Boy Wonder?"

"Do I? I guess I read. Everything. And remember all sorts of useless things."

"Not *useless*." I flick water in his direction. "So in theory,

Professor Woo, if two people were to engage in such forbidden activity in this vicinity, they would fly in the face of years of tradition?"

"A hundred thirty. And regulations. It would be *serious* breaking of the rules."

"Too bad."

Moonlight catches his impish smile and he turns to face me and flips a lock of my hair behind my shoulder. Wraps a strand around his fingers. "Does it make me shallow that I'm obsessed with your hair?"

"I didn't know you were obsessed with it."

"It's not just black. It's blue and brown and red. In the moonlight, parts are silver."

"How would you feel about me if I were bald?"

He kisses my forehead. "I *guess* you have other qualities. Meaningful ones. Like your shoulder." His hand glides along the bare skin there. "Your neck."

I push him gently back. "What if I were in an accident and got disfigured? Lost my mind? Not trying to be morbid. Just realistic. Nothing's certain in life."

His hand grasps my waist, drawing my body toward him until my thigh bumps his knee. "Remember how I said the timing makes no sense? But you're here. Like you'd finally shown up and I didn't realize I was looking for you." His voice has turned serious. "Maybe some people are meant to be a part of your life. And we don't have any control over when they drop in. Or over anything else that's going to happen that might take them away again. If I couldn't talk to you anymore"—his lips brush the tip of my nose and hover—"that part of me that needs to talk to you would die."

I kiss him.

His arms close around me, his strong hands grasping my back. My lips part, drinking down his hot mouth, his tongue that tastes of mint and plums. I slide my hand between us, along the planes of his chest, his ribs, exploring his body, those muscled abs. His firm fingers glide down my wet skin to my waist, then come up to thread into my hair and cup the back of my head.

I have no idea how much time passes, or when the stars begin to cluster so thickly overhead that the sky drips with their lights.

We separate at last, dizzy, breathing heavily.

"Why didn't we do that sooner?" I murmur.

"There's more where that came from." His voice is languid, lazy.

"You're so smug."

"Mm-hm."

We slip lower into the water, resting our heads on the ledge, listening to the soft song of crickets in the night. I want to stay in this warm moment with him forever.

But a thought from dinner stabs into my head. A connection clicks and I sit up with a soft splash.

"What did you call this place?"

"Hot springs?" He turns to look at me, his head still resting on the ledge.

"You used a different word. The Japanese word."

"*Onsen.*"

"This is what that tourist was looking for. He said it wrong. 'The outdoor *onsee.*'" And he took it out on Mei-Hwa, while her parents were running for their lives from a flood. My throat swells shut. I can't explain why it makes me so sad to realize the tourist had been in the wrong on two fronts.

"What's wrong?" Rick sits up, alarmed. "Did I hurt you?"

"No. Her parents—" To my horror, a sob escapes my throat. "*My* parents—"

"Come here, you." He pulls me to his chest and I sob against him.

"I'm so sorry," I choke out between hiccups. "I don't know what's wrong with me. This is our one night together and here I am raising the salinity of the hot springs."

His laugh echoes off the waters. "I have never met anyone like you, Ever. Don't worry. We're still having our night." He kisses the top of my head, my cheek. "What are you thinking about?"

I rest my head on his shoulder. I hadn't wanted to burden him, when he's already borne so much for Jenna. But this is Rick: solid, dependable. Maybe it's okay to lean on him. I try to pull together my thoughts, what it is that's been troubling me, not just tonight, but for so many nights.

"My dad's fifty-five. Older than most of my friend's parents. He didn't have shoes until he was nine. His mom cooked noodles with scraps of meat, because they couldn't afford more. When he first came to America, he admired the roads so much, because all he knew were dirt ones. When I was little and spit out meat, he ate it because he couldn't bear to let protein go to waste. And now Asia has built itself up, and meanwhile in the States, my parents have had immigration officers on their backs, and dried-out dragon fruit, and my mom sold her necklace to send me here to learn their culture, and every time I let them down, it's like I spit in their face like that tourist.

"I hate when they remind me, but they *have* suffered. Like Mei-Hwa's family. And no one cares. And tonight, when Sophie said I could be surgeon general—do you know what that would mean to my dad? He's always dreaming about big stuff like that when he's pushing his orderly cart—that's how he's kept himself going. That's how he injured himself; he walked right onto a spill at the Cleveland Clinic and never even saw it.

"But I don't have it in me to get there. And then I thought, what if I *didn't* become a doctor? What if I became a dancer instead? Even wanting it feels like I'm betraying them."

Rick combs through my wet hair, gentle, comforting strokes. "Do you think they want you to be unhappy?"

No matter how angry I've been, I have never doubted they want the best for me. The molecular biology textbook was for my future. My happiness.

"No," I admit. I lift my eyes toward a horizon I can't see. "But I can't talk to them. If they were American, maybe I *could*. Like Megan and her parents. If I were Chinese, maybe I'd want more of what they want, like my cousins in China. No confusing

American messages about individualism and self-actualizing. But they're seven thousand miles away, and even if we were standing in the same room speaking the same words in the same language, those seven thousand miles are always there. This *Great Divide*. Between us."

"It was the opposite with my family." His thumb skims my thigh, then disappears. "They were right about Jenna. And I couldn't hear them. Didn't want to. If I had, maybe I'd have gotten help for her sooner." He rests his nose in my hair behind my ear, inhaling me. "Maybe I wouldn't feel so guilty now."

"Guilty for what?"

"For being happy. Bigger. Like the biggest nesting doll, instead of the smallest version of myself. Not because of her, but who we were together." His voice catches. "I didn't know it was supposed to be like this. Between two people."

Because he's the eldest son of an eldest son of an eldest son, carrying the weight of his name. Not after his own happiness, but the happiness of others.

"Ever." His fingertips brush my bare stomach. "I know you think I'm not ready— "

"Sh." I catch his hand.

Then I draw it to my chest.

His touch is hesitant. Tentative. I place my hand over his, holding him to me.

"Ever, are you sure?"

*We're moving too fast*, whispers a small voice in my head. But I don't want to stop.

"I want you to touch me."

He palms the whole of it, setting me trembling. My fingers find him under the water, and explore, both of us learning each other's muscles and curves and contours. His mouth takes mine again and we move together in a haze of hunger and heat. At some point, I become aware he's pushed me into a corner. The stone edges press into the backs of my shoulders as he kisses my mouth, my chin, the back of my jaw, my neck, his hands still exploring under the water.

"I'm hot," I whisper.

He lifts me by my waist to sit on the edge. He stands between my knees, kissing me as I wrap my legs around his waist, cling to the short silk of his hair.

"I have a confession," he murmurs between kisses. "That first day, sitting beside you in the van, I wanted to kiss you then."

"Was that why you were such a jerk?"

"Was I?"

"Definitely. Where?"

"Where what?"

"Where did you want to kiss me?"

His voice is husky. "Everywhere."

"Then do it," I breathe, and his breathe quickens with an answering hitch. His lips graze my collarbone, presses to the tops of each shoulder. My hands curl in his hair as he lowers his head to my breasts. A laugh escapes my lips.

"Shh." He rises with a soft splash. His lips brush my ear, "Unless you want counselors joining us?"

"No and don't stop," I say, and he dips me gently until I'm lying flat on the stones, gazing past the eaves at the stars, legs still in the water. Bracing his hands on either side of my elbows, he kisses my lips again, a single, chaste point of contact that makes the rest of me burn with jealousy.

"Wait here," he breathes.

"Wait here for what?"

His mouth burns a line down to my belly button. It makes my body quiver like a tightly strung instrument. The splash of water echoes as he slips back into the pool.

And his mouth keeps descending.

Dear God. Is he—?

My stomach dips as his hands part my knees. He slides his shoulders between them, and his hands tuck under my thighs and take hold of my hips. He kisses a trail along the inside of each thigh, his breath warm on my skin, so near and intimate. My palms press the stones, all my body throbbing, unbelieving, as he asks permission to continue, and my whisper *yes* blends with the gurgle of the hot waters.

He takes his time. A slow burn that builds and builds, until I am clawing at the stones and my back arches and my toes splash and my body ripens under his grip.

Until the stars above explode into a billion supernovas of light.

# 33

When I come down for breakfast in the morning, Rick rises from a table for two by a window overlooking a rock garden. The hard body I explored last night is now safely clad in a green T-shirt and sports shorts. He pulls out my chair, and the mischief in his warm eyes, the quirk of those lips that did glorious things to me, makes me blush.

"You're up early," he teases. And when I simply drop into the chair, he feigns surprise. "Someone's in a good morning mood."

"I had a nice night." I open my all-Chinese menu. "You know, the Dragon would be proud. I can read which dishes are soups, meats, vegetables—"

"Nice? Your night was nice?" Rick grabs my waist, angling

for a kiss. My menu drops. "When we get to Sun Moon Lake tonight, I'll show you *nice*."

He kisses me and I tuck my hand into his hair that I am seriously crazy for. Our tablecloth is slipping and we're drawing attention from an older couple the table over, but I don't care. I want to see Rick no longer in control, but laid bare, drunk on pleasure. On *me*.

"Who knew Boy Wonder was so good with his tongue?" I murmur.

He smirks. "I won a speech contest junior year."

"Such a *waste* of talent."

"Hey, guys." Sophie swings a third chair up to our table, glowing in her orange-striped dress. "I got us a spot! I heard the typhoon was jamming up flights so I called the National Theater again and I was right! An acrobatic troop from Singapore had to cancel and now the theater's scrambling. Friday night when we get back to Taipei—it's ours! My aunt and uncle will be there and Li-Han's already agreed to move the whole talent show and open it to the public—now I just need to get the Dragon's okay."

"Wow, Sophie." I pull free from Rick to give myself space to breathe. So many good things are tumbling into my life. "I can't believe it. Yes, I can. The National Theater. You did it."

She swings her black hair over her shoulder. "They'll put posters in their box office windows and send an email to their list. They said we can even charge admissions."

"Seriously?" I scoot my chair forward. "Let's donate the

proceeds to Mei-Hwa's family. To all the families in her village impacted by the typhoon."

"A benefit concert," Rick says. "Perfect."

"I should have thought of it sooner." I hug him, then Sophie. "It'll be a small way to give back to her."

"And what about adding an auction?" Rick says. "It'll raise more money. Then anyone can contribute, even if they can't be onstage."

"Sophie, you can pull it together, I know you can. We could ask everyone to donate stuff. Even Xavier—" I wrinkle the hem of our tablecloth. "Maybe he'd be willing to give us some paintings."

Sophie's hand moves to her ear, involuntarily searching for his opal earring. A small cloud passes over her face.

Then she leaps to her feet. "There's the Dragon. Ever, come *on*."

The Dragon scoops salted egg halves onto her rice porridge as Sophie explains. I shift my weight from foot to foot and at one point, the Dragon sets a finger on her nose and a thumb on her chin, listening like Mom does.

"*Hǎo ba*," she says at last.

"We're on!" Sophie starts to drag me away.

"Ai-Mei," says the Dragon.

I turn back cautiously. "Wei?"

Her hawk-eyed gaze pierces. "This is a fine thing you girls are doing."

Picking up her plate, she continues down the breakfast bar.

"She won't think it's so fine when I walk onstage," I murmur as Sophie and I head back toward Rick. "Especially if our costumes are as sexy as you say."

"By then, it will be *too late*," Sophie sings.

"*Ai-Mei*." Li-Han hands me a green hotel slip as I reach Rick. *"Nǐ bàba dǎ diànhuà lái le."*

"My dad called?" I fight down a stab of panic. I still haven't spoken with him since the nude-photo call.

Li-Han hands a second slip to Rick, who frowns. "Jenna? I thought she didn't want to talk to me."

I resist the urge to tear both slips into confetti.

Aloud, I say, "Looks like we both have calls to make."

This resort has no fourth floor—the Chinese equivalent of unlucky thirteen because *four* sounds like *death* in Mandarin. My room is on the fifth floor, which means it's really on the fourth, and I'm feeling the weight of all that unluckiness as I press my door open.

He's not interfering with the talent show. No. Freaking. Way.

Not even if I have to eat a plane ticket home.

I check email first, to see if Pearl's sent warning. She has, my faithful sister. *Dad's trying to reach you. Not sure what about. They're speaking Chinese. Mom's worried.*

Dad picks up on the first ring.

"Hi, Ever." I picture him on the other end, under his

Cleveland Indians cap. His voice has calmed an order of magnitude since the nude-photos call, but that doesn't mean bad news isn't coming. "I asked the hospital to move my flight up a few days. I'm flying out tonight and will pick you up tomorrow afternoon, and we will fly out Sunday together."

It's better than threatening to fly me home, but not by much. He's come to supervise me in person for my last days.

"I won't be back on campus until late Saturday." By the time he figures out I'm at the National Theater, as Sophie said, it will be too late.

"Oh, okay." Dad sounds disappointed. "I'll pick you up on campus Sunday morning. Keep your cell phone on, okay? I'll text you on WeChat." I'd expected anger, but his voice is kind. Almost pleading.

Have I dodged a bullet? "Sounds good, Dad."

I hang up, but my hand stays on the phone. He's about to board a plane, and I'd forgotten to wish him safe travels. That family ritual, a pinch of salt over my shoulder, without which misfortune might ensue. My absentminded dad, dreaming his doctor dreams as he walks through life. He'll forget his luggage at the airport or walk into a wall without Mom to keep him focused on where his feet are taking him.

"Safe travels," I whisper. I hope it counts.

A knock sounds, and I open the door to admit Rick. He's slung his backpack on his shoulder, ready to go.

"She didn't pick up so I left a message. Everything okay?"

So we're both off the hook. I should embrace it. Chalk my

paranoia up to that lifetime of waiting for the other shoe to drop.

His hand lingers on my waist and I rise on my toes to kiss him. "Everything's okay."

By the time we disembark our buses onto the white-sand shores of Sun Moon Lake, our last stop, word of the benefit concert has spread. Debra and Laura offer to invite the Taiwanese officials they met as Presidential Scholars. More talent comes out of the woodwork, including an *a cappella* group and Spencer's Martin Luther King Jr. rendition, which Sophie adds to our growing performance list.

"Put me and the boys down for a seven-minute block." Marc winks, and refuses to say more. A warm breeze wraps its arms around us as the Gang of Five poses on the shoreline for another Take-Back-the-Trope photo: arms and legs raised for crane kicks, dragon fists doubled and cocked, teeth bared—Magical Martial Arts Gurus who have our entire bus roaring with laughter.

I laugh, too, and add their names to the list.

"You might have another calling as a talent scout." Rick kisses my hair.

I smile. "Maybe we can be a lot of different things."

Sophie and I find Xavier sitting against a palm tree under

low-hanging fronds, sketching on a pad on his lap. White waves surge up the sand to lap at his feet.

He flinches when he meets my eyes and his hand moves to cover his sketch.

"What do you want?" His tone is edged.

Sophie, clipboard in hand, bravely drops down beside him on the sand, unconcerned about her orange dress. I sit on her other side, letting her explain the auction, the goal to help the flooded village. Xavier doesn't speak, but he doesn't tell us to leave him alone either.

"I bet your stuff would go for a lot," Sophie finishes. "And it's for a good cause."

Xavier sets his pad on the sand. "My grandmother was Aborigine. Hence the curly hair." He flicks a curl with his pencil. Glances at me, then at his sandals. "I might have a few paintings."

"Okay, let me know." Sophie's all business, a front for those deeper things she can't say or show. "I'm inviting all the local families, plus my aunt's art collectors. I'll make sure your work gets seen by the right people. If you do it, I won't let you down."

His eyes flicker with surprise. A small smile. "I've never doubted that."

Mei-Hwa cries when I call her from Li-Han's phone. "Are you sure?"

"Absolutely. Lots of people want to help. They just need to know how."

"My parents won't believe it. My mom is nursing my new sister now—I will wait to tell her so she doesn't drop her! Please thank everyone. For all my village."

"I will," I promise. "You should be dancing with us, too."

"I have two left feet! But thank you, Ai-, I mean, Ever."

"It's okay to call me Ai-Mei. I like them both."

"*Hǎo de.*" She laughs. "*Xièxiè, Ai-Mei.*"

I search the crowds for Rick, finally spotting him in his green T-shirt by the bus's luggage compartment. His back is to me, body bent at an odd angle. He holds his phone to his ear. His body is webbed with stress lines I haven't seen since he returned from Hong Kong. His thumb digs at the insides of his fingers in a familiar, fidgety gesture.

Fear lances my heart.

I sprint over the sand toward him.

"Please, I can barely understand you," he's saying. "You're here? But how? Where?"

"What's wrong?" I catch his arm, slipping on sand. "Who's here?"

Rick lowers his phone to his chest, shoulders tensed like rocks buckling at a fault line. With a jolt, I see his fingertips are red with blood—from digging at those scars.

"She's here," he says, dazed. "She said she's been trying to reach me for days."

"What are you talking about?"

His eyes swing toward the road as a silver Porsche pulls onto the beach. A beautiful girl leaps from the back, stylishly cut black hair swinging at her jawline. Her crumpled black dress speaks of hours of travel.

"Rick!" Kicking off her sandals, she races over the sand toward us.

With a shock, I recognize her.

In person, she's even more beautiful than her photo: all clean lines with a perfect brow, a narrow nose, rosebud lips. Large, movie-star eyes.

In my mind, I'd built her up into a huge presence. But in real life, she's narrow-shouldered, tiny and fragile as gossamer. I'm horrified at the desperation she must be feeling, to have faced down her fear of flying and traveled so far.

"Rick, we need to talk." She stops before him, with eyes only for him. At her throat glitters the sapphire class ring on its chain. She's slightly out of breath, but her expression is composed, even lofty, like a princess—no wonder no one suspects how much she's buried deep inside.

But then her face crumples like a stage curtain crashing down.

Flinging her arms around him, she presses her face to his, and bursts into tears.

34

"Let's move people! Guests arriving in two hours!"

Sophie pushes through a slit in the backdrop curtain and onto the stage of the National Theater, her clipboard in hand. She's dressed for work in slacks and a white, short-sleeved blouse.

The theater itself is alive with sounds: the rattle of wheels as Spencer and Benji cart in their dragon drums, the clop of shoes as my dancers whirl in their flirty gem-color dresses: emerald, sapphire, topaz—every last stitch in place.

A fresh coat of wax on stage covers the scuffs and scars of prior acts and from my spot in the center, the left and right wings feel miles away. Six spotlights blend double halos over me as, from the technician's box at the back, a stage manager dressed all in black yells instructions. Sophie's arranged for the theater to film the entire show.

I'm standing before three tiers with 1,498 velvet seats, where the Mariinsky Ballet danced and Broadway shows have performed and Yo-Yo Ma played his cello. This should inspire cartwheels. It's the greatest night of my dancing career—and yet all of me aches as if I've been crushed under a collapsed bridge.

Sophie grips my arm on her way to a mic check. "He'll be here." She runs her hand through her hair and sighs. "I feel so terrible I never knew. None of us did . . ."

Rick left Sun Moon Lake with Jenna yesterday afternoon, afraid to leave her to make the trip back to Taipei alone. He called her grandparents in Hong Kong and is waiting for them to arrive.

The selfish part of me wanted to hang on as tightly as she did: *Don't go. I need you, too.* To demand that Rick draw hard lines, the way Megan's always pushed me to draw hard lines with my parents. But I couldn't. Not with Jenna where she is.

What did they talk about in those long hours on the ride back to Taipei? They stayed last night at the Grand Hotel. He would have carried her bag into the plush lobby of red carpet and columns. Did their years together come slamming back? Did he find there's no letting go of someone for whom you are breath and life?

And if *she* can't let go, will his lifetime of subverting what he wants to his roles as the eldest son of the eldest son of the eldest son, as a big brother and a boyfriend, allow him to let go himself?

I have to believe there's an order to this universe, even if we can't see it, and that its fundamental design is good. One human was never intended to carry another. Rick and this summer gave me the courage to take charge of my own future.

I can only hope that I've done the same for him.

And if he decides it's her, then this summer was about their destiny, not ours.

"Is Rick coming?" Debra asks, when I execute the solo instead of the stick fight for our dress rehearsal.

"He'll be here," I say.

The girls exchange glances. Maybe Debra was right, and I shouldn't have asked Rick to dance with us to begin with, or built our performance around the stick fight.

But I love it. Love dancing it with Rick. And if we don't go after what we love, then what's the point?

"He'll be here," I repeat. "And if not, I'll do the solo. Come on. We have the blocking down. Let's see if the auction people need help."

In the sunlit atrium of the theater, girls from Lena's Bible study are draping white cloths over rectangular tables and unfolding two dozen easels dropped off by Sophie's aunt. Other kids are setting out saran-wrapped platters of mochi, *niángāo*, and other offerings from Chien Tan's food electives on a dessert table.

Sophie snags three easels for Xavier. She sets out his painting of a pair of dragon boats on the Keelung River, angling it to best catch the light.

"He's so talented." She chokes. "I was so stupid, Ever."

A lump solidifies in my throat. "We all were."

"Hey, girls." Xavier arrives in a silky black shirt, tucking a long roll of paper deeper under his arm. "I brought the mural." His wavy hair is slicked back behind his ears. He spots his paintings and a muscle works in his jaw—I'm afraid he'll ask us to take it down. Or bolt.

Then he straightens the three old men in black hats, which Sophie's taken the liberty of labeling, simply, *Three Old Men*.

"When you put them up like that, it almost looks like a real artist did them."

"A real artist did." I move beside him. "But you haven't signed them."

His eyes meet mine, unreadable. "If anyone actually buys them, I will."

Xavier and Sophie hoist his mural onto the stage's backdrop. A lean green Chinese dragon flies through a collage of Chien Tan memories: the five interlocked gates to the National Palace Museum. A golden urn smoking with incense sticks. Dancers under strobe lights. Sun Moon Lake, the Chinese characters cleverly imbedded in its sun-and-moon-shaped body. A Y-shaped confluence of blue water flowing into gray water at the Taroko

Gorge, the blue peopled by Asian American kids, the gray teeming with black-haired families of all ages.

"It's an analogy." Xavier's elbow brushes mine. I've come to a stop beneath it. "It's us."

I tilt my head, reading without words. Us cutting our own path through the rock, until we merge with the larger river of life. The flow of water breaks my heart, but it also mends it again—everything art is supposed to do.

"It's brilliant." My throat is tight with gladness. "I love it."

He hands me a smaller roll of paper tied with a brown ribbon. "You told me not to sketch you, but I thought—you wouldn't mind these."

"Oh?" I unroll four sketches: Rick and me seated together on an orange rock in the Taroko Gorge. Rick and me with the glow of the night market behind us. Rick and me stick fighting on the edge of Kenting National Forest, my head flung back with laughter.

And one more. Sophie and me sitting by Sun Moon Lake, Sophie's head bent over her clipboard. My arms around my legs. We'd been talking about this moment with Xavier.

"You were right. About a lot of things." He touches the tiny bo staff in my painted hand. "That's what happiness looks like."

Sophie joins us. "I'm auctioning off your mural last of all."

"Anonymously," Xavier says. "Say it's some student's."

"Sure," Sophie agrees, then gasps as she catches sight of our painting. "It's beautiful."

"The colors." My throat aches with the release of so much

that's been buried deep away. "I've never seen such amazing colors."

Backstage, in the mirror-lined dressing room, I change into my ruby dress. Cap sleeves show off my arms and a black sash tied at the side accents my waist. The skirt modestly skims my knees but the silk clings to my body. As I face myself in a mirror, I instinctively hunch my shoulders, hiding my curves. Then I force myself to straighten.

Still, my stomach is taut with nerves, imagining all the eyes of Chien Tan on me, as I tuck my clothes into my bag. A glamour shot flutters down—the one Xavier returned. I feel the usual jolt, but for the first time, I allow myself to study it.

And a crazy thing happens: It's so much better than I'd feared. The light highlights my cheekbones at a flattering angle, the ballerina curve of my neck, my good posture. I would still rather throw myself under a rickshaw than have had these passed around—but I'm no longer mortified by the sight of my own body.

Sophie comes in and opens her makeup bag before one of the mirrors.

"It's nuts outside," she says.

I peer out the window. A crowd jostles against the five-paneled gateway of Liberty Square, waiting for entry. It's so large that it spills onto the street. A barrier of policemen in blue uniforms is herding them out of traffic onto the opposite sidewalk. Cars and motorcycles honk as they cut through like lawn mowers over a yard.

"It looks like half of Taipei has come out," I say.

"They have," Sophie gloats. "Debra said some government VIPs are coming. That's why they've beefed up security."

I know it's unlikely I'll spot him, but I still search for Rick's bulky shoulders among the crowd, his bo staff aloft.

Instead, from among the crowd across the street, a familiar Cleveland Indians cap jumps out at me.

Even among a hundred Chinese, I recognize his slouchy posture. The way he lowers his cap and hunches down. The extra distance from his eyes that he holds his folded paper map. Like a character from one performance walking onto the stage of the wrong story.

Dad.

I pull out my phone—sure enough, he's texted me:

Dad: I'm here at Chien Tan. Your classmate said you were at a picnic at Chiang Kai-shek Memorial.
Dad: I'm here at Liberty Square but it's blocked. There's a fundraiser at the theater.
Dad: Are you still at the Memorial? I'll try to get through.

He sent his last text twenty minutes ago. What was my classmate thinking, covering for me by sending him to the wrong tourist attraction in the right complex? I text him:

380

> Dad, I'm not there. Must be a mix-up. Meet you on campus tomorrow, k?

My text spins, spins, spins, then fails to send. No signal. Timing couldn't be worse. "Sophie, my dad's outside." I grab a black smock off a hanger and drape it around my dress. "He's looking for me. I need to run down for a few minutes."

"You can't." Sophie grips my arm. "He'll stop you. You said so yourself. This is your *grand finale*. Ever Wong's last dance!"

I hug her. "He won't stop looking until he finds me and I can't let him look all night. I'll tell him to meet me on campus tomorrow."

"What if you get stuck at security?"

"I'm a performer. They can't keep me out."

"But—"

"Here." I reach for her clipboard and unclip one of the backstage passes she's auctioning off tonight. "I'll get back in with this."

There's an unexpected spring to my step as I run down the theater steps into the growing dusk. Dad's here. Doofy Dad who took me ice skating when Pearl was born so I wouldn't feel left out while Mom focused on nursing her. Dad who taught me to drive in the school parking lot at peril to his own life and limb, who left the shores of Asia when he was a few years older than I am now to live his life away from family and friends.

I wasn't entirely truthful when I told Sophie I wanted to spare him wandering all night. I understand why Dad cried in *Mulan* when the Huns invaded China.

He missed home.

And I've missed him.

The five gates leading into Liberty Square are barred by blockades. Guests file through a narrow entrance, opening their bags and backpacks for inspection by security guards in blue. Squeezing by, I flash my backstage pass at a moon-faced guard. "I'm coming back in. *Wǒ hěn kuài jiù huì huílái le.* Don't forget me!"

He waves me through and I sink into the crowd that towers over me like a field of corn. I can't see beyond the faces coming at me. Under my feet, the ground vibrates with the rumbling of cars zipping by ahead. A cavalcade of mopeds speeds past, spewing fumes.

As I near the street, a white truck barrels through.

And when it passes, the Cleveland Indians cap is opposite me, across the street.

He's hemmed in by a tall man on his left and a family on his right, and squashed behind a large woman in a floral skirt who keeps bumping into him as the police press the crowd back from the street. The blue-striped shirt he wore to my graduation is untucked over his jeans. He squints at his map, then cranes his neck in several directions, maybe trying to find alternative routes into Liberty Square. He looks tired. In Ohio, dawn is breaking, and like me, he's never adjusted well to jet lag; he must have sat awake all night on his flight.

"Dad!"

A black car zooms by, leaving a vacuum that tugs at my skirt. Dad turns in several directions, seeking my voice.

"Dad, over here!" I wave.

His weary eyes meet mine, then light up like fireworks.

"Ever!" Waving, he tries to maneuver around the woman between him and street. "Ever!"

She shoves back. "Wait your turn!" she snaps in Mandarin.

I push eagerly toward him. He's still waving, grinning ear to ear. He sidles around the woman and rushes toward me, all of his attention focused on reaching me in that single-minded way of his.

Then everything happens at once.

Dad's face opens with surprise. He pitches forward, arms flailing for balance.

Into the street. Into the path of an oncoming car.

"Dad, look out!"

A horn blares without end. In the middle of the road, Dad freezes like a cornered animal. He's never been quick on his feet.

In the space between heartbeats, the collision plays out in my mind and heart. That body that's pushed an orderly cart for twenty years. The unforgiving impact of steel, the weight of too-many kilometers per hour.

It's a choice to leave the curb. A choice to risk not just tonight's performance, but all future ones. But it *is* a choice, not a forcing of my hand through a sacrifice, or threat of punishment, or even the weight of guilt and obligation.

And I make it with all my soul.

"Dad, *move!*"

"Ever, no!" he shouts. "Stop!"

Then I'm sailing over the street at him. To my left, the glint of chrome, the glare of headlights barrels toward me. My hand closes on his arm as another blare of horns takes out my eardrum.

**35**

The world is vibrations. Thunder. Particles.

Dad and I barrel into the woman in the printed skirt. She screams and my shoe flies off and my arm wrenches in its socket, shooting fire into my body. We're a tangle of hair and limbs hitting the sidewalk, rolling, bruising, as the horn falls in pitch behind us, then fades.

"Ever! Are you hurt?"

My shoulder and upper arm burn. I can't move it. The pain comes in waves that threaten to drown me but slowly I realize I'm lying on top of Dad. He gropes at the pavement. His glasses have fallen off and I snatch their wire frames off the ground. One thick lens is cracked, but I shove them into his hands and he fits them to his face.

"Ever." His face is more mole-speckled than I remember, his graying hair wild tufts on his head. "Ever, are you okay?"

Something is wrong with my body. But I scramble to my knees and wrap my good arm around him, which I cannot remember doing since I was a child. He smells like soap, like Tide, like newspaper.

Like home.

"You could have *died*," I sob.

All around us, people babble, prod, kneel, and fuss. But all my focus is on Dad's hand, hesitantly stroking the back of my head, another something I can't remember happening since my early years.

"It's just my ankle. Better than my head, thanks to you," he adds when I pull back.

A flare of pain washes my vision white.

"Ever!" Dad grips my arm as I cry out. "What's wrong?"

"Shoulder—" I grate. "My shoulder—"

"You've dislocated it." He grips my shoulder blade, his other hand my arm above the elbow. The worry fades from his face, replaced by a calm focus I've seen at parks and events, when he's kneeling before a medical emergency, and knows what to do. "Hold still, this will hurt."

With a wrench and pop, he jams my arm back into its socket.

The extreme relief collapses me against him.

"You'll be fine." He strokes my back with that tentative hand. "In a few weeks—"

"You lost this." A man hands me my shoe. "Paramedics are coming."

Sure enough, a white ambulance, red-cross logo and red lights flashing, is moving up the street toward us.

Dad grips my hand. His next words tumble out, as if he'd dammed them in his entire flight, his entire search for me, and he needs to get them out before the paramedics are upon us. "On the plane, I was remembering a time we brought you to the park. You were four. A man was playing a violin and you danced barefoot on the grass. Everyone came and watched you. A woman told us to enroll you in dance classes. That was when we put you in Zeigler's."

*All I wanted to do this summer was dance.*

Dad heard me.

That four-year-old day, I don't remember. I didn't even know that was the reason I'd ended up in the studio that became my second home. But the story is a gift. Dancing has always been a part of me—and Dad's seen that.

"I'm sorry I let you down." This reunion is nothing like Mulan and her father. I'm not bringing him the emperor's crest. From his point of view, he sent his elder daughter over the seas and she went berserk. He's not entirely wrong either. "I'm sorry about the photos."

"You talk to your friends and guidance counselor more than us," he says. "Sometimes, when you come home, you speak English so fast we can't understand. Sometimes we are scared we haven't raised you right. All we wanted was for you to have a better life. What if we came to America for that, and we lost you instead?"

"But don't you see?" I shift against him, pressing my shoulder into his chest. "I already have a better life. Because of you and Mom."

Dad's face spasms. I'm afraid he's going to cry.

"Do you feel that way?"

And then the paramedics are raining down a hundred questions on us.

"My ankle's broken," Dad tells them calmly.

"Dad, oh, no." Typical Dad, to keep that to himself. "But your work—"

"Let me worry about that."

They check his vitals. My ankle is tender, but unsprained. A paramedic hands me a white pill—prescription-strength ibuprofen—and a bottle of water. As another paramedic inspects his ankle, Dad jokes their ambulance is better equipped than some hospitals in the States. His voice is richer, more confident, than I remember.

And another amazing thing happens. They're speaking Mandarin—and I understood the gist of it.

The crowds have begun to thin, funneled into Liberty Square and the theater. A man in a white coat presses through, kneels beside Dad, and shakes his hand. His hair is tufty and grayish like Dad's.

"Andy, I came as soon as I got your text."

"This is Dr. Jason Lee," Dad introduces me. "We were in medical school together. He's the one who's been flying me out to consult for his hospital here these past few years."

"He's a treasure, your father." Dr. Lee squeezes my hand. "Thanks to him, we provide the best patient care in Taipei."

Dr. Lee takes charge, and soon Dad is seated on a stretcher, ankle temporarily wrapped. Despite his protests, they declare he's dehydrated from his long trip and put an IV into his arm. I gently rotate my arm. The pain has lessened but I know better than to ask Dad about the bo staff dance. It should be fine.

"*Wong Yīshēng?*" The head paramedic hands Dad an electronic tablet. "The city will cover your bill. Please sign here?"

Wong Yīshēng. *Dr. Wong.* He's using his proper title.

All these years.

Then Sophie's voice reaches my ears. "I need to speak to her. This is an emergency!"

Sophie appears from behind a paramedic, her face ready for prime time with faux eyelashes, deep blue eyeshadow, berry-red lips. A black smock covers her checkered dress. Her hair spills from its updo.

"Dr. Wong! Hi! I'm Ever's Chien Tan roommate. I heard you were safe—*so glad*! Um, since you're okay, can Ever come with me for an emergency school project?"

The trump card. Nice, Sophie. She shoots me a fearful look, while Dad removes his glasses and rubs them on his shirt.

389

"You should rest your arm, Ever."

"I just need a few hours, Dad." I slip another ibuprofen from the paramedic's kit.

Dad's eyes tell me he wants to protest. But then he nods. "Jason wants me to come to the hospital for X-rays and casting. I'll go to my hotel afterward. What's the project?"

"Just end-of-summer stuff." I automatically downplay. I give him another hug, then start after Sophie, who waves me on impatiently.

*Hurry, hurry!* twitch her brows.

But something tugs at me, holding me to this patch of sidewalk.

I turn back. Dad's watching me from the stretcher, that mole-speckled, spectacled face I can never penetrate. That gap between us that will likely always be there.

But I know now that the Great Divide is the enemy. Dad might never understand why *I* cried in *Mulan*, but maybe it isn't fair to demand that of him.

And if that Great Divide is ever to be bridged, or at least made smaller, I can only change myself. Not to give up my Americanness.

But to let them in.

I take a step back toward him, fingers wrinkling my black smock. He's never seen me dance outside my tame ballet recitals. For so many reasons, I've never been able to share this part of myself with him.

"I'm actually helping to run the fundraiser in there." I point to the orange swallowtail roof of the National Theater. "It's a talent show. I choreographed a dance. If you can pull your doctor strings and get them to discharge you, I'd love for you to come."

Dad blinks behind his lenses. "Oh." He tugs his IV from his wrist.

"Dr. Wong, please, be careful!" The head paramedic springs forward.

"If you could find me a wheelchair for now." Dad's already climbed to his feet, bracing himself on the ambulance door. I'd forgotten how stubborn he can be, too. "I'm going with my daughter."

# 36

The red velvet drapes muffle the roar of voices beyond. Completely unprofessional, I make an eye-sized slit and peer out. Chien Tan kids and counselors cram the front half of the theater, and the rest of the rows to the topmost balcony overflow with strangers.

"We're sold out!" I whisper.

"And the better our show, the more people will bid at the auction. They'll be in the right mood." Sophie hugs me. "He'll be here."

Program in hand, she slips out between the curtains.

The show runs an hour, plus intermission, and our number is the finale. Rick still has time. I refuse to worry. My ankle twinges—I seem to have injured it a bit after all, and I rub it, and take the second pill, hoping that will be enough to get me through. I smooth my braid to the bit of red lace at its end, then adjust the neckline of my dress. Every tuck and curve molds to my contours. There's no hiding my body in this dress, and instead of wishing for Megan's legs or Sophie's curves, I feel beautiful in my own right. Tonight, I'm showing what I can do, not just to Taipei and Chien Tan, not just to Aunty Claire and Uncle Ted—

But to Dad.

"*Dàjiā hǎo!*" The mic amplifies Sophie's welcome through the theater. "*Hel-lo, Taipei!*"

An answering roar shakes the stage beneath my feet.

I watch from the wings with Debra and Laura as Sophie announces each act: Chinese yo-yos, martial arts. Mike's comedy routine draws chuckles from the audience. A guy from Bus G flies through Rachmaninoff's *Études-Tableaux*, his body and hands digging into the piano keys with so much fire and passion that I understand what Rick understood when he switched from music to football.

At intermission, Sophie encourages everyone to peruse the silent auction in its last minutes. I cover my red dress in the black smock again and slip out to peek at the progress. Hundreds of people swarm the auction tables, marking up bid sheets, and then the auction closes. I smile at the crowd gathered around Xavier's easels. Xavier himself is seated beside them, wavy black hair falling into his eyes as he presses his chop to an inkstone, and sets his seal on each painting.

So he's sold them all. And carved his chop, too. *Three Old Men*, that slice of hope, is now cast like a die into the world.

As if he can feel my gaze, his eyes lift to mine, and he returns my smile.

The second half of our show kicks off with a bang. Spencer's nailed Taiwan—with their own independence close to heart, his thunderous "I Have a Dream" rendition gets a roar of applause that rattles the chandeliers.

"A vote for Hsu is a vote for you!" yells a voice.

Debra and Laura play a duet on zithers. A trio of kids and a counselor from Bus D improv a jazz number on keys, bass, drums, and a wind instrument hand-whittled from bamboo.

Then Sophie announces the Gang of Five, the last act before ours.

I duck into the dressing rooms, the hallway behind the stage, but Rick is nowhere. As I lean my bo staff against the wall, my stomach clenches. Five minutes to go before showtime.

He'll be here.

"Where's Marc?" Debra murmurs. "This is his act, but I haven't seen him today."

I bend my knee back and massage my aching ankle. "Haven't seen him all night," I admit.

Runway music blares through the theater, a mash of electronic piano and a synthetic beat that demands all our attention. I crane my neck at the stage as a tall girl in a short fur coat over fishnet stockings struts into the spotlight. Heavy black hair frames a strong face with cherry-red pouting lips and devastatingly made-up eyes.

"Whoa, she's stacked," Debra whispers.

She is—and proud of it. Her red lace bra is covered only by the middle button of her coat. She strikes an exaggerated model pose: arm up, wrist bent, chest out—to uncertain titters and a few whistles.

"Um, who *is* that?" Debra asks.

"I don't know." Sophie folds her arms over her clipboard. "Spencer's been passing messages for Marc. I haven't spoken to Marc myself." Her jaw clenches. "This had *better* be good or there will be bloodshed."

I stare at the girl. "She looks familiar." But I'm positive I've never seen her. A friend of Marc's? I still haven't met all five hundred kids, but a girl like her would have stood out. And where's the Gang of Five themselves?

The music accelerates as a second girl steps from the wings, small-boned and delicate in a pink gown embroidered in darker cherry blossoms and white, elbow-length gloves. She's followed by a third girl in leopard print, bursting with cleavage deep enough to drown someone. The heavy scent of perfume reaches my nose.

"Is that *Sam*?" I ask.

Debra gasps.

I stare hard at girl number one as a fourth and fifth girl in silk qipaos join the lineup.

I grab Sophie's hand. "I think that's *Marc*. And David."

"No!" she cries.

The first girl takes the microphone. Her warm contralto fills the theater.

"Ladies and gents, I'm Marquette, and I'm pleased to introduce the delicious Sammi, Vida, Ben-Jammin', and Petra. Welcome to the Ms. Chien Tan Beauty Contest! Contestants, please line up. Audience, prepare to cast your votes!"

The audience erupts in cheers and piercing whistles. Marc. And Sam, David—goatee shaved—Benji, and Peter. The Gang of Five, taking back the effeminate Asian male stereotype on their own terms.

I whoop so hard my throat aches. This is too awesome. Too crazy. Rick should be here to see this. I peer into the audience, wondering how our grown-ups are taking it. To my surprise, in the front row, the Dragon is clapping with her arms over her head. Two dignitaries flanking her are cheering equally hard.

Who'd have guessed?

The Ms. Chien Tan Beauty Contest goes way overtime as the would-be queens strut their stuff. But the audience is roaring. They vote down one after another, until, at last, it's down to Ben-Jammin' and Marquette, who rips off his fur coat and what turns out to be a faux-skin leotard to reveal . . ."

The Dragon's green qipao!

The Dragon herself rises from her front-row seat, her matching qipao sparkling in the glow of stage lights. Grinning, she raises her clasped hands overhead, shaking them as she turns a full circle, lapping up the applause. On stage, Marquette is crowned and the others lift him onto their shoulders and parade around, tossing confetti.

I dab tears from my own eyes. Marc's destroyed Sophie's careful makeup job.

"We will never top that," I say, turning to Sophie.

But she isn't here.

Instead, Rick emerges from the curtained wing. His damp black hair gleams like raven feathers over his black tunic and slacks, courtesy of Sophie. He drops his sneakers into the trash, but not before I glimpse their soles flapping like hungry alligators. He's holding his bo staff. Grabbing mine from the wall, he tosses it to me and I, too stunned not to, catch it.

"What happened to your shoes?" I croak.

"I ran all the way here from the hotel. Traffic was jammed up. Sorry I'm late. Just showered." He smiles. "Couldn't let Marc show us up."

"You ran your shoes off." I can't believe it.

"I bought them in Snake Alley. Got ripped off, looks like." He kneels to tie on his black dance shoes.

"Her grandparents' flight was delayed. I ended up calling her dad and both he and her mom flew out to be with her. She's with them now." He takes my hand, eyes suddenly serious in a way

397

that makes my heart lurch in my chest. "I told her I'd made a commitment to be here. I told her she needed to let me go."

Let him go.

Happiness wars with guilt. I know what that's cost him.

"Do you—do you think she'll be all right?"

There's a weight on him, the boy who shoulders his responsibilities with a maturity beyond his years, making a choice with no assurances that all will be well.

"We talked a long time. We both realized she's stronger than she or I gave her credit for. Flying here on her own surprised even herself. This was the first time we've really talked openly about her depression. I told her what you said about finding the right counselor—not from you, I mean, just the advice. She didn't say yes, but she didn't say no either. She gave this back." He holds up his knuckles. Light glints off the sapphire on the class ring from Jenna's necklace. "It's mine, actually."

So she let him go.

A choked sob escapes my lips. "I was afraid—"

I break off, unable to say what it was I'd feared. He draws me to his warm chest and wraps his arm around me. Puts his mouth to my ear. "When I was a kid, my teacher asked who didn't believe in life in outer space. I was the only one who raised my hand. Not because I didn't believe. Because after reading all those Usborne books, I was afraid to believe something so incredible could actually be true.

"When I'm with you, I just know. There's life out there. We could find it someday."

His amber eyes smile down at me. A miracle on the order of the Big Bang.

But Sophie is calling the audience back to order.

"My ankle's a little injured. My shoulder, too."

"What happened?"

"Just a twist." I center Rick's collar and kiss his frown before he can protest. "Don't worry. I can do this."

My dancers line up in the wings, black hair swinging free of bands or ribbons, the gem colors of their dresses and ribbons and fans hidden under gauzy black overshirts buttoned to their necks.

Debra flashes Rick a thumbs-up.

"Thank you, Marquette, and thank you, generous benefactors," Sophie says. "Our auction has closed and we will announce proceeds at the end of tonight's performance. For those disappointed folks who haven't won yet, we have one more item—this stunning mural behind me, which I will auction off after our grand finale. Again, all proceeds go to families in Taitung impacted by the typhoon."

I spin my staff a revolution to center myself.

"And now, ladies and gentlemen! I'm pleased to announce the international debut of *The Wanderer*, an original dance created and arranged by our very own Ever Wong!"

# 37

The opening notes of "*Lán Huā Cǎo*" play and my girls flow forward to form three identical bundles: a girl pirouetting, arms upraised, and four revolving around her like the petals of a black flower. Three stage lights halo over them. Their faces are neutral—for now. With languid motions, hips and arms, they form changing shapes to the soft beat of the drums.

One of my favorite aspects of choreography is that there is always a story. At least with me. The story of this dance has evolved each time we practiced, each time we added new elements.

As the music accelerates, the girls strip off their black robes and explode into sapphire, emerald, and orange. Silk ribbons erupt, blue fans snap open, jazz-hands wrist-flick. Their skirts and hair fan out like petals as they whirl: blues, greens, and oranges mixing across the stage.

Then Spencer's drums beat out a counter rhythm. Blues, greens, and oranges coalesce like a flower arrangement as I emerge in red, bo staff twirling. My heart pounds with stage fright. It comes with the territory, but this is different—Dad's in the audience.

And he's about to watch me dance. With a boy.

Keeping my focus on my dancers, I weave figure eights through them. Their silk ribbons whip against my arms and my feet stamp the floor to Spencer's counter-beat as I search for a home—do I belong to the ribbon dancers without ribbons? the fan dancers without a fan? the jazz dancers who clasp hands and knock me aside?

My dancers line up in an undulating wave, alternating blue-green-orange. They wall me out. My bo staff flies spinning in the air while I whirl in red beneath it, catch it, cast about for a place in line.

But I don't belong anywhere.

Then a fanfare of drums and vocalization herald a new-comer: Rick steps onstage, bo staff revolving to match mine. Stage lights glitter off his coal-black hair.

A murmur ripples through the audience.

Feigning outrage at this intruder, I leap at him. My staff whistles through the air as I bring it down on his with a crack that echoes. Bo in both hands, I fly into barrel turns across the stage then back around to him.

But at a sharp pain in my ankle, I cut the turns short. Expel a breath—*hang in there*. My dancers form a phalanx behind me, and we're sixteen advancing on one as I swing at Rick's head. He blocks. Counterattacks. Swings at my head, my feet, my waist as I dodge, give him ground.

*Crack, crack, crack!* Rick grins as he drives us all back. The cracks reverberate into my hands as he beats out our fight down the stage. My dancers, defeated at last, drop back to form a rustling choral line.

I forget the audience, my ankle, as I take center stage with Rick. With every swing of my staff, he mirrors me, every crack augmented by the drums. Neither of us get the better of the other as we feint and dodge, swing and cry out.

Crossing staffs, we spin a circle together, faster, faster, then Rick yanks my stick from my hand. Not to be outdone, I wrestle his staff free, tossing it aside with a clatter. His hands go around me, my hand glides down the side of his face, and my dancers loop a double circle around us, flowing in opposite directions in rainbow rings.

Then my ankle gives way.

I bite back a cry as I pitch forward. My foot slips on the waxed floor and I'm falling toward Rick, about to land at his feet in an undignified heap.

But smooth as silk, Rick seizes my waist. He lifts me into the air as if I were as light as a feather, spinning, spinning circles we didn't practice, blurring the lights into colors. I'm flying and I go with it—arch backward nearly double, hair whipping the air, arms and legs pliant, surrendered and free.

At last, Rick folds me into his arms, spins a final few circles, and lowers me to rest against him. His damp chest heaves against mine, both our hearts pounding louder than the dragon drums as we gaze at one another, the world spun away.

Only the thunder of applause brings me to my senses.

My dancers are bowing. Rick and I jerk apart to our clasped hands and drop our own bows. My heart thunders in my ears and I'm grinning so hard my face hurts. The audience beyond the stage is a blur of faces.

Except for the man who leaps from wheelchair to feet. His tortoiseshell glasses slip to the tip of his nose, and he shoves them back into place and keeps clapping as the audience follows him into a standing ovation.

Dad.

We take a second and third bow, but the clapping doesn't stop. Finally, at a pre-arranged signal from me, the drums swell for an encore.

Rick and I separate to retrieve our staves, beat out one last fight across the stage. My ankle holds. The audience clapping turns rhythmic and my dancers form a semi-circle behind us.

And as I lunge and whirl my bo staff, dancing to the ancient drumbeats, I feel all the parts of myself coming together: glad that a part of me is Chinese, a part of me American, and all of me is simply me.

At Xavier's request, Sophie auctions off his mural as the work of an anonymous student. I sit on a stool offstage while Lena wraps a bag of ice around my angry ankle. The bidders in the audience duke it out, higher and higher, until at last she declares it sold at US $7,100.

"Holy cow, his dad won it," Debra says.

"No kidding?" I crane my neck at the familiar-looking man with his military bearing, not a wrinkle on his snow-white jacket, his steel-gray hair parted at the side. But how ironic. He can't know it's Xavier's work he bought.

"I wish I could see Xavier's face right now," I gloat.

"Ladies and gentlemen," Sophie declares, "on behalf of the typhoon relief fund, all of us at Chien Tan thank you for your support. I'm thrilled to announce we raised over five hundred thousand NTs!"

US $16,000!

Even before the curtains hit the stage floor, we scream and hug, a tangle of sweaty bodies and stiff-sprayed hair: Debra, Spencer, Marc, Laura. Lena cries. Spencer high-fives the world. Sam kisses Benji. We're drunk on ourselves and our success.

Li-Han pumps my hand up and down, stops when I wince. "I'm proud of you guys. When you all first arrived, I thought you were a bunch of spoiled Americans—I, uh—"

"We were," I say, and hug him, too.

Sophie pushes through the curtain, yanking off one high heel, then the other. She tosses her clipboard into the air and raises her arms, glowing like the chandeliers.

"Sixteen thousand!"

I throw my arm around her neck. "Not bad for a girl with no talent!"

"Harvard Business School, here I come!"

Xavier climbs the stage steps toward us, a thumb hooked in his pocket as usual. But a new light illuminates his eyes. He fans a handful of business cards.

"Art collectors—and my *dad*." He shakes his head, disbelieving. "Someday, I'll tell him."

"I'm glad." I squeeze his hand fiercely. "So, *so* glad."

Sophie flips through his cards. "Not this guy." She crumples one card. "My aunt knows him. He's a scammer. But these two"—she presses them back into his hand—"are legit."

After a startled pause, his mouth pulls into a smile. "Thanks."

Then they head across the stage toward the Dragon. Bossy Sophie has outdone Beautiful Sophie tonight, but I'm glad she's both.

We are powerful.

We can be anyone we want to be—daughters, sons, mothers, fathers, citizens, human beings. We showed Taipei that tonight. And in the days to come, we will show the world.

A familiar hand falls on my shoulder.

My own hand reaches up to take it as I turn.

Rick smiles. "We did good."

"We did." I smile back, then spot Dad rolling off the stage elevator in his wheelchair.

"Hold on, Rick. Hey, Dad." I move toward him.

His arms surge as he rolls toward me. "Ever, your arm! When I saw you walk onstage, your ankle giving—"

"I had to do this."

"You might have damaged your body for good!" Dad holds a hand out for my ankle, which I place in his lap. He probes at it with expert fingers, then sets it down and rises onto one foot to check my shoulder. It aches, but nothing more, and at last he sinks back into his chair. "You need to rest that arm and ankle for the next month. *At least.*"

"I will," I promise. And I mean it. Some rules are no-brainers.

He takes hold of my hand in both of his. "You were wonderful. And you look so beautiful. Maybe you can teach me how to stick spin when we get home. I saw it in a kung fu film."

My throat swells. "I will."

Rick has been hovering in the background. Now, I lace my fingers through his and tug him forward. Dad's eyes open wide and I wonder how many more surprises he can bear tonight. But I only have one more.

"Hey, Dad." I smile. "Remember Boy Wonder?"

# Epilogue

Taipei's Taoyuan International Airport is jammed with thousands of travelers, but this time, the frenzy feels friendly, not frightening. There are things I won't miss about Taipei—too many mopeds, body-licking humidity—but I've grown to love the people, the night market, the street food everywhere. I will miss the intensity of my Loveboat friendships and am thankful to have them going forward. I will miss the anonymity of blending in, but perhaps I was never meant to blend in.

As for Mandarin, I have a new appreciation for my parents' bilingual abilities. I still can't read more than a few dozen characters. But the signs, newspapers, magazines are no longer random symbols. They're full of significance: doors, eyes, hands, men, meat, water, hearts, dagger-axes, earth, rain, trees, suns and moons, wood, fire, power, gold, and short-tail birds.

For now, it's enough to know there's meaning there.

I walk beside Dad in his wheelchair, and put my hand on his shoulder, new for the both of us.

He places his hand over mine and smiles up. "Ready to go home?"

"I'm ready."

I bring Pearl a third bo staff so we can practice with Dad, and I surprise Mom with a small purple dragon fruit I smuggled inside two pairs of socks in my suitcase. After years of being harassed by customs agents at the border, I figured she was due one.

Her normally stern face softens. "Ever, it's my—"

"Favorite. I know." I smile. It's not a pearl necklace, but I can at least show I was thinking of her.

A few weeks after my return home, after my jet-lag loopiness wears off, a jubilant reunion with Megan and Dan, and a call from Mei-Hwa—she's back in school thanks to us—I brew a pot of red oolong tea, and set three cups on the kitchen counter.

"Mom? Dad? Can we talk?"

At the dining table, Mom looks up from her stack of bills. Dad closes his newspaper and removes his spectacles, polishes them with the hem of his shirt, then returns them to his face.

In a summer of firsts, this is the first I've approached them with news of my own. I'd let them down in small ways all

408

summer, though they will never know the half of it. I'd let myself down at times, too.

But I'm still standing.

And now, I'm ready to let them down in the biggest way of all.

I slip into a seat across from them. "I did a lot of thinking in Taiwan," I say. "This won't be easy for you to hear, but I'm not going to Northwestern in September."

Dad's glasses come off again. Mom sets down her teacup.

"Everett—"

"Please hear me out. I don't want to be a doctor. I've always known that deep down but was too afraid to acknowledge it." I smile. "I get vertigo at the sight of blood. Not the most auspicious beginning for a medical career."

"That shouldn't stop you—" Dad protests, but I put my hand over his.

"I could overcome that—you raised me that way. The real reason is—" I take a steadying breath. "I want to dance. I want to create dances. And I'm good at it. I'm going to take a gap year and work at Zeigler's as a dance instructor, and apply to dance schools and scholarship programs for next fall. I have a film of the dance I choreographed in Taiwan that I'll use as part of my application."

"Dancing isn't practical for a career." Mom's as brisk as morning air. "*Starting over* isn't practical. What if you can't get a job after dance school? No medical school will want you then. No, you've worked so hard. You finish medical school, and dance on the side."

"Mom, you didn't hear me," I say. "I'm not going to medical school."

I pull out an envelope that came in the mail today, and push the letter from Northwestern toward them. A check is enclosed. "I learned to negotiate this summer from my roommate. I asked them to return our deposit."

Mom pushes aside her stack of bills and draws the letter closer. She raises her eyes to mine. With a pang, I notice new wrinkles in their corners, the lines on her forehead. They deepen.

"This is foolish."

Her worn hands land on the table and she rises.

"Dancing doesn't put food on the table! How can you do this to us? To your *father*? Are you still so ungrateful, after all we've done?"

"Paula—" Dad begins, but she shouts him down.

"This isn't what we raised her for. We gave up everything for her. Everything!"

I stay in my seat, my hands wrapped around my hot mug. At the start of summer, her words would have torn my soul to pieces. In the middle, I might have roared, "Then I'll just *starve!*"

Now, her glare still makes my stomach dip like I've hit the bottom of a roller coaster.

But then I ride forward over the next hill.

I would die for my family if it came to it. I would emigrate to a foreign country and give up dancing to unwrap blood-soaked bandages every hour of every day if it meant food and shelter

410

for my family. But because of them, I *don't* have to. I don't have to be Dad pushing a cart, reeking of antiseptic and longing to be somewhere else, the place where my soul lives.

"Mom, Dad, both of you were brave enough to come to America without your families. Dad gave up medicine so we could grow up here. That took courage, and I learned that from you. You gave up security and took risks so you could have bigger things. I'm doing that, too. I want to use my dancing to bring attention to people no one's paying attention to."

Mom storms from the room.

Dad still wears a stunned expression. But not of anger. Our precious bit of hard-won trust is still between us.

"She'll come around." He squeezes my hand, then follows her.

The long, painful conversation stretches over many days, interrupted by meals, work, Pearl's recital for her Mozart Sonata in C, which she nails, then her first day of middle school, and a tearful farewell with Megan. But it's a conversation I'm glad to have. For too long, I've hidden my love for dancing, those larger dreams, from my parents.

No longer.

Mom stops speaking to me. But I know that even if she's wrong about what I need, she wants the best for me in her own way. Dad says little, as usual, but instead of judgment, I sense support underlying his silence. Maybe it's always been there.

Dad understands what it means to give up your dreams. And I understand now that rejecting their wishes is not the same as rejecting *them*.

I wrestle with another kind of guilt. Am I that girl who shies away from science or traditionally male careers? But the answer is no. I love my parents for never seeing my gender as an obstacle to my career success. That gave me choices Sophie never saw for herself.

Because I *do* have a choice.

And I'm not making it blindly. I've looked all the way down the road, and I know I will be a thousand times happier dancing on a community theater stage than advising the Oval Office as surgeon general.

Sophie calls from Dartmouth orientation: her roommate, like Spencer, wants to run for office one day, and Sophie's already got her eyes on the presidency of the entrepreneur club. Xavier, to whom Sophie speaks once a week, turned down a spot at a fancy private high school in Massachusetts that his dad got him through a big donation, and moved to Los Angeles to work on a set for an indie theater, a gig he got from the buyer of *Three Old Men*.

"And you'll never believe this," Sophie says. "Jenna got into Northwestern's medical program."

"No!" I clutch my phone. "She got my spot."

"Marc called it, didn't he?" Sophie's exasperated. "One Asian girl's as good as another. But she deferred her acceptance."

"Really?"

"She's taking a gap year to work with a counselor first. She said she's not ready yet."

"I'm glad," I say. "On so many levels, I'm glad."

On August 24, Rick visits on his way to Yale, and Dad makes his own announcement over dinner. He's still using crutches, on light duty at work. "I've decided to retire from the Cleveland Clinic and pursue my consulting business full-time. Dr. Lee has been encouraging me to do this for a while, and he's gotten me another contract in Taitung."

I rise from my seat to hug him. "Dad, that's *great*. Congratulations."

"It's risky," Dad admits. "If things go south, I might make less than I did at the hospital. The timing seems wrong, with you not going to med—ur, switching directions. But I've been thinking about doing this for ten years. And you're so happy. Maybe none of us can hide who we are."

"We can't," I agree.

Rick offers to help Dad set up his remote office, and the two of them spend a busy few days in the study setting up a Wi-Fi range extender, power bank, and telepresence screen.

"Thank you." I loop my arm around Rick's waist and he drapes his around my shoulder as we admire the setup.

"Homecoming in October," Rick reminds me as Dad plugs in his desk lamp.

With Dad's back turned, I sneak Rick a silent kiss. "I'll be there."

Mom celebrates Dad's first contract by splurging on the

white interior shutters she's always wanted. "It will help Dad focus when he needs more privacy," she makes excuses. But as I dance by the living room to the rhythm of a song in my head, on my way to teach a class at Zeigler's, I catch her sitting on the couch, smiling at her shutters.

How far we've all come.

Opening the door, I dance down the steps and spin a pirouette. The sun is bright in a cloudless blue sky. I haven't just thrown open the shutters on my burglar's lantern. I've torn them off their hinges.

There's no more containing the supernova.

# Author's Note

Writing an English-language novel with three different Chinese dialects was trickier than I expected. I didn't have many precedents to draw from, so found myself making my own calls on how to navigate spellings, italics, and tone marks. I don't know that I've gotten it right, but hope I've at least come close to making the reading experience as seamless as possible.

The majority of Chinese-language dialogue in this novel is written in *Hànyǔ pīnyīn*, the official Romanization system for Standard Chinese. For Chinese words commonly used in the English text, such as *qipao, pinyin,* and *dim sum* (Cantonese), I chose not to use tone marks to blend them into the main English-language text. I made the same choice for proper names of characters and places, such as *Mei-Hwa* and *Ai-Mei*, which often appeared in English sentences, although they also sometimes appear in the same sentence as *Hànyǔ pīnyīn*.

Chien Tan is the spelling of the actual campus, and uses the Wades-Giles system, the formerly dominant Romanization system in Taiwan.

The *Hokkien* pinyin is based on Peh-ōe-jī Romanization, one of multiple systems for Taiwanese Hokkien.

# Acknowledgments

So many people have helped me through my writing journey of twelve years. There isn't ink enough to thank them all.

I am grateful to the following people who helped bring *Loveboat, Taipei* to life.

My HarperCollins team:

My brilliant editor Kristen Pettit, whose vision, energy, and creativity have made a beautiful book. Thank you for all the ways you are bringing change into our world.

Jenna Stempel-Lobell, Corina Lupp, Janice Sung, and Jennet Liaw for the incredible cover art and your other works.

Cindy Hamilton, Ebony LaDelle, Jane Lee, Sari Murray, Clare Vaughn, Michael D'Angelo, the Epic Reads team, Shenwei Chang, Jessica Gold, and all those in marketing and publicity who are bringing *Loveboat, Taipei* to the world.

My New Leaf family:

Jo Volpe, who, ten years before becoming my agent, encouraged me as a fledging writer when she sent me a hand-marked copy of my first manuscript. With you, the possibilities are endless.

Pouya Shahbazian who is pulling back the curtains into Hollywood for me.

Meredith Barnes for brilliantly bridging my many lives when I wasn't sure they could all fit together.

Mia Roman, Veronica Grijlva, Abigail Donoghue, Jordan Hill, Kelsey Lewis, Mariah Chappell, Hilary Pecheone, Cassandra Baim, and the whole New Leaf team. Suzie Townsend for your warm welcome!

My VCFA community:

Shelley Tanaka, A.M. Jenkins, Lyn Miller-Lachmann, Rachel Yeaman, Monica Roe, Gena Smith, Suma Subramaniam, Heather Hughes, Lianna McSwain, Laura Atkins. Susan Korchek for our conversations on dyslexia.

My critique partners: Sabaa Tahir, Stephanie Garber, Stacey Lee (a fellow two-Loveboater family), Kelly Loy Gilbert, I. W. Gregorio, Sonya Mukherjee. Your generosity and faith in me made this book happen.

My San Francisco writing community: SCBWI NorCal writers, Melanie Raanes, Angela Mann and all the booksellers at our beloved Keplers Books— I am so grateful for your friendship over these years.

My wise college friends and community: my roommate Judy Hung Liang, Chienlan Hsu, Emily Sadigh, Jennifer H. Wu, Paula Fernandez, Kavitha Ramchandran. When we met years ago, we wanted to change the world—and we're doing it.

Yang-Sze Choo and James Cham for years of patience and advice.

Olivia Chen for boundless creative marketing ideas for the bubble tea tour.

Jill and Nathan Schmidt for forging my gorgeous chops. I have been so proud to use them.

For invaluable professional feedback: Noa Wheeler, Anne Ursu, Lewis Buzbee, Jordan Brown and Cathy Yardley. Meghan Hopkins for your mental health sensitivity read.

Brian Yang, Bing Chen, Chris Kim, Eugene Wei and Pier Nirandara for support as I navigate Hollywood. Stephanie Yang, thank you.

For taking the time to dish about Loveboat: Carey Lai (your bo stick fighting tip changed the story!), Emily Yao, Eugene Wei, Jerry Chiang, David Lee, Dave Lu, Andy Wen. Ferdinand Hui for introductions. Tony Lin, my tour guide around the island of Taiwan.

My siblings, Byron and Liza Hing, for wise counsel and support, Colleen Hing Linde for faithfully reading every one of my novels, and Brooks Linde, for much needed prayers.

My parents, Ray and Barbara Lim Hing. It still means so much to me to make you proud.

My boys, Aidan and Alistair—you are my greatest joys.

My husband and best friend, Andy. I can't imagine who I'd be without you.

And the One who does everything in His own time.